DO YOU BELIEVE IN MISTER BONES?

I

BELIEVE

IN

MISTER

BONES

I BELIEVE IN MISTER BONES

WRITTEN BY
MAX BOOTH III

EDITED BY
BEN DEVOS

INTERIOR DESIGN BY
LORI MICHELLE BOOTH

COVER ART BY
TREVOR HENDERSON

INTERIOR ILLUSTRATIONS BY
BETTY ROCKSTEADY

PUBLISHED BY
APOCALYPSE PARTY

ALSO BY MAX BOOTH III

For Betty

Disconnect dem bones, dem dry bones
Disconnect dem bones, dem dry bones
Disconnect dem bones, dem dry bones
I hear the word of the Lord

—James Weldon Johnson, "Dem Bones"

"God Almighty, all these years I've gone around with a
SKELETON inside of me!"

—Ray Bradbury, "Skeleton"

ACT ONE
"BREAK MY BODY"

I believe in Mister Bones, and by the end
of this book so will you.

THAT'S HOW THE manuscript started, although
Daniel didn't know that yet. He thought he was still
reading a cover letter. Only nutcases copy/pasted an
entire book's text into the body of an email. Anybody who
knew shit about shit used attachments. Word docs,
usually—watermarked PDFs, if they were paranoid.

DO YOU BELIEVE IN MISTER BONES? the subject line
had read.

It'd caught his eye as he scrolled his phone on the
toilet. He assumed it was spam at first. Someone trying to
sell him dick pills. Most people, Daniel included, deleted
those types of emails without bothering to open them. But
there was something about this one—*who is Mister
Bones?*—that wedged a lemon of curiosity into his brain.
Plus, he'd initially misread the name as *Mister Boner*,
which was undeniably hilarious.

He read the first line, then registered how much text
proceeded it, and started scrolling, and scrolling,
surrendering long before reaching the end. This was a
fucking book submission. A long one. No title listed, either.
Not even a byline. The sender's email address was equally

3

cryptic: augustskeef@yahoo.com. Augustskeef? What the hell kind of word was that? First and last name, maybe? August Skeef? Augusts Keef? Either option sounded equally ridiculous.

He tried reading a few more sentences of the manuscript, but his train of thought derailed at the sound of someone else barging through the door. For a moment, he'd blissfully forgotten he was sitting in a shopping mall restroom. The sudden explosion of moist flatulence from the stall next to him shattered any delusion he might've constructed for himself while scrolling through his emails.

With one swipe of his thumb, he deleted the bizarre email, then finished his business and flushed. There were five sinks in the bathroom, and only one of them ever seemed to work. Which one that was, however, changed weekly—almost as if by design. They were all motion sensored, so Daniel stood in front of each basin waving his hand back and forth for a couple seconds. The last sink he approached ended up being the one that'd decided to be operational this weekend. It was always the last one he tried. Anything to make him look like a fucking idiot.

Cold water blasted from the faucet with the intensity of an industrial sand blaster, hitting the porcelain and splashing all over his stomach. There was no way these sinks were up to code. He doubted anything in this mall would meet any standard regulations. The front of his shirt was soaked. Considering how hot it was in this building, he didn't mind getting a little wet. But still. He'd need to dry off. Nobody wanted to buy books from a guy with wet hands. He went over to the towel dispenser and waved at the sensor. Nothing happened. He slapped it a couple times. He whispered a few desperate pleas. Nothing came out. It was empty. Of course it was. He wiped his hands on the back of his shirt and got out of there before the neighboring stall's occupant could confront him about causing a commotion. The man would soon find himself in the same predicament, and only then would he understand what Daniel had gone through.

By the time he exited the bathroom, he'd already forgotten about the unsolicited submission.

Their vendor table was in the middle of the mall, on the ground floor. If they'd gotten stuck upstairs again, they probably would have bailed before setting up. The mall only had one elevator. It was typically cramped and shook as it lifted and declined, like it might collapse under any amount of extra weight. Everybody always joked about how this place was haunted. Despite working in the horror genre, he didn't really believe in that kind of shit, but for this mall he could almost make an exception. The story went, sometime back in the early 1960s, while installing one of the elevators, an unlucky contractor got himself stuck between the elevator doors and then, as these things sometimes went, was fully decapitated. Now, supposedly, the poor fucker's headless spirit haunted the property. It was a good story. He kept meaning to turn it into a zine or something to sell exclusively at these little popup events. People around here would've eaten it up.

There were also two sets of escalators, but neither had been operational in all the time they'd been participating in events here. So, at least two years now, and they were still broken. Daniel'd once asked one of the ladies who operated the coffee shop in the food court how long they'd been out of order, and she gave him a look like she didn't understand the question, as if it was silly to assume there'd ever been a point in time when they *had* been functioning. The discolored caution tape blocking off the escalators didn't show much promise that maintenance planned on addressing the issue any time soon, either.

Reaching the table was a bit of a challenge. The mall was packed. Sweaty nerds cosplaying as their favorite slashers and oblivious, argumentative families doing their absolute best to block every conceivable pathway. Maneuvering around them was its own type of stupid sport. Weekdays, this place was dead, but on weekends when there was an event going on? Every goddamn person in San Antonio seemed to make an appearance.

The event organizer, Xiomara, knew their shit when it came to promotion. They hosted something at least once a month, sometimes twice, depending on how close in the year it was to Halloween. This was the second consecutive year Daniel and his wife Eileen had purchased the $1,000 vendor package, which reserved them table space at every Ghouls & Boils-organized event for the next twelve months. Xiomara first launched G&B as an annual festival every October—then, as it grew in popularity, expanded it into a full-time business. Eileen and Xiomara had gone to high school together. From the way Eileen once explained it to Daniel, they hadn't exactly been best friends or anything, but they'd been friendly enough to keep in touch post-graduation. Their shared interest in horror movies kept their paths slightly aligned, Eileen full-on embracing the horror lit community and establishing Fiendish Books with Daniel while Xiomara took a stronger interest in spooky merch like shirts and Funko pops, ultimately leading to the creation of Ghouls & Boils—now a bi-weekly multi-themed popup market featuring over fifty vendors at the American Utopia shopping mall *plus* a permanent brick and mortar located within the same building.

It was easy to spot Daniel and Eileen's table. For one thing, they were the only book vendor. Everybody else sold stuff like plastic DIY Halloween jewelry, low-quality bootleg art prints, used DVDs inexplicably marked at retail prices, and those tall Jesus candles with famous slashers like Leatherface and Ronald Reagan stickered over the holy savior. But also, their banner stand towered over the masses of sweaty mall customers like a lighthouse beacon guiding him to safety. On the left of the banner was their logo, a rotting zombie head deepthroated by a butcher's knife, courtesy of the cartoonist Betty Rocksteady, a weirdo Canadian who handled the majority of their artwork needs:

And to the right, in red goopy font, was the name of their press:

FIENDISH BOOKS

There was only one person browsing their selection, an older fella dressed primarily in blue denim, from his jeans to his buttoned-up jacket. Eileen remained seated behind the table, working on her laptop—most likely formatting the interior of an upcoming Fiendish publication—and that told Daniel everything he needed to know about the potential customer: he was a nutjob. Normally she would have been standing and greeting whoever approached their table and asking questions to help ensure the sale—unless the person turned out to be crazy, then she'd avoid eye contact and hope like hell they didn't try engaging in any further conversation. Daniel considered waiting until the guy left before officially returning to the table, but noticed Eileen had already spotted him and was motioning for him to hurry.

The moment he slipped behind the table, she said, "Gotta pee," and fled the scene before he could ask any follow-up questions.

He glanced at the denim guy and nodded. "How's it going?" he said, too many years of previous customer service jobs kicking in on instinct.

Unfortunately, the guy took this as an invitation to start a dialogue. He leaned over the stacks of horror books at their table and said, in a voice that sounded like steamrolled gravel, "You a publisher?"

Daniel gulped and weighed his options, then gave him another nod. "Yup."

"You publish scary books?"

"We, uh, try to." Daniel had to take a step back from him. He reeked of hard liquor and unwashed ass.

"Let me tell you something," the man said, "I've just spent the last fifteen years of my life living in Central Mexico. I have seen some shit. Some *real* shit. You know what I'm saying?"

"Uh, no, not really."

"I'm saying I've witnessed some shit that is *really* scary. The shit in movies? That doesn't scare me. But this shit? It's real-life shit. It's actually scary."

"Oh, okay," Daniel said, scratching the back of his neck, "that's cool, man."

"So what do you think? You want to publish it or what?"

"Publish . . . ? Did you write a book, or . . . ?"

I BELIEVE IN MISTER BONES

The denim drunk shook his head. "No, I'm telling you, this is *real* shit. But it could be a book. It'd be scarier than any other goddamn book out there, I fuckin' guarantee it."

Daniel despised getting caught in these types of situations, which always seemed to happen whenever they were vendoring somewhere. It almost felt like they were holding him hostage with the slim chance of them possibly buying something at the end of their interaction. That was never the case, of course. These types of people were never interested in actually supporting the arts. The sad, pathetic truth was they had nobody else to talk to anymore. Their friends and loved ones had stopped responding to their messages. They had run the well dry and were now desperate for any kind of human connection. Somehow that then became Daniel's responsibility. "Well, we aren't exactly open for submissions right now," he explained, "and even if we were . . . we'd only consider finished manuscripts—not, uh, pitches."

"What do you *mean*, exactly?" the guy asked. "You want me to, like, take something to a printer and get it bound?"

"What?" Daniel tried not to laugh, immediately failed. "No, I mean . . . a digital file. Microsoft Word or Google Docs or whatever you have available. You'd email it as an attachment."

"But there's no book."

Daniel shrugged. "I guess you'll have to write it."

"Hmm." The drunk studied a stack of Fiendish titles on the table between them. "Tell you what," he said, glancing back up at Daniel, "what if I just, like, compile everything into a list, and send that your way?"

"A list?"

"Yeah, a list of all the fucked-up shit I've seen."

"Like what?"

The drunk hesitated, as if afraid someone else might be eavesdropping, and whispered, "You don't even want to know, man."

"But I thought you *did* want me to know?"

"Would a list work, or not?"

Daniel shook his head, wondering if Eileen had already finished peeing and was somewhere nearby waiting for this guy to leave, just as he'd tried to do before she caught him in the act. "We don't take a look at lists. You'd have to write it as a book."

"But don't you think something like that would sell, though?"

"I don't know. It's hard to say. Even a book containing the craziest, scariest material isn't going to mean anything if the writing's bad."

"The writing?" Something in the drunk seemed to deflate.

"At the end of the day, yeah," Daniel said, "the writing is what matters most. It's what guides someone through the story. If the writing sucks, then nobody's going to read it."

"What if I've never written a book before, though?"

"Then, I don't know, I'd suggest practicing a lot. What kinds of books do you typically read?"

The drunk stared at him like he was being asked an impossible question. "I only read one book, sir."

Daniel was sure he'd misheard him. "You only read one book?"

But he'd heard correctly. The drunk nodded. "The Holy Bible."

Daniel waited for the drunk to start laughing. It didn't happen. "You only read the Bible?"

"Yes, sir. It's the only book that matters, far as I'm concerned."

"Then . . . why do you want to write one?"

The drunk shrugged. "I just don't know what else to do with all of these experiences I've had."

Daniel sighed. Goddammit, where was Eileen? Now *he* had to pee again. "Well," he said, biting his lip until the pain made him stop, "I guess I would have to strongly discourage you from trying to write a book, then, if you have no interest in reading books besides . . . uh, the one you mentioned."

"What do you mean?"

"I mean, man, it's pretty insulting to come here and tell me—a publisher—that you don't read books, all while trying to get me to publish something of yours, which you haven't even written. You don't get that?"

"Hmm." He glanced down at the books again, then nodded. "Okay, sir. Thank you for your time." He turned around and stumbled over to the next vendor table. The man's smell, sadly, decided to linger awhile.

Seconds later, Eileen slid up next to Daniel and said, "What a fucking nutjob."

She happened to say this just as three children approached the table, ages ranging anywhere from seven to ten, if Daniel had to guess. Although it was hard to tell for certain, considering all three were cosplaying as horror monsters: Freddy Krueger, the Babadook, and the Creeper from *Jeepers Creepers*.

"My mom says you're not supposed to say 'nutjob,'" Freddy Krueger said.

"Yeah," the Creeper added, "it's apple cyst."

"*Ableist*," the Babadook corrected.

"Oh."

"It's true," Daniel said, shaking his head sadly. "I'm always telling her that."

"I'm very sorry," Eileen said, holding back a laugh. "You're right."

"What does your shirt mean?" the Babadook asked, pointing at Daniel's chest.

He glanced down, having already forgotten that he was wearing his favorite T-shirt of all time, one that he frequently wore in public despite Eileen's protests.

Against black fabric, in large white letters, the shirt read: I CAME ON EILEEN.

"Oh," Daniel said, and nodded at his wife standing beside him, "it's, uhh, from a song."

MAX BOOTH III

Freddy Krueger picked up a book from their table—*Misfortunes* by Mindy Rose—and started flipping through it. "What's this book about?" he shouted. Then: "These drawings are very gross."

Misfortunes was one of the few *experimental* titles Fiendish had published. Its appearance closely resembled a children's book, which definitely seemed to attract the attention of children at popup events—something Daniel weirdly never anticipated, perhaps because he was an idiot. Every page was illustrated in color by Betty Rocksteady. As Freddy Krueger commented on, the art *was* gross. But it was also incredibly hilarious. The illustrations were accompanied by brief, one-to-two sentence "death predictions" written by Mindy Rose, some weirdo they'd connected with on Tumblr several years ago.

Examples of misfortunes found in the book consisted of entries like *You will die the exact same way as Amelia Earhart (suicide by cop)*; *Congratulations! You've just been cast in John Landis's segment of* Twilight Zone: The Movie; and *You will discover a snake in the toilet. The two of you will fall deeply in love and live together for 12 years, until one of you is diagnosed with a terminal illness and you decide to each swallow cyanide capsules while listening to your favorite album in bed.*

Not *exactly* for kids—but, not *not* for kids, either, as far as Daniel was concerned. The shit was funny no matter how old you were.

"It's a book that predicts how you're going to die," Daniel explained.

All three of the kids seemed flabbergasted by this concept.

"*What*?" Freddy Krueger said, and slammed the book back down on the table. "Why would you want to know *that*? You can't avoid death no matter what. Why would you want to *know*?"

The Babadook shook his head and yelled, "I avoid death all the time! It's easy!"

I BELIEVE IN MISTER BONES

"Even if you *try* to avoid it, it's still going to get you somehow." Freddy Krueger said. "Like . . . like . . . like what if it says you're going to die 'in bed' and then you stop using a bed . . . what if a bed then *falls on you from an airplane*?"

"Whoa," Daniel said. "I never thought about it like that."

"I would step out of the way," the Babadook replied.

"No you wouldn't! You wouldn't even see it coming until it was too late! You would be killed just like everybody else!"

"I want to die from AIDS," the Creeper said, matter-of-factly.

"Uh, what?" Daniel said, suddenly uncomfortable with this interaction. Where the hell were their parents, anyway?

"*Old* AIDS," the Creeper clarified.

"Old *age*?" Eileen asked, and the kid nodded inside his mask.

"You know," Daniel said to the Creeper, "that costume you have on? The person who made that movie is a convicted child molester."

"Huh?" the Creeper said.

Eileen nudged him with her elbow. "*Daniel.*"

"Victor Salva. That's his name, the guy who made *Jeepers Creepers*. Look it up sometime," Daniel said. "Seriously, it's pretty messed up. I'm sure he still profits from the franchise, too, and yet they continue releasing new ones every couple years."

"What on earth are you talking about, mister?" the Babadook asked.

"What's a child molester?" Freddy Krueger asked.

"How do *you* not know that?" Daniel asked. "You're literally dressed as one."

"I am?" he said, surprised.

Next to him, the Babadook started laughing at his brother and shouting, "You're a child molester! You're a child molester!"

"Molester! Molester!" echoed the Creeper, as all three of them seemed to lose interest in the book table and scampered off to the next vendor.

"What the hell is wrong with you?" Eileen asked, once they were gone. "Are you trying to get us arrested?"

"What do you mean? Of all people, shouldn't *children* be aware of the concept of child molesters? Like . . . they're the ones who need to watch out for that stuff! If anything, I'm doing a public service here."

"I'm sure your medal is in the mail."

"Also, wait," Daniel said, "come to think about it, for kids raised by someone who's already educating them about ableism, isn't it *extra* nuts that their mom wouldn't also be aware of someone as problematic as the *Jeepers Creepers* pervert? Where does this woman draw the line, right?"

Eileen stared at him for approximately ten seconds before saying, "I'm so glad we never had kids."

The rest of the day didn't see many sales. A few bites on their discounted back-issues of *Fiendish Tales*, mostly because they were cheap and the cover art caught the eye. That was fine with Daniel, though. The writers in the magazine had already been paid their one-time flat payment pre-publication, which meant there were no royalties to keep organized. Any magazine sales went straight back into the company—or, in situations like tonight, would pay for their dinner.

Loading out always felt a hundred times more miserable than loading in. When a vendor was setting up for an event, there was a certain whiff of optimism in the air. *Maybe all of this shit will sell,* they might think, *maybe the universe will provide a sign I am not wasting my life producing art nobody cares about.* This almost never happened, of course. Even on weekends with heavy foot

I BELIEVE IN MISTER BONES

traffic and customers with money to burn, there was always an embarrassing amount of stock left to box back up come Sunday evening. Maybe the solution was to bring less stock, but there was always that fear of running out, of not having that one perfect book for that one perfect reader. So they tended to overprepare, and they paid the price afterward.

While Eileen returned stacks of books to the empty boxes under their table, Daniel went out to their car to fetch the dolly. Nearly a decade ago, when they first launched the company and started vendoring at popups and conventions, the concept of requiring one of these things had never entered their minds. They'd instead lugged each box from their car to the venue, then back again once the event wrapped. It was a tiring, time-consuming process that they'd quickly grown to dread, but the idea to head over to Home Depot and buy an actual dolly didn't form until after vendoring at the city's first Alamo City Comic Con. The convention itself—that initial year, at least—proved to be more successful than anticipated, but it was the load-out experience that ended up forever traumatizing them. Once ACCC shut its doors to the public, vendors were told they had exactly one hour to pack their shit and get out before the warehouse's garage exits were locked, which was already an insane expectation, but now consider the fact that due to either poor organization or miscommunication or perhaps a little of both, this load-out period also happened to coincide with the San Antonio Zombie Walk—meaning streets were shut down, and none of the vendors could retrieve their vehicles from the parking lot several blocks away from the Henry B. Gonzalez Convention Center. Most of the vendors had dollies, and thus faced minimal trouble transporting their stock to the parking lot. Daniel and Eileen, on the other hand, were shit out of luck and forced to carry stacks of boxes around hordes of citizens in zombie cosplay who all insisted on being in character, which meant none of them understood what the words "excuse me" meant and instead tried to get in the way as much as possible. Some of these dorks were even lunging at people and pretending to take bites out of them. It was a nightmare. They each had to make this trip at least half a dozen times. Books are heavy, after all. And zombies, Daniel and Eileen concluded, suck ass. So after that, yeah, they finally went and bought a dolly for the company. They would never do another event without one—in fact, if the dolly wasn't actively in use, it would remain in Eileen's trunk, as the fear of forgetting it one day greatly outweighed the annoyance of always driving around with a large metal object sliding around in her car. And they certainly would never do another event during a goddamn Zombie Walk. After that night, the two of them could barely stomach zombie *movies*.

Outside the shopping mall, people were pissed. Some bozo had parked their van in front of the sidewalk ramp, preventing anyone else from rolling their dollies down it. The bozo in question was another vendor, someone far too oblivious of their surroundings to realize they'd need to share this space with others. Half a dozen different vendors lined up in front of the van with their own dollies, growing furiously more impatient by the second. Daniel considered hanging around to see what happened once the owner of the van returned to the scene of the crime, but at the same time he was starving and sick of being at this fucking mall, so he maneuvered around everybody and headed over to their SUV in the center of the parking lot. He popped the trunk and dragged out the dolly, then wheeled it back toward the mall just in time to overhear the blocked vendors giving shit to the van owner.

"Wow," one of them said, "I sure wish there was a communal ramp for us all to use right now."

"You know what I love?" another said. "Standing on sidewalks doing absolutely nothing while my children wait for me to pick them up from the babysitter."

I BELIEVE IN MISTER BONES

Daniel wheeled his dolly past them all and stole an amused glimpse of the bozo nervously loading several boxes of trademarked horror movie shirts into his van. He was drenched in sweat and something told Daniel it wasn't entirely from the exercise.

Back inside the mall, Eileen had already finished refilling the boxes with books and was nearly done folding up their tablecloths. "There you are," she said. "Another five minutes and I was afraid I'd have to call in a rescue team for you."

"You should see what's going on out there," Daniel said, and explained the situation as they layered the book boxes atop the dolly.

"Wow," she said, "some people have no clue, do they?"

"How'd y'all do this weekend?" someone asked behind them, causing both Daniel and Eileen to flinch. Xiomara— the main organizer of these shopping mall events. Shorter than Eileen, but also muscular in a way that secretly intimidated *and* aroused him. He was pretty sure they could knock him out with one punch, if it came down to it.

Eileen recomposed herself first. "Oh, I guess we did okay."

"Yeah?" Xiomara frowned, seeing through the lie. "I don't think we sold much, either. It's weird. Sometimes we can get this place packed with people, but that doesn't always translate to sales."

"If only we could force them to spend money," Daniel said. "Like, by gunpoint."

Nobody laughed at his joke and Daniel scratched his head, thinking, *What if I killed myself right now?*

"It can be tricky," Xiomara said, scratching their shaved scalp, "attracting the right balance of people interested in both the celebrity guests and our vendors. A lot of times, they only come to get something signed by one of those *Walking Dead* idiots or whatever, which I know is a disappointment to everybody else, but sometimes it also translates into extra sales, depending on the person and what, you know, the vendors have available." They paused long enough for it to feel weird. "Anyway, that's why we try to notify our vendors of each event's theme months beforehand, so y'all have time to prepare."

This month's theme was *The Lost Boys,* because Xiomara had dished out the cash to fly Corey Fieldman to San Antonio for the weekend. Unfortunately, Fiendish had yet to publish anything about vampires. Although, even if they had, Daniel doubted it would have made that significant of an impact. That wasn't how book readers worked. They approached tables because they liked to read, not because they were searching exclusively for stories that reminded them of a specific movie from the 1980s. Or maybe that's exactly how readers behaved. If he knew the secret formula, he probably wouldn't be wasting his time every month at this haunted shopping mall asking strangers, "What do you like to read?" and grimacing at one of two standard responses: *Oh, a little bit of everything*—which, of course, was a lie—or, *I wish I had the time*—which was one of the more infuriating responses to hear, because Daniel was sure they had plenty of time to binge twelve seasons of some insufferable sitcom they'd already watched a dozen times before.

"Anyway," Xiomara said, "I'm sure this is all stuff y'all are gonna be finding out first-hand soon. Isn't your festival coming up?"

"Kind of," Eileen said. "We still have another couple months."

"Plenty of time," Daniel said, although he had no idea what he meant by it. Plenty of time for *what*, exactly?

"Well, you know," Xiomara said, "if you guys ever need any help, or anything, I've had plenty of experience, as you know, and I'd be happy to lend a hand."

As they said *lend a hand*, they looked directly at Daniel and smirked in a way that made him uncomfortable and slightly hard. He readjusted his stance, hoping nothing was visible against jeans.

I BELIEVE IN MISTER BONES

"Um," he said, clearing his throat.

It wasn't the first time in recent years he suspected they might've been flirting with him. Not that Daniel was someone who others went after, often. There'd only been a few occasions, from his recollection. He'd once gone on a podcast where it'd quickly gotten out of hand, in a way that left him thinking, *Wait a second, did I just get sexually harassed?* Another time, at a bar, a woman had leaned into his ear and whispered, *You smell so good,* and left it at that. He hadn't minded that interaction so much. In fact, he'd ridden high off of it for weeks, months. To this day, he still applied the same coconut body lotion after every shower. And when it came to Xiomara, things became more complicated. The flirting wasn't *unwanted.* He would be lying to himself if he claimed he hadn't instantly found himself attracted to them on day one of Eileen introducing the two of them early on within their relationship. Not that Daniel was a cheater, or anything. He'd never betray Eileen like that. Besides, suppose the opportunity presented itself, and he *wanted to*, he wasn't built to be that type of person. He was way too fucking anxious to balance adultery. The stress would eat him alive. The confidence to please multiple lovers sounded like an alien skillset he'd never come close to touching. Once, while masturbating in the bathroom, he'd attempted to fantasize about all three of them being intimate together, but the logistics of a threesome—*even in his own imagination*—were so nerve-racking that he couldn't finish himself off, and gave up.

"Thank you," Eileen said. "That's really nice of you. We don't really know what we're doing yet, but I'll hit you up when we do."

"If y'all ever wanted to come over for dinner, or whatever, to help plan stuff, I'd be open to that, too," Xiomara said.

Holy shit, Daniel thought, *this is exactly how threesomes happen.*

"Well," he said, "we better get going," and quickly pushed the dolly away before anyone else could respond.

It would be another ten minutes before Eileen found an escape from the conversation and joined him outside. Only then did he remember they'd left their tables back in the mall, and he had to run inside to collect them. Fortunately, Xiomara was no longer anywhere in sight.

ON THE WAY HOME they stopped at the Burger Boy drive-thru and picked up dinner. The teenager standing out by the exterior menu taking everybody's to-go orders snuck a glance at the back of their car and said, "Wow, what's in all those boxes?"

"Children," Daniel answered matter-of-factly, and the teenager turned pale. "Little, cut-up children."

"Sir?"

Eileen slapped him on the arm and recited their order. He took their method of payment—the Fiendish Books company card—and swiped it, noticeably trying not to look at the boxes again. Daniel managed to keep a straight face until they pulled forward, but any longer and he would have broke.

"I hope that kid doesn't call the cops on us," Eileen said, as they waited for their food at the last window.

"Hard disagree," Daniel said. "You know how much press we'd get if we got pulled over for something like that? It's not like we actually have children back there or anything."

"No, but we have something far more criminal, at least in the eyes of Texas," she said. "*Books*."

He clutched his chest and pantomimed a heart attack. "Oh, the horror! The horror!"

Neither of them realized the drive-thru window had opened until it was too late. A girl the same age as the boy who'd taken their order stood inside the restaurant, holding their bag of burgers, clearly concerned. "Um, is he okay?"

Eileen shook her head. "Sadly, what he has can't be fixed."

It was dark by the time they made it to their apartment complex. They were both too exhausted and hungry to bother unloading the SUV again. "Let that be a problem for Tomorrow Us," Daniel suggested, and that sounded like a good enough plan to Eileen, so they left everything behind besides the food, Eileen's laptop, the tablet they used to process credit card payments, and the company's cashbox. Everything else wouldn't be worth stealing, unless they had the incredible misfortune of being burglarized by a lover of horror literature. In which case—fuck it. It'd just be less stuff they'd have to carry in tomorrow. Maybe the thieves would even go through the trouble of reviewing the books on Goodreads after they were finished.

The first thing Eileen did once they were inside their studio apartment was take off her bra and let out an exaggerated, relieved sigh. Daniel got a pot of coffee brewing. He'd been dealing with an annoying headache fueled by caffeine withdrawal for the past several hours, and he was desperate to get a few cups into his system so he could think clearly again.

The apartment was small and cramped. It consisted of one decently-sized room that worked as both their bedroom and living room. Near the front door was a television anchored against the wall. In front of it, an old couch they'd picked up from a neighbor's yard sale ages ago—probably the same yard sale they'd secured most of their dishes and clothes hangers. Behind the couch, against the opposite end of the apartment, was their bed: two mattresses stacked on top of each other. A nightstand on either side, with reading lights. A dresser so crammed with clothes that none of the drawers shut all the way. They also had a closet and a bathroom. There was a kitchen area, too, separated from the living quarters only by a marble counter, which was currently overwhelmed with stacks of half-packaged webstore orders they were behind on mailing out to customers. Every other inch of free space, outside of an adequate walking path, was reserved for book inventory and shipping supplies.

Daniel was in his early thirties and Eileen was in her late forties. Was this the kind of life either of them had envisioned when they were kids? No, obviously not, but what child ever correctly predicts their own future? Once you were out of your twenties, you were expected to have a house, a high-paying career with lots of benefits, a couple of kids, a savings account. That wasn't in the cards for them. Neither of them was interested in children. Eileen couldn't have them, anyway, even if they were. They ran an indie horror press together. There was no getting rich from that. Their living situation didn't allow room for a *dog*, much less another human being. Everything they made from bookselling either went back into the company or into their cost of living. Rent, groceries, the occasional movie. And the thing was, they were both content with that. There wasn't anything else they wanted to do. For them, this was probably as good as it would ever get, and that was perfectly okay.

They kicked their shoes off and changed into more comfortable clothing, then gathered their burgers and sat on the couch to eat and watch an episode or two of whatever new show they'd recently started streaming. The show didn't matter all that much, honestly. It was more like white noise. Something to fill a space. They'd both finished eating maybe ten minutes into the first episode, then got out their laptops and started working on company-related shit while the television continuing broadcasting to an empty audience.

MAX BOOTH III

Daniel's laptop was ancient and took ages to wake from hibernation mode. As it loaded, he threw away their trash and fixed them each a cup of coffee. Eileen was already zoned in on whatever book she'd been formatting all day. Whichever one that might've been. Daniel knew they'd overcommitted this year to how many books they'd agreed to release and it was already driving them batshit with stress. A publishing company as small as theirs—operated by two people in a studio apartment—should not have been taking on more than two, maybe three books a year. So why the fuck had they announced ten titles, on top of two additional issues of *Fiendish Tales*? The reason wasn't complicated, of course: they were very, very stupid.

Plus, there was the massive three-day book festival they were planning on launching a few months from then, featuring vendors from all around the world, but that was too terrifying to dwell upon tonight. Instead, he focused on small tasks. He checked the company's social media accounts and reshared pictures of Fiendish publications readers had tagged them in during the weekend. He checked the Fiendish Discord to make sure nobody had bombed their community with phishing links again. Nothing suspicious there. A few questionable selfies in the #toilet-talk channel, though, which was a channel where Discord members could only post if they were actively sitting on a toilet. Daniel had regretted creating it almost immediately, but people seemed to love it, so he reluctantly kept the channel around. He replied to a few emails from authors and deleted a ton of spam, including several unsolicited manuscripts. Their inbox got swarmed on a weekly basis despite the website clearly stating they were not open for submissions. Writers had the worst reading comprehensions than anybody else he'd ever met.

With the emails situated, he opened up the next book he was due to edit, took one look at the opening page and decided he couldn't possibly concentrate on something like that tonight, then hopped back over to social media and spent the next three hours attempting to understand the latest drama surrounding the horror community. He did not succeed.

Frustrated, he closed his laptop. He stared at the television for a bit, which had been autoplaying episode after episode of a show he couldn't recall the title of, nor could he remember why they'd decided to start watching it in the first place. It looked terrible.

He glanced over at Eileen, who was still formatting. "Hey," he said.

"Yo."

"Want to have sex?"

"With you?"

"Ideally."

She thought about it for a moment, then nodded. "Yeah, okay."

They washed out their coffee mugs, then took turns peeing and brushing their teeth. The bathroom was not big enough for two people, but the sink was installed just outside the doorway, near the dresser, so anyone could utilize the faucet while the toilet was in use. They undressed and got in bed—Eileen on her side, back facing him, an invitation to massage her shoulders, which he was happy to do.

She was full of knots, from stress, from the poor posture of always being bent over a laptop, who knew what. The only real exercise either of them ever seemed to get involved carrying books. Around the apartment, to the post office, to conventions. Always with the books. It was all they ever did. If it didn't involve books, then they didn't have any time for it. What was that old, stupid expression? Do what you love for a living, and you'll want to stop living? Something like that.

He was tired of rubbing her shoulders. His cock was already hard and he was desperate for it to be touched. He trailed his fingernails down her spine, over the curve of her ass, and moved them in gentle circles around the back of her thigh. She let out a soft moan. This was her spot, he knew, the one that made her melt when touched. She went to roll over, but Daniel wasn't anticipating the motion so soon, and paid the price with an elbow directly to the face.

He flew back against the bed and grabbed his nose. "Oh fuck, you kneed me."

"Oh shit, I'm so sorry," she gasped, then: "Wait, did you just say kneed?"

"No," Daniel lied, and inspected his hand for any sign of blood. It was clean. "I meant, you *need* me. Like, you desire me so much. Need."

She giggled. "You forgot what elbows are called, didn't you?"

"I actually meant knead," he clarified, "like, you know, what you do to pie crusts."

"Well shit. Now I want pie."

"I will go get us a pie if you knead me right now," Daniel said.

"I'm not . . . I'm not sure you know what that word means."

"I know what lots of words mean."

"How about I just play with your penis for a little bit?"

"That also works," he said. "But be gentle. I just got a new tattoo down there, and it's sensitive."

"You did not get a tattoo on your penis."

"It says BROOKS WAS HERE."

"Uh huh," she said, laughing and digging through her nightstand for something. She turned back around, this time exercising more caution with her elbow—or knee, or whatever it was called—and pressed a small, shockingly freezing object against his testicles. She turned it on and the vibration instantly made him gasp. "Too cold?" she asked.

"Uh, no, it's . . . it's good," he said, then gasped again when she leaned over and took the head of his cock in her mouth. "It's, uh, it's very good," he said again, then decided he should probably stop talking. Only then did he catch a whiff of his own balls, and remembered he'd spent the whole day drenched in sweat while selling books. He wished he'd taken a shower before they lay down. He wondered how she was managing to do what she was doing without grimacing. He debated telling her to stop, that she didn't have to do this, but this thought only crossed his mind for a couple seconds, then he stopped thinking altogether.

A few minutes passed and he took the toy from her and nudged her against the pillow. He spread her legs apart and softly rubbed her slick lips with his index and middle fingers, waiting for them to blossom against his touch, then slipped the vibrator into her and massaged what he was *pretty sure* was where her clit was located. Judging by the noise she made, he was correct. Unless she was just doing that to help his ego. Did he actually know what he was doing here, or was he fucking this up and she was too embarrassed to mention anything? He was never quite sure. Jesus Christ, was he remotely *close* to her clit? What the fuck even *was* a clit? How many years of marriage and he was still too scared to ask, "Is this okay? Does this feel good?" What kind of man was he, anyway? Also, what the fuck were they thinking scheduling ten books so close together? And why the hell had they announced this goddamn book festival? He didn't know how to run a festival. He didn't know how to do anything. This was going to be a disaster. The end of the company. The end of everything. His erection softened. Suddenly all he could think about was how he was no longer hard. This did not help it grow back. Miraculously, Eileen sensed something amiss and reached between his legs and squeezed his balls with enough strength to make him forget everything he'd just been worrying about. He tossed the vibrator aside and fucked her before anything further could corrupt the pathetic excuse he had for a brain.

Afterward, Eileen hurried to the bathroom to pee again. She collapsed on the toilet with the door wide open and waited for something to happen. Daniel sat at the edge of the mattress as he wiped himself off with a couple tissues. He could see her through the door, head leaning back, eyes closed.

"Did you really want me to go get pie?" he asked, flinging the tissues into a nearby trash can. He missed and had to stand up to retrieve them.

"Nah, that's okay," she said. "I'm pretty tired. Plus, my teeth hurt tonight."

"They hurt?" Daniel asked, stricken with panic. "Not from . . . not from *that*, right?"

"From what?" She opened her eyes and followed his line of sight, then laughed. "No, weirdo, I think I got something stuck in them earlier, at the mall."

"Oh, maybe from that kettle corn we were snacking on?" One of the Ghouls & Boils vendors always sold fresh kettle corn. This weekend they'd been doomed to table nearby. The smell was impossible to resist.

"I'm sure it's not unrelated."

He leaned against the doorway of the bathroom and waited. "You think you're going to pee anytime this century, maybe?"

"I'm trying."

"Do you want me to tickle you maybe?"

"I do not want you to tickle me, no."

"Okay, well." He clicked his jaw. "What if you just spread your legs a little, so I can pee between them?"

She stared at him like he was insane. "I think you can just wait your turn."

"If I wait too long, all this leftover cum solidifies over my urethra, and suddenly I'm pissing on the ceiling. Is that what you want? Pee all over the ceiling, like we're a bunch of astronauts?"

"I don't think astronauts pee on the ceiling," she said, laughing, evidently enough to prompt the blocked liquids to finally escape. "Oh, here we go," she whispered, pleasured in a way that he couldn't help but secretly suspect she was only *now* orgasming, here on the toilet, with zero assistance from Daniel, from her husband. But that was crazy thinking, right? And if it was true, so what? What did it matter? At least she was getting off *somehow*. Why would he ever try to deny her that?

She finished up, wiped, and surrendered the bathroom over to him without bothering to flush. He pissed on his wife's wadded-up used toilet paper floating around the bowl and experienced an odd sense of accomplishment. Together, their mixed urine appeared almost radioactive. It didn't matter how much water they drank during these weekend-long popup markets—by the end of them, they always felt drained and dehydrated. A sick part of him wanted to kneel over the toilet and take a sip. He shook the thought away along with his cock.

Just outside the bathroom, Eileen swished mouthwash from cheek to cheek, and once again Daniel felt ashamed with the hygiene of his own genitals. Would she be using mouthwash after fellating someone else? Did he want her *not* to use mouthwash after? What was wrong with him? He didn't have an answer to any of these questions. He wondered if he also typically utilized mouthwash after performing oral sex on her, then realized he couldn't remember the last time he'd gone down on his wife. Was she upset about that? Did she have a secret grudge against his laziness? Why hadn't she left him already? He vowed, right then and there, to eat her out the next time they got intimate together. He didn't say it aloud. He just thought it very intently and hoped he remembered later on. He wouldn't even rinse out his mouth afterward, either. It would be a symbol of his love and dedication. *Look at me,* the gesture would say, *I am not repulsed by the person I married.* Could she say the same?

Eileen spat into the sink, rinsed out her mouth from the faucet, then searched through the medicine cabinet until retrieving what she was after: a spool of floss.

"I didn't know we owned floss," Daniel said, flushing

away their combined fluids. It was a little depressing, watching everything vanish from the toilet. *One day that'll be me for real,* he thought.

"What are you talking about?" she said. "You don't floss?"

"No one flosses."

"I floss."

"I have never seen you floss."

She motioned to the string of floss wrapped around her fingers. "I am literally flossing right now."

"Yeah, but now you're just doing it to show off."

"No, I told you, I have a piece of popcorn stuck in my teeth."

"Isn't that what toothpicks are for?"

"We don't have any toothpicks."

Daniel threw up his hands, at a loss. "So we have floss, but not toothpicks? What kind of life are we living here?"

"A perplexing one," she mumbled, as she bent over the sink, focusing on her reflection in the mirror and digging between her teeth.

He caught one glance at the way her ass looked in that position, and couldn't resist the urge to approach her from behind and press his flaccid penis between her cheeks. He wished he was the type of man who could be ready to go for round two so quickly, but he wasn't. He didn't know what kind of man he was but he knew it wasn't that. There would be nothing down there for at least another three-to-four hours. It was still fun to stand like that, though.

Eileen didn't acknowledge his presence, instead too focused on removing the popcorn stuck in her teeth. He pressed himself harder against her as he leaned forward, peering into the mirror over her head as if he might somehow be of any help, and for a moment, in the reflection, it appeared as if his head had replaced Eileen's, and her body had become his—the breasts sagging over the sink; the smooth, hairless arms; the soft, creamy skin. This was Daniel's body. This was Daniel's skin. His cock started stiffening.

He cleared his throat and said, "I don't, uh, see anything."

"What are you, a dentist?" she asked.

He paused, then readjusted himself between her cheeks. "What kind of dentists have you been going to?"

"Wouldn't you like to know?" she said, and wiggled herself against his groin.

"I'm just saying, I don't see anything."

"It's not about seeing. It's about *feeling*."

"Oh, I feel plenty."

"Ah shit, I got it!" she exclaimed, removing the floss and spitting something out in the sink. "I swear to god, I thought that was going to be stuck in there forever."

He stepped away from her and retrieved his underwear from the floor, feeling stupid and embarrassed for having positioned himself in such a way. They weren't new lovers anymore. Married people didn't do spontaneous shit like that. They had too many other real-life priorities to stress out about. "I still can't believe you floss," he said.

"I still can't believe you *don't*." Eileen scooped up a housedress from the back of the couch and slipped into it, then started turning off all the various lights around the apartment. "I thought I saw you floss before."

"You must have hallucinated that," he said, "because it wasn't me. I wouldn't know how to floss if my life depended on it." Then, after a moment: "You know what? Teeth freak me out. I don't even like thinking about them."

She climbed into bed next to him. "You're afraid of teeth now?" He'd already turned on his own reading light. She followed suit and grabbed her book from the nightstand. Some library-borrowed Christopher Moore paperback. Meanwhile, Daniel held open Sarah Gailey's latest novel.

"I didn't say I was afraid," he said.

"But they freak you out?"

"A little bit, yeah." He thought about it, because he knew she was going to ask, and shook his head. "I don't

I BELIEVE IN MISTER BONES

know what it is about them. But there's something, though. Something I can't explain."

"You're too funny sometimes," she said, and then neither of them spoke for a while, each invested in their individual novels.

It wasn't until after they gave up reading and put everything away, after Daniel had closed his eyes and was seconds away from succumbing to unconsciousness, that Eileen said something else.

"I think I know what it is," she said, next to him in the darkness. "About teeth, I mean. I think I know what it is about them that's so unsettling."

Daniel didn't respond. He didn't want to have this conversation. Let her think he was already asleep.

But she told him anyway:

"They're the only part of the skeleton you can see," she said. "Everything else is hiding."

EILEEN WAS SNORING in no time. Daniel, on the other hand, never got any sleep that night. Not after hearing something like that. *The only part of the skeleton you can see. Everything else is hiding.* What the fuck? What kind of thing was that to say to someone before bed? It was cruel. Grounds for divorce. He tossed and turned for what he guessed was at least an hour, unintelligible anxiety bouncing around his brain like a pinball machine, until the urge to pee returned and he had an excuse to get up.

With a studio apartment, turning on any light during the middle of the night was hazardous. They'd long learned how to maneuver around the place in the dark without kicking over a stack of books or walking into a wall or piece of furniture. He made it to the toilet without incident, lifted the lid and let loose. For the first couple seconds, there was no sound of the urine stream landing anywhere. Not in the bowl, not on the floor, nowhere. Almost as if he was pissing into the void. He liked the idea. But he was also realistic and knew the pee was landing *somewhere.* He readjusted slightly to the right, then heard the familiar sound of toilet water. What had he just been pissing on? It didn't matter. At this time of night, certain things could be ignored and forgotten. Come the morning, he knew the rogue urine would be gone without a trace. How? He didn't know, and he didn't care to question the magic of the night. He didn't

I BELIEVE IN MISTER BONES

dare flush afterward. Even with the multiple fans in the apartment creating white noise, they were in no way strong enough to muffle the sound of their toilet flushing. Better to leave it percolating in the bowl. They tried to abide by the *if it's brown, flush it down; if it's yellow, let it mellow* rule, anyway. An easy way to build up mold on the porcelain, too—something they often ignored until the bowl was more black than white.

Daniel didn't want to return to bed. Any exhaustion he might've experienced at the popup event earlier had dissipated. The evening helping of coffee must've kicked in. That, or what Eileen had said about teeth, which was all he could think about now. Another negative aspect of living with someone else in a studio apartment: if one person was sound asleep, that meant either you also slept or you were forced to move around like a mouse. Which was what he did now, tiptoeing first to the kitchen for a glass of water, then over to the couch. He didn't want to turn on the TV and risk waking her up, so instead he curled up with his phone and started scrolling through social media. At this time of night, most of the people he followed were either asleep or from a vastly different time zone. None of them were saying anything worth his attention. Pictures of coffee, memes he'd seen a thousand times already, dramatic opinions about television shows he had no intention of ever watching. He hopped around a couple of his favorite subreddits. Nothing of interest anywhere. The world was ending. Fascism was on the rise. Middle-aged white women were upset about fast food service. A celebrity had said something problematic. Nothing Daniel hadn't seen before.

He set his phone down on the armrest and closed his eyes. The more he focused on trying to sleep, the less tired he felt. Instead of counting sheep, he started keeping tabs on each one of his teeth by pressing his tongue against them. He couldn't remember the last time he'd lost a tooth. Certainly not any since childhood. How many teeth did the average adult have in their mouth? He felt like he should've known the answer to this. A simple statistic any semi-intelligence person would be able to recite on demand. Not Daniel, though. He'd never paid attention to that kind of stuff. Not that he was better than anybody else. It just never interested him. Back in school, he could usually be found at the back of class, some paperback novel hidden inside the textbook the rest of the class was busy studying. Reading fiction had been his primary focus back then, and not much had changed since. Did he often find himself feeling stupid about basic shit, as consequence? Constantly. But at the end of the day, did it really matter that much? Weren't they all heading down the same path, anyway? It didn't matter what you did in life, what you chose to focus on, what you learned. The crimes you committed or the good deeds you did when nobody was looking. When you got right down to it, everybody was gifted the same one-way ticket to a grave. Underneath all this disgusting flesh, everybody was just a skeleton.

A skeleton.

He'd never thought of his teeth like that before. As part of his skeleton. But now that was all he could obsess over, thanks to Eileen's offhand remark as she drifted asleep. What was it, exactly, he found so unnerving about skeletons, anyway? Most living—*and dead*—things had one. They were just bones, right? And what was so scary about—

Bones.

There, that word. *Bones.* It struck a nerve, but he wasn't sure why. Not at first. He had to sit there on the couch with nothing but his thoughts for a while, examining the word in his mind space like someone might rotate a newly acquired video game item in their character's inventory screen. Not that Daniel had much time for PlayStation nowadays, but man did he miss it sometimes. Any gaming systems they might've once owned had been long pawned by now. Either to pay rent or make up for

I BELIEVE IN MISTER BONES

royalties they had to borrow to pay rent. In the end, the decision had probably been beneficial in more than one way. Daniel wasn't someone who could simply play a game for a half hour and then call it quits for the day. He leeched onto things. He got addicted. He obsessed. Which meant he fell further behind on publishing duties. Which meant Eileen got frustrated, since a delay in production on Daniel's end meant a shorter deadline for Eileen's portion of work—she couldn't begin formatting a manuscript, after all, until after Daniel and the author had wrapped on the editorial side of things. Which meant their authors got pissed—or, at the very least, disappointed. And that was, of course, Daniel's worst nightmare: their authors upset with them.

All of that was to say: removing certain distractions from his life, it wasn't such a bad outcome, even if the circumstances leading to the decision hadn't been the most ideal.

But he didn't want to think about video games.

Tonight was all about bones.

Not just because of what Eileen had said, he eventually realized. Her weirdo comment had functioned more as a reminder. But a reminder for what?

The email he'd gotten earlier.

The one he'd noticed while at the mall, fucking around with his phone on the toilet.

DO YOU BELIEVE IN MISTER BONES? the subject line had read.

It didn't take him long to find it again in his trash folder, half-buried with a dozen obvious phishing scams he'd deleted without bothering to open in the first place. It was past midnight and he was wide awake. At the very least, maybe this book would put him to sleep. He certainly never expected to stay up the rest of the night reading it in its entirety.

Which was, of course, exactly what ended up happening.

MAX BOOTH III

Daniel fell asleep early that morning, just before dawn, seconds after finishing the last sentence of the *Mister Bones* book. Like he'd been in a trance, unable to look away until there was no more text to consume. The cell phone he read it on, at this point its battery percentage crossing over into single digit territory, slipped out of his hand and landed somewhere between the couch and the coffee table. His neck stretched in a position he'd later regret. Although he did dream, he would not remember the contents of the dream upon waking—only the feeling it gave him. And that feeling was uneasiness. That feeling was . . . unrest. Beyond these vague, displeasing sensations, he couldn't remember anything else about what he might've dreamed. And, if he *could* remember, he would have wished to forget as soon as possible—to forget that, in this dream, he was in a hole. A grave, the dream version of him concluded. No coffin protection from the insects and all the other subterranean *things* that dwelled under the ground, that waited under our feet. Just a hole in the dirt that someone or something had buried him in. He couldn't move. He couldn't make a sound. His body was pinned by six feet of earth. Grains of soil that felt weightless when falling between one's fingers but cosmic when dumped over their horizontal carcass. In the dream, he tried to break loose. He tried to rise from the mound like an old-school movie zombie. He didn't have the strength. He was helpless. The dirt was crushing him, flooding orifices until he was more dirt than man. One by one, he heard the sound of every bone in his body snapping. But it didn't hurt. It didn't feel like anything at all. In dreams, pain stopped existing. But no, Daniel didn't remember any of that. He'd always had trouble recalling his dreams. They tended to fade from memory seconds after regaining consciousness. The dreams weren't for Awake Daniel. They were for someone else, someone he'd never have the privilege to meet.

I BELIEVE IN MISTER BONES

Heavy footsteps eventually woke him up. *Intentionally* heavy footsteps. The kind of footsteps an annoyed person might initiate while trying to make someone else aware of their irritation. The foot-stomper was clearly his wife. What she was annoyed about, however, took a little longer to figure out. First he had to acknowledge the immense pain bursting from his neck. Trying to move only spread the awfulness throughout his shoulders. This was the usual consequence of falling asleep on the couch. He'd done it many times in the past, and on every occasion expressed surprise when he woke up feeling like shit. He would never learn his lesson—about this, and about many other things too numerous to list here.

Eileen was still stomping around the apartment. His vision hadn't quite adjusted yet to make sense of the context. He reached toward the coffee table for where he assumed he'd left his cell phone, but came up empty, leaving him nowhere else to direct his gaze but at his frustrated wife as she stepped out of the apartment, leaving the door wide open. He remained where he lay and waited for her to return. When she did, she was drenched in sweat and carrying a folded-up table.

"Oh, shit," Daniel said, realizing too late what was going on, "why didn't you wake me up to help you?" He sprung off the couch and glanced around the floor for some clothes to throw on.

"I tried," Eileen said. "You made a grouchy noise and rolled away from me." She leaned the table against the wall, next to two other tables she must've brought in while he was asleep.

"Well, shit, let me go get the rest." He was nearly finished wrestling his shoes on.

She shook her head. "It's fine. That was the last of it, anyway." She nodded to the other book boxes next to the tables, stacked haphazardly like chaotic Jenga blocks.

For a moment, both of them stared at the work she'd done without him. He knew full well he'd been the one who suggested leaving everything in the car last night, that it'd be easier to unload in the morning once they'd had some rest. Although she claimed she'd tried waking him up, something told him she hadn't tried very hard. He wasn't a deep sleeper. Immediate cynicism theorized whether she actually tried, if instead she'd set out to make him feel bad for not helping. Even Daniel knew this was a stupid idea. Eileen wasn't that kind of person. He was just tired, and his neck hurt, and he couldn't shake this weird, uneasy feeling that'd carried over from sleep. Those kinds of factors could make anybody think the worst about the people they loved the most. Brains were conditioned to lash out when they felt mistreated. It didn't matter who was responsible for the abuse.

Still, he couldn't help but ask, "Are you sure you tried to wake me up?"

The look she gave him made him regret opening his mouth. "Do you see anybody else here I could have mistaken for you? I shook your shoulder. I called your name. I said, 'Daniel, wake up.' I offered to make you some breakfast. I told you the coffee was ready. You were out cold. How long was I supposed to wait for you?"

"Wait—what time is it, anyway?"

"It's almost one."

"Oh, shit," he said, convinced he was late for something but oblivious to what, exactly, that could've been. This was a frequent feeling—this suspicion of displaced tardiness, of being perpetually behind on everything. He imagined most folks in the publishing industry would've been able to relate. There was no solution other than to quit everything, which Daniel tended to consider multiple times a day. What stopped him from following through with it was the fear of not having any other interests or talents in life. He'd spent so many years doing nothing else but being a publisher that it was highly likely there was nothing else of him left. Was this a depressing thought? Maybe. Would it go away—or, at the very least, weaken—with a fresh cup of coffee? Without a doubt.

He made it to the kitchen, fetched a clean mug from the cabinet, and stared dumbly at the empty pot. He turned back to Eileen, who was back to work unloading the boxes she'd brought in by herself—returning books to their rightful shelves, promo materials to their individual containers.

"I thought you said there was coffee," he said, weakly.

She paused and glared at him in disbelief. "Yeah, there was. This morning. I drank it all waiting for you to get up."

"Oh." He set the empty mug on the counter, unsure how to proceed. Only seconds before, he'd been operating in a reality where the coffeemaker still contained enough for him. For this fantasy to shatter so quickly and easily, it had a temporary paralyzing effect on his cognitive abilities. Yet he was conscious that, from Eileen's perspective, he must've looked like a malfunctioning robot. By now he was sure she was used to these moments. He forced himself to snap out of it, and proceeded to brew a new pot. As the black liquid dripped into the glass canister, he helped her finish up emptying the boxes, then stored the containers in the closet with the rest of their miscellaneous shit. They had to push the door shut together to keep it from bursting open again.

"We really oughta look into renting a storage unit one of these days," Daniel said, somehow already out of breath.

"We have," Eileen said, plopping down on the couch, "and we can't afford it."

"You know, most publishers, they have . . . like, whole offices. They have actual space."

She side-eyed him while scrolling Facebook on her phone. "We'll be lucky if we can pay off the venue for the book fest."

A familiar burning sensation yawned in his gut. "I thought we'd already paid that."

"Only the deposit. We still owe another twenty-five hundred."

"Wait, holy shit, really? When's the deadline to turn that in?"

"As long as they have it, like, two weeks before the event, I think we'll be okay."

"Are we . . . you know, going to be able to?" Daniel asked, hating how clueless he sounded. Eileen was the one who handled all of the accounting—both for the company and their personal lives. She'd worked as a bookkeeper in a previous life and understood how that kind of shit worked. Daniel was helpless when it came to numbers. It was a foreign language to him that he'd tried to understand and failed. Or maybe he'd never really tried as hard as he liked to think he had. Maybe he'd given up on math at the very first instance of frustration, and never looked back.

"It would help if we sold some more badges soon," she said. "I know LSI is due to pay us next week, but after royalties I'm not sure how much is going to be leftover." LSI referring to the print-on-demand company that distributed all of their retail orders besides ones made directly through the Fiendish webstore.

"Then I guess we need to sell more badges," Daniel said, feeling stupid for stating the obvious. Easier said than done. "When's the fest promo supposed to arrive? Soon, right?"

"I think next week," Eileen said. "Xio said they'd come with us if we want, to hand stuff out."

Daniel gulped, wondering what it'd be like to spend an entire day with Xiomara. "Since they've done it before, it might be a good idea."

Since starting the monthly popup events at the mall, Xiomara had racked up a ton of experience utilizing local promo. The thing they swore by the most involved literally walking into every public business around the city and asking to leave a stack of postcard-sized advertisements or hang up a flyer. The concept of not just interacting with

I BELIEVE IN MISTER BONES

hundreds of strangers but practically *confronting* them with such an awkward request terrified Daniel to the very core. Eileen thought it wouldn't be too bad, but she also seemed immune to the same crippling anxiety that controlled most of Daniel's life.

"What else do we have to do today?" he asked, still unable to shake that certainty of being late for something. "Did we have anything planned?"

"I don't think so," Eileen said. Still seated on the couch, she scooped up her vape pen from the table and started pressing its little boost button over and over until it was charged enough to take a couple hits. "I just have some freelance stuff to get done. What did you have in mind?"

The coffee had finally finished brewing. He retrieved the clean mug he'd already gotten down from the cabinet and fixed himself a serving. "I don't know. I'm kinda tired. Just hanging around sounds good to me."

"Are you feeling okay? You slept pretty late."

"I was up all night. Couldn't sleep." He thought about telling her how she'd spooked him with the teeth line, but knew she'd never let him live it down. "I ended up reading some submission instead."

"What submission?" she asked, half-hypnotized by the faint cloud of vaporization drifting out of her mouth. "I thought we weren't open right now."

He shrugged as he sipped the coffee. "I don't know. Some random one. We got it yesterday at the mall and I deleted it, then last night I was bored and decided to take a look."

"Is it any good?"

"I don't know. It's different."

"What's it about?"

"Hard to describe," he said. "Anyway, it's not important."

"Do we know the author?"

He shook his head. "There wasn't even a name listed. No byline or anything. Just the email address, which was weird and I think nonsense."

"Weird how?"

"Augustskeef."

"Excuse me?"

He spelled it out for her. Then said, "Maybe the author's name is August Skeef? But c'mon. That has to be one of the worst names I've ever heard, if so."

She rolled her eyes. "Perhaps they were too ashamed from ignoring our guidelines that they couldn't bear the thought of identifying themselves. Cowardice by, uh, anonymity."

"It also wasn't attached," he said, finding the whole thing funnier the more they discussed it. "The whole book was in the body of the email. No cover letter, no intro. Just straight to the story."

"And you read it?"

He stopped laughing and found himself blushing. "I couldn't sleep."

"It must not have been too bad, then, to have still gotten your attention despite its flaws."

"I don't know about that."

"Wait," she said, pausing as her mouth attempted to catch up to her brain, "you threw it away, and then took it out of the trash."

"Yeah, so?" He had no idea where she was going with this.

"You are literally Tabitha King," she said. "Remember, she took *Carrie* out of the garbage? Look at what happened to them because of that. Maybe this book will be our *Carrie.*"

"This is no *Carrie*," he said, then: "You know, I've never thought about it, but why the hell was she going through her husband's trash like that?"

She took a long hit of her vape and said, "You think I don't go through your trash? You think I don't read all the crumpled-up balls of paper you chuck from your typewriter out of frustration, because you so desperately want to become a professional novelist so all of your dreams can come true and you can support your family and you can stop working at the god*damn* laundromat and stop teaching snot-nosed punks high school English?"

"Wh-what?"

She got off the couch and stormed toward him in the kitchen, raising her fists. "You think you're better than Tabitha fucking King?"

"No, ma'am," he said, and took a nervous drink of his coffee.

"Name one book she's written."

"What?"

She reached forward with both hands and grabbed his nipples. "Name one fucking book written by Tabitha fucking King or you're going to lose these."

He managed to set the coffee cup down while only spilling a tiny bit. "I don't think I can."

"Wrong answer." She started to twist his nipples, and he screamed.

"Wait! Wait wait wait!"

She paused without releasing her grip. "Yes?"

"Didn't she co-write that one with Michael McDowell? The dude who wrote *Beetlejuice?*"

"What was it called?" She started twisting his nipples again.

"*Beetlejuice?*"

She let go of his nipples and snaked her hands down the front of his pants until she got a good grasp on his testicles. "If you fucking say that name one more time and summon a perverted ghost, I'm going to rip your balls off. I'm going to rip them off and I'm going to eat them, but not in a sexy way. In a scary way. And not in a scary-sexy way, either. In a scary-scary way."

"Wait, was he a ghost?" He wrapped his arms around her and held her against his chest. "I always thought he was more of a demon."

She relaxed her grip for a second. "You thought *who* was a demon?"

"Ummm . . . *Beetlejuice?*"

Panic widened her eyes and she squeezed his balls tighter. "Was that a third time?"

"I—"

"*Did you just say his name three times?*"

"I'm sorry! I didn't mean—"

"You know what happens now, right?"

"I'm afraid to guess," he said, absolutely rock hard.

Three and a half minutes later, as Daniel wiped the leftover cum from his softening penis while still standing in the kitchen, Eileen shouted from the bathroom, "*Candles Burning!*"

"What candles?" he asked, picking up the mess she'd made when bent over the counter only a moment or so beforehand.

"That was the name of the book she wrote with Michael McDowell. *Candles Burning*. She finished it after he died."

"Wow, I can't believe you remembered that."

She exited the bathroom, still nude, and held up her phone. "I had to look it up."

THE UNSOLICITED SUBMISSION was barely a novella. Daniel copied it from his email into a blank Microsoft Word document and checked the word count. In the world of publishing, most books were first categorized by a length statistic. Sometimes publications followed slightly different guidelines, but generally people agreed that anything over fifty thousand words qualified as a novel. Less than fifty thousand but more than seventeen thousand? Now you were in novella territory. Works between seven and seventeen thousand were called novelettes, and most folks in the industry viewed them as poison. Too long to sell to an anthology or magazine, and too short to print as a standalone. Below seven thousand was your standard short story. Less than one thousand? Micro fiction, or sometimes it was labeled flash fiction.

This submission—which Daniel had decided to call *I Believe in Mister Bones* since it lacked an official title—exceeded eighteen thousand words by just a couple sentences. If they decided to publish it, he doubted it would be long enough to fill out a spine, meaning it'd end up looking more like a chapbook. That was okay for selling through the Fiendish webstore and at popup events, but terrible for doing business with legit brick and mortar bookstores. Without a proper visible spine, shops couldn't shelve it unless they faced the cover out. Face-outs were preferable, of course, but booksellers tended to get grumpy when they didn't have a choice in the matter, which resulted in less overall sales.

Daniel wondered where he might suggest revisions on the manuscript to potentially expand the material. So far he'd read it in full once, and skimmed through it a second time. There was one peculiar chapter missing from the manuscript altogether. The title of the section was still there—"WIND CHIMES"—but below the title, in brackets, lingered only one italicized word: [*REDACTED*]. The chapter title itself was peculiar, as every other chapter followed a specific formula: listing someone's first name, then where the character was from. For example, the first chapter after the narrator's brief introduction was titled "STEPHEN, FROM BALTIMORE." Which made the redacted chapter all the more puzzling. Why *wind chimes*? What had this chapter consisted of before it was deleted? Daniel theorized it'd accidentally gotten carried over from a previous draft, and its inclusion here had been unintentional. But who knew? Maybe the chapter was pretty good, and could be added back to increase the word count.

If they could get it to at least twenty thousand words, that might've been enough to generate a spine. Additionally, if they could find room in their bank account, Daniel could also hire their go-to artist Betty Rocksteady to come up with some interior illustrations. There were a few scenes in particular that Daniel thought could've made for some real gnarly artwork. Hell, worst case scenario, Eileen could just get generous with the formatting and force the book to be longer than the word count justified. There were always workarounds to this kind of shit.

Assuming they accepted it.

Neither Daniel nor Eileen had the mental bandwidth to take on another book. Already for this year they had ten titles scheduled, not to mention two issues of their magazine *Fiendish Tales*. Next year they had three other books contracted. Daniel was hoping to keep it at that

I BELIEVE IN MISTER BONES

number, to massively pump the breaks on constantly overcommitting and killing themselves from exhaustion. Not to mention the fact that publishing was expensive, and only seemed to get pricier every year they continued. Between paper costs, book binding, and shipping rates, nothing about this industry was getting any more affordable. They didn't even know how they were going to pay off the venue for their book festival, and here he was debating whether or not to accept another manuscript?

Besides—they weren't open to submissions. This author, whoever they were—*August Skeef?*—had rudely ignored their submissions page, which stated in huge bold font: **WE ARE NOT CURRENTLY CONSIDERING UNSOLICITED SUBMISSIONS. ANY MANUSCRIPTS EMAILED TO US WILL BE DELETED UNREAD**. So why should he reward such behavior? He should have never read the book in the first place. Also, it wasn't like the book was *incredible* or anything. He'd read plenty of other novellas of much superior quality, both in prose execution and story ideas.

Yet.

There was something about this thing he couldn't stop thinking about, and this reaction to it, this lingering attachment, it would have been stupid to ignore. Because if Daniel was experiencing this after-effect, then that meant other readers would, too. Readers who would pay them money to read it. People wanted to read what others were talking about. They wanted to be involved in the conversation. FOMO was a very real thing in the book world, as it was everywhere else. All it'd take was one deranged vlogger claiming how much it'd fucked them up, and they'd be set.

Would it really fuck someone up, though? Daniel didn't feel psychologically scarred, or anything like that. It wasn't that kind of book. The ideas it presented were certainly weird and skin-crawling, yes, but its atmosphere never felt intentionally *spooky*. Instead, it came off as more . . . *educational?* Which, the more he thought about it, took on its own unique form of spookiness. So maybe he didn't know what he was talking about, after all.

The book didn't contain any dialogue, for one thing—not exactly a *red flag*, but the first time Daniel noticed its absence he let out a heavy sigh. Readers liked dialogue. Sometimes they skipped straight to it, glossing over important narrative paragraphs altogether. Daniel didn't approve of this behavior, but it wasn't like he could make people change how they processed text. Social media had rotted people's brains. Attention spans were nonexistent.

Once you got into the book, it made sense why the author hadn't bothered utilizing dialogue. This wasn't a typically-structured story. The narrator—who remained unidentified throughout the novella—was essentially a historian who had dedicated their life to documenting reported incidents involving the titular Mister Bones. Who Mister Bones was, exactly, was never quite explained. He was *something* that resided in a realm known only as Marrowland, which sounded astonishingly cheesy when Daniel said it out loud. His origin was unknown, as was his species, or biology, other than that he was made of bones. The bones of what, though, was unclear. He was a walking, animated skeleton, but a skeleton unlike anything anybody had ever seen. A one-of-its-kind monstrosity.

Physical descriptions of Mister Bones were kept ambiguous and inconsistent, due to the nature of how he traveled from Marrowland to "our world." In most of the recorded incidents, any actual sightings of Mister Bones occurred in dreams only, which Daniel knew made the whole thing feel sorta like a Freddy Krueger knockoff, and if it'd stopped at that he would have brushed the whole thing off as unoriginal trash, but of course there was more to it.

The lore wasn't overly complicated, which Daniel appreciated. Essentially, there was a . . . a *thing,* an evil presence named Mister Bones. He seemed to somehow simultaneously exist everywhere and nowhere. He could

I BELIEVE IN MISTER BONES

be summoned from Marrowland, but summoning him was never a good thing, it was always a mistake. Summoning Mister Bones made you, the summoner, a target.

How one summoned Mister Bones—now, that was one of the details Daniel couldn't stop thinking about, one of the reasons this book stood out to him as something interesting and refreshing. All you had to do was break a bone while actively thinking about him—about Mister Bones. He had to be on your mind at the specific moment the bone fractured. The pain, the intensity, the *blasphemy* of violating the ultimate anatomical taboo, it disturbed him out of wherever he hibernated—conjured him back into existence, until he finished the one task he was hellbent on accomplishing:

Collecting every single bone from your miserable little body.

How he did this wasn't thoroughly described. The summoner was asleep during the process, so of course the recorded incidents would be fuzzy here. What *was* known was he didn't acquire them all at once. He took his time, collecting a few here and there every time his target succumbed to a fresh slumber. The dreams were always graphic and horrific. The summoner maybe never got a chance to see Mister Bones in the corporeal world, but they sure as hell encountered him in their unconsciousness while the bone heist unfolded, and there was nothing they could do about it. Everybody had to sleep. Sooner or later, it happened to us all. You could drink coffee or pop uppers or tape your eyelids open but all that shit was just delaying what was already pre-programmed.

Delaying Mister Bones from taking what now rightfully belonged to him.

Because those bones . . . they *did* belong to him now.

They were his price, his *reward* for having yet again been summoned away from his home, from Marrowland.

It often took the summoner some time to realize their bones were being stolen, too. Mister Bones was slick. He was a seasoned veteran. He didn't just empty out the limbs, rendering them floppy and useless. Instead, he *replaced* the stolen bones with fake ones before they ever woke up. But what were the fake bones made out of? What did "fake bones" even *mean,* right? Another detail stranded in the depths of ambiguity. Some substance of Mister Bones's own creation. There was a chapter halfway through the book that detailed someone performing an autopsy on an alleged victim of Mister Bones—titled "DOCTOR ZWEIG, FROM NEVADA." The pathologist character described the material as rubbery and clay-like, unlike anything he'd encountered in all of his professional years. Any further investigation by the pathologist was not included in the chapter, and the character was never mentioned again. Expanding a bit on that character, spending some more time with him and his work, that could've been a smart way of increasing the word count a little bit—just enough to fill out a spine on the paperback release. Daniel made a mental note to bring it up once he finally got in contact with the author. August Skeef or whatever their name ended up being.

So that was the gist of what Mister Bones *did,* but what *was* he, exactly? A ghost? A demon? Some kind of mythological god? The narrator did not speculate one way or the other. Instead, they walked the reader through each recorded incident in chronological order, while stressing heavily that these events were only the ones they could confirm without any shred of doubt, implying that the exact number of Mister Bones's victims could very well be in the hundreds, if not thousands. There was no three-act structure. There was no *resolution.* It was all matter of fact. There was something named Mister Bones, and throughout history, people all over the world had accidentally summoned him. Once summoned, their lives were made a living hell until either the ensuing madness drove them to suicide *or* their bodies simply ran out of bones necessary for survival. Nobody had ever gotten the

I BELIEVE IN MISTER BONES

best of him. Every incident ended the same, more or less. Which could be considered *boring*, maybe, or it could also be interpreted as cosmic horror at its finest. Everybody unlucky enough to run into Mister Bones soon discovered just how insignificant their lives really were, and how once a certain sequence of events was triggered, there was not a goddamn thing they could do to stop the inevitable.

The whole thing was sorta beautiful, the more Daniel thought about it.

They were at an IHOP near the apartment consuming their weight in pancakes, eggs, and coffee. Daniel had his phone out, eyes glued to the screen as he slowly scrolled through a document. *The* document. The same one he'd been reading and re-reading for the last week. It was so bizarre, he kept thinking, how it continuously felt like he was experiencing the novella for the first time, as if the words and sentences were somehow rearranging and evolving between each reading.

Fingers materialized between his face and the phone.

Eileen's fingers.

Snap.

He glanced up at her and wondered how long she'd been talking to him. He hadn't heard a word she'd said. And, weirdly, he didn't feel bad about it like he normally would've. Like any decent person would've. He'd never admit it aloud, but he honestly wasn't all that interested in what she had to say right now. Not just her. Anybody. He needed more time to study the *Mister Bones* book. To figure it out.

"What?" he said. If he sounded cold, he couldn't tell. And besides, coming off as rude was only a natural consequence of someone snapping their fingers in your face.

"I thought we were going to finalize the panel ideas,"

she said, referring to a tiny notebook next to her half-eaten flapjack stack.

He turned his phone off and rested it on the table face-down, afraid the mere sight of the screen would lure him back into temptation. "Yeah, I know. I was waiting on you."

She laughed at his all-too-obvious bullshit of an explanation, then spun the notebook around so he could properly read what they had listed. "So, right now we have eighteen panels."

"Nice," Daniel said. "That's perfect."

She raised her brow at him, amused. "Well, no, it's not."

"Oh." He shrugged and shoved a forkful of pancakes into his mouth. "How many can we have?" he asked while chewing.

She held up one hand with all fingers extended.

"Five?" Panic forced him to swallow the pancakes prematurely.

"Plus ten more."

"So . . . fifteen? We can have fifteen panels?"

She nodded while sipping her coffee.

"That the weirdest way you could have answered that." He leaned over the table and scanned the list. "So, we need to cut three panels. Easy."

"I was thinking maybe the wrestling one," Eileen said.

For a brief second, Daniel forgot all about the book waiting for him in his phone. "What are you, crazy? That's the best panel idea we have."

"But we're not hosting a wrestling festival?"

"Yeah, but trust me. People are going to love that one." The panel in question was called Horror Writer Royal Rumble, and the idea was for panelists to speculate on who in the horror genre was the toughest son of a bitch to ever live. In his head, there would be discussions mapping out imaginary fights between writers like Shirley Jackson and Mary Shelley, Stephen King and Dean Koontz, Thomas Ligotti and Nic Pizzolatto, etc. It'd be the perfect amount of chaotic silliness needed to close out the weekend. By then, nobody would want to be serious. They'd be exhausted, disoriented, ready to go home. So why not send them packing in a good mood?

"Okay, then which ones do you think we should cut?" Eileen asked.

Daniel scanned the list again. The Royal Rumble they were keeping no matter what. When initially brainstorming the programming, they'd settled on a few ground rules that would help them stand out from the many other conventions out there that focused on horror literature. The biggest difference being that their festival would be marketed to fans of the genre, rather than creators. Most of these other fests catered to other writers. All of the promotion was directed to them, and so was the programming. While there was nothing wrong with that, in theory, that still wasn't the type of event Daniel and Eileen wanted to organize.

The main issue with a writer-focused festival was, of course, the exclusion of readers. Obviously writers were also readers, but reading wasn't the reason they attended the event. They traveled there to improve their craft and network with others in the industry. Which resulted in the vendor rooms at these things becoming a ghost town for the majority of the weekend. It was Daniel and Eileen's theory that if they instead threw all of their promotional efforts into advertising the Fiendish Book Festival as a celebration of the horror genre for all fans of spooky literature, that would attract a bigger crowd eager to spend money at each table. Another decision they'd made early on, which a lot of these festivals seemed allergic to doing, was to make the vendor room free to the public. Removing this barrier would convince so many more people to come give the event a chance. And, if they found anything appealing about checking out the panels and live readings, they could easily purchase a badge—either beforehand or during the weekend.

Which meant the programming had to also align with their other promotional efforts. They needed to attract not just writers but all horror aficionados. This was why most of the panel ideas in Eileen's notebook consisted of things like GOOSEBUMPS NOSTALGIA and FAVORITE URBAN LEGENDS. They made sure to include a couple craft-based panels, mostly to appease the writers who did plan on attending—stuff like HOW TO BREAK INTO HORROR and HOW TO RESEARCH STORIES—but those were the minority. For the most part, the programming would center around a more general interest in the genre.

"I think we could merge the WITCHCRAFT and OCCULT panels," Daniel said. "They're kind of the same thing, right?"

"Easy," she said, and made an adjustment with her pen. The ink was dark purple, and along its plastic casing a cheap buy-promotional-stationary-in-bulk website had printed FIENDISH BOOKS in red font. "That leaves two more to eliminate." She sucked in a breath. "I know you probably don't want to hear this, but I think we should remove the DUCKS panel."

"Oh, god," Daniel said. The DUCKS panel had originated from an inside-joke in the Fiendish Books Discord. One of the members had purchased a zombified rubber duck and posted it in the #general-discussion channel requesting name recommendations. Five days later and still nobody could decide on the best choice, resulting in Daniel having to rename the channel #ducks and create a separate #general-discussion area now that the old one had been completely overwhelmed with duck content. Since a good chunk of the current badge holders were also recognizable names from the Discord, Daniel thought it'd be fun to moderate a whole panel about the damn things. But Eileen was right. It wasn't worth the headache, if the schedule didn't allow for it. "Yeah," he said, "it has to go."

She crossed it out, and a small part of him died inside. "Okay, one more?"

I BELIEVE IN MISTER BONES

He scanned the list again, and the answer was obvious. "We should cut the AI panel." The tentative title they'd given the panel was FUCK AI AND EVERY TALENTLESS HACK WHO USES IT, which was admittedly too long to print in a program book.

"Are you sure?" Eileen said.

Daniel nodded and held out his empty coffee mug for the IHOP server approaching them with a fresh pot. As she topped both of them off, he said, "Our whole mission statement is being a celebration of horror, right? A panel discussing AI would be the antitheses of that. It'd just bum everybody out."

The server, now finished pouring the coffees, paused at their table and said, "Oh, god, I'm sorry, but that whole AI stuff really freaks me out."

"It freaks us out, too," Eileen said.

"I know this guy from school," she said, "he got expelled because he kept making AI nudes of all the girls in his class. I think he might've gotten arrested?"

"I wonder if that technically qualifies as possessing child pornography," Daniel said. Both women stared at him with disgust. "I mean, *would* it? If so, he could be in some real, long-term trouble."

"As he should be," Eileen said.

Daniel chuckled nervously. "I'm not arguing that! I was just wondering if having AI child porn resulted in the same repercussions as having, like, *real* child porn . . . you know?"

The server gasped and strode away from them.

"What the hell did I do?" Daniel asked.

"I don't know," Eileen said, "but I'd recommend not saying 'child porn' so loud in a public restaurant."

She made a good point. "Okay," he said, "so, do you agree the AI panel should be cut?"

Eileen nodded overly enthusiastically. "After what just happened, yeah, I think you've more than made your point." She crossed off the AI panel from the list. "That brings us to fifteen, which should be perfect."

"And there's still room for readings?" Daniel said.

"Yeah, the way we have things scheduled, we'll go panel, reading, panel, reading, panel, reading, et cetera."

"Perfect." This was exactly the way they'd discussed handling things when first deciding to organize the festival. Too many other conventions overlapped their programming, forcing attendees to choose between two-to-three events at a time. It wasn't fair to the badge holders and it certainly wasn't fair to the panelists and performers. Sure, this meant that they couldn't host as many panels or live readings as they might've liked, but in the end they speculated it would make for a more satisfying weekend overall. "What do we do next? With the programming, I mean."

"I guess we need to start emailing people to see who wants to be on what," she said.

Meaning, specifically, the vendors, guests of honor, and everybody who had already purchased a badge up to that point. Ethically, Daniel wondered if they were making a mistake by not offering to comp badges for those volunteering to participate in panels. But at the same time—they hadn't even sold thirty badges yet, and he knew at least ninety percent of those who had bought one already were interested in being on panels. If they comped all of them, he wasn't sure how they'd actually make any money outside of book sales from their own vendor table. Maybe if more casual fans started buying badges they could consider it, but it didn't seem too likely at that point. They *were*, however, comping Fiendish authors. More of their authors present meant more people promoting the books at the Fiendish table. That was the hope, at least.

"Okay," he said, "I guess when we get home we can just . . . like, bulk email everybody the list we've come up with, and ask them to reply back with their top three preferred panels. I think, as long as everybody can get at least one thing, they'll be happy."

"Same with the readings," Eileen reminded him.

I BELIEVE IN MISTER BONES

"Depending on demand, we have to give them either a panel slot or a reading slot, not both."

"Or maybe nobody will want to do anything," Daniel said, "and you and me will be running around pretending to be famous authors on each panel. How's your Stephen King impersonation?"

Eileen mimicked snorting a line of cocaine from the table and said, in a nasally voice, "Anybody over two hundred and fifty pounds is so morbidly obese that they are literally evil. Hello, my name is Stephen King and I have literally zero concept of what people in real life actually weigh."

"Nailed it," he said, laughing, then noticed a couple sitting across the aisle giving them a mean look, and laughed even harder.

A lull in their conversation followed, which they took advantage of by finishing the rest of their now-cold breakfasts. Eileen excused herself to the bathroom while Daniel took care of the bill with the company card. They had, after all, discussed almost nothing else besides company-related stuff during the meal—surely enough to satisfy any audio-recording devices secretly installed on their phones by the IRS. He sat in the waiting area at the front of the IHOP as he waited for Eileen to finish in the bathroom, thought maybe he'd check his messages or notifications but instead found himself opening the *Mister Bones* book again. He stared at the opening sentence and read it a couple times. *I believe in Mister Bones, and by the end of this book so will you.* First person, but who was the narrator? The author, or some unnamed protagonist? Either were equally unknown. Augustskeef. August Skeef. Augusts Keef. What were the other alternative words he could scramble from that nonsense? He was still building up the nerve to respond to them. Not that he was afraid. It was more like he was unsure whether or not he gave enough of a shit to follow through. If this breakfast meeting had been any inclination, they had more than enough other projects occupying their time. But, with that said . . .

There was something about this fucking book.

And it was going to drive him crazy trying to figure out what it was.

"You ready?" Eileen asked, having somehow spawned in front of him as he scrolled through the manuscript.

"What?" he said, spooked, and stuffed the device back in his pocket, feeling weirdly guilty. "Yeah, let's go."

"Okay," Eileen asked on the drive back to the apartment, "what is this book about? The bones book." She was driving, and he'd been trying his best to resist pulling out his phone again. Not that she'd asked him not to look at it, or anything. There was this weird sense of shame he always experienced when spending time focused on a cell phone screen while in the presence of others. At some point in the past, he'd conditioned himself into believing such behavior was impolite.

"Well, that's kinda complicated," Daniel replied, and winced at his own response, feeling like he was already on the losing side of an imaginary argument that hadn't officially started yet. "It's not, like, a standard story. The way it's written is very untraditional."

"Untraditional how?"

"Hmm. I guess it's written . . . almost like a warning."

"A warning? To whom?"

"To the reader."

"Oh. That sounds kinda cool," Eileen said. From the center console, she dug out her vape pen and took a hit, then passed it to Daniel. "What is it warning the reader about?"

"Mister Bones," he said, and set the vape down without using it. He didn't like to get high this early in the morning. Eileen could be stoned twenty-four-seven and still function perfectly normal. Not Daniel, though. He was too much of a lightweight, and anxious enough while sober. Add a brain-altering chemical to the mix and things quickly started spiraling out of control.

She followed up with a question he expected, but hoped she wouldn't ask, if only because he still wasn't sure how to explain it. "And who is Mister Bones?"

"I'm not sure," he said. "He's like . . . a cryptid, or something. Wait, how would you define cryptids?"

"How would I define them?"

"Yeah, like, if someone had never heard of cryptids before—what would you say so they understood what they were?"

"I don't know. Just, like, some weird animal, I guess?"

"But is Bigfoot an animal? That's a cryptid, too, right?"

"Even humans are animals . . . the most dangerous animal of all, some might say," she whispered, more to herself than him, and he knew the vape was already doing its job.

"What about something like the *Babadook*? Is that a cryptid?"

"The Babadook?" she said, reaching for the pen again and giggling. "You mean the one from the hit motion picture *The Babadook*, or are we talking about a completely different Babadook?"

"Uh, the first one."

"From the hit motion picture *The Babadook?*"

" . . . Yeah."

"I don't know if he's a cryptid, but I'm pretty sure he's a queer icon."

"I've seen those memes, too."

"I don't remember what he did in the movie to deserve that title, though."

"If I remember right, it was something stupid, like Netflix accidentally added it to their LGBT category, or something, and then Tumblr went wild with the screenshots."

"Plus."

He glanced at her, perplexed. "Plus what?"

"LGBT plus."

"Oh," he said. "Well, yeah, that's what I meant."

"Aren't cryptids supposed to be, like, animalistic in nature? Something resembling an animal. And they're not always represented as fictional, right? Like, a lot of people believe in Bigfoot or the Mothman or whatever."

"Do you think people really believe the Mothman exists?"

"Of course they do," she said. "I mean, come on, there's a lot of people out there convinced drinking water turns you gay."

Imitating an outraged lisp, Daniel exclaimed, "It *doesn't*?"

"Don't be homophobic," she said, not a trace of humor in her tone.

"I don't think I was," he said, terrified he'd gone all these years not realizing he was homophobic. "Anyway, if the Babadook isn't a cryptid, what is he?"

She shrugged, taking another hit from the vape as she waited at the intersection next to their apartment complex. "I don't know. It's been forever since I watched that movie. I guess . . . just, like, some kind of . . . uhh, I don't know, *mysterious entity*, or whatever. Wait, why are we talking about the hit motion picture *The Babadook* again?"

"Because you asked about the submission we got."

"It's about the Babadook?"

"No, it's about Mister Bones, which is . . . *maybe* similar to the Babadook," he said. "I like what you said, though. Mysterious entity. That's perfect. Like the boogeyman or something."

"Well, what's the deal with this Mister Bones dickhead, then? I assume he's the bad guy, right?" The light turned green and she veered left into their complex. Miraculously, nobody had stolen their reserved parking spot.

Before heading inside, they walked across the lot to retrieve the mail. It was chilly out, but a nice chilly. The exercise felt good—a necessary boost post-pancakes, a food

I BELIEVE IN MISTER BONES

that could taste so delicious one minute and then turn their stomachs into concrete before the next one started.

Along the way, Daniel continued filling her in on the book.

"The way it's written, it's almost like a long . . . uh, history lesson, I guess. Like a historical record of this thing called Mister Bones, a document chronicling his various sightings throughout time."

"What is he, exactly? What does he do?"

"Some kind of skeleton," he said, struggling to remember the specifics now that he was being forced to concentrate. "Like . . . a skeleton, but not quite a skeleton. You know what I mean?"

"Does it seem like I know what you mean?" she asked, handing him a stack of packages from their mail slot.

He gritted his teeth, annoyed with his own inability to describe something he'd been thinking about off-and-on for almost a week now. "He steals bones."

"Mister Bones steals bones?" She shut the mailbox and locked it, then took a handful of the mail from Daniel so they both had an equal balance in each of their arms. "Whose bones does Mister Bones steal, exactly?"

He shrugged, already convinced he needed to reread this thing again. "Anybody's. It just depends on who summons him."

"Wait." She paused mid-stride and glanced at him in the middle of the apartment complex parking lot. "How does somebody *steal* bones? You mean, like, after they're dead? Grave-robbing or whatever? Jesus Christ, could you imagine being a grave-robber? How exhausting would that be?"

"No, he steals them while you're still alive. When you're asleep."

"Okay," she said, "I admit that's pretty cool. But how does he do it?"

"He replaces them with . . . uh, fake bones."

"Fake bones?"

"Yeah."

"Now, what the hell does that mean?"

63

NOBODY EMAILED BACK the first time Daniel responded to the *Mister Bones* submission. A week later, his inbox remained empty. Well, not *empty* empty. No publisher's inbox was ever light on unread messages demanding their immediate attention. But it was empty of the one email Daniel was waiting to receive. The one from augustskeef@yahoo.com.

This baffled him more than the content of the actual book. Writers spent most of their time refreshing inboxes waiting on good news. For someone not to respond to a publishing inquiry one week after Daniel sent it . . . he didn't know what to think about that. To be fair, it wasn't like he'd emailed an acceptance or anything.

The message had been brief, but concise: *Hi, August, I am interested in discussing your manuscript. Can you confirm it's still available?* What he expected was to hear back from the author within twenty-four hours with an enthusiastic *Yes!!!* Or anything, really. Anything but silence. Unless the author had already sold it elsewhere, and was too chicken-shit to admit it. Not that there was anything wrong with simultaneous submissions. Some presses prohibited them in their guidelines, and Daniel never understood why. It wasn't like the presses were paying the writers to hold it for any exclusive amount of time.

Besides, this author had already proven they didn't

have much respect for publishers' guidelines, considering they'd submitted it to Daniel in the first place.

Whoever this author even was. The email address didn't offer many clues. Nothing that Daniel could research. He'd tried searching "augustskeef" and all of its variations online. Nothing worthwhile. According to Urban Dictionary, "skeet" could mean "to steal." Additionally, "skeefing" meant "skeeting while cheefing" which Daniel then translated to mean "ejaculating while smoking a lot of marijuana." Beyond aggravating. It was as if the author had zero intention of ever getting published, like they were purposely trying to get rejected. Maybe frustrating indie horror publishers was this author's kink. If that was the case, Daniel hoped they were having the orgasm of their life right now.

He checked his spam folders daily, sometimes hourly, in between fidgeting with other mundane tasks. Sometimes he scrolled through the manuscript searching for any identifiable details he might've missed on previous readings. There was nothing there. Nothing beyond the novella. What was this author's goal? Why the fuck did they send it to him? He wanted to forget about it and move on, but for whatever stupid reason he couldn't.

A week after sending his first response, Daniel sent a follow-up. *Hi! Me again. Just confirming you received my previous email? Thanks!* Within seconds of clicking SEND, his inbox's bolded unread tally increased by one digit. The briefest rush of endorphins flooded his brain before registering the new email's subject line: Delivery Status Notification (Failure). He clicked on it despite already knowing what the message would say:

Address not found

Your message wasn't delivered to **AUGUSTSKEEF@YAHOO.COM** because the address couldn't be found, or is unable to receive mail.

MAX BOOTH III

In the week since Daniel had sent his first response, this email address had either been deactivated, or . . . or what? They'd blocked Daniel from contacting them? The only reason he could imagine getting blocked again went back to the author having already sold the novella to another press. It would be a silly reason to block him, but at least Daniel could make some sort of sense out of it. A lot of people—himself included—loathed confrontation. They tried to avoid it however possible. Sometimes they took extreme routes to do so, such as what may have happened here. If that's really what happened. Daniel remained unconvinced. He googled around to learn whether or not a person was able to tell if they'd been blocked by someone else, and from what he was able to gather, the answer was no. It was more of a silent exile. The blocked party could continue sending the emails and never quite grasp why nobody ever replied. Which implied the notification failure Daniel received had nothing to do with getting blocked, and he was wasting energy worrying about reasons someone might've done so.

Meaning the email address no longer existed.

To be on the safe side—perhaps the author's email server had experienced a fluke glitch—he waited another day and then sent a third message to the same address. This time, instead of a direct reply, he drafted the email as its own unique message, complete with a different subject line. He even sent it from his personal account instead of the Fiendish Books Gmail. The same automatic failure notification generated his inbox.

Why would someone submit a book, and then deactivate their email? They hadn't deactivated right away, of course, otherwise Daniel would have gotten the failure notice after replying to the author last week. But he didn't. Not until he attempted to follow up a second time did it pop up. Meaning, for whatever reason, Daniel replying to the submission had done something to the author to warrant a full-on account deactivation.

I BELIEVE IN MISTER BONES

He racked his brain coming up with possible explanations, and ultimately settled on Occam's razor: people were fucking bizarre, and often did things for seemingly inexplicable reasons. Continuing down this impossible investigation would only put him further behind on real tasks he was responsible for accomplishing. Books needed to be edited. Books needed to be promoted. Author emails needed to be answered. Festival badges needed to be sold. There was always something that needed to be done. A small press publisher never had the luxury of a free moment. There was no such thing as a completed to-do list. When one job was checked off, three others took its place, and so on, forever, until Daniel and Eileen finally quit, if such a day would ever come, if such a day was even possible at this point.

He decided to send out one last hail mary before moving on with his life, and crossposted the following status across the half-a-dozen social media accounts he struggled to maintain relevancy on:

Sorry to post this here, but if you recently submitted a novella to Fiendish, I am trying to contact you and your email address no longer seems to be active. Specifically referring to a "Mister Bones" submission. If that doesn't make sense to you, then you aren't who I'm attempting to reach. If it does make sense to you, please either DM me or email me as soon as possible.

Within five minutes of publishing the post, he had to scramble to edit in an addendum: *And, no, we are NOT currently open for submissions. Please stop asking me this question.*

He knew the phrasing made him sound like a dick, but sometimes a firm tone was necessary when dealing with overeager writers.

Daniel checked his comments and DMs throughout the day as he worked on other projects, but nobody offered any useful information. All he received was a mix of authors continuing to inquire about submitting their own work, and other dickheads making jokes that involved the name Mister Boner, which Daniel supposed was inevitable. A title like that was practically designed for ridicule. He recalled reading an interview once—or maybe he'd listened to a podcast—with that one obnoxious author talking about his book *We Need to Do Something*. His name was Max Brooks, if he remembered correctly. The original title of the novella, which involved a possibly-supernatural tornado trapping a small suburban family in their home— had been *A Violent Wind*. But, after Brooks posted the title page on his Twitter account, numerous comments immediately generated below cracking a variety of fart jokes. It got to where he couldn't even celebrate the fact that he'd finished a new book without seeing another fart joke in his notifications. Brooks was so embarrassed that he had no choice but to change *A Violent Wind* to *We Need to Do Something* and delete the initial announcement, hopeful nobody remembered its original title—which made it funnier that Brooks would bring it up himself on the podcast, practically unprompted.

Daniel had always viewed this decision as cowardly. *A Violent Wind* was a great title, and so was *I Believe in Mister Bones*. Sure, that wasn't the official name, but it was the closest thing to one this book had so far.

Daniel forgot all about the Other folder. Over on Twitter— or whatever the site was called now—whenever someone you didn't already follow DM'd you, their message typically got placed in a folder marked Other, which took a couple extra thumb movements to access compared to the general inbox tab. Users weren't notified of these messages. He had to remember to occasionally check, which he seldom did. Most of the time, the Other folder consisted of cybersex spam and authors promoting book discounts or demanding to know when Fiendish would re-open for

I BELIEVE IN MISTER BONES

submissions. Honestly, he preferred the OnlyFans messages out of the two. At least those typically offered a brief glimpse of nudity before he clicked DELETE.

But sometimes the Other folder contained something useful, which was why he still bothered to check it. When he remembered to do so, at least. Which he didn't until a couple days had passed after cross-posting the public status seeking the vanished *Mister Bones* author.

They were driving to H-E-B, the central grocery store chain in San Antonio—Eileen behind the wheel, Daniel riding shotgun and aimlessly scrolling his newsfeed trying to catch up on the latest controversy in horror publishing. Some nobody micro press had announced a new book containing an obnoxiously transphobic premise. A portion of the internet gave them shit for it. Another portion praised them for it. Now the publisher couldn't stop posting delirious rants about woke culture canceling talented cisgender men. Real boring shit.

Daniel was about to put his phone away when his Twitter inbox blinked a blue digit at him. One of Fiendish's authors, a San Antonio local named Johnny Compton, had DM'd him to check if they thought his book would still be ready in time for the book festival. It had already experienced a couple delays—none of which were the author's fault, the blame laid solely on Daniel—and he was understandably worried about it hitting their targeted release date. Daniel replied that everything was running smoothly now, and to rest assured Daniel and Eileen wouldn't be stupid enough to spend all of this money hosting their own festival and *not* get one of their most-anticipated titles out in time for it.

In reality, though, Daniel was a little concerned. At least the book had already been story-edited. He just had to finish going through one last proof for typos before handing it over to Eileen for interior formatting. There was still time to get it finished. It would be close, but there was still time. Of course, Daniel would have preferred to have gotten it proofed and formatted months ago, to allow more time for reviewers to start building the pre-release hype train, but that no longer seemed as feasible. This was what happened when you scheduled ten books in one calendar year. You fell behind. You started compromising. You never stopped hating yourself.

It would be okay, though. It had to be okay. They'd figure it out. Daniel just had to focus. No more distractions. No more bullshit. When they got home later, he'd get out his laptop and start working and not stop until he'd finished proofing Compton's novel. Then he'd move on to the next projects they intended to launch at the festival, like the upcoming issue of *Fiendish Tales* and whatever else needed to be done that had already slipped his memory since the last time he reminded himself not to forget.

All good, Johnny replied. *Just excited! Let me know if there's anything I can do on my end to help.*

Thanks, Daniel typed back. *Updates soon!*

Then, just as he was about to close out of the app, he noticed the Other folder near the top of the inbox tab. When he maneuvered over to the filtered messages, the unsolicited submission wasn't on his mind. In all honesty, he'd already given up hope of ever learning more about the book and its mysterious author. What else could he have done? He'd tried everything he could think of trying. He wasn't a detective. He was a publisher—and, again, in all honesty, not a very good one at that. It was time to move on from books he'd never get the opportunity to work on and regroup on the ones he'd already contracted. The ones with real deadlines.

Which was why he was so blindsided when he screened the only unread message waiting for him in his Other folder. The sender's username was nonsense, an undecipherable combination of numbers. Their message consisted of a single line. It was a question Daniel had read before, one he knew by heart.

I BELIEVE IN MISTER BONES

Do you believe in Mister Bones?

According to the timestamp, it had been sent only a few hours after Daniel's social media post. He didn't think before responding. Instincts guided his fingers to type out: *Are you the author? Did you email me?*

While waiting for a response, he clicked over to the user's profile. It was brand new—created just this month, according to the statistic beneath their username. No public posts, no likes, no shares. The bio section was blank. The avatar was the same gray humanoid outline assigned to every account lacking an uploaded profile picture. A burner account, most likely. Was somebody fucking with him?

The inbox folder on the bottom of his screen blinked to life. The user had already responded, but with another question instead of answering anything Daniel had asked them:

Did you read it yet?

Daniel replied, *Yes.*

The user's next reply arrived seconds later.

What did you think of it?

Daniel stared at the question on his phone and concluded he was definitely talking to the person who had written the book. Nobody was more desperate to hear feedback than a writer.

"Dude," Eileen said, "are you coming in or what?"

He glanced up from his phone. She stood outside their car, staring at him from the open driver's door with a collection of recyclable bags draped over her arm. They were parked at the grocery store. He had zero memory of them arriving.

"Um," he said, because his brain hadn't fully caught up to speed yet, "yeah, sorry, one sec."

He unbuckled and got out of the car, one hand gripping the cell phone tight enough to send a wave of cramps through his fingers.

"Everything okay?" Eileen asked, as they walked across the packed parking lot toward the front of the store.

"Yeah," Daniel said. "I'm okay. I was just talking to somebody."

He scanned the lot nervously, forever paranoid a car was about to hit them. It baffled him how pedestrians could be so careless walking in and out of grocery stores. So many of them had their eyes glued to their phones as they stepped directly in front of traffic, seemingly content under the assumption that the giant boxes of steel death blasting past would honor the right of way. Even Daniel, who very much wanted to check his inbox again, would not dare look at his phone until they'd safely made it inside.

They collected a shopping cart under the awning. Eileen stuffed the recyclable grocery bags under the little shelf at the front of the cart reserved for fragile items like fruits and eggs. Inside, the store was bursting with noise. It was overcrowded as usual, children running wild, employees blasting music from their phone speakers, shoppers standing completely still in the middle of aisles as they texted others. Daniel didn't enjoy being another person staring at his phone as they maneuvered around the store, but he was left with no choice. The author was online *right now*. He had to continue the conversation. At the very least, he tried to remain aware of his surroundings and only check it when nobody else was within his orbit.

The last thing the unknown user had sent him was: *What did you think of it?*

Daniel had been contemplating his answer to this question since exiting the car. He still wasn't sure how to respond. What *did* he think of it? Did he actually *like* it? He must've, in some way. It'd sunk its hooks into him. That couldn't be ignored.

He typed back, *It's very interesting,* then put his phone away and grabbed a carton of coffee creamer for the cart. Eileen had been talking to him since entering the store, but he had no idea what she was saying. Once in a while he nodded and went *uh-huh* or *right* and that seemed to satisfy her enough.

I BELIEVE IN MISTER BONES

Then she said, "Are you even listening to me?"

And he paused and said, "What?"

She pointed at the dairy cooler again. "We also need milk."

"Oh. Right." He fetched the milk like an obedient husband.

"Who are you talking to?" she asked, amused. "You look . . . weird."

"I look weird?" He touched his face, as if that might somehow give him any indication of how he looked. He felt clammy.

"A little."

Some lady behind them cleared her throat, so they moved away from the dairy section and headed toward the next aisle.

"I think the author of *Mister Bones* reached out to me."

"Oh, shit, really?" she said. "Do we know them?"

He shook his head. "I don't know. They're using a burner account and haven't told me their name yet."

"Why . . . why would someone do that?"

"I don't know," he said, shrugging. "The internet is a strange place."

"Have you *asked* them who they are?"

"Not yet."

"Hmm. Maybe you should do that?"

"Okay, yeah, good point." He got out of his phone again. The user hadn't messaged him back yet.

Daniel typed, *Who are you?* and clicked SEND.

Three seconds later, they responded: *I'm a believer.*

He chuckled in the middle of the aisle, unable to prevent the obvious Justin Bieber joke from entering his head. This was officially getting too corny for him to handle.

Are you the author of the book or not? Stop wasting my time and tell me what this is all about.

He felt ridiculous giving this person so much attention, which was possibly exactly what the user was hoping to accomplish. Perhaps this was someone Daniel had crossed in the past. A disgruntled author trying to play a prank on him, or something. Or maybe one of the other small press publishers he sometimes feuded with online. There were too many to narrow down to just one.

"What did they say?" Eileen asked as they continued shopping. They were in the canned vegetables aisle now, on the hunt for store-brand green beans.

"Nothing yet." There was no way he could recite her the *I'm a believer* line with a straight face.

"Let's say it is the author, and they're legit," she said. "Do you think this is really a book we should publish?"

"I don't know. Maybe. Probably. Yeah, I think we should."

"Next year?"

He bit his tongue, resisting his true opinion, which would be to somehow put it out this year—not only that but in time for the festival. She'd kill him if he said that, though, so instead he said, "I haven't thought about it."

"It's weird how secretive they're being about everything, though," she said.

"Yeah, I know."

"Makes you wonder what they might be trying to hide."

"Maybe they're just concerned about their privacy," he said, even if he barely believed the theory himself. "Who knows, maybe they've dealt with stalkers or something in the past." He pulled out his phone. Another message awaited him.

I'm available for the next 10 minutes. After that, you'll never hear from me again.

The message was followed by a strange link, inviting him to a video call. According to the timestamp on the message, they'd sent it to Daniel six minutes ago.

Every logical instinct in him screamed DO NOT CLICK THAT LINK, YOU IDIOT.

Daniel shook all logic away and told Eileen, "Shit, they want to call me."

I BELIEVE IN MISTER BONES

She glanced over her shoulder, both hands gripped around the shopping cart handle. "Call you? What are you talking about?"

"I—I gotta go."

She laughed, but there was no amusement in her tone. Only concern. "What? Where are you going?"

"Just outside. I won't be able to hear shit in here."

She stared at him a moment before responding, then said, "Okay. Let me know what's going on when you're done."

He had maybe three minutes left to join the call, assuming the user was serious about what he'd said, and Daniel had no reason to believe otherwise. He took off running at full speed through the store, dodging oblivious shoppers and awkwardly maneuvering around sloppily-stacked merchandise displays. At one point, someone called him an asshole, and he dramatically shouted, "It's okay! I'm a book publisher!" as if that somehow explained anything—although, in a way, he supposed it did.

In a way, it explained everything.

There was no opportunity to catch his breath once he made it outside the H-E-B. Daniel couldn't remember the last time he'd properly exercised. The consequences of prolonged sedentariness were felt immediately. Bent over on the sidewalk in front of the grocery store, he pressed the video link and followed the site's directions to log in to the call. He didn't have any earbuds handy, so the conversation would have to broadcast over the phone's speaker. Not ideal, but it wasn't like he had much of a choice given the current circumstances.

Daniel gained access to the call. His own face appeared in the small box at the bottom of his screen, and he saw how pale and out of breath he looked. He straightened up and tried to compose himself. The other user's screen remained blacked out. Both the video and audio were disabled on their end. Their activity status, however, displayed that they were currently in the call. Meaning what? They were watching him. Listening to him. Still hidden.

"What the fuck is this?" he said, embarrassed by the gasp of breath he had to take afterward.

No response.

"Are you gonna fucking say something or what?" Daniel asked, one hand to his hip while the other held out the phone in front of his face. Shoppers entered and exited the grocery store giving him looks like he was someone to be avoided. Like he might be deranged. Dangerous. He ignored them and focused on the dark screen observing him. "If there's a point to any of this shit, get to it or I'm hanging up."

The red X indicating the user's disabled audio transformed into a green checkmark. A muffled, male voice emitted from the speaker, barely intelligible over the generic parking lot noises:

"Do you believe?"

He sounded sleepy, on the verge of falling asleep.

"Do I believe? Do I believe in *what?*" A stupid question. Obviously Daniel knew what he meant. "Dude, are you gonna show yourself or what?

"I didn't believe at first," the tired voice said. "I thought it was all bullshit. I thought it was a hoax."

Daniel took another deep breath and tried to calm his tone. "Listen, dude, I applaud you for the crazy marketing campaign here, but typically this stuff is reserved for the audience, not the publisher. I've already read the book, right? That's why I was trying to contact you in the first—"

"I didn't write it."

"What are you talking about? Why are you bothering me with this shit?"

He noticed a woman passing him with a small child in her shopping cart. She gave him a look like, *Really? You're using that kind of language with children present?* He faked a smile and shrugged. She returned the smile with a middle finger and the child started clapping and laughing, then they continued through the store's automatic entrance.

Into the phone, he shouted, "Who the fuck are you, then?" He didn't care if he sounded angry. He *was* angry, goddammit. Someone was fucking with him and he was sick of being the brunt of some unknown joke.

"I'm just like you," the voice whispered, and now the video icon changed from red to green, replacing the void of Daniel's screen with the caller's webcam POV and revealing a sickly gaunt man seated in front of his computer. "I'm just like you," he repeated.

"What . . . what does that mean?" Daniel asked. All of his anger drained like pus from a boil. He didn't know how to comprehend what he was staring at. This person, this man, was not well, and Daniel suddenly wished he'd never checked his Other folder and replied to his DM. He wished he'd never laid eyes on the human staring back at him. He wished he'd never resurrected the unsolicited submission from his trash folder.

Due to the man's severe malnourishment, his age was indiscernible. He could have been in his early twenties or his late sixties. He breathed long and heavy, wheezing with each exhale from lungs that sounded wet and clogged. His cheeks were caved in and his skull protruded against the skin of his forehead. His scalp and face were shaved down to the flesh. He wore a dirty white tank top; anything below that was out of the webcam's angle. He sat indoors, possibly a living room, but it was too hard to tell for certain. Behind him, no less than a dozen wind chimes hung from the ceiling, which blocked from view any other recognizable furniture or decorations.

The wind chimes were perfectly still.

Daniel was reminded of the redacted "WIND CHIMES" chapter from the manuscript, and thought, *Holy shit.* He stood on the sidewalk staring at his phone screen, waiting for a response. Shoppers dodged him with their carts. He paid them no attention. As far as Daniel was concerned, nothing outside of this video call currently existed.

"What do you mean, you're just like me?" Daniel asked again, voice weaker. His knees felt rubbery and wouldn't stop shaking. "What do you . . . what do you *mean?*"

"Have you broken anything yet?"

"Broken *what?*" Daniel said, but of course he knew. He paused, took a breath. "No. I haven't broken anything."

"What are you waiting for?"

"What the fuck does that mean?"

"Don't you believe?" he asked. "I thought . . . you believed." His voice grew sterner: "*I thought you believed.*"

Daniel studied the stranger's features again, and wondered not for the first time if he was conversing with someone genuinely out of their mind. "You look unwell, man. Do you need me to call someone? Where, um, where do you live, exactly?"

"He doesn't always have to take them," the man whispered, gazing off screen at something Daniel hoped never to see. "It's not about the theft. It's never been about the theft."

"Okay," Daniel said.

"He only steals them because he doesn't have any other choice. Because we don't believe enough. But it's better if he doesn't have to. It's better if we give them to him ourselves. If we make an offering. If we prove our faith."

The phone was overcooking in Daniel's hands and felt hot to the touch, but he didn't dare let go. Not now. "Who, uh, who are we talking about here?"

"You know who."

He was right, of course. Daniel *did* know. It was just too ridiculous to take seriously. Too silly to entertain as anything other than a prank. "You can't be serious," he said.

I BELIEVE IN MISTER BONES

The man held up his left hand to the webcam. His thumb and index fingers were missing. At the base of each phantom joint were scabbed-over nubs. "When it comes time to test your faith," he said, "are you going to be prepared? Because he'll come, either way. He *will* collect what belongs to him."

"What the fuck," Daniel said.

Then the man leaned aside and attended to something off-screen. Daniel heard him struggling but couldn't tell what, exactly, he was doing. Enough time passed that he debated whether or not he should hang up and join Eileen back inside the grocery store.

"Dude, are you still there?" he said, hoping he wouldn't receive an answer.

But of course he did:

"I'm almost ready," the man whispered somewhere off camera.

"Almost ready for *what?*"

As if the man had been waiting for Daniel to pose this question, the computer—a laptop, he guessed—swiveled around until it faced the opposite side of the room. Daniel spotted a garage door in the background, finally giving an answer to where this man was talking to him from. He was standing now, and with his full midsection in frame, Daniel had to hold back a gasp. He had never seen someone so thin before. Perhaps in photos on old schlock websites of Holocaust victims, but nothing else. Nothing like this.

In front of him, between his body and the laptop, was some sort of mechanism that Daniel struggled to comprehend initially. It was long, and consisted of steel spirals, like a tube, or a roll of some kind. Its design didn't make any sense. Not right away. The roll was elevated, with nothing beneath it, each end balanced over a wooden plank to prevent it from falling to the floor. Next to them, on its own table, appeared to be some kind of giant motor.

"What the fuck am I looking at here?" Daniel asked.

MAX BOOTH III

"This?" He pointed to the mechanism between them. "This is a torsion spring." Then, intuiting Daniel had no idea what that meant, added: "You ever wonder how garage doors can so effortlessly lift up and down?" He sounded less tired now. Reenergized. "It's because of these bad boys. Extremely strong torques. Very dangerous. Don't worry. I'll demonstrate in just a moment."

"I, uh, I think I need to get going. My wife is waiting on me."

The man leaned forward, over the torsion spring, squinting at the camera. "You wanted to know about Mister Bones, right?"

"The . . . the book?"

He smiled and shook his head. "This is about far more than a book." In his hands, he fiddled with some type of long strap. "This is about . . . *so much* more than a book. But to understand, to truly understand, you have to believe. You have to have faith."

Daniel stood in front of the grocery store, staring at his burning-hot phone with its decreasing battery percentage, paralyzed with the utmost certainty that he was about to witness something truly and irrevocably fucked up. "Hey, man," he stammered, voice so weak he wasn't sure if the phone even picked it up over the wind, "why don't you tell me your address?"

"Did you know," the man continued, "that the strongest muscle in the human body is the masseter muscle?"

"Wh-what?"

"And did you know," the man said, swinging the strap back and forth in his mutilated hands, "that the masseter muscle is in direct collaboration with the jawbone? In fact, our jaws would be rendered pretty useless without the masseter muscle, wouldn't you say?"

"Okay," Daniel said.

"I'm telling you this so you understand why the equipment here is necessary."

I BELIEVE IN MISTER BONES

"The . . . the equipment?" He stared at the torsion spring again, trying to make sense of everything and failing miserably.

"It's easy to remove your own finger bones," the man said. "Shit, most of your bones, if you have the right willpower, you can remove with a simple pair of shears, maybe a hacksaw. But something like the jawbone? Well, that's not so simple. That takes work. Work most people don't have the tenacity for. Faith isn't for slackers, is what I've come to realize. Faith requires sacrifices. To believe in something like this? To really, sincerely believe? It requires not just *a lot,* you understand. It requires *everything.* Are you following me? Do you understand what I'm telling you? Don't answer. I don't need you to answer. I need you to watch. It's the only way you'll get it. It's the only way you'll learn."

"Learn . . . what?" Daniel asked, on the verge of crying.

And the man said, with a twinkle in his eye, "That there are things in this world far more important than bones."

Then he stuffed a portion of the leather strap into his mouth, hooking the other end under his chin. Daniel remained standing on the sidewalk, legs weak, unable to look away as the man connected a thick wire to the strap and pulled it taut against the bottom of his chin. After that, he brought out a roll of duct tape and proceeded to wrap it across his lips and around the back of his skull until at least half of the tape had been unraveled, successfully trapping part of the strap inside his mouth, while the other part remained against his chin.

Tightly wrapped around his jawbone.

What the fuck what the fuck what the fuck, Daniel thought, pacing around the sidewalk now, watching as the man then connected the other end of the thick wire to the torsion spring between them. This wire was long, its exact length hard to tell as it seemed to spool at his feet out of frame. What did this mean? What the fuck did this mean? The man gave Daniel a thumbs-up with the one hand of his that still possessed a thumb, then he leaned over and pressed a button on the giant motor next to him.

Over the phone's speaker, a loud grinding noise erupted as the torsion spring started twisting at a speed that Daniel could only describe as *menacing*. With each rotation, it wrapped another portion of the wire connected to the man's jawbone. Very quickly the wire shortened as the spring consumed more of its length, leading to its inevitable conclusion. Daniel didn't want to watch. He didn't want to see this. Yet he was helpless. He couldn't look away. He wouldn't dare.

The man stood with his hands folded across his back, maintaining eye contact with his computer screen, watching Daniel watch him, begging him with his expression not to hang up the call.

He wouldn't. Goddammit, he wouldn't.

Then, just as the strap's wire was finally running out of extension, the torsion spring started to slow down, until it was rotating in an awkward, cartoon-cat-on-piano-keys motion. *Is it stopping?* he wondered, but the sound coming from the mechanism didn't advertise a logical conclusion—instead, it sounded somehow worse than before, like it was straining with all its strength, and now the man was wincing and making a noise, a terrible unmistakable noise of someone who's realized they've made a mistake, that they want to stop before it's too late but it was obviously too late now, too late with a noise like that, with a motion like that, and there it was, the split-second from no-return, the blink-of-an-eye explosion as the torsion spring burst apart—a reaction so quick, so sudden, that it took his phone a moment to process anything had happened at all, but when it finally caught back up, Daniel could piece together the details, could see the chaotic mess of springs, yes, but more importantly he could see the man standing in the same spot as before, this time without the lower half of his face intact, although not completely removed, no, it still hung there by a tendon or two, teeth and tongue and whatever else draped against his chest, as if teasing him, as if saying *you're not quite there yet*, and somehow, Jesus Christ, *somehow* the man was screaming, he was screaming without a jaw, without a mouth, a river of blood pouring from his exploded face, he was screaming so goddamn loud that Daniel dropped his phone, dropped it to the sidewalk except *no wait this wasn't the sidewalk this didn't look anything like the sidewalk this looked like the parking lot he dropped his phone on the black pavement of the grocery store parking lot because somehow he wasn't on the sidewalk now, he'd moved away from it and now he was in the middle of the parking lot, staring at his dropped phone, thinking holy shit, thinking holy fuck, and wait a second what was that he heard coming from the phone's speaker, what was it he heard under the man's jawless screaming? wind chimes, he heard wind chimes, all the wind chimes in the man's garage rattling at once, but what was hitting them, what was setting them off? jesus fucking christ who else was in the garage with this man on his phone? what was coming for him? what the fuck was coming?*

But of course he knew.

He'd known all along.

Mister Bones, Daniel thought, a split-second before the car slammed into his body, sending him hurling across the parking lot and landing directly on his left wrist.

He heard the snap before he felt the pain.

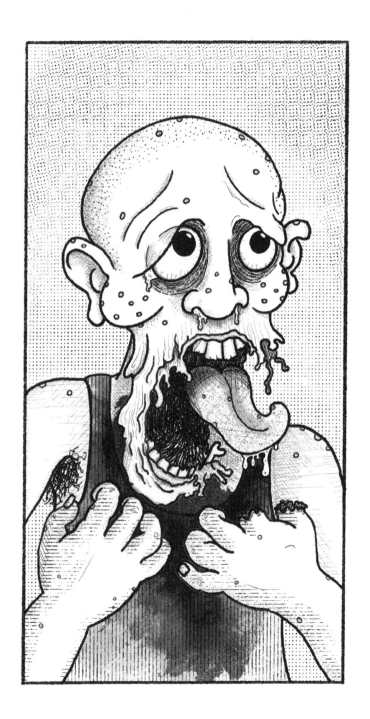

IT TOOK EILEEN a while to find him. Daniel would have called, but the car that hit him also ran over his phone, shattering it against the same pavement that snapped his wrist. Because it *was* broken—his wrist—there was no doubt about that, as he sat on the sidewalk unable to bend his wrist, as his hand quickly swelled and blossomed into a sickly purple. His spine also ached, but he didn't think it was anything too serious. He didn't think anything was broken. Not there, at least. The car hadn't plowed into him at full speed, thankfully—and, for that, he supposed he needed to be grateful for the grocery store's incessant speed bumps that he'd often cursed during previous visits. It'd hit him hard enough to knock him off his feet, but it didn't take much speed to do that with someone actively bent over reaching for a dropped item.

Surrounded by concerned and nosy pedestrians, Daniel couldn't help but find a little humor in what he'd done, considering how many times he'd judged others for maneuvering this parking lot with their eyes glued on a device. *One of these days,* he often thought, *some idiot is going to get hit out here.* Well, technically he hadn't been wrong.

He'd told someone his wife's name, and they rushed inside so an employee could call her over the intercom. Personally he wanted to just go inside and get her himself, but everybody kept going, "Don't move, you shouldn't move, you should stay seated," and he figured a bunch of strangers knew about these kinds of things better than he did.

The car who hit him belonged to some guy who made his annoyance with the incident no secret. He parked off to the side and stood on the sidewalk with the other growing group of people, and kept muttering things like, "I have milk in my trunk," and, "My meats!" every couple minutes. Daniel felt bad about the milk. He knew how much milk cost nowadays. He finally told him it was okay to leave.

"Oh," he said, "and get arrested for fleeing the scene? I don't think so, pal."

"Wait," Daniel said, something dawning on him, "has anybody even called the police?"

The crowd went quiet, and everybody scanned each other's faces, as if to ask, *Oh, I thought you did?*

As Daniel suspected, nobody had called in the accident. This was already feeling like more of a hassle than necessary. His wrist was screaming and his brain was going apeshit trying to comprehend the video call he'd just participated in, and he couldn't focus on either of these disturbances with everybody surrounding him like he was the main character of the day. Fortunately, Eileen emerged from the store a moment or so later, sans groceries, bug-eyed and freaking out. Less than five minutes after *that*, they were in the car and driving to the nearest emergency room, leaving everybody behind, including the man who'd hit Daniel with his car full of milk and meats.

The one thing they knew about ambulances was they were expensive. A friend of theirs once got stabbed in the leg by a total stranger, just some total nut job strolling down the street that he happened to bump into, and he ended up getting charged over eight thousand dollars for the ambulance ride to the hospital. No thank you. Eileen was perfectly capable of driving him, once she calmed down and processed what had happened. Well, as best as

I BELIEVE IN MISTER BONES

she could. During the drive, he attempted to fill Eileen in on what transpired during the video call, but he was in too much pain to make any sense, not that what happened made any sense to begin with, and he was sure she chalked up everything he was saying to being the nonsensical ramblings of a lunatic—which, okay, maybe wasn't that far off.

At the hospital, she had him take a seat while she went up to the front desk and checked him in. The ER's waiting room was packed, barely a vacant chair to be found. He managed to find two unused seats directly beneath one of the overhead televisions blaring old game show reruns at a volume loud enough to rattle his skull. Half the waiting room couldn't help but stare at him, since he fell upon their line of sight as they tried to watch TV. He kept his wrist in his lap, and his eyes on his wrist.

Neither of them had any health insurance, which was the norm for most of their publishing peers. Daniel and Eileen seldom sought the services of medical professionals. It'd been a decade-plus since either had gotten their teeth checked, or their vision examined, or anything. They did manage to keep up to date on vaccines, thanks to seasonal discounts provided by local drugstores, but that was about it. The receptionist read the "N/A" on Daniel's form and gave them both looks like they were lowlife pieces of shit. Did she know that they had no intention of ever paying whatever outrageous bill they tried mailing to them after today? More importantly, why would she care, anyway? It wasn't like hospital receptionists worked off of commission or anything. Daniel's broken wrist would not affect her paycheck.

They didn't end up doing much for him. Not that there was much *to* do. The X-Ray confirmed that the bone was fractured. Luckily not in a way that required anybody to physically straighten it back into place, but fractured all the same. It would only heal with time. He walked out of the hospital five hours later with a thick cast and a prescription for painkillers. It was getting dark out, but the pharmacy across the street wasn't scheduled to close for another hour or two, so they rushed over and picked up the Vicodin. As they waited for the pharmacist, a thought suddenly occurred to Daniel, and he asked Eileen, "What did you do with the groceries?"

"I just left them in the cart, back in . . . like, the frozen food aisle, or something," she said. "Wasn't like I had much of an opportunity to pay for them, or anything."

"I wonder if that guy who hit me made it home before his milk and meats spoiled."

"I still can't believe you told him to go."

Daniel shrugged. "It wasn't his fault. I was the dumbass standing in traffic."

"A parking lot," she reminded him. "Not traffic."

"I've never taken Vicodin before," he said, trying to spy on the pharmacist over the counter. "Have you?"

"It makes you feel smooooooth." She said it with a hint of nostalgia, caught back in some memory from before they'd ever met each other. He bit his tongue and resisted the irrational irritation he felt from the reminder that she'd once lived a life before him, that she had experiences he'd never share with her. Jealousy never made much sense, but this specific type of jealousy would always seem especially asinine. And yet, there was no getting rid of it. Not completely.

"Well, that would be a welcomed change of pace from how I am currently feeling," he finally said, shaking the envy loose and focusing on the pain in his wrist, like a thousand knives piercing his skin, a thousand teeth—teeth being the only visible part of the skeleton, at least under normal circumstances. Sometimes other bones were visible, right? Sometimes jawbones were ripped off. Sometimes fingers were removed. The skeleton could only be guarded so long, it could only protect so much.

He popped one of the painkillers the moment they got back in the car, swallowing it down with a Coke Zero purchased before leaving the drugstore.

I BELIEVE IN MISTER BONES

"Well," Eileen said, starting up the engine, "it's too late to do anything about your phone today, so we can do that tomorrow."

"I'd be fine if I never had a phone again."

She side-eyed him, incredulous. "Yeah, right."

"I don't need bones, and I don't need phones."

"We don't have anything at the house, obviously, so what should we get for dinner?"

"I don't need food, either."

"Everybody needs food."

"Maybe I'll go on a fast. No bones, no phones, no . . . " He paused. "What's a food-related word that rhymes with bones and phones?"

"If only you had a phone so you could look this up on the rhyming thesaurus."

"Fuck. Maybe I need a phone, after all."

"And what about bones?"

He shook his head. "Nah, I don't need bones."

"Oh really?" She leaned over and gave his crotch a soft squeeze, still parked at the drugstore. He scanned the lot in a fluster of panic, paranoid someone was watching.

"Do you think there's a bone in my dick?" Daniel asked, hopeful that was exactly what she believed. He rarely got the chance to be the smart one in their marriage.

"Um, it's literally called a boner." Eileen rolled her eyes and put the car in reverse.

He opened his mouth to correct her, then decided not to. It would be better to let her have this one. Maybe sometime down the line, at a public gathering, he would bring it up again. But not now. Not after he'd just taken a Vicodin. He would need her to not be mad at him tonight. So he suggested they get some Taco Bell instead, since it was in the same parking lot at the pharmacy, so that's what they did, and they only felt a *little* guilty for patronizing Taco Bell while living in San Antonio, a hub of delicious hole-in-the-wall Mexican restaurants.

They got their food, and they drove home, and neither

of them talked about the video call from earlier this afternoon. He had already caught her up to speed back at the hospital, when they were waiting on someone to take a look at his wrist. Had she believed him? Hard to say. Did he believe himself? Even harder to pinpoint, really. So much had happened so quickly. He kept trying to recollect what he'd witnessed, but it all felt so chaotic in his memory, so jumbled and nonsensical.

Back at the apartment, Daniel got out his laptop and fired up Twitter. Since his phone was kaput, he hadn't gotten the chance to get back online post-accident. A pathetic portion of his brain had already fallen into withdrawals from the deprivation. He was confident that, just as the manuscript author's email account had deactivated shortly after Daniel expressed interest, the guy who'd hopped into his DMs would also have vanished. He expected to find a page that said *This user no longer exists,* was almost *hoping* to find that, but the page was fine, and the DMs were still in his inbox. There had been no additional messages sent since Daniel received the invitation link. No activity on the user's page of any kind. This, somehow, felt far more foreboding than a deactivated account. It served as evidence that Daniel hadn't imagined the interaction leading up to the video call. Everything was still here, waiting for him.

He debated a long time about whether or not he should send the guy another message—and, if so, what the hell he would type. What was there to say to someone after witnessing them rip off their own jawbone? Assuming that's what really happened. Eileen was confident that it had been a prank, some kind of deepfake trickery or practical effects sleight-of-hand. Maybe she was right. The probability of her theory being correct was far greater than the opposite being true.

But, at the same time . . .

Eileen hadn't been on the other end of that call.

She hadn't seen what Daniel had seen.

I BELIEVE IN MISTER BONES

She also hadn't read the book like he'd read the book.

She didn't understand the significance of this broken bone.

He'd told her, he'd tried to explain, and she'd seemed concerned, sure, but not concerned *enough*. Daniel had broken his wrist while *actively thinking about Mister Bones*. Maybe the book was just a book and maybe the guy who'd ripped his jaw off was just an internet troll, but the cast around his wrist and hand was very much real, as was the fractured bone hidden inside it. The fact that this had happened while everything else was going on, *while thinking about Mister Bones*, was too fucking spooky to ignore. Even if none of this meant anything, he would be a fool to not be a little superstitious about the whole thing, right? He was a horror publisher. Half the books he worked on involved characters too stupid to know when to be paranoid about something before it was too late, before the evil caught up to them and ripped them to shreds. It was practically Daniel's *job* to take this shit seriously.

Then the Vicodin he'd taken back in the drugstore parking lot decided to finally kick in, and a beautiful, transcending cloud of numbness swallowed him whole. He fell asleep soon afterward, seated at one end of the couch with his computer in his lap, head tilted forward, broken wrist dangling toward the floor like an offering to anything within reach, anything hungry and gutsy enough to come up and take a bite.

But the man from the video call did not leave his thoughts for long. One could argue that he'd never left at all—not really, not completely. It was more like he'd gone into hiding under threat of the painkiller, waiting for the perfect moment to re-emerge, waiting for Daniel to drift off into the fog of unconsciousness. Then, there he was again. The man from the video, the man in the garage of wind chimes, the man with the straps and wires wrapped around his jaw, stuffed into his mouth and trapped there by layers and layers of duct tape. This time not staring at Daniel through a computer webcam but at Daniel here in the garage with him, Daniel who had somehow joined him in this mysterious room in this unknowable house in this unplaceable town. The man stared at him with eyes not of horror or fear but of desire, of lust. Beckoning Daniel forward. Begging for his touch, his intimacy. His *closeness*. He had no choice but to comply. He *wanted* to step forward. He wanted to touch this man, wanted to wrap his fingers around his restrained jaw, wanted to rip it clean from his eager skull. He wanted to do this more than anything else in this world. Daniel reached out and only then did he get a good look at his own body for the first time. Only then did he see his hand, did he see his arm. The flesh and muscle had been stripped clean—as if they'd never been there at all. There was bone and nothing else. The very bone he'd fractured outside the grocery store. Only now it was no longer broken. No longer broken but also no longer a traditional bone like the kind he might expect. It was different now. It was improved. It was *realized*. His arm was longer than he remembered it being, longer than he'd ever seen any arm on any person he'd ever known. He was still several feet away from the man in the garage and yet he was still able to touch him, was able to stroke his skeletal fingers across his face, was able to softly squeeze his chin and test its resistance. He could pull it off so easily. He could detach it like it was nothing. Then—a noise behind him. The wind chimes were moving. He glanced at them, trying to determine the source of their disturbance, but there was nothing there, nothing he could see. He turned back to the man in the garage, but something was different now. This wasn't the same man in the garage he'd been examining only seconds previously, this was someone else, someone new, someone . . . familiar, yes, familiar, but how did Daniel know him? Where had he seen him before? In the mirror, of course, he had seen him in the mirror because this *was* Daniel, this man in the garage, this was *him* who was gagged and waiting, waiting for . . . waiting for who? If this was him, then who was *he?* He raised his arm again, his impossibly long arm without flesh or muscle, his skeleton arm, and he grabbed his own jaw, looked into his own eyes, and apologized. And then, and then, and then—

HIS WRIST STILL ached the next morning. Daniel had asked the doctor at the emergency room how long the pain would last, and she'd shrugged and made a face that suggested an answer along the lines of, *Depends how big of a pussy you are, I guess.* Out loud, though, all she'd said was, "It can vary."

He woke on the couch, where Eileen had left him, injured arm still dangling from the side without any support. Slowly, he lifted his arm and held it against his chest. He couldn't stop sweating. His left pinky and ring finger were numb and tingled with movement. He associated the feeling with lying on his hand too long, but that clearly wasn't what had happened here. He supposed it made sense that the same affliction could strike with leaving his fingers hanging like he'd done. Upsetting the blood flow, or whatever. Or maybe this was one of the many unexpected side effects one experienced after breaking their wrist and having to put on a cast. Daniel didn't know. He wasn't a doctor. He wasn't anything.

He was barely a publisher, honestly.

Sometimes he thought about how wild and insane it was to run your own business. There was nobody to fire you once it became clear how shitty you were at your job. You either kept going out of stubbornness or admitted defeat. Unfortunately, Daniel and Eileen were two very stubborn people.

I BELIEVE IN MISTER BONES

"Wait until you see the email we got this morning," Eileen told him, seated at the kitchen table with her laptop.

Fear seized his muscles. Speculation zeroed in on the *Mister Bones* author having finally responded—because, if the maniac on the video call had been telling the truth, then he *hadn't* been the author, which meant the real author was choosing to remain anonymous and was still out there somewhere. "Wh-who?" he said, needing her to say it out loud.

But, instead, she said, "Lenny Kaufman."

Daniel relaxed. "Oh. What did he want?"

"He says he never got that anthology we mailed him."

"What? He already said he got it, didn't he?" Daniel felt around—with his good hand—for his cell phone, before remembering the fate it'd been dealt the day before. He gave up and pulled out his laptop.

"Now he says he didn't, *plus* . . . " she said, with a smile across her face, "he also says he never received a copy of Lauren's book."

He cocked his head at her, still waiting for his laptop to re-emerge from hibernation. "Why would we have sent him that?"

Eileen shrugged.

"Did he ask us to send it to him?"

Another shrug.

"Lauren's book is a *novel*. Why on earth would we have ever sent that to him?"

A third shrug. "I was going to ask you the same thing."

Lenny Kaufman was a mystifying person. The first time Daniel met him, he had been vendoring for Fiendish at the World Horror Convention in New Orleans. Daniel was standing there, a little nervous since this was one of the first writer events he'd ever attended, when this tiny little gremlin of a man scurried up to his table. Daniel told him hello, but the man didn't acknowledge him, verbally or otherwise. He hovered over their selection of books, scanning the titles and picking up anything that included short stories—just anthologies and collections, since they hadn't launched *Fiendish Tales* yet. Daniel took one look at the stack of books held against the man's chest and thought, *Oh shit, I'm about to make a huge sale, maybe investing all of this money in travel and lodging and everything else hadn't been a colossal mistake, after all.* Then the guy spun around, still holding the books, and wandered off without a care in the world. "Hey, wait!" Daniel had shouted, and some other vendor next to him grabbed Daniel's shoulder and shook his head and said, "Don't you know who that is? That's Lenny Kaufman." And Daniel had said, "Who the fuck is Lenny Kaufman?" The vendor let out a condescending laugh and explained that Lenny Kaufman was the most famous editor in the horror community. He was most well-known for compiling an annual "best-of" reprint anthology series, which was why everybody sent him complimentary copies of their anthologies and story collections. Lenny Kaufman didn't pay for books. He took them, and you were expected to be grateful for the opportunity—for the slightest chance that he might consider reprinting one of your stories. Of course, he also discouraged electronic copies of these books, expecting everybody to mail him physical paperbacks. Over time, Daniel developed a theory about Lenny Kaufman's operations. Most of these reprint anthologies tended to feature the same authors every year. The table of contents were more predictable than fatphobia in a Stephen King novel. It was clear to Daniel that Lenny Kaufman wasn't reading many, if *any* of these hundreds of complimentary anthologies. So what the fuck was he doing with all of these books, right? Well, Daniel did some research on Google Maps, and there were not two but *three* Half-Price Books within an hour's drive of Lenny Kaufman's mailing address. Half-Price Books being, of course, a retail store that purchased used books. This whole thing was a fucking scam and anytime Daniel brought this up with anybody, they looked at him like he was a maniac. They never even gave him a chance to bring up his *other* theory about Lenny Kaufman's best-of anthologies. In the beginning of every book, he spent several dozen pages giving shout-outs to novels and other publications released in the past year. Mini-reviews that barely read like reviews. The *why?* here was more obvious than the Half-Price Books shenanigans: once an author discovered their work had been spotlighted in a Lenny Kaufman anthology, there was no way in hell they weren't going to buy a copy to brag about. Do this enough times and you immediately make a profit before the anthology's even reached the doorsteps of its readers. Daniel wasn't crazy. He just understood hucksters better than most.

Laptop finally awake, Daniel clicked over to the Fiendish Books email tab and checked the thread from Lenny Kaufman. He scrolled back up to the beginning of the conversation and refamiliarized himself with the conversation. It'd started with him requesting a review copy of the latest anthology Fiendish had published, along with his mailing address. They responded back, "No problem," and sent it out to him a week or so later. Fast forward two months later, and the editor of the anthology messaged Daniel on Twitter letting him know she'd run into Lenny Kaufman at a recent event, and he was claiming he'd never received a copy of the anthology. Daniel logged into their mailing software and searched the tracking code for the package they'd mailed out, confirming it should have arrived at Lenny Kaufman's house shortly after his initial request. So he sent a follow-up email to Lenny and included the tracking code, and said, "You should have already gotten this book, but here's the tracking in case you need it for some reason." Lenny responded back a couple minutes later with, "Oh, it appears I did get it." That should have been the end of the interaction.

Except now he'd emailed again this morning, claiming he'd never gotten it after all—and, on top of that, he'd never received a novel neither of them had ever discussed sending, which was a little like telling a waitress he'd never gotten pancakes after ordering an omelet at Waffle House. Why had they sent Lenny Kaufman the anthology in the first place? Mostly for appearances, honestly. Daniel never for a second thought Lenny was going to actually read the thing. But sometimes a significant portion of being a publisher involved doing things that were never going to see results, anyway. But you still did them, because you were dumb and you didn't know what else to do.

"I have the perfect response," Daniel muttered, diabolically.

"What's that?" Eileen asked.

"I'm going to say, 'Oh, I see, I see. PDFs attached.' Then I'm going to add a smiley face."

"You're going to give that man a heart attack."

"Fingers crossed," Daniel said, then realized how hard it was to type with a broken wrist, and proceeded to keyboard smash with just his right index finger. Giggling, he said, "Eat shit, Lenny Kaufman."

After the email was sent, the amusement vanished and was replaced with loathing—but not for Lenny Kaufman. For *himself*. Pettiness embarrassed him, and yet . . . most of his DNA consisted of this emotion. He *thrived* on being petty. It sucked.

He got up to fix himself a cup of coffee. There would be no breakfast today. The idea of eating anything made him want to hurl. The pain in his wrist had swallowed the desire to consume food. Coffee, on the other hand, there would always be room for coffee. He could break every bone in his body and still desire a hot cup of coffee poured down his throat, as long as it was so scalding that a cloud of steam drifted out of his mouth afterward.

She asked how he was feeling, and he answered honestly: like shit. Although he didn't bring up the numb fingers. He thought it would sound stupid and she would look at him like, *No shit, that's what happens when you break your wrist,* as if this was a side effect everybody was already aware of except for Daniel. He didn't mind admitting that he was an amateur when it came to breaking bones. This was all new to him. There was a lot for him to learn still.

"What do we have to do today?" he asked, hoping the answer would be nothing, that he hadn't forgotten a list of plans and he could just pop another painkiller and zone out on the couch until everything stopped hurting so much.

"I guess we need to go get you another phone, right?" she said, eyes glued on her own laptop as she worked on some formatting project.

He grimaced. Fuck. "Oh, yeah." Then: "Wait, can we even afford that right now? The fest venue still needs to be paid."

"We'll figure it out. You need a phone."

"Does anybody actually *need* a phone, though?" Daniel asked.

"You know, you say that, but you look at yours more than I look at mine."

This was true, of course. Eileen had a personal Facebook account and that was it. Daniel had an account pretty much everywhere. *However,* Daniel was also the one who handled all of the Fiendish Books socials. If not for him, there would be no activity, no promotion— everything would remain dormant, Tumbleweed City, USA. He chose not to bring that up, though. He was sure there were many things she did he never considered that helped the company stay alive.

So they got dressed, and Eileen drove him across town to their cell phone carrier's store, located in a strip mall with a Goodwill, Mexican restaurant, and a pet shop.

These phone places stressed him out. Most businesses did, he guessed. Anywhere that required talking to a representative and answering questions, really. Shit, even ordering food at restaurants often spiked his anxiety. This time, though, he hoped would be different. He'd swallowed a Vicodin before leaving the apartment and his brain had already entered a pleasant fog. An hour later, they walked out of the store with a brand-new phone, and Daniel had no memory of anything anybody had discussed while inside.

Out in the parking lot, they took turns hitting Eileen's vape, then decided a person should take advantage of being high while in the proximity of a pet shop, so they locked up the car again and headed into the store on the far left of the strip mall. Normally he would have declined to smoke with her while they were out in public, but the painkiller sponging his nerves made this idea far more appealing than it would have while sober.

A foul odor hit them the moment the automatic doors slid open, which was to be expected. Daniel couldn't remember ever entering a pet shop that didn't smell like animal shit. At least the weed and Vicodin made it somewhat tolerable. A peppy girl with pink-dyed hair greeted them and asked if there was anything she could help with today. Eileen rubbed her face, speech delayed, and replied, "No . . . no . . . we . . . uh, we are good. Thanks."

Daniel forced a smile and nodded at her, and they proceeded to browse. As if guided by magnets, they drifted toward the puppy pit—which was exactly what it sounded like: a pit full of puppies napping and play-fighting. Eileen let out an, "Oh my god, oh my god," and Daniel tensed up, thinking, *Fuck, we can't afford to get a puppy, what are we doing here?* Then he saw one of them yawn, and he also let out an, "Oh my god, oh my god."

Terrified he was seconds away from buying a puppy, Daniel spun around and searched for something else to focus his attention on. More dog stuff. Toys, treats, little adorable sweaters. He left Eileen at the puppy pit and stumbled to the other side of the store. Not really on the hunt for anything in particular, just letting the drugs work their magic and moving on autopilot. Until he saw the display against the far wall, and his feet stopped moving.

I BELIEVE IN MISTER BONES

There were several shelves featuring a truly bizarre range of creatures, confined in various tanks and habitats pressed side-to-side. He forced himself to inch closer for a better look, unable to believe what he was seeing wasn't some hallucination birthed from the marijuana/painkiller combo coursing through his system.

He saw earthworms piled on top of each other, writhing as one conglomerate mass.

He saw snails.

Beetles. Spiders.

Crabs. Shrimps.

Snakes and snakes and snakes.

And, in the middle of the display, perhaps most baffling of all, he saw the purple, luminescent tank of several jellyfish.

Could pet stores sell jellyfish? Obviously this one was doing so. Surely they were better educated on the laws than some random customer tripping on psychoactives and opioids. He was overwhelmed with the urge to buy one and take it home and love it forever. Unfortunately, he didn't know the slightest thing about jellyfish upkeep. He imagined ensuring their survival was not cheap. He didn't even know how they'd been able to buy him a new phone earlier. There was no way they could afford a jellyfish.

Still, though, he couldn't figure out why the store had paired all of these creatures together. There was *something* about them that made sense. Something that he found inexplicably desirable.

Then he noticed the display sign above the shelves, near the ceiling, painted in thick green font:

PETS WITHOUT BONES!

Then, below that, in smaller yellow font:

LIL' CRITTERS YOUR KIDDOS WON'T BE ABLE TO CRACK IN HALF!
YOU'LL THANK US LATER!

"What the fuck," Daniel whispered.

His left pinky and index fingers started vibrating with numbness.

The pink-haired clerk appeared next to him, with a box of fish food she intended to stock nearby. "Finding everything okay, sir?"

He gasped, startled by her presence. "Uh, yeah. I guess so." Then he nodded at the display. "What's, um, what's the deal with this?"

She followed his gaze at the display, then glanced back at him like she didn't understand what he meant. "Sir? Were you after a pet without bones?"

"I . . . I am not, no."

"They're great for children," she said, emphasizing the sign above the display. "Hard to crack something without bones, you know."

A panicked sweat dripped down his lower back. "But why . . . why . . . why . . . ?"

He didn't know how else to phrase the question. She stared at him, trying to decipher his words and failing miserably. Luckily, she didn't have to answer, because Eileen swooped in to save the day.

"Then why do you have snakes?" she said.

"Excuse me?" the clerk asked, further confused.

Eileen softly tapped one of the reptile terrariums. "This is false advertising."

"Ma'am? What are you—?"

"Snakes. They have bones."

The clerk shook her head, disgusted by the mere

thought of snakes having bones. "Um, no, ma'am, I'm pretty sure they don't."

"Look it up then. I don't know what else to tell you."

Everybody was quiet for a moment. Nobody knew what to say. Daniel desperately wanted to leave, but it was clear Eileen wanted to see this conflict play out a little more, so he remained standing next to the boneless pets display thoroughly spooked out of his gourd.

Finally the pet shop girl got out her phone and pulled up its mobile browser. "What am I supposed to search?"

Eileen smirked in a way that made her look both cocky and incredibly hot. "Try 'do snakes have bones?'"

She transcribed the question into her phone, then squinted at the screen for a moment before freaking out and stammering, "I-I-I'm sorry, but I-I-I need to call my ma-ma-manager!" She fled toward the EMPLOYEES ONLY backroom.

Left alone in the shop, they inspected the boneless pets display again. Daniel had never felt more stoned in his life.

"How easy do you think it'd be to shoplift one of these jellyfish?" Eileen asked, and they stared at the tank's purple glow pondering the idea.

"I think it would not be easy," Daniel answered, several minutes later as they were heading out the door, empty-handed.

But by then, she had already forgotten the question.

Daniel slept like shit that night, despite popping another Vicodin before crawling into bed. He didn't have any issues falling asleep initially. He passed out like an exhausted baby long before Eileen had turned off her work light. Usually it was the other way around, and he was the one going to sleep long after she'd called it a night. It was sort of nice, closing his eyes without the sound of her snoring next to him—and, embarrassingly, equally discomforting.

A person got used to certain noises over the years. He'd conditioned himself to adapt to her heavy snores. They were his white noise. Some people needed fans. He needed his wife's undiagnosed sleep apnea.

But that wasn't why he slept like shit.

Or, at least, he didn't *think* that was the cause of it.

Some uncertain amount of hours after drifting off, Daniel sprung awake with the absolute certainty that something was wrapped around his leg. Not just *something* but . . . but a goddamn *jellyfish*. There was a goddamn *jellyfish* wrapped around his goddamn *leg* and he didn't know how it was possible but he'd never been surer of anything in his life. There was the pressure of something—of *tentacles*—constricting around his calf. Crawling, burning, *stinging* . . .

Somehow one of them must've followed them home from the pet store, or maybe Eileen had been trying to hint at something with the shoplifting comment—could she have stolen one from the tank and smuggled it all the way back to the apartment without Daniel noticing? Could he have really been so oblivious? Not to mention, was his wife capable of pulling off such an abnormal heist? Had she ever stolen anything before? At least once, that he could remember. They'd committed the crime together, like a modern Bonnie and Clyde. Except instead of stealing money or lives, all they'd done was walk out of a gas station with two fountain drinks of Diet Coke after deciding the line was too long to wait. The moment had been exhilarating, and after they got home they'd fucked like they used to when they first started seeing each other, and in that moment Daniel could imagine a life where they thieved together regularly, gradually upping the ante until finally, at long last, they were running out of a bank shooting pistols toward the sky and screaming, "Yee-haw, motherfucker!" But that never happened. As far as Daniel was aware, neither of them had ever stolen anything again. Except for possibly the jellyfish violently hugging his leg.

I BELIEVE IN MISTER BONES

He bent his knee up and felt toward his leg in the dark. No jellyfish. No anything. It was almost disappointing. Just a phantom hugging. Not quite a cramp or a charley horse or whatever. This was something different. Less of a painful spasm but more of a . . . lasting *tingle*. He was reminded of the numbness in his pinky and index fingers, an affliction he was beginning to fear might be permanent. But at least the fingers could be blamed on the broken wrist. The same couldn't be said for whatever was going on with his calf tonight. When he moved his leg back and forth, the tingling didn't go away, but it did become more bearable. As long as he kept it in constant motion. Not really the best solution for someone trying to fall back asleep.

Next to him, Eileen's snores abruptly stopped, and she sleepily asked if he was okay.

"I think so," he whispered, as if afraid of waking the neighbors, "just something weird going on with my leg."

"Something weird like how?" Eileen whispered back, matching his secretive tone.

"I don't know." He tried to concentrate on the ungraspable sensation. "Like there's . . . insects or something, inside my flesh, crawling around, pulling the skin all tight and making everything feel . . . uh, weird."

"Wh . . . what?"

"I don't know. Go back to sleep. It's fine."

"Doesn't . . . um, sound like it's fine . . . " She reached across the bed and felt his calf up and down, inspecting it.

He waited for her to diagnose the issue, but when she didn't say anything he grew impatient and said, "Does it feel weird to you?"

"Seems okay," she replied, drowsy. Then: "Maybe it's the Vicodin."

That idea hadn't occurred to him. "You think so?"

In the darkness, he could feel her shrugging. "Maybe it gave you restless leg syndrome. Who knows."

A few moments later the apartment was greeted by the

return of Eileen snoring, and Daniel shifted in bed hoping he'd fall back asleep before the odd tingling grew too intense again. He closed his eyes tight and tried not to imagine worms writhing inside his flesh, begging to burst out through his calf and spill out onto the mattress. He tried so very hard.

THE BOXES OF promotional material for the book festival arrived a few days later. For the last week the tracking had remained stagnant in Dallas, which was the worst place anybody or anything could be held hostage, as far as Daniel was concerned. Easily the shittiest city they'd ever set foot in. At a certain point they'd concluded the packages had gotten lost or destroyed, and had reached out to the promo company notifying them of the mishap. Nobody with support bothered to respond. Daniel had tagged the company on Twitter through the Fiendish account, and someone replied back asking him to DM them the order information, but after he'd done that the company had proceeded to ghost him. Then, today, here they magically were, stacked on top of each other in front of their apartment door, as if they had never been stuck in some unreachable limbo.

They'd purchased two types of physical promo: one hundred flyers, and five thousand double-sided postcards. The goal was to disperse every last shred of this stuff throughout San Antonio far enough in advance that the whole city would be properly prepared to attend, but not too early that they'd end up forgetting about it once the fateful weekend rolled up. In addition to handing the promo out locally, they'd also start including a postcard in every online order. It wasn't outside the realm of possibility that one of them would convince a customer from out of town to attend the festival. Most of their *current* badge holders weren't native to Texas, after all. Plus, they'd ordered five *thousand* of these things. Plenty to spare.

The flyers contained the festival artwork smack in the middle of the paper: Betty Rocksteady's logo for Fiendish Books, the zombified head deepthroating a butcher's knife, but revised here so the blood dripping out of its mutilated neck vaguely resembled the Alamo. Within the blood pattern, it read FIENDISH BOOK FESTIVAL, followed by the year. Beneath that, they had their FIENDS OF HONOR listed, aka the "named" authors they hoped would generate some buzz among horror aficionados. Nobody too famous or anything, just well-known enough so certain readers might stop and go, "Oh, yeah, I know them," when hearing about the festival.

The Fiends of Honor for the inaugural FBF were Jack Lyons, Rick Jenkins, and Jessica McHugh. The last one, Jessica, was someone they'd personally published. Her novels *The Green Rabbits* and *Witches on a Train* were both Fiendish titles. When designing the festival and deciding to name it after their press, it was an easy decision that each year they'd include one of their own authors as a special guest. A way to spotlight their books and thank them for trusting Daniel and Eileen enough to work together. Rick Jenkins had published one notable book years ago and everything afterward had seen progressively shittier sales through embarrassingly incompetent micro presses, but he'd managed to somehow wedge himself into the indie horror community as a person of note, and other writers seemed to love him—or, at the very least, they were convinced Rick could help their careers if they kissed his ass enough—so they'd decided what the hell and invited him. Jack Lyons was undoubtedly the most famous of the bunch, and one of Daniel's favorite writers. Plus, he lived in Texas, so they just had to buy plane tickets for two of the guests instead of all three. If only the trio could have also bunked together in the same hotel room, too, but that was an expense they couldn't think about until closer to the festival. The hotel wouldn't charge them until the day of check-in, anyway. They had some time to figure out how they'd pay for the rooms—once they paid off the rest of the festival venue's rental costs, of course.

On the flyer, beneath the listed Fiends of Honor, they'd printed relevant info about the event plus a scannable QR code leading to their website. At the top of the flyer, above the festival artwork, in huge red font: WEEKEND-LONG BOOK FESTIVAL FOR HORROR FANATICS, along with another reminder of the date. On either side of the artwork they'd stuck little descriptions intended to excite passersby, such as SPOOKY BOOKSTORE! PANELS! LIVE READINGS! HORROR CONTESTS! They still weren't quite sure what kind of "contests" they'd be hosting. Something simple and inexpensive, preferably. A horror trivia competition, most likely. A mix of easy questions like *What kind of car is Christine in Stephen King's* Christine? (1958 Plymouth Fury) and aggravatingly difficult ones like . . . well, okay, he hadn't been able to come up with any aggravatingly difficult ones yet, but there was still plenty of time. Most likely, he'd forget until the day before the festival, then panic and either plagiarize some online quiz or slice his wrist open with a box cutter to avoid having to do anything ever again.

The front side of the postcards were similar to the flyers, but on the back of the postcards they'd made space to add a box listing out their spooky bookstore vendors, which consisted of small presses like Fiendish Books (obviously), Bizarre Goon Books, Caliginous Press, Doomsday Dinner Press, Graveyard Doors Media, Haunted Scraps Books, Hysteric Pancreases Press, Kaiju Spirits Books, Nosy Birds Publications, and Pus Palm Press, as well as several authors tabling solo.

The only small press application they'd ended up rejecting had been one from Fracas Books. Much like Fiendish, Fracas was operated by a husband-and-wife duo named Tommy and Sabrina. Probably one of the more popular small presses in the scene these days, too. Fracas had started up just a few years after Fiendish. They started off as a literary publisher specializing in the short-lived alt-lit movement that briefly took the internet by storm. Once that faded, and the horror industry started seeing a resurgence, they were quick to hop onto the next bandwagon. Plus, on a personal level, Daniel despised the people who ran it, and would have rather dropped dead than give them a spot at his festival. There had been an . . . *incident,* some years back, that made him want to vomit whenever he dwelled on it—which was, sadly, often. The woman who co-owned Fracas, she used to host this absolutely dreadful podcast, and she'd asked Daniel to come on as a guest one night. This was before he'd decided they were terrible people. They hadn't been *friends* or anything, but friendly enough to consider each other acquaintances in the publishing field. So he agreed to guest on the podcast, and immediately regretted it. Sabrina was drunk as fuck before the recording even began. Despite being an audio-only show, she'd still insisted on enabling webcams so Sabrina and Daniel could see each other during the conversation. He remembered Sabrina had been sitting on the floor in her living room, with the laptop on what he presumed to be a coffee table. In the background, her husband Tommy paced around the house drinking a can of beer, completely in the nude, dick and balls flopping around without a care in the world. The two of them kept arguing about something during the recording. It was difficult to decipher what, exactly, they were both angry with each other about. The whole thing felt so goddamn awkward, and Daniel wondered why Sabrina didn't just apologize and reschedule the podcast. Then, miraculously, Tommy disappeared into the bedroom. Daniel figured, okay, now they can actually do this show for real. Except Sabrina never seemed interested in asking him any questions pertaining to Fiendish or anything else publishing-related. Within two minutes of Tommy going to bed, Sabrina was asking Daniel how big his dick was, and speculating what it'd be like to fuck each other. Daniel was recording his end of the podcast at the kitchen table in the apartment he shared with Eileen, who was seated on the couch reading a book during all of this. Thankfully he had been wearing earbuds, because he had no idea how Eileen would have reacted if she overheard the way Sabrina was behaving. All Daniel could think to do was nervously laugh and try to change the subject. Even with Eileen not present, he would have felt uncomfortable. This was not the kind of conversation he agreed to participate in. But the more he tried to get her to talk about other things, the stronger she resisted, until she was literally suggesting he expose himself to the webcam. She first said it like she was joking, but then kept repeating it until it sounded like a firm demand. *Seriously,* she said, *why don't you just show me your dick? What are you afraid of?* He'd told her no, that was quite okay, he'd rather not, and maybe had even said something cringeworthy like, *Um, ask me at the next convention we go to! Maybe it can become part of the programming*—anything to get her to drop the subject and move on, but of course she didn't. Not until he finally said, *Look, I don't want to talk about this,* and she stared at him like he was some kind of buzzkill, but finally, somehow, she changed the subject—nearly an hour into their talk. The next morning, she messaged him and let him know she had decided to cut most of the recording that made "them" sound bad. He asked her how she thought people would have responded if they'd heard the conversation unabridged—then he asked her how they would have responded if their genders had been flipped. *What if you were a man*, he'd said, *and I was a woman?* In response, all she typed back was: *Lol yeah.* He blocked both her and her husband plus the Fracas Books accounts without a second thought. Fuck all of them.

Besides, as far as vendors went, Daniel figured they

had a good balance between Texas creators and out-of-staters. Hell, Kaiju Spirits was flying all the way down from *Toronto* for this event. The pressure to not fuck everything up was immense. Which was why they'd invested in all of this promotional material. Now all they had to do was hand it out—a task that seemed infinitely easier back when Daniel had full use of both wrists.

Fortunately, Xiomara made good on their word to help out should Eileen and Daniel need an extra hand, and that was literally what they needed now: an extra hand. They showed up at the apartment early Saturday morning with a full printout of local businesses they'd previously established as being both promo-friendly and nonallergic to spooky showmanship—experience they'd gained from advertising their own popup events. The plan was to first hit up all of the shops spread out around the city, then—assuming they had time to spare, depending on how kindly traffic treated them throughout the day—park somewhere downtown and hoof it around on foot. Xiomara had mapped out the driving spots to form a perfect circle around the outer edges of San Antonio. They'd even programmed the route into their phone's GPS with each business filtered as a designated stop. Daniel had no idea how he and Eileen would have handled this chore, but it would've been wise to assume nowhere near as organized or sensible.

"You guys got everything packaged like I suggested, right?" they asked from the kitchen, helping themself to the last cup of coffee in the pot and a sausage kolache they'd brought with them. Daniel had intended on pouring the remaining coffee into a to-go thermos before leaving, but felt it would have been rude to point that out now. He would survive. Probably.

"With the rubber bands?" he said, seated at the couch, and tapped the bulked-out backpack at his feet. "Yeah. We separated the postcards into small stacks. Good idea."

"What about thumbtacks? Tape? Scissors?"

He patted the bag again. "All accounted for."

I BELIEVE IN MISTER BONES

From the sink next to the bathroom, Eileen proceeded with the finishing touches of her makeup and said, "I think we have everything."

"Sick," Xiomara said. "It's supposed to be pretty nice out today, too. Should be fun. Y'all excited?"

Eileen laughed and focused on her eyeliner, leaving the responsibility of answering up to Daniel. All he could do was shrug and say, "Sure."

Xiomara nodded their chin at him. "You doing okay, man? How's the wrist treating you?"

Daniel studied the useless limb resting in his lap. Every finger on his left hand had gone numb by now. He could still move them, if he focused, but movement sparked a tingling jolt that he preferred to avoid. The pain in his wrist had also numbed, although Daniel found himself missing the pain. There was something about this new sensation that he found difficult to trust, and even more difficult to voice aloud without sounding like a basketcase tethered to the nearest psych ward.

"Well," he said, struggling for coherent phrasing, "it's definitely a relief that you're coming with us today. I don't know how much help I'll be besides lugging the bag around on my back."

"Shit, man," they said, "that's the worst part of the whole thing, you ask me. It might not seem too heavy at first, but it starts to drag, plus your back gets all sweaty and gross? No thank you." They finished off their kolache, then approached him in the living room, eyes still on his wrist. "So what happened, exactly? Eileen said you were in front of an H-E-B?"

"Yeah, that's right," Daniel said, wishing he could make eye contact with Eileen to gauge exactly much she'd told them, but they were blocking his line of sight. "I, uh, dropped my phone, never really saw the guy coming until he hit me." Then, not knowing what else to say, he stood up, turned around, and slightly lifted his shirt to show off the bruise fading against his spine.

"Holy shit."

"It was way nastier looking, the first couple days after the accident."

"Did you break any ribs?" Without warning, he felt their fingers softly caressing the collision blemish. Goose bumps scattered up his back—a tingling unlike the one he'd been experiencing in his fingers and legs. This was more pleasant. Surprising, yes, but pleasant. Embarrassed, and afraid Eileen might've witnessed the interaction, he shook away from the touch and pulled his shirt back down.

"No, the doctor didn't seem to think so," he said. Xiomara stepped back a bit, but eyed him like they knew he'd enjoyed their fingers on his back. Of course he had. Any reasonable person would have found them attractive. But also, at the same time, Daniel liked to believe he wasn't a scumbag. Not that there was anything wrong with someone rubbing a bruise on your back. In theory, at least. But the thing was, the caress hadn't *felt* innocent.

"Yeah," Eileen said, puckering her lips in the mirror before applying a round of lipstick, "but that doctor wasn't exactly the most attentive person in the world."

As further explanation, Daniel told them about the coldness the hospital staff had given off once learning of their health insurance status—or lack thereof.

Xiomara shook their head, flushed with outrage. "Do you even *know* someone who has health insurance nowadays? Because I sure as fuck don't."

Daniel had to think about it. "Honestly . . . I don't think I do." He held his wrist to his chest, hating how it felt when his arm was swinging downward.

Xiomara squinted at his cast, leaning forward for a closer look at what was written on it in huge black marker. "What . . . what does that say?"

Instead of saying it out loud, he held up his arm so they could read it themself:

I BELIEVE IN MISTER BONES

THANKS FOR THE FREE BONES, SUCKA!
—MR. BONES

"Eileen wrote it on me when I was asleep the other day," he told them, ignoring the chuckle fest erupting from over the bathroom sink.

"He got so freaked out," Eileen said, on the verge of hysteria.

But Xiomara didn't join her in the laughter. They appeared too puzzled by something, and continued studying the arm graffiti, until finally coming out and asking what was perplexing them the most: "Does that say BONES or BONER?"

Along the drive, they tried to fill Xiomara in on the Mister Bones fiasco. If it'd been up to Daniel, he would have never brought it up at all, but the floodgates certainly opened after they spotted Eileen's prank on his cast. Which, yes, as Eileen claimed, *had* freaked him out when he woke up from his Vicodin-induced nap and spotted it on his arm. His first thought obviously hadn't been, *Oh, geez, my wife sure has pulled a fast one on me—what a crackup!* Instead, it'd been something more along the lines, *Holy shit I'm going to fucking die.* Technically true, either way. He just hoped the cause of death wasn't going to involve some Babadook dork from a haunted book submission of all things. *Babadork?* No, that was stupid. He was glad he hadn't said that joke out loud.

Eileen hadn't read the book yet, nor had she been the one on the video call with the man who'd potentially ripped off his own jaw, and Daniel was growing agitated that she kept insisting on summarizing the story to Xiomara. If it was going to be discussed, then he ought've been the person in charge of educating others. He wasn't an expert, or anything, but at least he was treating the situation somewhat seriously. Not *too* seriously, though. He was cognizant enough to understand how silly all of it sounded.

"Let me see if I understand this correctly," Xiomara said, as they idled at a red light, "in this book that y'all got, there's this monster that goes around stealing bones from people's sleeping bodies, and he can *only* be summoned when someone breaks a bone *while* thinking about the monster."

Okay, maybe Eileen had done a better job explaining the context than he wanted to admit.

"Yes," he said from the back seat. Eileen was driving and Xiomara was riding shotgun. He kept trying not to look at how smooth the back of their neck was. Goddamn, why was he such a creep? "That's pretty much it, yeah." Then, because he wanted to feel like he'd contributed something, he added, "And he replaces the bones with fake bones. Like, a rubbery material that only pretends to be authentic. And the victims spend all this time going crazy, paranoid about what's inside them and obsessing over it until it's too late, until . . . until the *monster* has collected the entire, uh, skeleton."

"A horror story about people scared of what's inside their own bodies?" Xiomara said, then chuckled about something. "Bet you anything this author is trans as fuck."

"What are you talking about?" Daniel asked.

"That is the most trans-coded premise I've ever heard in my life, babe."

"Shit, you're right," Eileen said, setting down her vape now that the light had turned green. "I didn't even think about that."

"It's okay," Xiomara said, patting Eileen on the shoulder like *there, there*. "It's not your fault you're a basic cis bitch."

Eileen nodded back at Daniel in the back seat, briefly meeting his eyes in the rearview mirror. "Daniel thinks the same thing's happening to him. You think he's trans, too?"

I BELIEVE IN MISTER BONES

Xiomara glanced over their shoulder at him, expression unexpectedly sincere. "Well, Daniel? Are you?"

It wasn't that Daniel believed his bones had literally been stolen and replaced with some alien substance like in the novella. That would have been insane. He *knew* that would have been insane. But *something* weird was going on with his body. That much was undeniable. Something he couldn't keep blaming on the broken wrist. He could also stop pretending everything was just a side-effect of the Vicodin. The prescription had dried out. He hadn't taken a painkiller in several days, and still the bizarre sensations persisted.

He barely slept anymore. The restless leg syndrome bullshit woke him up several times a night. It'd get so bad he had to stand up and walk around in the darkness to battle the phantom jellyfish aggressively humping his calves. Grinding, crawling, pulling, *burning*. It was usually around then that he'd start thinking about the *Mister Bones* book again, and reflect on the similar circumstances some of the characters went through in the text that he was presently living through, and he'd experience this abrupt, terrifying certainty that the legs he was currently utilizing to stand no longer belonged to him, that they were not strong enough to hold up what little of his skeleton remained, and suddenly his legs would start wobbling, shaking, and he'd collapse on the couch drenched in sweat and out of breath.

Fortunately, Eileen was asleep for most of these outbursts. This felt like a horror that needed to be kept as private as possible. If *he* felt nuts about the whole thing, then what would others think? Except, he hadn't been as secretive about the fears as he would've liked. She was his wife, after all. She picked up that things weren't right. He folded, told her about how he thought the restless leg syndrome and the broken wrist and the numb fingers were all connected, how it felt like something was . . . *off* inside him that he couldn't quite readjust. He never claimed there was a monster stealing his bones. He never voiced that concern aloud. He knew what happened to people who believed in those sorts of things. Instead, he'd suggested that the car crash had afflicted more nerve damage than the emergency room doctor had cared enough to investigate. This seemed like a far more reasonable theory than . . . than the alternative. Could it be confirmed, though? Well, not with their current finances. Seeing a real, non-emergency-room doctor would cost real money. Real money neither of them had. Same thing as far as a therapist was concerned, assuming Eileen's theory was closer to reality—that a lot of this was possibly psychological, perhaps from whatever traumatic shit the deepfake dickhead on Twitter had streamed for him over the phone, perhaps from the stress of running the publishing company and preparing for a massive book festival while their bank accounts trickled closer to single digits.

All of it would have to wait.

And, besides, whatever was going on with him, it wouldn't last forever, right? It'd go away. It'd heal itself. Just like his broken wrist. He just needed to rest, to give it more time. Things had a way of working themselves out. He had to believe that was true.

The list of businesses on Xiomara's route consisted of tattoo parlors, pawnshops, vape shops, coffeehouses, sex shops, toy shops, comic book shops, mom & pop pizzerias, beauty salons, vintage clothing stores, and panaderías. They also hit up a hipster donut bakery because it was the middle of the afternoon and goddammit, a donut sounded incredible.

I BELIEVE IN MISTER BONES

Most of these places Daniel had no idea existed until today, and he'd lived in the area over a decade. Xiomara and Eileen were locals, though. They'd grown up here. They knew all the right spots to hit. The ones that'd been around since childhood and had somehow managed to survive all this time, plus the new places that'd blossomed in the wake of previous closures and land expansions. Well, *Xiomara* knew about these spots. Eileen had never explored the city like her friend had done over the years. A hermit of a person, just like Daniel.

If the parking was crammed or nonexistent, Eileen would stay in the car with the engine running, maybe circle the block if necessary, as Xiomara and Daniel ran into the business or string of businesses depending on whether or not they'd stopped at a strip mall. Most of the time there was some kind of parking available, and Eileen joined them. Daniel kept the bag of promo material slung over his back, with the zipper pulled halfway down, and Eileen and Xiomara would take turns pulling out stacks of postcards to leave out on retail counters once granted permission from the staff on duty. Daniel noticed a can of pepper spray dangling from Xiomara's side, and joked that they could blind anybody who refused their requests to hang up promo. "Don't think I won't do it," Xiomara had responded, and winked in a way that made Daniel deeply turned on.

As Xiomara guaranteed, all of the places they hit up acted enthusiastic about the festival, and were more than eager to help spread the word. Time and time again this city surprised Daniel with how much it loved weird, spooky shit. They couldn't have asked for a better stomping ground to run a small press. Maybe one day they'd even come up with the funds to open their own horror-themed bookstore, and shit could really kick off.

By the time they got hungry for lunch, the backpack had been emptied twice. Luckily, Eileen had stored the box of extra postcards in her trunk before leaving the apartment. Most businesses still had several hours before standard closing times, so they decided to go ahead and make the trip downtown. Eileen and Daniel would have to come down here, anyway, but it'd be better to take care of it now when they had the extra help. Xiomara didn't seem to mind. They said it was a good workout, that it did wonders for the calves. He'd seen their calves, and would have to agree. Meanwhile, Daniel had spent most of the day trying his hardest not to think about his own legs at all—but there was a moment, every time he stepped out of the car, where he feared there would be no support when his foot connected to pavement, and his legs would give out like silly putty and send him crashing to the ground. The cartilage in his legs felt too fragile, untrustworthy. So far they seemed to still be working, but for how long? How much more weight could he put on his legs before they finally crumpled?

Once downtown, Eileen parked in the garage of the festival venue and showed Xiomara around the building, since they were unfamiliar with the location when she'd tried explaining it.

After seeing it, though, something clicked. "Wait," they said, "I think this place used to be a bowling alley, right?"

Eileen nodded, looking up at all three stories of the structure. "Something like that, yeah. Now it's just a bar and an event space, really. I heard there's a lot of dance studios that teach here, too."

"How much are you paying for this again?"

She told them.

"Dang, that's a pretty good deal for downtown."

"Yeah, we thought it'd be a lot more."

As the two of them talked, Daniel stood off to the side, back leaning against the concrete wall, convinced he needed the extra support for preventing his own skeletal collapse. Did they realize how sweaty he was? Did he look clammy? Could they tell how much he was freaking out on this sidewalk as they chit chatted about shit that didn't matter when his bones were cursed?

I BELIEVE IN MISTER BONES

"What about the hotels?" Xiomara asked. There were hotels surrounding the venue—one on either side, and one directly across the street. "Were they cool about offering room discounts?"

"Only one of them," she said, referring to the SpringHill on the other side of the street. "The other two basically implied they didn't want to take a chance on an unestablished group. I also think maybe our name scared them a little."

"Well, fuck them," Xiomara said. "Let them regret their mistakes once they see how packed the SpringHill is, right?"

"Exactly." She looked back at the garage, trying to make up her mind about something. "I'm pretty sure we can just leave my car here and it'll be fine."

"You don't have to pay?"

"From what I remember, it's free on weekends."

"Well, shit," Xiomara said, grinning, "isn't this place just perfect?"

Gus's World Famous Fried Chicken was only a block or so away from the venue. An easy walk. Along the way, they encountered a couple shops cool about dropping off promo—a few bars, an erotic toy store, a tattoo parlor, a small shack that only sold sombreros. They hung up flyers and put out stacks of postcards at them all, and as they headed toward the fried chicken restaurant, Daniel couldn't help but feel optimistic about this festival. Sure, his body was potentially going through a nightmarish transformation, but at least there was reason to believe they weren't wasting their time, energy, and money putting together this goddamn event. Because if these businesses were expressing interest in the festival, then surely that would translate into their customers also getting excited, right?

Right?

Believing anything else would only deflate them, kill their momentum. There was not much else going for them these days, so latching onto manic hope felt like their only option.

They ordered a couple baskets of chicken strips to split for the table—one medium heat, the other on the spicier side. Xiomara had requested the latter. Daniel and Eileen were stereotypically white when it came to handling hotter foods, which Xiomara made sure to point out over and over as Eileen scrambled for her cup of water between every bite of the medium-tiered strips. Weirdly, the heat wasn't affecting Daniel all that much. Normally he'd be dumping a bucket of ice water over his face while steam shot out of his ears like a cartoon character. He was having trouble tasting much of *anything* lately, truth be told. There was a certain tastelessness to most of the food and drinks he'd consumed in the last couple days. Too stressed out to focus on anything, he assumed. Were taste buds connected to bones? That was all the tongue, right? Which was a muscle. At least he was *pretty sure* the tongue was a muscle. But what the fuck did he know about tongues? What the fuck did he know about *anything*? Why would that be giving him trouble, anyway? Why would *anything* be giving him trouble besides his wrist, which was undeniably broken, beyond a shred of doubt? What a medical professional had *not* confirmed, or even *acknowledged,* was a much higher list—including, but not limited to, the sudden loss of his taste buds, or the ongoing restless leg syndrome that he'd never in his whole goddamn life experienced until recently, until snapping his wrist, until . . . until . . . until Mister Bones. Whatever that meant, exactly, in the real world. Daniel didn't know, but that didn't make it any less of an active worry rotting his brain while both awake and asleep. There was no such thing as time off from these troubles. There was no punching the clock and going home for the day. The tingling didn't go away. The vague certainty that *something* was very much wrong didn't waver. If anything, it only got stronger with each passing day.

"So, have you heard from that guy since he ripped his

jaw off?" Xiomara asked, as the lunch neared its end and they were all sitting there feeling fat and ready for a nap. Then, catching the ugly side-eye from Eileen, added, "I mean, *allegedly* ripped his jaw off."

Daniel shook his head, and hoped he didn't sound as disappointed as he felt. "Not a word."

"Do you think he . . . uhh . . . really did it?" They leaned over the table, all conspiratorial. "Like . . . do you think he died?"

"Xio, come on," Eileen said.

They shrugged and forced an innocent face. "What? Are you telling me you aren't curious?"

"No, I *am*, but . . . " Eileen trailed off, then sighed. "Don't you think something like that would have been in the *news*, at least? Wouldn't a man ripping off his own jaw with a garage door spring make headlines somewhere?"

"Has anybody checked to see that it *hasn't*?"

"I have," Daniel said. Omitting that he'd checked every day, multiple times a day, since the incident transpired. "I haven't been able to find anything."

"Well," Eileen said, "there ya go."

Xiomara wasn't convinced. "You know, not everything goes viral on Twitter, or whatever. Remember my cousin Victor? We were so afraid it was going to be in all the newspapers and bring great shame to the family, but they didn't even print the obituary. The world is full of strange, stupid shit, and there's not enough room to pay attention to everything. Sometimes, you know, people just hit their capacity levels."

"Wait," Daniel said, "who's Victor?"

Eileen groaned and buried her face in her palms.

"My cousin," Xiomara said. "He died a couple years back. On the Fourth of July."

"Holy shit, I'm sorry," Daniel said.

They shrugged, like it wasn't a big deal. "We weren't that close, it's fine."

"What . . . what happened?"

"Dumb motherfucker got drunk and someone dared him to shoot a bottle rocket out of his ass."

Daniel nearly choked on his water. "Holy shit, what?"

"Dude was so wasted, he stuck it in the wrong direction. Shot straight into his colon, erupted him from the inside-out."

This time he did start choking.

As they walked around downtown handing out festival promo, Xiomara returned the conversation to Mister Bones. They were curious about the situation in a way that Daniel wished Eileen would try out. Instead, Eileen had acted strangely apathetic about everything. She was concerned about his injury, yes, and possibly even troubled by the gradual unraveling of his mental state, but she didn't seem that interested in discussing the specifics of the man from the video call—or, for that matter, the contents of the *Mister Bones* book. She'd listen to him if he felt like talking to someone about it, but there were never any follow-up questions, never any attempt to understand what he was going through. Was it fear that drove her away from engaging in any of this stuff, or boredom?

Xiomara had him walk them through the video again, prompting him to recall details he'd nearly forgotten. Like the wind chimes.

"What do you mean," they said, an amused smirk across their face, "like, he just had them hanging all over the garage?"

"From what I could tell, yeah, they were everywhere."

"What the hell? That's weird, right?" They glanced at Eileen, as if they felt obligated to keep her included in the conversation. "You ever see wind chimes in some fool's garage before?"

"Can't say I have," Eileen said, pressing the crosswalk button a couple more times. It didn't seem to make the light change any quicker. Then, to Daniel: "You never mentioned wind chimes before."

"I just remembered," he said, blushing. Why did he feel like he was being accused of something? "Actually, in the book itself there's a deleted chapter, or a *redacted* chapter, and the title at the top of the page says 'WIND CHIMES.' But the rest of the chapter is gone. You think maybe it's related to what that guy was doing? It would have to be, right? Who even buys wind chimes anymore?"

"If the garage was shut, what made them go all crazy?" Xiomara asked.

"That's what I'm wondering," he said. "I mean, I only got a small view from my phone. Maybe there was a window open somewhere, and a breeze got in."

"Or maybe he had a fan running," Eileen said, and they both glanced at her, surprised to hear her contribute something resembling even an inkling of a theory.

"I don't remember hearing a fan," Daniel said, "*but*, again, I was on my phone, listening through a speaker, in front of H-E-B."

"Yeah," Xiomara said, "probably not the most ideal circumstances to watch some fucker rip off his own jaw."

"What *would* be?" Eileen asked, horrified.

"I don't know. Home theater set-up, something along those lines. I feel like you probably want privacy. Plus a good sound system. Decent microwavable popcorn. The works." Then, to Daniel, they asked, "Do you think he really believed in this Bones dude?"

"I think he was insane," Daniel replied, which he knew didn't actually answer the question.

"Well, yeah. He ripped off his jaw. *Allegedly*." They winked at Eileen, who scoffed. "Wait, Eileen, if this guy didn't really do what Daniel saw, then what do *you* think happened? That he faked it? Like, he was trolling him?"

"Uhh . . . AI?" Eileen suggested.

"Can AI do *that*?" Xiomara asked, flabbergasted.

"I don't know what it can or can't do," Eileen admitted,

and Daniel could hear the frustration threatening to burst from her body. "Maybe it was some clip of a horror movie Daniel didn't recognize and it fooled him. Does it sound right? No, not really. Does it sound plausible? Barely. But what's the alternative here? That some maniac tracked Daniel down on Twitter, someone also cursed by the same haunted book, and physically removed his jawbone as an offering to some . . . some what? Some *demon*? What the fuck is this thing supposed to be, anyway?"

"He's like the Babadook," Daniel reminded her.

"Right," Eileen said. "Some fucking Babadook? I can't believe that, and I don't think Daniel believes that, either. I don't think anybody remotely sane believes something like that."

"I never said I believed," Daniel said, but she was already talking over him, not listening.

"Which means," she continued, "whatever Daniel saw wasn't real. Somehow it was faked. Someone, for whatever reason, is trying to fuck with him. They sent him a prank book submission, and now they're stretching the joke as far as they can take it. Which is why my suggestion is to stop taking it seriously, and move on. Don't give these assholes an ounce of space in our heads. Because they'll just leech on and continue to abuse us."

Abuse *me,* Daniel almost corrected. Not *us.* Nobody had contacted Eileen. She hadn't read the book. She hadn't broken a bone. She wasn't involved in any of this. Not directly. She was a bystander, a witness. But before he could say anything, Xiomara thankfully cut in with their own comment:

"Wait, this guy is like the Babadook?"

Downtown was not booming with promo-appropriate businesses like Xiomara had advertised. Most of the places they passed were hotels, or private offices, or fancy

I BELIEVE IN MISTER BONES

restaurants that wouldn't allow them through the doors without a reservation on the books. It wasn't a total waste of time, though. There were a few oddity shops and arts & crafts shacks that allowed them to leave stuff out.

"The places you really want to avoid," Xiomara explained, "are the fast food franchises. Subway, Starbucks, Whataburger, whatever. Franchises have very strict regulations when it comes to this shit, and all of them are assholes about it. The answer is always no. Sometimes you might get an employee pitying you and taking a stack, but don't be fooled: the moment you walk out the door, their manager's tossing that shit in the trash. That's why I don't bother fucking with them, anymore. You do this long enough, you start developing an instinct based solely on vibes whether a place is going to be cool or not. Like that place, for example." They pointed at an old house across the street, which had been renovated into a business. A sign out front declared itself THE JUNK DRAWER, with a subtitle beneath it reading: WE SELL THE CRAP YOU'LL NEVER END UP USING. "That place," Xiomara continued, "is going to be dope."

A bell rang as the three of them entered, and a nearby cat wearing a necktie let out a terrified screech before fleeing for cover.

"Oh don't you mind Detritus," an older woman from behind the checkout counter said, attention half-focused on some overly loud mobile game in front of her face. "He don't scratch none."

"Good to know," Eileen mumbled, as they all took in the store.

It was appropriately named, was Daniel's first thought. There was no clear theme here of what they sold. Just...stuff. *Junk*. Tables and shelves piled high with the most random odds and ends one could imagine. It looked less like a legitimate business and more like a flea market self-contained to one particularly unhinged hoarder's bungalow. A flea market felt like the perfect comparison, the more he surveyed the place. It quickly became obvious flea markets were where the owner had purchased most, if not all, of this junk, with the sole intention of doubling their retail prices here in the city proper, where tourists might get duped into believing they were purchasing high-end antiques.

Eileen approached the woman at the counter. She already had a thick stack of postcards equipped in either hand, held up like peace flags. "Hi," she said, then cleared her throat when the woman didn't look away from her phone. "Hello."

The woman sighed and set her phone down on the counter and said, "Can I help you?"

Then Eileen gave her the speech all three of them had been reciting throughout the day: "Yes, we are going to be hosting a book festival here soon in San Antonio, and we were wondering if you'd be okay with us leaving some promotional materials out for your customers?"

She stared at Eileen for a moment, mouth agape, then erupted into a wheezing coughing fit. After composing herself, she snapped, "You're doing *what* now?"

While Eileen dealt with the confused clerk, Daniel browsed the shelves of garbage with Xiomara. There was an assortment of shit here that he couldn't make heads or tails of. On one display alone he spotted an American-flag-decorated flask, a coverless Holy Bible, a dozen shrink-wrapped DVDs of *Wedding Crashers,* and the telephone toy from *Skinamarink.*

Behind him, Eileen continued explaining what a book festival was to the clerk. "It's a festival for publishers and authors to sell books. We are hosting it on St. Mary's. It's free to the public. We have flyers?"

"Oh," the woman said, "I thought you said *hook* festival." She started cracking up. "I was thinking, what kind of maniacs throw a festival for hooks."

"I'm sure those exist, too," Xiomara said over their shoulder. "I bet there are festivals for most things.

I BELIEVE IN MISTER BONES

Everybody has *some* kind of hobby—right? There's gotta be some hook fanatics out there."

The clerk leaned over the counter, cocking her head in a classic *I'm-old-and-hard-of-hearing* pose. "I'm sorry—did you say something, sir?" She paused. "I mean, ma'am?" Another pause. "I mean . . . sir?"

Xiomara winked at the woman, then turned their attention back to the shelves of nonsense.

Eileen tried repeating her sales pitch about the promo material, but it didn't sound like she was getting through to her. Daniel and Xiomara started laughing about how frustrated Eileen sounded, when something crossed his line of sight. He must've spotted it at the exact same time as Xiomara did, because they pointed at it and said, "Hey, how weird is that? Weren't we just talking about those?"

Daniel reached forward and picked up the wind chime and held it at eye-level with a numb hand that couldn't stop shaking.

The "tubes" were small, ceramic mushrooms painted shades of blue, pink, and white. A handwritten price tag hung from the clapper. Almost fifteen bucks. He had never owned a wind chime in his life, and up until this very second, had never so much as *considered* purchasing one.

"I'll take this," he told the woman behind the counter.

She ended up allowing them to leave a stack of postcards, after all.

TWO WEEKS BEFORE the book festival, Daniel and Eileen hopped on a video call in their apartment for an interview with the *Alamo City Weekly*. They sat on the couch, with Daniel's laptop on the coffee table in front of them. It should've been an exciting moment: at long last receiving some recognition from their local alternative newspaper. A milestone for the company.

And yet, there was no buzz or thrill for them that morning, as they waited for the reporter to grant Daniel's account access to the call. The last time he'd participated in a video call, he'd witnessed some lunatic rip his own jawbone off. Eileen might prefer to imagine someone had tricked him with a deepfake, but Daniel no longer bought into that theory. If he was being honest with himself, he never had—not genuinely. What he'd seen had been real. He knew it to be true with all of his heart.

Understandably, this app had given him a mild case of PTSD. Not just this specific app, but the entire concept of . . . phone calls? Video calls, at the very least. He'd been dreading this moment for days now, ever since the reporter had reached out via email about scheduling the conversation. There was some comfort that Eileen was joining him, at least. This time, if something insane happened, she would also be present. He wouldn't have to rely on his own awkward testimony to convince anybody of anything. Plus, Daniel was in no way in the right state

I BELIEVE IN MISTER BONES

to be answering questions. He'd pretty much stopped sleeping at this point, outside of the odd twenty-minute brain reboot that hit him every couple hours. He'd need Eileen to do most of the heavy-lifting for this interview, and hope the reporter asked questions that either of them could answer and weren't centered on his exclusive knowledge or experience.

Of course, the very first question asked by the reporter pertained to the many, many wind chimes hanging throughout their apartment. He'd foolishly hoped their bodies would block them from view. Eileen turned her head toward him like, *This is a 'you' question, buddy.* Which . . . okay, fair. She hadn't been the one staying up every night ordering wind chimes off of Etsy with money neither of them could afford to spare. That was all on Daniel.

"Oh, you know, just . . . uh, decoration, that kind of thing," he mumbled, trying to figure out a comfortable position to rest his arms and legs. None of his limbs felt . . . *natural* anymore. Like rubber hoses sloppily crammed into skin pouches. He didn't understand how he could still move them at all, at this point. Any given moment his body would stop obeying commands directed down from his brain, and he would go limp, unable to move, or talk, or breathe. Alone in a recalled husk with just his maddening thoughts to keep him company. No, not quite that, either. His thoughts wouldn't be keeping him company. He *would* be his thoughts. There would be nothing else left that belonged to Daniel. Could he say for certain that every thought entering and exiting his mind didn't carry with it some nefarious bias implanted by a malicious outsider? Could *anybody* claim that, and still maintain a straight face?

"I don't think I've ever seen wind chimes inside before," the reporter said, squinting at his webcam like it might somehow improve his perception of their apartment.

"Oh?" Daniel said, and debated shutting the laptop

without another word. Instead, he said, "There's a Thai restaurant near us with bamboo ones inside the lobby. They're pretty cool." He shyly glanced at Eileen. "Right?"

"Um," Eileen said, "yeah, sure, I've seen those."

"See?" Daniel said to the computer. "All perfectly normal." He forced a smile that lasted only as long as it took him to worry about whether or not his teeth were still teeth and not . . . something else. "Anyway . . . we wanted to thank you for reaching out to us about this. It means a lot."

The reporter returned the smile. "It's our pleasure, believe me. Getting to help spread the word about something as cool as a horror book festival? Ten-year-old me would be ecstatic right now."

"You were a horror fan as a kid?" Eileen asked.

He nodded, enthusiastically. "Oh, yeah, for sure. My parents let me read Stephen King way too young, so I've been pretty corrupted for a while now."

Daniel resisted the urge to make a jerk-off gesture. Thankfully, Eileen took the lead. "Yup, we hear that all the time from people in the community. It's a very common origin story for horror fans."

The reporter tried to cover up a look of disappointment, and Daniel knew he thought he'd somehow been special for reading Stephen King as a kid. "Anyway," the reporter said, "in case I forgot to mention it, this conversation will be recorded. Easier to just transcribe later on, instead of scrambling to take notes as we're talking."

Eileen nodded. "Makes sense to me."

There was a gap of silence, and Daniel realized they were waiting on him to say anything. So he said, "Okay."

"Great!" The reporter glanced at something off-screen. A list of questions for him to ask, Daniel presumed. "So, uh, anyway . . . I thought we should start off with a bit of clarification. I was reading up on you guys, and it looks like you also publish books, too. Is that right?"

I BELIEVE IN MISTER BONES

Daniel immediately wanted to strangle himself.

In an exaggerated chipper voice, Eileen replied, "Yes, that's right. Fiendish Books is a small press we started, uhh . . . "

"Back in 2012," Daniel mumbled, internally adding, *The year the world was supposed to end.*

"Wow," the reporter said, "I didn't realize you guys had been around so long."

Daniel let out a bitter chuckle. "That's okay. Most people don't."

"So, do you just publish local authors, or . . . ?"

"Nope," Eileen cut in, "we've published people from all over the world. It's not just a local thing."

"And how much do you typically charge them?"

"I'm sorry?" she said.

"Some of our readers might be interested in also getting published with y'all, so I thought maybe your rates might make for a good advertisement."

Daniel buried his numb face in his numb hands.

"Oh," Eileen said, "well, we don't charge writers to publish with us. In fact, no publisher should charge writers to publish them. Money goes *to* the writer, not the other way around."

"Oh, wow, okay, that's fascinating," the reporter said.

Daniel managed to hold back from saying, *Is it really, though?* Instead he fussed with the drawstrings from the hoodie he was wearing. He'd thrown it on before the call so he'd have long sleeves on. Anything to hide the markings he'd drawn all over his body—little Sharpie circles around spots on his skin he suspected might've served as insertion points while unconscious.

"So, the press started in 2012, you stated," the reporter said, "how did that come about? Did you two already know each other? Walk me through how the publishing company started."

"Well, let's see." Eileen paused to think back, as if the two of them hadn't answered this question a thousand times before, as if the information wasn't readily available on their website's ABOUT US page. "Before Fiendish, we were both volunteering for another press—which is no longer around. It was owned by another man. He'd put out a call for volunteer editors. Back then, Daniel and I were just starting to submit short stories to markets, so we were already subscribed to his newsletter because of that. We saw the call for volunteer editors, and Daniel sent in an application. Meanwhile, I'd already seen some of the books they'd put out, and . . . well, not to toot my own horn *too much*, but I knew I could have done a much better job formatting them, so I also emailed the publisher and let him know his interior designs could really use some help, and I'd be willing to volunteer there. So, that's kind of how Daniel and I both got started in . . . you know, the whole indie horror community thing. Volunteering for this other press. Helping out there introduced us to this whole . . . labyrinth of small presses and indie authors that we never even knew existed until then. We did that for . . . I don't know, I want to say about a year, but it was always a little bit frustrating, doing all that work while someone else profited from it. We'd always talk about what we might do differently, if we were the ones in charge of everything, and finally we decided to go ahead and do it." She looked to Daniel. "Am I missing anything?"

He shook his head no and said, "Sounds about right." He didn't add what else he was thinking, that the whole thing had been a huge mistake, that they turned out hardly any better than the shitty publisher the two of them had volunteered for in the beginning of their careers. He didn't voice his fear that Fiendish had accidentally become a publishing factory, pumping out title after title without enough energy to properly promote anything. He didn't tell the reporter that both Daniel and Eileen were wasting their lives working on books only a few hundred people might ever read, and that estimate was being generous. Nobody wanted to hear him say what he was really thinking. Not even Daniel wanted to hear it. So he didn't say anything else. He bit his tongue with teeth that felt slightly out of place in his gums and he wrapped the hoodie's drawstring around fingers that'd lost all feeling outside of a dull, predictable numbness.

"And you guys only publish horror?" the reporter asked, completely oblivious to the mad symphony erupting in Daniel's mushy skull.

"Yeah," she said, "that's what we try to focus on."

"Do you find that limiting at all, with reaching readers?"

She shook her head. "No, if anything it has the opposite effect. Leaning into a niche genre like horror, it only helps us attract the type of people who *do* like that stuff. If we were trying to publish every genre, we would be trying to hit a much broader audience, and small presses don't have that kind of reach. It's smarter, we think, to embrace the weirdos who like the same kind of stuff we do."

"And that's horror?"

"Yeah, horror."

"Well, you know I have to ask this next question, then," the reporter said, annoyingly giddy with anticipation. "Why horror?"

Daniel hated that question. Everybody hated it. There was no easy answer. Nothing that could be confined to a brief interview response. He could write out an entire essay exploring *why horror* and still would struggle with solidifying a satisfying explanation. "It's just cool," he said.

"Yeah," Eileen said, "it's pretty cool."

The reporter waited for an elaboration, and when he didn't get one he let out a nervous laugh and moved on. "Let's talk about this book festival. Can you tell me a little more about what it is?"

"Sure," Eileen said. "No problem." She glanced at Daniel, but all he could think about was how this interview could have easily been conducted over email. She took a sip of coffee and said, "It's meant to be kind of like those old Scholastic Book Fairs we all used to do as kids, but more for adults who love horror."

"That sounds so awesome," the reporter said.

"Thank you, we hope it is." She went on to offer a condensed version of everything they'd already posted on the Fiendish Book Festival page. Daniel zoned out. He could hear her talking, but the words stopped sounding like words and evolved into more of a white noise.

The two of them continued the interview for another ten minutes or so, and Daniel tried his best to nod and go, "Uh huh," and, "Yeah," every once in a while. If either of them noticed he'd mentally checked out of the interview, they didn't say anything. At least nothing he picked up on while pretending to be listening.

Then, at long last, it was time to wrap things up.

"I want to thank you once more for talking with me," the reporter said. "I'll get this all typed up today or tomorrow, and it should go live a week before the festival."

"Sounds perfect to me," Eileen said, and nudged Daniel's leg.

"Uh, yeah, perfect. Thank you."

"Before we end things, was there anything else you wanted to get out there that I maybe didn't ask about? Anything else you were hoping to promote or let folks know about?"

"Hmm, I don't think so, but thank you," Eileen said.

"Okay, well then great—"

"—Actually," Daniel said, "yeah, there might be something you can help us with, if you're interested."

"Oh?" The reporter appeared genuinely surprised, as did Eileen. "Sure, absolutely. What were you thinking?"

"We got this submission a while ago," he said, ignoring the sigh from Eileen next to him, "and we've been having the hardest time trying to track down the author."

The reporter blinked a couple times, not understanding what was being asked of him.

"We want to accept the book," Daniel continued, "we'd like to print it through Fiendish and put it out and all that. But, their email address is no longer active, and they forgot to tell us their name when submitting the book."

I BELIEVE IN MISTER BONES

"Oh," the reporter said, "that's kind of weird, right?"

Daniel nodded. It *was* weird. He was sure they could all agree on that point, even Eileen. "Yeah, definitely weird. I've been trying to track down the author ever since they submitted it to us, and I've had no luck. So I thought, I don't know, maybe we could shout it out in the interview? Like . . . 'by the way, if you wrote a book called *I Believe in Mister Bones* and sent it to Fiendish Books recently, please email us as soon as possible.'"

"It's called *I Believe in Mister Bones*?"

"Well, no, not really," Daniel admitted. "That's the title I gave it. The submission didn't have an official one when it was sent to us."

"No author name, *and* no title?" The reporter's voice cracked with amusement. "What exactly were they expecting to happen here?"

Daniel hugged his chest and rocked back and forth on the couch. "Yeah, I'm not sure."

"Well," the reporter said, dragging out the word, "obviously it was effective, though—right? I mean, it's gotten you trying to track them down. I bet it's usually the other way around, isn't it?"

"Are you going to do it?" Daniel asked. "Put the message in the interview, I mean."

The reporter bit his bottom lip before responding. "I can't make any promises, but sure, I can try, yeah. But I'll tell you now, the odds of my editor allowing something like that to stay in aren't exactly in your favor. He can be pretty ruthless with the red pen, *if you know what I mean.*"

He leaned toward his webcam, facial expression resembling someone who'd just told a naughty joke and was waiting on the rest of his party to catch up.

"You *do* know what I mean, right?" he said, once nobody else reacted.

"Uh," Daniel said.

"Of course we know what you mean," Eileen said.

The reporter grinned and exclaimed, "That's what I'm talking about! Hell yeah!"

After the video call ended and Daniel had closed his laptop, he turned to Eileen and said, "Wait, what *did* he mean?"

She was already in the process of charging up her vape. "I don't even think *he* knew what he meant." Holding the device up to her lips, she added, "Fucking weirdo," before taking a hit. Then: "Why did you ask him to do that?"

"To do what?"

"You know what."

Of course he knew. "I don't know. Why not? It's not like we have any other ideas at this point, right? If it doesn't work, then oh well, at least we tried something new. And if it *does* work, well . . . "

"I didn't know you were still trying to *find* this person," she said. "I thought you had given up."

The question had him searching for something nearby to throw across the apartment. Unfortunately, there was nothing within reach. He glared at her with the intensity of someone with laser-beam vision. He couldn't remember ever being so angry at her. "What are you talking about? How could I *give up?* Do you think if that was an option for me, I would've by now? Do you think I want this to happen to me?"

"You want *what* to happen to you? You still haven't said it."

"Do I have to at this point? I mean, come on, Eileen, do I really have to fucking say it?" It struck him that he'd just said "come on, Eileen" without any hint of irony, and he had to choke back a laugh. This was not the time.

Tears had formed in the corners of her eyes as she waited for him to put words to the illness they both knew he thought he was suffering from. "Yeah," she said. "I think you need to."

He slumped back against the couch, overcome with a deep sense of shame. This shit was embarrassing to talk

I BELIEVE IN MISTER BONES

about. "If you'd read the book, I don't think I'd have to say it. You'd know."

"I know, and I'm going to, I promise I'll read it. I've just been busy trying to format all of this other shit, the last thing my brain wants to do is look at *more* text. But I will, okay? I will. And, until then . . . you're here, I'm here. So talk to me. Tell me."

He closed his eyes and tried to fall asleep. No luck. "Come here," he whispered.

"What?"

"Come sit down." He licked his dry, flaking lips. "Please."

He kept his eyes shut, but heard her returning to the living room, felt her weight as she joined him on the couch.

"I'm here," she said, voice softer now, gentler.

He pulled off his hoodie, accidentally taking off his shirt with it, and tossed them both to the floor. He held up his left arm, indicating the cast, refusing to make eye contact with the Mister Bones signature she'd scribbled on it. He closed them tighter, like an infant feigning sleep. "Can you take this off for me?"

"Do you think it's time?" Eileen asked. "How long did they say you had to keep it on?"

"Trust me. It's time."

"Okay." Then, "Do I just cut it off?"

"There should be scissors on the coffee table."

He knew they were there. He'd been eyeing them off and on during the interview, but with different intentions. She scooted forward and retrieved them, then settled back in the cushion. He could feel her watching him, unsure of how to proceed. He held out his arm again and told her, "It's okay. I'm ready."

"Are you sure?"

"I'm sure."

"Okay," she said, nowhere near as confident as he sounded, and proceeded to split the cast lengthwise, beginning at the bottom of the wrist and working her way

139

up to the palm. Now he opened his eyes, nervous and excited to see what awaited beneath. The cast cracked open like a shell, revealing Daniel's pale, slightly-atrophied wrist. The relief he felt was immediate as air touched his previously-confined skin. Cooling, calming. He imagined the sensation being similar to coming home from a long day at work and finally being able to take off his bra, not that this was something he'd ever experienced himself, or ever would, but it was the comparison that came to his mind, the one that he latched onto. The stitches were gone at this point. An ugly, ridged scar served as the only evidence of their past presence.

"Jesus, that smells," Eileen said, tossing the mutilated cast onto the table, along with the scissors.

"Does it?" Daniel's sense of smell had vanished around the same time as his taste buds. "Like what?"

"Like sweat, and dirt . . . like you need to wash it with lots and lots of soap. How does it feel? Does it hurt?"

"It doesn't hurt," Daniel said, without touching it. Nothing in his body had hurt for quite some time now, although that wasn't to claim that he felt *good*. Instead, everything was numb. Everything *tingled*. Awkward, claustrophobic. Like his skeleton no longer correctly fit in his flesh. Like it was aching to escape.

And where did it all start? Where had he first allowed this bizarre ailment to violate his person? The fracture. The first blasphemy.

He let his wrist rest in his lap, undisturbed. Too afraid to examine it any closer. "Would you feel it for me?" he asked her. "Would you tell me . . . you know, if there's anything strange?"

He hoped she wouldn't need him to elaborate on what he meant by *strange,* and to his relief she didn't ask. Slowly, she extended her arm out and delicately touched the scar on his wrist.

"Feels pretty gross," she said.

Daniel shook his head, resisting annoyance.

I BELIEVE IN MISTER BONES

Everything so easily irritated him lately. It was a struggle to remain calm and collected. "Not that," he said. "The bone. Feel the bone."

Like she hadn't known what he'd meant the first time. Why would he want her to touch the scar? Who gave a flying fuck about the scar? The whole thing was about bones. It had always been about bones. Hadn't she been listening to a goddamn word he'd told her? Hadn't she been paying attention at all?

She gently clasped her fingers around his wrist, fingertips near the area of the snap. Her nails were jagged, discolored.

All the anger and annoyance throbbing in his temple dissipated.

"You stopped getting your nails done," he said, voice weak.

"I decided it was a stupid expense," she said, taken aback by the observation.

"But you love doing that." She'd once told him she viewed it as her one silly extravagance. A little treat just for her. "You should go back."

"There are more important things to worry about than my dumb nails."

"But they look nice, and you like them." He reached out with his right hand, and took her fingers in his grasp. "You should at least do them before the festival next week, right?"

"I'll think about it."

"You should make the appointment."

Her lips broke into a subtle smile. "Maybe I will. Now tell me what I'm looking for here."

"Just tell me what you feel," he said, suddenly conscious of how many small circles he'd drawn on his body with black marker. Circles marking spots he suspected where something had been inserted into his body. Inserted and withdrawn. With his shirt off, there was no hiding how nuts he'd become over the last couple weeks. It was difficult to ignore how out of control everything had gotten, but they would try their best, anyway.

Eileen pressed her thumb down on his wrist bone. Anticipation influenced a wince, but Daniel didn't feel any pain. The tingling numbness that had consumed his body briefly spasmed, and he was reminded of the jellyfish they'd seen displayed at the pet store, but the sensation wasn't anything too unbearable. In a way that he found impossible to articulate, it was sort of pleasurable. He half-expected her finger to rip through the skin and burst the bone open, to crumble it like stale bread. Maybe a sick part of him was even *hoping* for something abnormal to occur, anything to provide some sort of external evidence that he hadn't lost his mind, that something really was wrong with him. Acknowledgement from Eileen might've cured Daniel, judging by how desperately he craved it.

"It feels fine to me," Eileen said—and then, as if reading his mind: "I'm sorry."

"It's a good thing, right?" Daniel said, unconvincingly.

"Yeah, but . . . " She sighed, clearly not believing he truly felt that way, either. "I know you expected something different."

"Something different like what?" he asked, wishing she'd be the one to say the words out loud. To give voice to what was a delusion at best, terminal illness at worst—or was that the other way around? He touched his wrist with his other hand, rougher than Eileen had dared pressing down. It felt fine. Like a standard, healthy-ish wrist of someone in their early-to-mid thirties. Maybe healthy wasn't the right description for someone who spent most of their time on Earth hunched over a laptop, teasing the gods of carpal tunnel syndrome. Healthy enough for someone with his profession. Erase the ugly scar and it would've been difficult to guess the bone had recently been broken at all.

Defeated, he tucked his healed arm between his left

thigh and the armrest of the couch, then sat there with his jaw tilted toward his chest, sulking.

"Did you feel anything?" Eileen asked, still seated next to him. He wished she'd get up and go find something else to do. Leave the apartment altogether. Just for a little bit. Tears felt inevitable at this point, and he would have preferred solitude upon their arrival.

"Nothing that you didn't feel, too."

"It doesn't hurt, or anything?"

He shook his head. "It's just numb, and tingly. Like when your foot's asleep."

"I hate when that happens."

He looked her in the eyes, serious. "My whole body feels like that."

"Your whole body feels like . . . "

"Like it's asleep."

There was something in her face that screamed *does not compute*. "What do you mean, your whole body?"

"I mean, my *whole* body." He couldn't conceive of a clearer explanation. "My arms, my legs, my hands, my feet . . . my stomach, back . . . even my face. Like all of my skin has been . . . readjusted, you know? Like it was all taken off my skeleton, then put back on slightly wrong . . . except I know it's not my *skin*."

"It's your bones."

He grabbed her hand and squeezed it tight. "It's my bones."

"You think they've been stolen."

"Maybe. I don't know." He rubbed his impossibly tired eyes. "Something is happening when I'm asleep. I keep having these dreams . . . and then, when I wake up, I feel different. I feel . . . *less*."

Eileen glanced around the apartment. "The wind chimes haven't gone off once, though, right? Wouldn't they have woken *me* up, at least?"

"I don't know how any of this works. It just seemed like a good idea. The redacted chapter in the book . . . it must have been there for a reason. It must have said something important . . . "

"What do you think about us taking some of them down?"

"What? The wind chimes?"

"Yeah, sure, why not? If they're not doing anything, anyway . . . "

A blade tensed in his gut. "I'd rather keep them up."

"It just makes it hard to walk around here, is all I'm trying to say. I'm always bumping into them. They're bothersome."

He wanted to bash his fists into the coffee table and cry out for her to leave his fucking wind chimes alone. They were *his* property and she would keep her goddamn fingers off of them. The anger was instant, like a lighter conjuring flame. He managed to extinguish it just as quickly and compromised by giving her hand another intimate squeeze. "If it's okay with you, I'd like them to stay just a little bit longer." Then, because he knew she'd want more commitment than that, suggested she give him until after the book festival.

"Well," Eileen said, "it would be nice to have them gone *before* then, otherwise they're going to be in the way as we pack everything up to take downtown."

Daniel bit into his tongue with teeth made out of who knew what. "Can we talk about this next week?" The wind chimes were staying. He didn't know how to make that any clearer for her. He'd stumbled upon that one in the thrift shop for a reason. None of this was accidental or random. It *meant* something. The guy from the video call, the one who'd ripped his jaw off, he'd decorated his garage in a similar fashion. Clearly he'd known something. Maybe he'd read the missing chapter. Maybe he knew the secret.

But one look at her face told him she wasn't ready to drop the conversation. She was dedicated to picking at this wind chime issue like a scab until he caved in. That wasn't going to happen. What *would* happen was Daniel would

I BELIEVE IN MISTER BONES

eventually lose control of his temper, and he'd snap and yell and say some shit that he would regret, then she would snap and yell and say some shit she'd regret, and they'd spend the rest of the night not speaking to each other from opposite ends of the apartment, then in the morning they'd pretend like nothing had happened and continue on about their day like they were a happy couple, like they weren't both miserably depressed and crippled with stress and anxiety, like Daniel wasn't being stalked by some goddamn Babadook bozo every time he nodded off, like his bones weren't becoming rarer by the day, by the hour, by the minute. By the second.

He didn't feel like losing his temper. He didn't want to fight. He didn't have the energy for it. He didn't have the *passion*. Bickering required stamina. So he did the only thing he could think of that might halt the fight in its tracks—not stop it entirely, but certainly delay its arrival for an insubstantial period of time. He took his healthier hand and caressed her cheek, running his fingers down her neck and resting them on the back of her left shoulder where he started giving her a lazy massage.

"What are you doing?" she asked.

"Distracting you from the wind chimes."

She smiled, and he knew he had her.

"Oh, you think it's as easy as rubbing my shoulders a little bit?"

He feigned contemplation, then nodded. "Yes, yes I do."

"Hmm. You might be right."

"Why don't we do this properly?" With his feet, he pushed the coffee table out more, creating ample space for Eileen to sit on the floor. He made sure to set down a pillow first. The carpet in their apartment was not kind to uncushioned butts. They had learned this from experience.

She got down on the floor, sitting between his legs with her back facing him. He slowly pulled off her T-shirt and tossed it in a pile of laundry across the room that desperately needed to be washed. Neither of them had any plans of going out soon, so she hadn't gone through the trouble of putting on a bra today. Her back was smooth and pale. He felt goose bumps rising against his fingertips as he brushed them around her shoulders. She shivered and let out a soft gasp.

"You okay?" he asked, knowing she was.

"Just sent a chill down my spine, is all."

"Well, I can stop, if this is too extreme for you."

"I think I'll be able to handle it."

He realized he was smiling, and that it wasn't forced. Nobody could see his face right now, anyway. This smile was just for him.

He continued massaging her, starting soft and gentle, slow, lightly using just his fingertips, before evolving into a harder rub, really working at the knots in her upper back. She'd let out a gasp or moan here and there as the pressure intensified, but he had no plans of stopping until she told him she'd had enough. Eileen had a greater pain threshold than he did. She could tolerate the kind of shit that would send him sobbing in the shower.

"Oh shit," she said, wiggling against his touch, "right there, right there . . . "

"I can feel it," he said, referencing the rat king of knots practically pulsating in her left shoulder. "You want me to go harder?"

"A little," she said, then: "Not too much."

"Understood," he said, and sat forward to collect a new gust of strength. His fingers, still asleep, were becoming increasingly difficult to control. He flattened his left hand against her shoulder, and started digging his palm into the knot, twisting it left and right, all while holding her right shoulder with his other hand to stop her from squirming around too much.

"Oh my god," she cried out, softly.

"Keep going?"

"I don't know."

I BELIEVE IN MISTER BONES

He kept going. Not only that, but he started pressing down even harder. She cried out louder, but never said stop, never said that's enough. She was hurting, he knew, but not because of him—because of the knots inside her back, and he was going to fix it. He was going to cure her. Just as he wished she could do for him. He was going to help.

He slightly stood off the couch, putting all of his weight into his left arm as he dug into her knots, ignoring the pained noises escaping her clenched jaw. "A little more," he whispered, "I got this . . . I got this . . . "

And then something peculiar happened.

All of that weight Daniel applied to his arm finally gave out, and it *snapped*.

In the exact same place as he'd snapped it back at the grocery store.

"*Oh fuck oh fuck oh fuck.*"

Unlike the previous instance, however, this snap was silent. It didn't puncture the skin, either. It was less like a bone had been broken, and more like a hose had been bent.

His left hand was twisted all the way back, so his fingers were slapping against the back of his forearm.

Hanging there like a discarded rubber glove.

"*Holy shit holy shit holy shit,*" Daniel cried out, fleeing to the bathroom.

As he ran, half of his arm flopped uselessly at his side.

Back in the living room, Eileen shouted, "What's wrong? What happened?"

There was no time to answer her questions. He wouldn't have known how to respond even if he'd wanted to, anyway. How the hell was *he* supposed to know what was wrong or what had happened? How was he supposed to know any goddamn thing right now, the condition he was in?

He collapsed recklessly on the tiled floor, crushing the cartilage connected to whatever resembled his knee bones these days. His face was barely in the toilet before everything in his stomach came spewing out of not just his mouth but also his nostrils. Hot, burning liquid hit the bowl and ricocheted back into his eyes. It'd been so long since he'd properly vomited that, for a moment, he genuinely didn't understand what was happening. He thought he was dying, that this was his body's way of officially calling it quits and shutting down the factory.

"Daniel?" Eileen asked, somewhere nearby. "Jesus Christ, are you okay?"

If he wasn't actively puking, he would have laughed. Did it *look* like he was okay? Did it look like he was *remotely* okay?

After he finished emptying his insides, he flushed the toilet and leaned back against the wall, blindly reaching for the toilet paper roll beside his head and using every remaining square to wipe his face clean.

"Daniel?" Eileen said again, and his eyes followed the source of her voice. She stood in the doorway, still topless, tears in her eyes. She was scared out of her mind, and that made two of them. "Daniel, please, say something."

He raised his left arm and said, "Do you see now? Do you see?"

But before he even looked at his arm again, it struck him how easily he'd been able to flush the toilet, which he would have had to use his left hand to do.

"See *what,* Daniel?" Eileen asked, fully crying now. "What am I supposed to *see*?"

Reluctantly, he looked at his arm, still raised like it was about to shatter Eileen's sense of reality.

But of course it was fine.

His arm wasn't bent.

It wasn't snapped.

It wasn't anything but a regular arm with a little scar along the wrist.

He banged the back of his head against the wall behind him, and said, "I can't fucking do this anymore."

And the way Eileen was staring back at him, he figured she was thinking something similar.

IT TOOK SOME RESEARCH, but Eileen found a
doctor they could afford. Someone in their community
Facebook group recommended him, after she posted a
desperate plea in the middle of the night for budget-
friendly medical options. This guy—Doctor Zambrano,
according to the DIY-looking WordPress site advertising
his services—was a professional, certified general
practitioner who worked at a decent-sized office closer to
the city, but also opened his own home to the public every
Sunday on his day off. Strictly pro bono work, a service to
the poor and uninsured. She heard getting an appointment
wasn't always the easiest. The Sunday slots filled up fast.
And yet, somehow, she managed to book an opening on the
next available Sunday—the Sunday before the inaugural
Fiendish Book Festival.

Daniel felt equally impressed and useless. He'd done
nothing but lie around moping and going over his body
with the black Sharpie again, searching for more insertion
points that might've sprung up since previous inspections.
Once in a while he'd look at his new phone and scroll
through the *Mister Bones* manuscript, as if some clue
might leap out to him and piece everything together once
and for all. There was nothing, of course. Just a mediocre
book full of unexplained mysteries. Meanwhile, Eileen was
actually trying to come up with a solution. She found a
doctor he could see, long after he'd concluded medical help

would not be an option for him. She'd also managed to format an entire book during this time. He still hadn't finished editing the book he'd been working on for the last two months. There was zero chance of it coming out for the festival now. Johnny Compton, the author, had sent numerous emails demanding updates, and Daniel had ignored them all. Ghosting authors was one of the worst things a press could do. Daniel knew that. Everybody knew that. Knowledge of his wrongdoings didn't prevent him from doing wrong. It just made him feel shittier.

Doctor Zambrano's home was located on the outskirts of San Antonio, several miles out on some remote farm-to-market road. It might've been harder to miss if not for the truck parked in front selling fruit pies, fresh-farmed eggs, and cold drinks. The website had included the fruit pie truck with the directions listed on the homepage. Doctor Zambrano's sister evidently baked them every week and sold them while he tended to his patients. The house was old and looked frail, like a strong-enough wind could easily collapse its foundation. Eileen and Daniel had already decided they would try to buy something to help express their gratitude for the generous services being provided.

The driveway expanded into a gravel parking lot occupied with several other vehicles. Before getting out, Eileen propped up the windshield screen and cracked all of the windows. It was only March and the weather was scorching. Not a great sign for this upcoming summer.

The website had directed patients to walk around to the back of the house, so that's what they did. There were a couple chickens roaming aimlessly in the front parking lot. Daniel tensed as they passed. Chickens had always freaked him out. All birds, really. There was something in their eyes that reminded him of dolls. He didn't trust them for a second.

Unfortunately, the back yard exhibited a much larger chicken population. They were everywhere, flocking around a dozen or so people waiting for their names to be called inside.

"There are too many chickens here," Daniel said, in a way that he thought implied they should turn around and leave.

Eileen interpreted his statement another way, and said, "I know! Aren't they adorable?"

She rushed toward a group of them—to do what? *pet* them?—and they dispersed in a frenzied panic.

"What the hell are you doing?" Daniel asked in disbelief.

Someone nearby cleared their throat dramatically—a youngish woman wearing a short dress—then tapped a narrow, wooden sign sticking out of the grass that read:

PLEASE DO NOT INTERACT WITH THE CHICKENS NO MATTER WHAT THEY TELL YOU

"Oh," Eileen said, after scanning it, "sorry about that."

"It's okay," the woman said. "The first time I came here, I tried to do the same thing."

The right side of her head, neck, and shoulder appeared to be horrifically disfigured. The skin of her face was melted, as was the hair on her scalp. She only had one eye, half a nostril, and most of her lips intact. Everything else on her face had been burned off some time ago.

"Right?" Eileen said, not acknowledging the woman's disfigurement. "How could you not want to pet a chicken?"

Daniel stood off to the side and tried his best to look at

anything but her face and failed. She noticed him looking, and he had no idea if he was supposed to look even farther away or now embrace the fact that he was looking. His eyes widened and he said, "Uhhh, yeah, chickens, huh?"

She laughed and said, "It's okay. I know I look crazy."

"No, no," Daniel said, unconvincingly.

"What happened?" Eileen asked, and Daniel clenched his asshole, wishing she had a better gauge on how to speak to people.

"Oh, you know, the usual," the woman said, brushing the left side of her hair back. "Botched suicide attempt."

"Oh, wow, sorry to hear that," Eileen said, then realized how that sounded, and added, "I don't mean that I'm sorry it didn't work. I just meant I'm sorry you experienced something tragic and painful."

The woman grinned with half her lips. "Isn't that what life is all about, though? Tragedy and pain."

"I don't know about that," Eileen said, for the first time in this interaction showing some sense of discomfort. "No, I don't know if I'd say that."

"It was an oven, if you're interested," the woman said.

"An . . . an oven?"

She nodded, then stretched her right leg forward and hiked up her dress, emphasizing a tattoo on the front of her thigh, just above the kneecap. A bell jar, with a heart inside it.

This is what she told them: "I used to be obsessed with the writings of Sylvia Plath—back when I was a depressed teenager. I still am, I mean—depressed, that is. No longer a teenager, though. And I don't read poetry all that much anymore. Especially not Plath. Don't worry, I'm aware of the way she wrote about people of color, and I do not endorse it. *Stranger Things* fan fiction is where it's at for me, these days. But as a depressed teenager, I wasn't as educated as I am now, and I didn't realize her writing was considered so problematic. All I knew was I could relate to her poetry in ways that nobody else seemed to understand.

I also knew I desperately wanted to die. I had read many, many times about how Sylvia Plath had committed suicide by sticking her head in the oven. It was probably the first thing I ever learned about her, and I'd always found the act admirable. So, when I decided I was officially sick of being alive at the ripe old age of sixteen, I decided to go out the same way. Only, like I said, I was sixteen and not very bright, and I guess I didn't quite understand the differences between gas and electric ovens. As it turned out, Sylvia Plath died from carbon monoxide poisoning, which is not something you can achieve with an electric oven—an electric oven being the kind we had in our family kitchen. I remember trying to figure out which temperature to set the heat to ahead of time, and finally settled on four hundred and fifty, since that was the highest our oven would go. I don't remember how long I lasted. I don't remember much, to be honest, other than thinking, 'Wow, how on earth did Sylvia Plath last so long without giving up?' Because I only lasted like five minutes before pulling myself out and losing consciousness on the kitchen floor. My mom found me later and called nine-one-one, and here I am now, helplessly dependent on a daily dose of pain medication otherwise everything starts hurting again in such a way that I can no longer function in normal everyday society, and then people get annoyed with me for crying, 'Ow, my face,' and, 'Ow, my skin.' I know nobody wants to hear that. They've told me plenty of times, believe me."

"Oh," Eileen said. "Okay."

Daniel said nothing.

Then, miraculously, the door at the back of the house creaked open, and a man stuck his head out to shout, "Daniel Addams! You're up, jabroni."

"Well," he stammered to the burned girl, "that's me, sorry," and hurried toward the back door, with Eileen close on his heels.

The man who called them in turned out to be Doctor

Zambrano himself. He did not have any additional staff besides his sister who was busy selling fruit pies out by the street. As he led them toward his examination room, he listed every pie she had for sale and kept talking up what a great deal they were when multiple pies were purchased together.

The examination room was nothing more than their kitchen. There wasn't anything special about it other than a wheeled cart containing an assortment of equipment and medicine that Daniel couldn't begin to decipher. Otherwise it was a standard kitchen. On the countertop, next to a pile of drying dishes, was a tray of tiny plastic cups each containing a bite-sized pastry. Under the cupboard overlooking the tray, someone had duct-taped a sign that read:

Fruit Pies
Free Samples

Beneath the text, there was a scannable QR code for anybody who wished to subscribe to the Zambrano's Fruit Pies newsletter. All new subscribers received a coupon for half-off their first order, the doctor told them as Daniel got situated at the kitchen table. Eileen stood off to the side, arms folded across her chest and butt leaning against an unoccupied counter space.

The doctor glanced at Eileen, then at Daniel in his seat, then back at Eileen. "So," he said, "I take it you are the mother?"

"Um, I'm his wife," Eileen said.

"Oh." Zambrano cleared his throat and pulled the shirt collar from his throat. "Well, you know what they say. Every good wife inherits exceptional maternal instincts."

"Who said that?" Eileen asked.

"What?"

"Did somebody actually say that, or did you just make that up?"

"Umm." The doctor started pulling his shirt collar, like he was suffocating. Daniel noticed sweat spots spreading at his armpits, and he wondered if this was why most of them opted to wear large lab coats. "Somebody said it," he finally said. "One of my patients. I can't tell you who, though. Due to, uhh, confidentiality agreements. I could lose my license even telling you this much, as I'm sure you know. Anyway," he turned back to Daniel, then referred to a clipboard in his hands, "what seems to be the trouble today, Mr. Addams? I must admit I greatly admire the shirt you're wearing today."

"Oh, thanks," Daniel said. He was wearing the I CAME ON EILEEN shirt again.

Behind them, Eileen sighed and said nothing.

"Where did you get it?" the doctor asked.

"I don't remember. Somewhere online, I think."

"What was the website, specifically?"

Daniel shrugged. "I'm sorry. I don't remember."

The doctor squinted at the clipboard and frowned. "It says here you're having some trouble with your . . . bones, is it?"

"It's . . . well, it's complicated," Daniel said, and proceeded to recite a condensed version of the last month or so, omitting the unsolicited submission and any other overly fantastical elements. The doctor didn't need to hear about Mister Bones and speculate over his existence. Daniel had already made up his mind there, and as far as he was concerned it was no longer up for debate.

What *was* important to get across seemed simple enough: his body was experiencing something highly unusual and difficult to explain, particularly in his skeleton. He couldn't come right out and claim his bones had been replaced with an unknown substance while asleep, but he could certainly hint at something along those lines with complaints like, "My bones feel out of place," and, "My skeleton doesn't want to get along with the rest of my body."

The numbness was one of the first things he led with, of course. Describing the sensation as not completely numb, but feeling like everything was asleep. That ever-persisting *tingling*. How it never went away anymore. It was always there—*everywhere*—reminding Daniel that he was in danger, that he was doomed, that the skeleton crammed into his meat suit was officially under new ownership.

He told the doctor about breaking his wrist outside the H-E-B, how this whole mess kicked off with that initial fracture. Then he told him how, just under two months later, Eileen had removed the cast from his arm and he'd given her a shoulder massage. He described how the massage had come to an abrupt end with his face in the toilet and Eileen hovering above him with tears streaming down her cheeks.

It was at this point that the doctor stopped nodding and going, "Uh huh," and glanced over at Eileen. "Ma'am, did you witness your son's arm—I'm sorry, your husband's arm—bend back in the way he has just described?"

She opened her mouth, but no words came out for a moment, then she said, "Well, I didn't *see* it happen. I definitely felt something strange against my back as he was massaging me, but . . . "

"But you didn't witness it with your eyes."

"No. I didn't witness it with my eyes."

Zambrano appeared to contemplate this response for a while, then he said, "Okay," and scribbled his pen on the sheet of paper attached to the clipboard.

"Okay what?" Daniel said. He was losing his mind sitting here after telling him all of that. He needed a better response than *Okay* or he was going to tackle him in this kitchen and cram one of the fruit pies down his throat. "Okay, you understand what I said? Okay, you think I sound insane? Okay what?"

"Okay, I've listened to what you've said and I've taken note of everything," Doctor Zambrano replied, still studying the contents of his clipboard.

"Well, what do you make of it?" Daniel asked.

"Unsure at this time. But let's inspect you a little further, shall we?"

"Um, okay."

"Okay what?" Zambrano said, mimicking Daniel's tone from a minute ago. "Okay, you understand what I just said? Okay, you agree to let me inspect you further? Okay what?"

Behind him, Eileen made a noise like, *Uh oh, this guy is crazy.*

Daniel bowed his head in shame. "Okay, you can inspect me further."

"Excellent!" Doctor Zambrano set his clipboard down, and Daniel stole a quick peek at the paper he'd been scribbling on since the start of their appointment. At the top of the page he'd written in huge blocky letters: FRUIT PIE IDEAS. Below the title, he'd drawn one large circle and aggressively traced over it until the shape resembled the cursed well from *The Ring*. Inside the circle he'd written the word *HUCKLEBERRY???* and underlined it several times.

Daniel wondered if Eileen had also seen the paper, and what they were meant to do in a situation like this. Could he afford to be picky right now? It wasn't like they were *paying* for this appointment, after all. So what if the guy was a little weird when it came to fruit pies? It didn't discredit him as a medical professional, right? He desperately wished he could ask Eileen this very question without the doctor overhearing, because he did not have the answer.

It was too late to stop the appointment. The doctor had already retrieved a stethoscope and was pressing it against his chest and telling Daniel to inhale and exhale deeply. "Like you've just consumed a bucket of blueberries and you forgot you're allergic," he advised, tone genuine in a way that he thought the idea couldn't be anything but helpful. Daniel visualized himself eating several dozen blueberries that would later attempt to suffocate him to death, then took in a breath and let it out. "Perfect," the doctor said, excited. "That's perfect."

Next he pulled out a flashlight, and took a gander inside Daniel's mouth and ears.

"How do my teeth look?" Daniel asked.

"Apologies, but I'm not a dentist." Doctor Zambrano grimaced. "All teeth repulse me, you understand."

"Oh, sorry."

"Perfectly okay, sir," the doctor said, suddenly wielding a rubber hammer. "I'm going to strike your leg now. Do not be alarmed." Before Daniel could respond, or fully process what he'd been told, Doctor Zambrano struck his knee with the hammer and made a comic-book *KA-POW!* noise with his mouth. Nothing happened. The doctor kneeled so he was eye-level with Daniel's knee. "Hmm," he said. "Maybe this works better when your leg is hanging. Unfortunately, I do not own a chair tall enough for such a procedure. Let's move on."

The doctor instructed Daniel to remove his shirt and pants. Daniel hesitated, wondering if he really wanted to strip in this weirdo's kitchen.

"Oh, I'm sorry," Doctor Zambrano said, then glanced at Eileen. "Maybe it's better if you stepped out of the room, ma'am. This young man might not be comfortable taking off his clothes in front of you."

"We're married," Eileen said.

"Is it a modern or traditional marriage, ma'am?"

"It's fine," Daniel said, and undressed to his boxers.

The doctor immediately took a photo of Daniel with his cell phone. The flash was enabled, as was the camera noise. The following five seconds were occupied by a terrible, awkward silence. Then he cleared his throat and stuffed the phone in his pocket and started his inspection of Daniel's body with a cartoonishly large magnifying glass he'd removed from another pocket. "Tell me something," he said a moment later, "did you make these circle markings yourself, or did they suddenly appear without your consent?"

"I, uh, drew them," Daniel said, embarrassed. Earlier that morning, he'd scrubbed his skin with soap and hot water in the shower, but the long-lasting power of the Sharpie was undeniable.

"And for what purpose did you draw them?" the doctor asked. "Is this some new fad I'm unaware of? Is this what all the jabronis are doing on TikTok nowadays? Also, are you aware these circles are the exact same shape as my darling sister's fruit pies that we have for sale outside? Please explain."

He couldn't think of a good lie quick enough, so he told the truth. "I think maybe these are the spots where my bones are being removed and replaced with something else. I was trying to keep track of them all."

"Oh, I see."

"You do?" Daniel went wide-eyed with excitement. "What do you see?"

The doctor shook his head. "No, I don't see anything besides the circles. If there were other markings here you were trying to preserve, they've either healed and faded, or you hallucinated them." He straightened his spine and looked Daniel in the eyes. "So, you're telling me these bones in your body have been swapped, is it? With what? And who is doing this swapping? Are we talking aliens here? Secret government experiments?"

"Uhh," Daniel said.

"You might as well just tell him," Eileen said.

"Tell me what?" The doctor looked at each of them, puzzled. "The answers to the inquiries I just posed, I hope."

"Well . . . " Daniel struggled to begin, fully aware that the chances of this guy calling the nearest mental hospital would increase significantly once he finished. "Have you ever seen *The Babadook?*"

I BELIEVE IN MISTER BONES

Doctor Zambrano scoffed. "Of course I have. What kind of question is that? The Babadook is a queer icon."

As briefly as he could manage, Daniel filled the doctor in on the details he'd previously omitted. He told him about the unsolicited manuscript and Mister Bones and the dreams he'd been having. He told him about the guy who'd contacted him on Twitter, and what he'd witnessed during their video call. He told him about how everything was connected to how he'd been feeling lately. That there was something violating him every night—some kind of entity, Mister Bones or another presence—something physically replacing his bones with an alien substance. That Daniel was sure, sooner than later, this would lead to his demise. There were only so many bones in the human skeleton, after all. There would come a time when he was no longer himself, but something else.

To his credit, Doctor Zambrano listened to Daniel without interrupting. He nodded along. He said, "Uh huh, uh huh," when appropriate. Then, once Daniel had finished, the doctor asked Daniel if he was lactose intolerant.

"Uh, I don't think so."

"Perfect." Zambrano turned around and opened the refrigerator. He pulled out a half-empty carton of milk, then held it up to them with a proud grin across his face. To Eileen, he said, "Ma'am, would you mind fetching a clean glass in the cabinet behind you for your son—husband?"

"Oh," Daniel said, "I think I'm okay, but thank you."

"Nonsense," the doctor said. "This is necessary for your recovery."

"Milk?"

He nodded. "Has nobody ever told you that milk builds strong bones?"

"I thought that was an old wives' tale," Daniel said.

The doctor glared at him, offended. "Please, I will not allow blatant misogyny in my kitchen office." He glanced at Eileen and said, "I apologize, ma'am."

"Uh, it's okay," Eileen said.

He took the glass from Eileen and filled it to the brim, then set it on the table for Daniel. He also grabbed one of the fruit pie free samples and rested it next to the glass. "Trust me, this will really complement the milk."

Daniel studied the glass of milk and the fruit pie sample with disgust. Even back when he used to have an appetite, he'd never cared much for drinking milk. Still, the doctor stood over him, watching with anticipation. To be polite, Daniel ate a small bite and took a sip.

"Well?" Doctor Zambrano said.

"It's delicious, thank you."

He clapped his hands several times, full of glee, and took a seat across from Daniel. "This is very good to hear. I'm glad you gave it a try. As you know, my sister sells these pies just outside the house, should you be interested in partaking in more than just a free sample."

"I remember. Thank you." While it was true Daniel and Eileen had talked about buying one on the way out of here, he'd already changed his mind. There was zero chance he was leaving this place with a pie. At this point, he doubted the doctor was even a real doctor. This whole thing felt like a bizarre scam to sell baked goods.

Eileen must've been thinking along similar lines. "Umm, not to be rude or anything, but I was curious where you earned your medical degree?"

The doctor immediately appeared flustered. He stood and started pacing around the kitchen. "Intentionally or not, ma'am, but that was quite rude indeed!"

"I was wondering the same thing, actually," Daniel said, and the doctor redirected his outrage to him.

"You, too, question my credentials!" As if punishing Daniel, Zambrano scooped up the glass of milk and fruit pie sample. He stuffed the sample in his own mouth and furiously chewed, then downed the rest of the milk in one vengeful gulp, all while maintaining eye contact with Daniel. Lines of milk streamed down either cheek and stained his shirt, but he didn't seem to notice or care.

I BELIEVE IN MISTER BONES

"Um, I think we should get going," Eileen said.

"Yeah," Daniel said, pushing himself off the table to his feet. He gathered his clothes from the floor and started redressing. To the doctor, he said, "Thank you for, um, your time."

"Sit down, sir!" Doctor Zambrano placed the now-empty glass in the sink, then gestured to the table. "Please, I insist."

"Well, you're kind of scaring us," Daniel said, "so I think we'd rather just leave."

"You'd rather leave than be diagnosed?" The doctor wiped milk from his chin. "Interesting strategy, if you ask me. And you *should* ask me, by the way. As I am a doctor." He cast Eileen an evil side-eye and added, "A *real* doctor."

"I didn't mean to imply you weren't one," Eileen said, and looked at Daniel like *can we please get the fuck out of here already?*

But Daniel was stuck on what he'd said. "Diagnosed?" He sat down, as instructed. "What do you mean, diagnosed?"

The doctor expressed the smuggest smirk known to man. "You think you're the first person to come in here with these symptoms? You think this isn't the most basic, textbook medical case I've seen all week?"

Daniel didn't know how to respond to that, so he didn't.

Instead, Eileen said, "Well? What is it then?"

"I think you both better have a seat," Doctor Zambrano suggested. Then, once all three of them were sitting at the table, he continued: "Have any of you jabronis ever heard of something called fat embolism syndrome?"

A tremendous shame overwhelmed Daniel. "I know I'm overweight, but . . . "

The doctor shook his head. "Not that kind of fat." He noticed Eileen typing something into her phone. "Please, ma'am, do not insult me any further by looking up the definition as you sit in my kitchen office. I am preparing to explain what it means right now."

Eileen laid the phone screen-down and said, "Sorry."

"Now, I understand I am speaking to two jabronis who do not have medical degrees, unlike myself—is that right?" Zambrano waited for them to give him a vocal confirmation. "Just to clarify, you are both admitting that I am a certified medical professional?" Once again, he waited for Daniel and Eileen to mutter yes. Then he said, "Something happens when you break a bone. Well, a lot of things happen, to be fair. But there's one specific thing I wish to talk about here. When a bone breaks, little pieces of fat enter the bloodstream. Fat emboli, it's called. Most of the time, the fat is so small that there's no reason to be concerned. It doesn't conflict with anything. Notice I said *most* of the time, and not *all* of the time."

"We noticed," Eileen said.

"Yeah, me too," Daniel lied

"Good, thank you for noticing," the doctor said, sincerely appreciative sounding. "Now, *sometimes* the fat emboli can cause all types of complications. It can create blockages, make it hard to breathe, develop skin rashes, and make the patient . . . if you'll excuse my lack of more sympathetic phrasing: cuckoo for Cocoa Puffs."

"There is surely a better way for doctors to phrase something like that," Eileen said.

"Unfortunately, this is the official phrasing we were taught in medical school, which I believe you already admitted that I graduated from, if I'm not mistaken."

"Please," Daniel said, "what are you trying to say? That I'm insane?"

"No, I would never use that word," Doctor Zambrano said. "*Deluded,* though? Absolutely."

"Deluded how?"

The doctor chuckled. "Well, deluded like believing the Babadook is stealing your bones every night, for one thing."

"I didn't say he was the Babadook," Daniel whispered,

feeling the anger steam out of his ears like his head was a tea kettle. "I said he was *like* the Babadook."

"Babadook-adjacent," Eileen suggested, helpfully.

"In any case," Doctor Zambrano said, "let's say the fat emboli that entered your bloodstream after breaking your wrist ended up being more severe than most cases, and this stuff reached your brain—some of your symptoms here would align with others who have suffered similar incidents. Altered mental states. Irrational behavior. Extreme paranoia. Peculiar delusions . . . "

"Jesus Christ," Eileen said, "what does this mean? Is there anything we can do?"

"Wait," Daniel said, not as convinced as his wife, "it's *that* easy to diagnose? Just like that, I have this disease I've never even heard of before?"

"Well, no, it's not that easy. I'm just making a guess here." The doctor's eyes lit up like *eureka*. "Actually, thinking back to those circles you've drawn, this stuff can also create rashes all over your skin. They may be gone now, but I don't doubt *something* was once there. Perhaps you had spotted splotches caused by fat emboli in your bloodstream. Difficult to really say, now that they've vanished." To Eileen, he asked, "Ma'am, did you see these rashes?"

She shook her head no.

"They weren't rashes," Daniel said, and held back from claiming that they hadn't vanished like the doctor stated. He was sure the insertion spots were still there. They just weren't the easiest to locate. But if he looked at them under a certain light, at a specific angle, and instead of staring directly at them he relied on his peripheral vision to bring them into focus, he would have seen the anomalies right away. But he didn't want to get into that right then and risk sounding even crazier than he already did.

"Do you think that's what's going on with him?" Eileen asked the doctor, full of bottled-up hope. "That he has this fat embolism thing? Oh my god, can it be treated? It's not . . . fatal, right?"

Zambrano scratched his ear. "Oh, yes, it's most definitely fatal. I mean, it's not *always* fatal. I believe the percentage is actually quite low, come to think about it, but that doesn't mean it *isn't* fatal. People have died from this, oh yes indeed, and they will continue to die from it. As to whether or not Daniel here has it, I suspect it's a possibility, but there is a distressing detail here that provides plenty of doubt."

"What detail?" She seemed to deflate in her chair as she listened to him.

"As best as my memory can recollect—in the past, when someone has been diagnosed with such an extreme case of fat embolism syndrome, the cause is usually from breaking either the pelvis or a long bone, often within the leg. But Daniel here has only broken his wrist. I'm not convinced the break would have been severe enough, if you want my professional opinion. I'm not *un*convinced, either, mind you, but it's certainly given me pause. Also, enough time has passed that the fracture has already healed. That's important to keep under consideration. In fact, it probably shits on my entire theory. Pardon my gratuitous language. My parents were circus people."

"Well, how can we tell for sure?" Eileen asked, desperate. "Isn't there some kind of test we can run, or what?"

"There are tests, yes, but nothing more we can do here with the limited amount of equipment in my kitchen office. He'd need to get X-rays done to rule out other possibilities . . . an electrocardiogram . . . lots and lots of blood tests. All very expensive stuff, which is why I don't offer them here. My best suggestion would be to make an official appointment at my day job—I can give you the address— and get some of these tests scheduled as soon as we have an opening. I assume, since you're at my house, you do not currently have any health insurance?"

"We don't," she said.

The doctor nodded. "I'd advise brainstorming a way to

change that, then. Get a new job with benefits. Beg strangers online to support a crowdfunding campaign. If you're going down this route, you're going to need all the help you can get. Assuming that's even what's wrong with him." To Daniel, he added, "With you, I mean." He coughed into his fist. Some of the fruit pie he'd eaten earlier shot out of his mouth and landed on the table. He picked it up and ate it again and acted like neither of them were watching. "Like I said, I remain unconvinced either way. For another thing, you seem to be breathing decently enough. The jabronis on their last leg from this ailment are usually suffering some pretty gnarly respiratory issues."

The doctor's pocket started beeping—an alarm on his phone, which he took his time shutting off. "Well, that concludes all the time I can afford to give you today."

"That's it?" Eileen asked. "What do we *do?*"

"What do you do?" Doctor Zambrano glanced around the kitchen, like he'd never heard a more offensive question. "You leave my house. You figure out a way to get treatment at a better-equipped hospital. You remind yourself the Babadook isn't real. You love each other every day. You watch your favorite movies and read your favorite books. You listen to your favorite songs. You laugh at your favorite jokes. You pick beautiful flowers when you come across them. You give yourself a little treat every twenty-four hours. You ignore all of the bad news beyond your control. You avoid doomscrolling on your cellular devices. You rise and you shine. You give yourself permission to cry. You give yourself permission to smile. You remind yourself that you are merely a human being—nothing more, nothing less. You take advantage of the fruit pie sale my sister is hosting outside. What you don't do is stay here asking me any further questions. I have a dozen other patients scheduled before I can go to sleep, and they've all been waiting patiently. I have one young lady out there, bless her silly heart, who tried to kill herself with an electric oven when she was a teenager, and if I don't restock her pain medication soon she's going to start wailing so loud that the local wild dogs will mistake her for part of their pack. And nobody wants that—not her, not the dogs, not anybody. Do *you?* No, you do not. Another thing you *do* need to do: continue drinking lots of milk. This is a doctor's order. You don't even need health insurance to consume dairy products. It will make your weak, jabroni bones stronger and you will forget all about them being fake. Fake bones do not exist, but *neglected* bones do. So drink up, and why not have a nice fruit pie to go along with it? They really do complement each other. My sister is outside right now. You won't miss her. We've chosen her parking lot specifically so nobody can miss her. So please don't give me that excuse later on when you don't buy anything and I question you about it, because I will question you. I strongly encourage you to patronize her business. My sister works exceptionally hard baking these pies and I would hate to see it all go to waste. I love my dear sister with all of my heart, you understand. Growing up, we were all we had. Our parents were absent. They left us alone most nights to work at the circus. They had their own priorities. My sister and I made lives for ourselves. We baked pies. We read medical textbooks. Sometimes we kissed, but it was never anything serious. It was casual. There was nothing weird about it at all. I also encourage leaving her company a five-star review, unless you are able to leave a higher star, then I encourage you to leave whatever that maximum number of stars might be. Zambrano's Fruit Pies. That's the name of the company. Zambrano's Fruit Pies. I've now said the name of the company twice. You have zero excuse not to remember it. We're on all the review places. Zambrano's Fruit Pies."

The doctor gestured to the door, drenched with sweat and panting, gasping for breath.

Daniel and Eileen got up and left without another word, too terrified to respond. Before piling into the car, Eileen ran over to the fruit pie truck and secured them a cherry pie to eat later that night. Daniel wasn't hungry, but Eileen served herself a slice since she was curious. She ate all of two bites before throwing the rest away. It was the worst pie she'd ever eaten in her life.

At some point after Eileen had given up on the pie and dozed off on the couch, Daniel curled up next to her and closed his eyes, hopeful the sound of whatever was streaming on Netflix would be loud enough to drown out any unpleasant thoughts that might attempt another nocturnal infiltration of his brain. These thoughts were getting more ambitious and rambunctious with their raids—like there was less protection in place, like his skull had softened, like it wasn't *quite* the same skull he'd been slowly developing since the womb.

Daniel couldn't remember the last time he'd intentionally slept. These days he forced himself awake until he physically could no longer keep his eyes open, and then he just sort of passed out. But tonight he wanted to cuddle with his wife. He wanted to rub his shoulder against hers and pat the fat of her thigh and give her cheek a soft kiss before nodding off into the same dreamscape that she was presumably already occupying. Sleep had been nothing but horrible, no-good misadventures lately, but for whatever reason, here on the couch next to her in this specific morsel of time, Daniel was struck with the most convincing gut instinct that sleep would be safe right now— that his dreams wouldn't harm him. That it would be okay, albeit momentarily, to drop his guard.

He found himself back at the doctor's house. It was daytime, yet the sky was *dark* despite the sky's absence of clouds. It was the kind of temporal ambiguity experienced during eclipses. All at once, everything felt *off*. There was no breeze. There was no *noise*. No traffic sounds, no animal chirps, no anything. But there *were* animals—oh, yes. *Chickens.* He spotted them behind the doctor's house. At first, he thought there were only a couple of them, but the more he tried to count, the more he realized it was useless. Every time he focused, their numbers seemed to expand. Hundreds of chickens marched aimlessly in this yard. Daniel was the only person here. He didn't know if he was supposed to let himself in through the back door or what. It'd said on the website to wait for someone to call your name. He didn't want to break the rules and let himself in uninvited. So he sat on the grass with his legs folded and waited patiently for something to happen. It didn't take long for his presence to attract the attention of a nearby chicken. As it neared, Daniel noticed half of its face had been burned off. Half of its beak was melted shut. It only had one eyeball left, which stared intensely at Daniel, as if it knew him, as if they were ancient enemies. Daniel reached forward and gave its head a little pet, then pulled its remaining eyeball off as if it were attached by Velcro. He threw it in his mouth and swallowed without chewing. The chicken did not react. It remained standing in front of him, expecting something further. Then, the side of its beak that wasn't grotesquely disfigured slightly opened, emitting a voice muffled by radio static: *My mom found me later and called nine-oneoneoneoneoneoneoneoneone.* The beak did not shut. Instead, it opened wider, as if being pried apart by some invisible force, tearing the section of its face that had been sealed together. The feathers disintegrated, exposing its skull. Except, this wasn't a chicken's skull. It was far too big to fit inside of a chicken's head. Not a human's skull, either. Closer, but not quite. Its eye sockets were too wide. Its unlatched scream was too deep. No, this was something else. This was something otherworldly. The rest of the chicken's body melted into the grass. The skeleton left behind didn't make any sense to Daniel, until he realized he was looking at something lying on its stomach with its head tilted up. The rest of the skeleton seemed to stretch endlessly through the back yard,

I BELIEVE IN MISTER BONES

connected to the other chickens. The chickens were decoys. They were frauds. The chickens were the flesh protecting this creature's bones. The chickens were the flesh the chickens were the flesh the chickens were the flesh. Then, quite suddenly, the back door swung open, and Doctor Zambrano stormed outside with a fruit pie in either hand. His face was smeared in either gore or fruit pie innards or maybe there wasn't a difference between the two. *Daniel Addams!* he shouted, voice that same muffled radio static. *Your time has comecomecomecomecome—*

EILEEN SPENT THE next morning calling every doctor listed online with advertised payment plans for uninsured patients. Doctor Zambrano's legitimate office downtown was the first place she contacted, and the earliest free spot available ended up being a month out. Daniel, flat on his back in bed hypnotized by the wind chimes dangling over him, suggested perhaps Zambrano *did* have available spots, and was waiting for them to rate his sister's pie business five stars on Yelp or whatever before agreeing to proceed.

"You didn't taste that pie," Eileen said. "At the very most, I could maybe consider giving it three stars, and even that would be generous—dishonest, even."

"One thing I've always admired about you is your food review ethics. In fact, it's probably why I married you."

"Aww, thank you, honey," she said, flipping him off while she dialed another doctor. She didn't have any better luck there, or with any other office who answered the phone that morning. Everybody was booked this week. When asked why nobody had anything sooner, one grumpy receptionist reminded Eileen that they were in the middle of flu season.

"You aren't the only person who's unwell today," the receptionist added, before hanging up.

"What a bitch," Eileen said under her breath, and tried a few others before giving up and booking Daniel an

I BELIEVE IN MISTER BONES

appointment two weeks from then. Then, to Daniel, she asked how he was feeling.

"Oh, you know," Daniel replied, "deluded . . . paranoid . . . the usual."

"Nobody is saying you're making any of this up."

"When was the last time you looked up the definition of 'delusion'?"

Daniel didn't want to talk about this shit anymore. Maybe he never did want to talk about it. He couldn't remember. Memories tended to blink in and out of focus during severe bouts of sleep deprivation. Every time he started nodding off, he snapped back awake, convinced he'd heard one of the wind chimes dancing. Eileen claimed she never detected any noise. She slept peacefully each night. He spent most of the time either beside her in bed as she snored, or on the couch combing through the *Mister Bones* manuscript with earbuds in, listening to the least calming music he could find while chugging cup after cup of coffee. System of a Down seemed to do a good job there. If only they'd released more than five fucking albums. He knew what sleep would get him, and he didn't want anything to do with it. Not until he figured out how to stop this shit, until he came up with a real, workable solution. These doctors, they weren't going to help him. They'd be quick to slap a dozen different "delusions" on his medical rap sheet, though. Anything to protect the fantasy that their bones were safe. Anything to convince Daniel all of this shit was only in his head.

Part of him wanted to release the *Mister Bones* manuscript online without permission. If nobody was interested in claiming the text, then would anybody be upset about him violating a number of copyright laws? And if someone *did* get upset . . . at least then Daniel would finally know who'd written the goddamn book. No great fisherman ever played by the rules. He was pretty sure he'd heard someone say that once. He'd never fished in his life but wasn't that what this would be? Fishing for an author. Baiting one out of hiding. Reeling in his own augustskeef. If they wanted him to remove it, then they'd have to contact him. They'd have to *speak* to him. They'd have to explain what the fuck this was all about. They'd have to tell Daniel how to end it. Because there had to be a way, right? Other than the fate of the man who'd contacted him on Twitter. There had to be another option. Otherwise, what was the point of any of this? Why bother doing anything at all?

After the festival, he decided, that's exactly what he would do. He'd give it a brief copy edit, then beg Eileen to format it enough so it looked presentable as a PDF. They wouldn't go as far as printing a copy. He wasn't interested in profiting from the novella—not anymore. He just wanted it out there. He wanted it to reach enough people that the person responsible for its existence would be left with no choice but to come knocking on his door.

After the festival.

Despite this plan in the back of his head, the next couple days were spent as if they *didn't* have a massive book festival to kick off first-thing Friday morning. Eileen worked on freelance formatting work, and Daniel pretended he was still editing Johnny Compton's debut novel. He had yet to answer any of Compton's recent emails. He hadn't even bothered opening the last half dozen. Compton was justifiably pissed. Daniel had accepted the novel over a year ago, with the intention of launching it during the inaugural Fiendish Book Festival. He was a San Antonio author, so he wouldn't need to get a hotel room or do too much driving. It was the perfect time and event to publish this book, and Daniel had fucked everything up. Compton's wasn't the only title embarrassingly behind schedule. Everything was behind schedule. Naturally, the *Mister Bones* manuscript and the wrist fracture contributed to these delays, yes, but the truth was he'd been behind schedule long before stumbling upon the unsolicited submission in his inbox. They'd committed to way too much for a small press of their size to handle without capsizing.

It would be a goddamn miracle if they survived the weekend.

Wednesday night, long after Eileen had fallen asleep, Daniel sat at the kitchen table with his laptop out. *I Believe in Mister Bones* was pulled up—the Word document he'd copy/pasted the original email into. The glow from the screen was the only active source of light in the apartment. His dehydrated eyeballs greedily slurped up its piercing illumination and begged for more, more, more. He used his right hand to scroll text while his left hand lackadaisically played around with one of the ten box cutters they had floating around their living and work quarters. At this point, every chapter of the manuscript had been memorized. Not word for word, or anything that intense, but the general beats.

There was a particular section near the end of the book that Daniel found himself drawn to more and more lately. It was titled "EMMA, FROM WATERLOO" and it documented an encounter Emma experienced with a deeply troubled man one early morning on a walking trail near her home sometime in the late 1980s.

She'd noticed him on the trail ahead, mumbling to himself and pacing around a tree, and considered turning around to avoid confrontation. The only problem with this new plan was she'd been on her way back home when she spotted the suspicious mumbler. To turn around now would mean, at the very least, tacking on an extra two hours to her morning stroll, which would make her late for work and potentially fired by a boss who was not known for exercising sympathy when disciplining tardiness. No, she would just have to proceed down her normal route, and pray that this weirdo wouldn't latch on to her scent.

MAX BOOTH III

The man's mumbling ceased as Emma neared. He turned around and stared at her with bloodshot eyes. If he was aware of the drool dripping from his chin, it did not seem to bother him. She debated breaking out into a sprint, but before she could make up her mind the man was lunging forward and dragging her off the trail into the nearby woods. She screamed and flailed like she was on fire and it did no good. Nobody heard her. The man's grip was inescapable as he taped her mouth shut and bound her hands together. He tried to do the same to her feet, but she was kicking too wildly for him to get them under control.

When he spoke to her, it was in a whisper. His voice was demanding, authoritative. Emma stopped fighting back and listened to what he had to tell her.

During that fateful morning in the woods outside her home in Waterloo, Emma learned all about the boogeyman.

Including the boogeyman's name.

And, when the stranger finished his lesson, he informed her of the purpose for this unexpected rendezvous. Mister Bones, he told her, exceeded the realm of mere folklore. He had accidentally summoned this entity firsthand, through circumstances that he refused to elaborate on, and had come to suspect foul play within his own skeleton. The boogeyman was violating him every night, helping himself to bone after bone, and the stranger understood with perfect clarity that if he didn't do something desperate soon, this whole thing would end with the most predictable outcome imaginable.

Which was what led to him devising a theory: that maybe, just maybe, if he could somehow *pass* this weird curse on to someone else, Mister Bones would finally leave him alone. Maybe the boogeyman was like a bug attracted to the brightest light in the room. All the stranger had to do was redirect his attention to someone brighter, someone *fresher*—someone with a greater collection of unclaimed bones stored in their future carcass.

I BELIEVE IN MISTER BONES

What happened next even Emma could see coming—as could the reader of the manuscript.

The stranger propped her up against a tree, so she was on her side with her bare kneecaps digging into the bark. He held both of her feet together, locked under his armpit, and charged forward. Both legs instantly snapped at a ninety-degree angle. The pain blasted through her body like jolts of lightning, rendering her unconscious.

When she came to, it was late afternoon and the stranger was long gone. A passing jogger heard her screams in the woods and, after assessing the situation, dialed the emergency number from a nearby payphone. Two days later, Emma overdosed on morphine while in the hospital. The nurse assigned to her room reported the patient had been complaining about weird, outlandish nightmares prior to the suicide.

The stranger from the walking trail was never found—not by the Waterloo police department, nor the book's narrator. *His fate,* the chapter concluded, *remains a mystery to this day.*

Later, sometime between midnight and dawn, Daniel found himself standing over the bed staring down at Eileen as she slept. She was nude, which should have struck Daniel as strange. Eileen never went to bed without a housedress or some form of pajamas on. Sleeping naked gave her bad dreams, she'd once told him. And yet here she was, exposed beneath the wind chimes—wind chimes which hung from every square inch of the ceiling, yet somehow didn't bump against his head as he moved around the apartment, as he hovered over his wife studying her chest as it lifted and fell with each heavy breath. In his hand he gripped the box cutter he'd been fooling around with at the kitchen table. The blade was already peeking out of its plastic shell. He had no memory of bringing it over here. He had no memory of leaving the table at all. His body was moving on autopilot. The hand holding the box cutter extended toward the bed. He didn't need to bend or kneel. His arm was long enough to reach anything in this apartment. It was one of the many benefits of shedding his flesh and fully embracing his skeleton. There was nothing artificial under the threat of ripping as he stretched. His new, streamlined autonomy could be manipulated with versatility. The tip of the box cutter entered Eileen's flesh just above her left breast. The blade sunk in like he was stabbing butter. A square of her chest folded back, revealing a rib cage that beckoned to him like buried treasure. Her snoring never paused. She remained fast asleep. He dropped the box cutter on the bed and made a fist. Skeletal fingers contorting around skeletal fingers. He punched Eileen's rib cage once, twice, three times before cracking through the bones. She flinched only slightly, in a way one might flinch at a gnat, and said, *Are you coming to bed?* before resuming snoring. He dug around inside her body a little longer, then removed his hand. In it, he now held the still-beating heart of his sleeping wife. He opened his mouth wide and shoved the heart down his throat. He was able to swallow it without chewing. Back in bed, Eileen moaned and whispered, *What are you doing what are you doing what are you what are you what—*

72.

THURSDAY MORNING HIT and Daniel couldn't breathe.

He woke in the kitchen, with his face smashed down on his laptop's keyboard. The *Mister Bones* document had been significantly altered halfway through the "EMMA, FROM WATERLOO" chapter with nonsensical letters and symbols inadvertently added while conked out. He closed the computer without attempting to fix it. The sight of the Word doc alone was enough to make him sick.

Something in his chest felt wrong. Congested, maybe— or *rearranged*. Like something had been digging around inside him and forgot to put everything back in its correct order. Forgot, or didn't care enough to bother. A sign—no, a message: *This body doesn't belong to you anymore.* Loud and clear, as far as Daniel was concerned. Shit, he didn't fucking want this miserable body, anyway. It wasn't like it'd ever done him any good. So go ahead and take it. What did he care?

It took him a moment to realize how badly he was wheezing, and once he *did* notice, it was all he could focus on.

"You sound terrible," Eileen said, spooking him in his chair. She stood at the coffee pot behind him, stirring creamer into a cup.

"My chest is all fucked up." His throat felt clogged with some mysterious fluid. It was the *thought* of something wet building up in his throat more than the actual sensation that sent him spiraling into a deep coughing fit. The implication of what it could mean, the fantasy of what it could be.

"Yeah," Eileen said, sipping her coffee, "my allergies are bad this morning, too. Let me get you some meds."

He was coughing too hard to argue that this had nothing to do with allergies, that this was clearly something far more elaborate and personal.

Eileen dug through the medicine cabinet and brought out a handful of pills for him. She set them on the table next to his laptop: a Zyrtec, a Mucinex, and two Sudafeds—otherwise known as a Hill Country Cocktail. Remove all other context from the last month or so, and he'd be willing to understand why Eileen presumed these issues were allergy-related. The area of Texas they lived in was notorious for something called cedar fever. The pollen count on local juniper trees grew out of control this time of year, afflicting flu-like symptoms on the vast population. It usually started hitting people around December, and lasted through the end of spring. There was no real cure other than pumping your body full of daily antihistamines and hoping for the best. Living here was great.

Eileen filled him a glass of tap water, and he swallowed the pills down his increasingly-clogged throat. It wasn't like they could make matters *worse*. Besides, just because Daniel was busy processing this whole Mister Bones clusterfuck didn't mean he wasn't also simultaneously experiencing an allergy attack. Two things could be trying to kill him at once. In fact, it felt likelier that even *more* things were after him—things he'd never discover until it was too late.

Neither of them wanted to voice the thing they were both thinking, how those suffering from fat embolism syndrome started experiencing difficulty breathing toward the end. But *was* that the problem here? Doubtful, Daniel thought. He'd researched it some more at the apartment.

I BELIEVE IN MISTER BONES

Too much time had passed since the wrist break. It didn't make any sense. Sure, it *sounded good*. It provided logic to an otherwise-irrational scenario. But that was about all it did.

"You might want to shower here soon," Eileen said. "We gotta get going in less than an hour."

He wasn't surprised to learn he smelled. He hadn't bathed since Sunday morning, before his appointment with Doctor Zambrano and his sister's fruit pies. When a person lost their sense of smell, they also started slacking on hygiene. At least that was the case with Daniel. But of course there was more to it than that, wasn't there? He didn't *care* if he reeked. He didn't *care* if he looked filthy. Appearances no longer mattered all that much to him. His biology was being rebuilt from the inside out, for crying out loud. Who gave a shit about how he smelled?

"Wait," he said, registering what she'd told him, "where are we going?"

She reminded him they'd agreed to pick up two of their guests of honor from the airport this afternoon.

The idea of leaving the house sounded physically impossible. "Can't we just, like, buy them an Uber or something?"

"I don't think you'd be asking that question if you took a look at our bank account right now."

"Hold up. Did we ever pay off the venue? What about the hotel rooms? Are we completely fucked or what?" He hadn't worried about any of this stuff in weeks, too preoccupied with the status of his own skeleton for anything external to warrant concern.

"The venue is paid. We should have enough for the hotels, too. First quarter royalties for Lauren's book saved our butts. We just have to hope for enough sales this weekend to pay her back before she starts asking why we haven't already emailed a statement. Now, are you going to get up and shower, or am I going to have to fetch a sponge and scrub you up and down here in the kitchen?"

"Why do you need *me* to do this?" He knew he sounded like a whiny baby, but goddammit he *felt* like a whiny baby. "You're gonna be the one driving, anyway—right? What am I gonna be doing besides taking up valuable car space?"

"I still think you should come with," she said, and started rinsing out her empty coffee mug in the sink.

"But *why*?"

"Because . . . you haven't been out of the house since Sunday. Think of it as a practice run for this weekend. Plus . . . you're practically the face of the company. Everybody knows you. Nobody knows who I am."

"People know who you are. Come on. Don't give me that crap."

"Not like you. I don't do social media stuff like you do and you know it."

"Okay, but who cares? What does that have to do with anything?"

"Don't you think it'd look a little unprofessional if you weren't there when they got off the plane?"

Daniel laughed. He couldn't remember the last time he'd let out a real, genuine laugh. "Do you think I give a flying fuck what someone like Rick Jenkins thinks?"

"You probably should have thought about that before inviting him as a guest of honor and offering to pay for his plane and hotel," Eileen said, and stormed out of the kitchen area to get dressed.

He sat at the table a moment longer, then sighed and headed into the bathroom.

As usual, Eileen made a valid point. Inviting Rick Jenkins had been a moment of weakness—of *desperation*. Daniel had never liked the guy. The first time they ever met—at some convention years ago—he'd detected an overwhelming stench of narcissism. He possessed the ego of a man so far up his own ass that his breath reeked of shit. Aspiring extreme horror writers followed him around at events like he was their father and they craved his approval. People tended to believe that he was *somebody*

I BELIEVE IN MISTER BONES

in the industry, that he could make or break careers. That he had any power whatsoever. This was all by design, Daniel knew. Sometimes he suspected he was the *only* person who understood what'd happened here. How Rick Jenkins had launched a podcast dedicated solely to investigating cliquish gossip within an incredibly niche bubble of the indie horror community, making himself the go-to authority when it came to both bullshit petty drama and legitimate controversy. All the while he'd feign annoyance at becoming the person everybody came to first, as if he wasn't the motherfucker to assign himself hall monitor duty in the first place. With the launch of his podcast, Jenkins had successfully rebranded himself as Horror Cop. The up-and-comers and plankton of the industry both feared and worshipped him, disillusioned into believing he was something more than an off-brand Jerry Springer.

And still, despite all of this knowledge, Daniel had chosen to invite him as a guest of honor for their inaugural book festival. The fate of the festival was too shaky to abide his own personal code of ethics. Other writers would travel to San Antonio purely for the opportunity of networking with Jenkins. Badges needed to be sold, and this was one of Daniel's strategies of doing so. Did that make him feel like an incredible hypocrite? Infinitely, yes. He regretted the decision immensely, and yearned for the ability to turn back time just far enough to prevent the email from being sent. He was spineless then, and he was spineless now—in more ways than one, thanks to Mister Bones's nocturnal visitations.

Eileen was right. Inviting him had been his decision, not hers. She didn't care for him any more than he did. It wouldn't be fair to make her pick him up by herself.

So he showered, and he got dressed, and together they drove to the airport. Miraculously, he even managed to scrub the Sharpie circles off his flesh.

Daniel straggled enough at the apartment that when they finally did make it to the arrivals section, both guests of honor were waiting on the curb. Eileen had cleverly booked tickets for each of them so they'd land in San Antonio around the same time. Luckily, neither of them had brought along much luggage, or Daniel's presence really would have hindered the preexisting space in Eileen's SUV.

Rick Jenkins wore dark sunglasses, a baseball cap snug tightly around his scalp, and a jacket with the collar unfolded over his tucked-in chin. When they approached him outside the airport, he vocalized in a hushed, secretive tone. Daniel had to force back a pitiful laugh as he helped him load his suitcase into the trunk.

Meanwhile, their other guest of honor—Jessica McHugh—shouted, "What's up, you beautiful cunts!" the moment Eileen and Daniel stepped out of the car, and gave them both a big hug. The three of them had known each other virtually for years now—over a decade, at the very least, before they'd even launched Fiendish Books. They'd published two of her novels and several short stories since then, but had never officially met in-person. Until now, anyway. Daniel returned the hug, and he meant it. It felt good finally meeting someone he'd worked with for so long. Plus, he knew Rick Jenkins was in a rush to leave, and his poorly-hidden impatience made this embrace with Jessica all the more satisfying.

Eileen got back behind the wheel, Jessica took shotgun, and Daniel and Rick climbed into the back seat.

"Hey, you're not sick, are you?" was the first question Rick asked, once they were all safely in the car and driving off. The question was directed to Daniel, whose breathing had only worsened since that morning.

"No, it's just allergies," Daniel explained.

I BELIEVE IN MISTER BONES

"Allergies to *what*?"

He shrugged. "Seasonal allergies. Nothing to be concerned about."

Rick squirmed in his seat. The sunglasses remained on his face. "If you're sick, you need to tell me. I have too many public appearances scheduled this year. I can't afford to let down my fans."

"It's a thing around here, in San Antonio," Eileen tried to explain. "The pollen count gets really high. It's nothing contagious."

"How far away are we from the hotel?"

"Not that far."

"Hmm. Okay." He pulled out his cell phone and started scrolling through it, evidently done with speaking to the rest of them.

From the front passenger seat, Daniel spotted Jessica rolling her eyes and doing a jerk-off motion, and smiled. At least they'd invited *one* cool person to the festival. He hoped Jack Lyons wouldn't be a grumpy asshole, either, but he wasn't due to make it into San Antonio until sometime tomorrow afternoon. Driving in from Nacogdoches, or one of those other Texas towns with funny-sounding names.

"You know," Rick said, eyes still on his phone, "I heard that you'd rejected the vendor application for Fracas. Isn't that a little odd, seeing as I'm your guest of honor?" Fracas Books had published the majority of Rick's later-year novels.

"Maybe so," Daniel said. "We could only accept so many vendors. Our venue has very limited space for tables. They sent theirs in pretty late, it was only fair to give priority to others." He omitted what else he wanted to say, which would have been, *Plus, even if they were the* only *vendor to apply, I still would have rejected their phony asses.*

"I guess it's a good thing I brought my own stock with me. Would hate to disappoint my fans over an avoidable discrepancy like this."

"I personally love to disappoint my fans," Jessica said. "It's why I got into this business."

Rick made a face like his brain was breaking.

"Well, you're doing a bad job at it," Daniel said, then cleared his throat. "At disappointing them, I mean. People love your shit. That new one we put out? We still hear people talk about it at the popups we do here in town. "

"Hell fucking yeah," she said. "Fiendish forever, baby."

"People also talk about my books," Rick said, and everybody fell silent. Then, after an extraordinarily awkward gap, tapped Eileen on the shoulder and said, "Hey, is your car AC broken? I'm burning up back here."

Eileen shrugged and said, "Welcome to Texas."

Guests of honor dropped off at the hotel, they returned to the apartment and accepted the miserable fact that they could no longer put off the remaining tasks needing to be accomplished before tomorrow. Eileen had been delaying them, she said, because trying to do *anything* in here with all of these wind chimes gave her a headache. And Daniel had delayed them because he'd forgotten they needed to be done.

Like most of the work that went into publishing, nothing they had to do this afternoon was glamorous or exciting. They had to organize and pack boxes. That was basically it. Not really the type of shit an audience would want to watch characters doing on the big screen.

Eileen printed out an inventory sheet of every Fiendish publication in print, and together they combed through the stock piled haphazardly against their living room walls. For the older titles that never seemed to sell much, they boxed three copies of each. Newer titles, between five and ten, depending on the width of their spines. Books that typically sold well at events they'd bring at least ten copies, and fifteen copies of books written by authors who would also be attending the festival—like Jessica McHugh's two novels, for instance. If they sold out of a specific title, one of them would make a note of it and restock before returning the next morning. The venue was booked from Friday through Sunday, and it wasn't like they'd need to personally stay at a hotel. It was maybe a twenty-minute drive from their apartment, assuming traffic was in a generous mood.

Books weren't the only items they had to pack. They were the organizers of the festival, after all, which meant it was also their responsibility to bring along tablecloths and signage and anything else to ensure the event ran smoothly. The plan was to show up to the venue tomorrow a good two hours before the advertised vendor load-in period so they had plenty of time to get everything else prepared. They'd have to push the vendor tables in a giant U-shape and drape them with cloths before setting down seat assignment placards for the small presses and authors arriving at 10:00 a.m. They'd have to lug in all of the audio equipment—microphones, speakers, and a mixer—and test it out before any of the panels started. There were sandwich signs and flyers to display both inside and outside the building. Not to mention boxes of snacks purchased in bulk from Costco and jugs of water they'd have to pour into coolers situated on all three floors. Plus, since they were also working the weekend as Fiendish Books the *publisher*, they'd have to find a spare minute to set up their *own* table display—ideally before everybody else started showing up and distracting them with a thousand questions.

Eileen did not hide her annoyance with the wind chimes as she transferred boxes from one side of the apartment to the other. Daniel didn't find them irritating in the slightest. They were easy to avoid, and so what if they did brush against their heads every once in a while? It wasn't like they were *painful*. If he could move around the apartment with his back slightly bent, then so could she. It wasn't like she was any taller than Daniel. This was all a big overreaction on Eileen's part. The wind chimes were fine. The apartment was safer with them than without them. He wished she'd understand that already.

Once in a while, he'd steal a peek at her when she wasn't paying attention, and wonder if she would've been willing to let him break one of her bones. Nothing too crazy. Like a finger or something. Just to see if the curse could be passed on and forgotten. He knew he'd sound insane if he asked her, that she'd react like he was asking to murder her or something. It was just a test he wanted to conduct. A goddamn experiment. And if it *did* work, if Mister Bones abandoned Daniel and set his sights solely on Eileen, then the solution would be simple. All they'd have to do was find another person for Eileen to pass the curse onto. Let it be someone else's problem for once. After the festival, maybe he'd approach her. Once she was no longer so stressed about this weekend. She'd see that he was making sense, that this could logistically *work*—that they didn't have any other options. That they were running out of time.

Everything they packed was collected in several intimidating piles near the front door. It might've been easier to load everything into Eileen's car *now*, but the parking lot of their complex wasn't the most trustworthy area to leave valuables overnight. They'd have to do it first thing in the morning.

"Is that everything?" Daniel asked, body weak and trembling. All he wanted to do was curl up into a ball on the couch and watch mindless television.

Eileen shook her head and stared at him in disbelief. "Dude, we still haven't packed the swag bags."

"Oh my god." Daniel glanced at all the swag bag shit on the floor between the bed and couch. "What if we just didn't do it?"

"What are we going to tell the companies that bought sponsorships from us? That we were too tired to include the free merchandise they mailed us?"

I BELIEVE IN MISTER BONES

"Well, they have an ad in the program, right? Isn't that enough?"

"We have to pack them. You know that."

"Maybe we should take a break, and start on it later tonight. Aren't you tired?"

"I already told you—everybody's meeting up at the bar by the hotel after dinner. We were going to go say hi to everybody and hang out."

Daniel had zero memory of her talking about this. "I'm not going to a bar tonight."

"What?"

"There is not a chance that's happening. You never told me about this."

"I told you multiple times."

How was he supposed to argue with that? It wasn't like either of them had any proof one way or the other. She could say that she told him all day and he could counter with *no you didn't* and neither of them would get any closer to believing they might be wrong—which she was, of course. He would have fucking remembered something like that.

Then she held up her cell phone, showing a text she'd sent him yesterday reminding him of the planned get-together at the bar Thursday night. He'd reacted to the message with a thumbs-up. *Fuck.*

"Are you sure that's me you texted?" he asked, grasping for straws.

"Yes, I'm sure it's you. What kind of question is that?"

"I'm still not going." He didn't understand why she'd possibly *want* to leave. They weren't bar people. They didn't socialize. They were hermits, and proud of it. "If you want to go by yourself, then by all means, have fun. But I'm staying home."

"I told everybody you were coming."

He shrugged. "I don't know. Tell them I'm dying, I guess. When they hear how I'm breathing tomorrow, it'll be easy to believe." For emphasis, he sucked in and exhaled a wheeze that sounded disgustingly wet.

She licked her lips, straining not to utter what was really on her mind, and instead said, "Regardless, these swag bags still need to be packed."

He glared at the items, having once again forgotten they existed. "Okay, fine. How are we going to do this?"

"Well, first it would be great if we could take down some of these goddamn things so I can think." Referring to the wind chimes.

He gritted his teeth, or *whatever* was stuffed into his gums. "You can think just fine with them staying up."

"We can't even take them down for a little bit? Just until we're finished?"

"No." He knew he was being stubborn and irrational, but he didn't care. The idea of removing them paralyzed him with fear. "They have to stay. I'm sorry."

They stood in a standoff for a minute or two. Daniel wasn't going to budge on this. He felt zero sense of urgency when it came to tomorrow's festival, unlike Eileen, which is why he knew she'd fold first.

"Okay, fine," she said, coldly, "have it your way." Then, under her breath, she added, "As usual."

Not for a single second did Daniel consider ignoring the comment. "What the fuck is that supposed to mean?"

"Nothing," she said. "Nothing at all." She moved past him and started separating the boxed merch—items their paid sponsors had mailed them in bulk, like bookmarks and coasters and pens, all stuff they'd have to include in every badge holder's complimentary swag bag tomorrow morning.

But Daniel wasn't ready to move on. He stood behind her, hands on his hips, rage pulsing through his veins. "No, I don't think it meant nothing. I think it meant a big fucking something, actually."

Eileen slammed a box of merch to the floor and turned toward him. "What do you think I meant by it, Daniel?" she shouted, tears welling in her eyes. "When do I ever get a say in anything? When do *you* ever do anything *I* want to do?"

I BELIEVE IN MISTER BONES

Daniel took a step back. "We're literally about to pack all of these swag bags, which is something I've already stated I don't feel like doing."

"Are you serious?" Eileen started laughing like someone having a nervous breakdown, and Daniel wondered if that's exactly what this was. "Swag bags for a festival *you* wanted us to do. For a publishing company *you* wanted us to launch."

"Oh, what are you talking about? You wanted to do these things just as much as I did."

"These were *your* ideas," she reminded him. "Not mine." She wiped tears from her face. "I don't *dislike* doing this stuff. Sometimes I even enjoy it, when you're not making every goddamn thing difficult and acting like *I'm* the one forcing you to participate."

He handed her the box of tissues, and she yanked them out of his hand. "I think, maybe," he said, "that you—"

"—And these fucking *wind chimes*, I swear to god," she said, blowing her nose, "I told you how much of a headache they've been giving me. This apartment is *too small* for stuff like this. And you won't even consider taking them down? Not even while we're packing stuff? Packing stuff for the festival *you* wanted to do? A festival you wanted to do because *why*, again?"

"A festival *we*—"

"—Was it to make a difference in the horror community, as you wrote in the newsletter? Or was it really just to show up some asshole you secretly hate?"

"What asshole—"

"—Have we really been losing our minds all year to put this together because you thought it would be satisfying to make someone else's festival . . . what, look *inferior*?"

"It isn't that—"

"—I mean, Jesus Christ, isn't that why you wanted to start the fucking *press* in the first place? It wasn't to provide a home for unheard voices. It wasn't to make an impact on the genre. Or whatever else you've said in interviews. You just wanted to make someone else feel bad. You wanted to demonstrate that you were better than them."

"I don't think—"

"—And you expect me to go along with it all, and I help and I help and meanwhile everybody tells you what a great job you've done. Nobody tells me *shit*, Daniel. Nobody even knows I exist, and that's the truth." This time, when she blew her nose, it sounded as gross as his lungs. "So yeah, dude. I want to go out tonight. I want to see these people and talk to them and be a person they remember, a person who means something."

"I never—"

"—There has to be *some* upside to spending all of my time working on this stuff. There certainly isn't *money* in any of this, so what is there? There has to be something, right? There has to be. All while listening to you give me shit about every little pushback, too. Every question I ask you is answered with disdain."

"I don't—"

"—Disdain for me, when *you're the one* who set all of these things in motion. You're the one who decided, hey, let's commit to all of these highly stressful projects. Let's do everything and then hate each other while doing it. Don't you see how unreasonable you're being? Don't you see how impossible you are to deal with sometimes?"

"I'm not—"

"—I mean, Jesus Christ, I know you're going through some stuff. I know you've not been well. I understand that. Even while trying to get you help, you've treated me like it's my fault. Like I'm the bitch insisting you see a doctor. All while you lie around taking pity on yourself, leaving me to handle fucking *everything*."

"I haven't—"

"—And maybe it's selfish for me to say, but trying to take care of both you and the company without any help? It's been exhausting. I'm fucking *tired*, Daniel. Okay? *Okay?* I'm *tired*."

I BELIEVE IN MISTER BONES

Daniel didn't remember what he said in response, which was maybe a lie, but a necessary one to keep himself from cracking. All he knew was, shortly afterward, Eileen got dressed and told him he could pack the swag bags himself, that she was leaving early to see who was already at the bar.

Then she was gone, slamming the door hard enough to make the wind chimes gasp.

As Daniel expected, packaging these swag bags were a pain in the ass. So much crap had been mailed to their address. If they were ever stupid enough to host another festival in the future, he'd need to remember to enforce a strict "one unique item per sponsor" cap for the swag bags. For each item they'd requested, at minimum, one hundred copies, to account for each badge holder's swag bag and leftovers for passersby who decided to buy a membership during the weekend. A lot of these sponsors mailed multiple kinds of things, which meant some of these boxes contained three-to-five hundred items that Daniel then had to separate into their individual piles.

It took some doing, but he eventually came up with a system. He cleared enough room in the apartment to unfold the three plastic tables typically reserved for popup events. He pushed them against each other, end to end, like a train, then dumped out every pile of swag bag merch in their own rows, essentially creating an assembly line. On one end of the table train—the end he dubbed the starting line—he'd gathered all of the empty Fiendish Book Festival tote bags they'd gotten silkscreened at a local SATX printer. On the opposite end of the table train—the finish line—he'd set out a large cardboard box, which he intended to fill with packed tote bags. He also set out piles of Fiendish merch to include in the bags, along with the programs they'd gotten printed. All in all, maybe fifteen total piles of crap. Each bag would need one piece from every pile. This was going to take him all goddamn night.

He decided to take a break before officially beginning. Watch something on TV for a little while. Then he'd get started. He'd knock it all out and by the time Eileen returned home, she'd forgive him for everything he may or may not have said, and she'd apologize for everything she definitely said.

He surfed the streamers for a while, searching for something, *anything* that might medicate his dumb brain. Nothing sounded appealing. Nothing he hadn't already seen a thousand times before. He surrendered and turned on *New Girl*—back to the beginning: season one, episode one. It wasn't the best show he'd ever seen (*Columbo*), but it also wasn't the worst (*Mrs. Columbo*). It was perfectly tolerable. Sometimes entertaining, sometimes mundane. Exactly what he wanted. Halfway through the third episode, he even got up and started packaging the swag bags while watching from across the apartment. A TV show to distract his brain and a dull, repetitive activity to keep his limbs busy. Piece of cake. He should've started doing shit like this weeks ago. Maybe next he'd try teaching himself how to knit. Probably would have done wonders in preventing the argument him and Eileen had engaged in earlier. She'd still be here, even. They could be watching and packaging together. Instead he was—

Someone knocked on the door.

13.

XIOMARA STOOD OUTSIDE the apartment, lit only by the exterior security lights installed between apartments. They wore an oversized hoodie with a cartoon squirrel on the front. In one hand they held a greasy bag of fast food, and in the other juggled a cardboard carryout tray containing two fountain drinks. He couldn't smell the contents of the bag, although he was sure it gave off a delicious aroma.

He was surprised to discover the sun was already down. How long had he been packaging the swag bags? What *time* was it?

"Xio?" he said, standing in the open doorway. Of all the people he expected to see when he opened the door, they were low on the list. Honestly, nobody ever knocked on the door unless they were getting a delivery, and even then most people just left the package nearby and shot over a text notification with a photo of the package like it was being held for ransom. "Eileen actually isn't here right now, if you were looking for her."

They shook their head and said, "Actually, I just saw Eileen."

"Oh?"

"Yeah, she invited me to hang out at some bar everybody's at tonight. I stopped by and had a drink or two, but . . . " They glanced around, visibly nervous about something. "Could I come inside, maybe?"

"Um." For the first time since hanging them all up, it occurred to Daniel just how strange the wind chimes in their apartment might appear to a stranger. Not that Xiomara was a *stranger,* of course. But it wasn't like they were someone who hung out in Daniel and Eileen's apartment. Come to think about it, he wasn't sure they'd *ever* entertained a guest here. The only visitors he had any memory of entering the apartment were maintenance workers employed by the complex. And, while it was true that Xiomara was in no way a stranger, they were Eileen's friend, not Daniel's. He didn't think the two of them had ever been alone in the same room together. Not for a minute, not even for a second. Not *intentionally*, or anything. There just had never been a reason for it to happen. So what the hell would Xiomara be doing here *now,* evidently already aware that Eileen wouldn't be around to greet them? The vibes felt strange, mysterious— *exciting.*

"So," Xiomara said, when Daniel never continued his thought, "is that a yes, or . . . ?"

"Oh, um, yes, of course. Come on in." He stood aside, and let them enter. There was no way he was going to tell Xiomara *no*. Not until he found out what they could possibly want with him, at this hour, without Eileen present. His brain spun with speculation. Was there some deep, dark secret about his wife only Xiomara knew? Had Eileen accidentally murdered a drifter back when they were both in high school together? In that moment, anything felt possible. "Um, excuse the mess," he told them. "We're in the middle of getting ready for the festival."

But their eyes were naturally focused on what hung from the ceiling, rather than the mess below. "Whoa, that's a . . . that's a lot of wind chimes."

"You like them?" he asked, desperate to hear *somebody* praise these things.

"I mean . . . " They laughed. " . . . No, not really."

I BELIEVE IN MISTER BONES

"Yeah, Eileen doesn't much care for them, either."

They nodded at the TV. "*New Girl*, huh?"

"You a fan?"

"A little too pro-cop for my tastes."

"Oh. Sorry." Disappointed and ashamed, he took the drink tray from them and set it on the kitchen table. "What's all this, anyway?"

Xiomara took a moment to remember the bag of food in their hand. "Oh, yeah. I thought maybe you might be hungry. I know I was." Then: "Sorry, I don't have your phone number, or I would have called to see what you wanted. Cheeseburgers cool with you?"

He nodded, and resisted the urge to tap his belly. "Cheeseburgers are always cool with me, yeah," he said, and—because he still didn't understand what was happening—added, "I'm sorry, but what's going on here, exactly? Did Eileen send you?" He wondered where he'd laid his phone down last. Silent mode was undoubtedly enabled. Who knew what kind of calls or texts he might've missed since Eileen stormed out of the apartment.

Xiomara frowned at him, concerned. "Are you okay, dude? You sound . . . not great."

It took him a moment to remember how bad his wheezing had gotten. He'd almost gotten used to it. "Yeah, it's just allergies, or . . . uh, something."

They raised their brow. "Something like that Bones freak messing around with your ribs?"

"Possibly," he said, and smiled. It felt good not being the one to bring him up first.

"Anyway . . . " Xiomara placed the food on the table next to the drinks. "Like I said, I met Eileen at the bar. She was already a few drinks in. We talked about the fight y'all had. It sounded . . . you know, ugly. A bunch of people from the fest are there, too, and I'm not sure she should've been saying some of the stuff she was saying. Not with them around. I mentioned that to her. You know. Suggested she cool it a bit. She didn't like hearing that, of course. So then *we* got into a fight, so I decided to bounce. But . . . " They pulled out a set of keys from their hoodie pocket and tossed them on the table with the food and drinks. "I did end up taking her keys before leaving. The rate she was going, it didn't seem like a smart idea to let her drive home tonight. So I thought maybe I'd swing by here with some late-night burgers, help you finish up with anything that still needs to be done, then I'll drive you downtown so you can bring Eileen home in her car. What do you think?"

"What kind of stuff was she saying, exactly?"

"Nothing too . . . uh, specific. But still. Aren't they people you work with, too? Just felt weird to be putting them all in that position. Trust me, it was embarrassing, but not because of you."

"Did she tell them about . . . uh, you know?" He tucked his left wrist against his chest, instinctively.

"Mister Bones?"

He nodded, already convinced the whole bar was laughing at him.

"Nah. Nothing like that."

"Okay, good," he said, and realized he had no idea what other dirty laundry Eileen could have been airing to people if not Mister Bones. What else *was* there? "Um, anyway, thanks for bringing food. I can't actually remember the last time I ate something."

"Anybody ever diagnose you with ADHD, Daniel?" Xiomara asked.

"What?" he said, panicked and paranoid. "No, why?"

They smirked. "No reason. Let's eat."

"Do you want me to turn off *New Girl* first?"

Xiomara glanced at the TV, then back at Daniel with a disgusted grimace across their face. "I mean . . . it's not like I don't *not* want you to turn it off."

I BELIEVE IN MISTER BONES

The two of them sat across from each other at the small table separating the kitchen from the living room. The burger *looked* appetizing, but predictably tasted like paper. Xiomara seemed to enjoy theirs, at least. He wished he could still taste things. At this point, he'd resigned himself to the fact that his taste buds would never return. Regardless, his stomach felt hollow and aching. Food would help.

"So, I gotta ask," Xiomara eventually said, and Daniel groaned.

"Ask what?"

"I remember you telling me about the wind chimes in that guy's video. I assume that's why you have them hanging up, too."

"Yeah, I guess so. Plus, there's that chapter . . . "

"Right, the one that got cut," they said. "Like a deleted scene."

He nodded.

"What do you think they're going to do, exactly? Alert you if this Mister Bones jackoff shows up?"

"I don't know," he said, then admitted something he'd been denying to himself for days now: "I don't think they actually work all that well."

"What do you mean?"

"Every time I fall asleep, he still shows up. In my dreams, but also . . . beyond that. Enough to fuck with my bones, at least. Enough to replace them." He balled up the wrapper from his finished burger, then nodded to the wind chimes. "And not once have I heard these things going off. Neither has Eileen. At least not without one of us bumping into them first. If he's physically entering this apartment, then . . . I don't know. He's able to move through objects without disturbing them, I guess. Probably invisible, too, since Eileen's never seen him while I was asleep." He tossed the wrapper toward the trash can and didn't come remotely close to making it in. "I sound fucking crazy right now, don't I?"

"Well, yeah," Xiomara said, "don't you think I'd sound pretty fucking crazy if I told you something like that?"

Daniel considered. "I'd probably be forced to restrain you with a straitjacket myself, yeah."

Xiomara smirked. "Now, don't go making promises you can't keep, Daniel." The smirk vanished within seconds after they realized Daniel didn't know how to respond, replaced by an expression of total embarrassment. "Sorry, that was stupid."

He shook his head. "It wasn't stupid." Then, desperate to reroute the conversation, brought things back to the wind chimes. "I've been thinking about these things a lot. Eileen wants me to take them down. I don't really have a reason to keep them. They just . . . *feel* good. They aren't doing shit to protect me, but at the same time . . . it's nice to have them, anyway. Does that make any sense?" He self-consciously picked up the box cutter from the table and started fooling around with it. Desperate for something to focus on right now.

"Sure, like a safety blanket kind of thing," Xiomara said. "Or when teachers used to tell kids to put a textbook over their heads in the event of nuclear war."

"I thought that was about earthquakes."

"Two things can be true." They slurped down some of the Diet Coke in their fountain cup. "So, you think this creep is invisible? That's how he can move around undetected?"

"I don't know what I think, really, but—"

"Wait, you said he can enter your dreams, too? Like what? Some kinda Frederick Krueger?"

"*Frederick*?"

"Freddy to his close friends, I guess," Xiomara said, and Daniel couldn't help but laugh. The noise that emitted out of him sounded like the inside of his body was unraveling all at once, he knew, especially judging from the look of concern suddenly across Xiomara's face. "Are you okay?"

I BELIEVE IN MISTER BONES

He shrugged. What an impossible question to answer. "I haven't been doing much laughing lately, I guess. But yeah. Kinda like . . . *Frederick* Krueger, but different. It's hard to explain. I've never been able to remember my dreams very well, and lately it's been even more difficult to grasp onto any clear details. I just wake up knowing he's been in my head, and then I feel a new oddity somewhere in my body. A new part of me is suddenly numb and weird and . . . *changed,* you know?"

"Oh, trust me. I'm well-versed in the body-feeling-weird department," Xiomara said.

"Because you're nonbinary?" Daniel asked, feeling like a fucking idiot the moment the words left his lips.

They chuckled. "Among other things, yes. Anyway, in that book submission y'all got, none of this shit was ever explained?"

"Nope," he said. "It's all pretty ambiguous."

"Do you think maybe I could read it?"

"You-you want to read the book?" He hadn't even been able to convince Eileen to do that. "Why?"

"Um, because it's turned you into a crazy person?" Xiomara replied, like they couldn't understand why Daniel was confused. "Clearly it's at least *interesting.* Who wouldn't want to check something like that out?"

Daniel sunk into his seat. Despite the fact that they'd just joked about him being crazy minutes ago, hearing it again—*now*—felt like a punch to the face. Maybe because this time their tone sounded more sincere, not a trace of humor detected. "I can email it to you, sure," he said. "I don't know if it's even good anymore. I don't think it really matters. I'm never going to track down the author. They clearly don't want to be found."

"What was the name they gave you again? Augustus Gloop?"

"August Skeef."

"Yeah, that shit was definitely a fake."

Daniel set the box cutter back down on the table. He

had lost track of how long they'd been sitting there. They'd both finished their burgers. And, if the sound of their individual straw slurps were any inclination, their drinks were each running on empty, too. There weren't any clocks hanging up in the apartment, and he had no idea where he'd put his cell phone, so as far as the actual *time* went right now he could hardly wager a guess.

"Well, I should probably get back to work," he said, referring to the swag bags still needing to be packaged on his makeshift assembly line. He'd gotten through maybe half of the merch before Xiomara showed up at the front door.

"Oh shit, right, yeah, sorry," they said, following his line of sight. "Just let me know what needs to be done. I'm here to help." They stood from the table and removed their cartoon squirrel hoodie, revealing only a tank top beneath.

For a moment, he couldn't take his eyes off their body, but managed to recover quick enough and cleared his throat. "Uh, thank you again for coming over."

"My pleasure, dude," Xiomara said, smirking like there was no way they hadn't spotted him checking them out. Then they nodded to a paperback Daniel had left on the kitchen table. *The Dangers of Smoking in Bed* by Mariana Enríquez. "Have you read this yet? Fucking great anthology."

"I'm only a couple stories into it," he admitted, "but yeah, I love the way she writes." Then, because Daniel was an intolerable nerd who couldn't help himself, added, "Although, it's a *collection*, not an anthology."

"What do you mean?" they said, amused.

"When all the stories are written by the same author, it's called a collection. It's only an anthology if all of the stories are by different people."

"Bullshit. I've never heard that before."

"I'm just telling you what I know."

"But what about *Creepshow*?"

"What about it?" he asked.

I BELIEVE IN MISTER BONES

"Or *Trick r' Treat*, or *Cat's Eye*, or *Tales from the QuadeaD Zone*, or—"

"I don't understand what you're asking."

"Every segment in *Creepshow* was directed by George Romero and written by Stephen King. Nobody calls it a *collection*. It's an anthology, babe."

There was something about the way they'd called him *babe* that made him feel like he was on a cloud. "Okay, maybe you have a point," he said, blushing, then led them over to the tables. "So, anyway, it's nothing too crazy. We're just putting one item from each pile here into all of the tote bags. It's more tedious than anything."

"That's it?" they asked.

"I, uh, sure fucking hope so."

"Let's knock this bitch out then." They punctuated this last sentence by cracking their knuckles, and Daniel winced, which they unfortunately noticed. "Oh, sorry, are you one of those weirdos who get grossed out when they hear knuckles cracking?"

"Nah, it's not that. You're fine." He instinctively covered his right hand over his left knuckles.

"Then what is it?"

"I used to be able to crack mine, too," he said, feeling so goddamn silly, "but since my accident I haven't been able to do it. Not even on my right hand." To emphasize his point, he tried to crack them now. Nothing happened.

"Whoa, that's weird."

"Not only that," Daniel said, "but also—" He jerked his head to the left, then to the right. "—I haven't been able to crack my neck, either. Same with any of the other bones in my body I used to crack. My back, my knees. They've all, uh . . . I don't know, changed on me, or something. They're not right."

"They've all been replaced, you mean," they said, in a tone that he found impossible to decipher if it was sincere or mocking.

He shrugged, like *what else would you call it?* "I mean

. . . maybe? *Something* has happened to them. They wouldn't just . . . stop being able to do that all of a sudden." He slumped, defeated and tired of talking about his body. "Or maybe they would? What the hell do I know, right?"

Xiomara reached forward, gesturing to his hands. "Can I feel?"

"I'm sure they will feel normal to you. I've already had Eileen check, and she didn't notice anything strange."

"Well." They surveyed the apartment. "Eileen doesn't appear to currently be here, so . . . "

They made a valid point. He surrendered his hands over to them, and they softly pressed their fingers up and down his own. Their nails were painted a mixture of yellow, white, purple, and black. Natural, not acrylic. Their touch didn't feel good, but it also didn't feel *bad*. His hands were too numb to understand the difference. Contact with anything—Xiomara's fingers included—only managed to send tingling ripples through the impacted area. It was a *distant* feeling. Like they were touching something not quite connected to him, but also not quite disconnected, either. All this time and somehow he still wasn't used to the sensation.

And yet, despite the numbness, it was still oddly pleasant to be touched by another person. He wasn't sure someone had ever massaged his hands before. Was that even a thing people did? It must've been. He only wished he could experience it with his original skeleton still intact.

"What do you feel?" he whispered.

"You're trembling," they said, concerned. "Is this painful? I'm not hurting you, am I?"

"No, you're fine. It's okay."

"Do you want me to try your neck?"

He heard the question, but his brain couldn't process what it meant. "Wh-what?"

"You mentioned you were also having neck issues, right? I don't mind. If you want."

Say no, you fucking idiot, his brain screamed, *do not*

I BELIEVE IN MISTER BONES

allow your wife's childhood best friend to give you a neck massage in your otherwise-empty apartment.

He opened his mouth to say those very words, only something else slipped out instead: "Um, sure, if . . . if you want to, sure."

They were just going to rub his neck a little. It wasn't that big of a deal. Besides, where was Eileen, anyway? She'd ditched him to go get drunk. Drunk at a bar where she was apparently shit-talking him? He had no reason to feel guilty about a goddamn thing right now. It wasn't like the two of them were going to fuck each other.

"It might be better if you removed your shirt," Xiomara suggested. "Just so I can get a better grip. If you're comfortable with that, of course."

"Yeah, that makes sense," he said, embracing their shared delusion on where this might or might not be heading. He took off his shirt, back facing Xiomara. They were both still standing by the assembly line of festival swag, and though he wasn't actively looking their way he was still aware of their height differences. Which led to him asking the question that sealed both of their fates: "Would it be easier if I sat down on the bed?"

"Mmm," they said from behind him, pretending to consider the question, "yeah, maybe so, good idea."

At first, only Daniel sat on the bed, while Xiomara stood over him at the edge, knees pressed to either side of his spine. He felt silly sitting there with his shirt off. Aside from Eileen, he couldn't remember the last time in the past decade he'd been topless around someone. He'd never cared too much for being perceived. It made him sweat and get fidgety. He cursed himself for agreeing to this massage so eagerly, and wished he was at least drunk like Eileen so he'd have something besides himself to blame.

"You definitely feel tight," Xiomara said, then, suddenly next to his ear, whispered, "Why don't you lie down on your stomach?"

He didn't respond. He didn't need to. Not verbally, at

least. He did as they suggested, then waited as they climbed onto the bed after him, straddling his lower back as they continued rubbing his neck. Brief shockwaves of numbness shot out from either direction between his shoulder blades. He didn't realistically think Xiomara would be able to feel any of his bones through the fat and muscle under his skin, but he admired that they still wanted to try. It also occurred to him that Xiomara most likely didn't believe they'd hit bone, either. That this was all an excuse to get into bed together. An excuse for them to touch him, for him to touch them. But he hadn't touched them. He was being good. This was just a friendly massage, and nothing more. The erection conjuring in his pants was unrelated.

"Daniel, would you mind, maybe, doing me next?"

His whole body tensed as he said, "Um."

"Sorry, it's okay. I didn't mean to—"

"No," he said, against his better judgment, "yeah, of course, I don't mind. You did me. It's only fair I, uh, return the favor."

"Say no more," Xiomara said, already wiggling off of him. They lay down on their own stomach and waited for Daniel to sit up.

For half a second he debated also straddling their lower back, but feared he'd crush them under his weight. He remained at their side, knees bent, sitting on the back of his legs. He hesitated, hands hovering over their back like he was preparing to attack, not quite sure how to begin. He'd massaged Eileen's back plenty of times. But Xiomara was not Eileen. Xiomara was not his wife. They were his wife's *friend*. What the fuck were they doing here?

"Is something wrong?" Xiomara asked, face buried in his pillow.

"Not at all," he said, unconvincingly.

He started by touching the areas of Xiomara's skin exposed between the straps of their tank top. He pressed down gently, nothing too hard, vividly reminded of the last time he'd given Eileen a massage, of what had happened to his left arm after applying too much pressure. He could've done the same here. He could've leaned all of his weight on his left arm until it bent against Xiomara's back. He could've forced them to stare at the curse rotting his bones. It would have been irrefutable proof that something was going on inside him.

But he'd tried showing somebody before, hadn't he? Eileen. Back in the bathroom, when he was emptying his stomach into the toilet. The moment she walked in, suddenly the bent bone in his arm straightened out. Like it'd never been corrupted. Like Daniel had hallucinated the whole thing. Playing right into what Eileen already believed. Mister Bones was fucking with him. The mysterious substance he'd inserted into Daniel's body had a twisted sense of humor.

So no. He wasn't going to try repeating the incident here with Xiomara. He was going to continue touching their back delicately and listening to them softly moan into his pillow. He was going to continue pretending like this was all perfectly natural, that Eileen would have been completely okay with everything if she barged in through the front door and caught them like this in bed. They were just two pals rubbing each other. It wasn't like *both* of them were topless, or anything that brazenly stupid.

The words spilled out of his mouth before he could process them: "Do you want to take off your tank top, too?" Then quickly added, "You know. For a better grip."

Now it was their turn to tense up, and Daniel wondered if he'd ruined whatever mistake they were about to make.

They turned away from the pillow, making eye contact with Daniel. "Actually, I prefer to keep that on." Then, after a beat, they grinned. "We can take something else off me, however . . . "

"Um," he said, helpless to do anything but watch as they rolled over and unbuttoned their jeans. They started to wrestle them off, then paused and glanced back up at Daniel, dead serious.

"You want to do this, too—right?" they asked.

"What? Take my pants off?"

A smile broke through. "I'm just trying to make sure what we're about to do here is mutually desired."

He almost asked, *What are we about to do?* but stopped himself. He wasn't going to play stupid here. He knew what they meant, and he knew that they knew he wanted this to happen just as much as they did. He had for a while now. Years, even. Maybe since the first time Eileen introduced him to them. He'd never cheated on his wife before. He'd never seriously even considered it. But still. There had always been this uneasy feeling whenever he and Xiomara were around each other. This instant attraction that made him feel antsy, like if he didn't distract himself when they were together he'd spontaneously combust. A crush. He had a stupid fucking crush.

"Daniel?" Xiomara said, uncertain. "Are you okay?"

He lunged forward, eager, manic, and kissed them on the lips. To his relief, they kissed back, tongue coiled around tongue, hands sliding over curves, and suddenly it was like the two of them were starving for each other, ravenous and desperate for their touch.

He helped Xiomara remove their jeans and underwear and then they helped him do the same, and there they were, in the bed that he shared with Eileen, both of them stripped nude save for Xiomara's tank top. He tried to work his way under the fabric to feel their chest, and they patiently guided his hand down between their legs instead. They were already wet. His finger, numb and tingling, slid into their hole like it'd always belonged there. They arched up against his touch, moaning as he massaged them from the inside.

Everything was happening so fast.

At some point they'd started stroking his cock. He hadn't even noticed at first. Suddenly it was just . . . *happening*.

The two of them hand-fucked each other with a shared,

I BELIEVE IN MISTER BONES

frenetic rhythm, as if they were trying to start a fire together, to catch a spark against their flesh and fully pyro out of control. Neither of them was going to be satisfied until detonation was achieved right here beneath the wind chimes Eileen had so vocally loathed.

He tried not to think about anything besides what was currently happening. He blocked Eileen out of his mind and focused on Xiomara in bed next to him. The way they were smiling and writhing against his touch. The speed in which their hand jacked him off, showing no signs of slowing down or tiring out.

It was then, noticing their hand, that a strange, alien seed of an idea blossomed.

It dawned on Daniel, in that moment, how weak certain bones in the body really were. How little strength was required to snap something. It was a recurring paranoia he'd found himself dwelling on since receiving the *Mister Bones* manuscript in his email. The fragility of all bones, yes, but particularly the phalanges. Fingers and toes. Little earthworms poking their heads out of the skeleton. So unprotected, so innocent. It would take nothing at all to break one. He just had to get a sturdy enough grip, and a sturdy enough determination.

Would Xiomara understand why he had to do it? What if he asked first? Would they be agreeable, or would they storm out of the apartment offended? It would just be one finger. Something useless like the pinky. They could pick the hand, for all he cared. Just as long as he heard something snap—and, obviously, that they were thinking about Mister Bones when it mattered most. Which meant he wouldn't be able to do it without asking first, or at the very least giving *some* kind of warning. Anything to bring Mister Bones back to the front of their mind. Then he'd take one of their fingers, and he would snap it back with one abrupt motion. The sound of it cracking would sound like a gunshot in his tiny apartment. Would Xiomara scream afterward? Would they cry? He assumed so. He certainly would, if their positions were reversed. But he'd already broken his share of bones. Now it was someone else's turn.

"Fuck, fuck, fuck, oh *fuck*," Xiomara moaned next to him, squirming as he fingered them, and he realized they were coming. Their grip around his cock tightened like they were trying to rip it off his body, and for one beautiful, aggressively erotic moment he hoped they did exactly that. *Yearned* for it, even. Needed it more than he'd ever needed anything else. *Do it,* he thought, but did not say, *Jesus Christ fucking do it*, and then he, too, was coming—ejaculating all over the bed, all over Xiomara's quivering thigh and exposed stomach, barely missing the tank top they'd insisted on not taking off. Coming so hard it hurt, so intense that he swore his skull was vibrating against his brain.

He removed his fingers from between their legs and scrambled for a nearby tissue box. He wiped himself off first and then collapsed back into bed to tend to Xiomara. They remained flat on their back, out of breath and relaxed with a post-orgasm glow. He wiped the cum off their flesh with the gentleness of a skilled artisan, then took care of the few visible spots on the bedsheet before balling up the tissues and tossing them to the floor behind him. He'd properly dispose of them later, when it felt appropriate to get up. The two of them stared at each other, smiling, absentmindedly rubbing their bodies. He ran his fingers along the length of their arm, toward their hand—the same hand they'd just had wrapped around his cock—and lifted it up to massage their individual knuckles.

"I can't believe we just did that," Xiomara whispered, smiling ear-to-ear like a character in a romance novel.

"It was nice," he said, and meant it, despite the guilt of adultery already bubbling to the surface. He was too distracted by their hand to let any other negative feelings overwhelm him. Maybe later, once he was alone with his thoughts again. "You have really beautiful hands, you know that?" Typically, he felt uncomfortable complimenting others, especially when it came to their physical appearances. There was a fear that the other person might be offended—or, worse, amused. But not tonight, not now. He'd found a hitherto unearthed confidence hidden deep inside him, something that felt almost like autopilot as he moved and spoke.

"My hands?" Xiomara said, surprised to hear it. "I've never much thought about my hands, one way or the other."

"I think about hands all the time," he said. "My hands. The hands of others."

They laughed. "You got a hand fetish, babe?" Then, worried Daniel might be hurt, added: "I mean, no judgment here. I can see how hands can be sexy, given the right set of circumstances . . . "

"Fingers, too," Daniel said, only half-listening to what they were saying as he extended their index finger out, rubbing it softly with his own fingers. "Beautiful fingers."

"Um, thank you?"

"You ever think about how weak they are, though?" He released his gentle grip on their index finger and extended out their pinky next. "How easy they are to . . . you know . . . break?"

"Well, I am now," Xiomara said, no longer so amused. Their body stiffened, but they didn't pull away.

"Let me ask you something, Xio," he said.

"Oh-okay . . . " They were staring at him like he'd suddenly turned into a complete stranger. But to be fair, how well had the two of them ever known each other, anyway?

"What do you think about any of this stuff that's been going on with me?" Daniel asked.

"What do you . . . what do you mean?"

"I mean . . . do you . . . you know?" He gripped their pinky tighter, and fear flooded their eyes. "Do you believe in Mister Bones, or not?"

Xiomara tried to pull away, but it was too late. He was already in the process of bending the finger back.

"*What the fuck are you doing?*"

They screamed—*loud*. The sound spooked him and he let go, no idea whether he'd succeeded. He didn't *feel* it snap. But would he have?

Suddenly a foot smashed into his face, and he flew off the bed.

When he sat back up, Xiomara was already standing and frantically searching through their jeans pocket for something. They were crying and shaking and shouting stuff like, *Get the hell away from me*, and *What the fuck is wrong with you?*

"It's okay," he tried to say, although he feared his voice was drowned out by the rising volume of Xiomara's panicked sobs. He climbed up to his feet and approached them, both hands raised with their palms out. *I mean no harm.* "If you would let me explain, you'll understand what I'm trying to—"

"Fuck off!" Xiomara screamed, finally locating what they were digging for in their jeans. By the time Daniel realized what they'd just equipped themself with, they were already squeezing the trigger and blasting his face with a gust of pepper spray.

His first thought was, *Holy fuck my face is on fire my fucking face is on fucking fire.* His second and third thoughts were very similar to his first. He tumbled back against the assembly line of tables and flipped over them, sending all the swag bags spilling to the floor with him. The wind chimes above him rattled like a snake from where the back of his skull had collided.

His fucking face was on fucking fire.

When he got back up, Xiomara was fully dressed and running toward the door. At least he was *pretty sure* that's what he saw. Keeping his eyes open longer than a couple seconds felt impossible. It was like there was fucking *sand* under his eyelids.

I BELIEVE IN MISTER BONES

"Just *wait!*" he shouted, then fell into a coughing fit. His throat tasted like battery acid. It felt ghoulishly ironic that *this* he would be able to taste, unlike the burger Xiomara had brought him earlier. He doubled over, leaning onto the couch, blinking long and hard but it was too late, Xiomara was already out of the apartment, out of his life. A life that, if it already wasn't ruined, he'd just ensured would be soon enough.

If he could've fought through the pepper spray long enough to ask just one question, he would have asked them whether or not he'd managed to break their finger.

Because something told him he'd failed. He'd fucked up. He didn't use enough force. They'd wiggled away too easily. He'd let them wiggle free before the job was done.

The *job?* Who the fuck was he? Breaking someone's finger wasn't his goddamn *job*. That was the work of monsters—of boogeymen. Was Daniel a monster now? A *boogeyman*? No, of course not. He'd just . . . had a moment of weakness. Something had made him do it. He hadn't thought it out clearly. Something was inside him making him do things he didn't want to do. It was that simple. It was certainly preferable to the alternative—that he'd chosen to do this of his own freewill. Not just the attempted finger snap but also the stuff before. The adultery. He'd never cheated on Eileen. He'd never even fucking thought about it. There was no way he would have caved that easily. That wasn't the type of person he was. He was better than other men. He was different. He wasn't a cheater. He wasn't a monster.

He was almost relieved his eyes were too fucked up to see his own reflection in the mirror. He would have seen a liar.

Water sprayed from the sink faucet into his eyes. He tried his best to rinse out the pepper spray but this shit didn't seem to be going anywhere. Somehow the burning only intensified. He gave up and stumbled through the apartment until he was seated at the kitchen table again, still nude, face dripping with water, tears, and snot. There was a crying noise in the apartment and it was coming from him. He had fucked up. The swag bags were scattered everywhere. All of the boxes they'd left by the front door had spilled to the floor and burst open. Eileen was at the bar drunk and telling everybody how terrible of a person her husband was. Xiomara was fleeing the apartment convinced that Daniel was some kind of serial killer. Would they notify the police of what had transpired—or, infinitely worse, would they post about the incident on Twitter?

It seemed somewhat insane to think about how not even ten minutes ago he'd been receiving the best handjob of his life.

How quickly everything had backfired.

Why hadn't he asked Xiomara first? What the fuck had he been *thinking*? This had not been the decision making of a rational person. He'd acted spontaneously. Something in him screamed *BREAK THEIR BONES* and he'd obeyed without hesitation.

Something in him . . .

Something like whatever had replaced his skeleton.

Something in him like a curse, a haunting.

Something in him like a monster, a boogeyman.

Like Mister Bones.

This motherfucker was synced into him somehow. He'd laced Daniel's insides with his evil DNA and now it was rotting everything that made Daniel who he was. It wasn't just the bones he was after but all the rest, too. Daniel was no longer Daniel. He belonged to something else entirely now. Something that had no problem fucking their wife's best friend, something that was eager to attack others. Something that got off on the prospect of hearing someone scream, of hearing someone cry.

Mister Bones was a part of Daniel, and there was nothing Daniel could do about it. He could break the bones of a hundred different people. He knew it would make no difference. Not at this point. Mister Bones had dug in too

I BELIEVE IN MISTER BONES

deep. He'd put in too much time and energy into claiming this body for his collection.

Daniel was fucked. It was plain and simple. There was no use fighting. Fighting back would only worsen the situation. It would only prolong the possession.

The skeleton inside him was no longer his, and soon enough nothing else would be, either.

Unless . . . unless *what?*

Unless he removed it himself? Removed *what?* Removed . . . *it*. Removed the intruder. The bones. The skeleton. Officially rejected it from his body. Told it *no thank you.* Told it *get the fuck out of here and never come back.*

Daniel could do it. Why not? He'd been stupid and deranged enough to launch a small press. He could evict a malignant skeleton from his rotting body. What would that mean, though? Where would that leave him? A melting pile of goo? So the fuck what?

Who wanted a body, anyway?

Not Daniel.

Not anymore.

Fuck bodies. They'd never done him any good. Overrated trash. A burden to the soul.

Something told him you didn't need bodies in Marrowland, which was where he intended on going.

To finish this fucking shit.

To do what he should have done weeks ago.

He didn't know how long he'd been holding the box cutter, or when he'd slid it open, but there it was in his right hand, blade emerged from its plastic case, ready to pounce. Ready to feed.

Where to start? At least that was easy enough to answer.

Where does anybody ever start other than at the beginning?

Daniel moved the box cutter to the scar across his left wrist and buried the blade into his flesh.

He did not scream, he did not cry, he did not make a sound.

He didn't even remove the blade from his wrist as bright, red blood streamed down his arm and over the kitchen table.

Instead, Daniel kept the blade planted inside him, exactly where it was meant to be.

He sawed back and forth, shredding the skin away like wrapping paper, digging to the one thing no human was ever meant to witness:

Their own skeleton.

All around him, the wind chimes erupted with noise, as if they were screaming—or laughing.

INTERMISSION

Daniel Addams, publisher of San Antonio's Fiendish Books, dead at 33

Daniel Addams, co-founder of the horror-themed publishing company Fiendish Books, died this past Thursday. He was 33 years old.

No cause of death was disclosed.

The small press shared the news on their social media accounts, describing Addams as "dedicated to literature" and "passionate about the horror genre."

> **@FiendishBooks**
> We regret to announce the unexpected passing of our co-founder and editor, Daniel Addams. He was fiercely dedicated to literature and extremely passionate about the horror genre. At this time, the future of Fiendish Books is unclear. Please be patient as we attempt to gather our bearings and figure out what happens next. Thank you.

MAX BOOTH III

Addams established the company with his wife, Eileen Addams, in the summer of 2012 "during a night of copious alcohol and terrible nachos," according to the Fiendish Books website.

Since launching over 10 years ago, the company has published nearly 40 titles, including novels, novellas, and anthologies. Some of the books released by the press include *Witches on a Train* by Jessica McHugh, *Above* by Lauren Lough, and the potato-themed anthology *Tales from the Spud* edited by the Addamses.

Fiendish focuses on horror fiction only, rather than a wide variety of genres. "It's smarter," Eileen Addams told *The Weekly* earlier this month, "to embrace the weirdos who like the same kind of stuff we do."

The married couple had been planning to launch an inaugural horror literature convention called the Fiendish Book Festival. Sources have confirmed the event was canceled in the wake of Addams's death.

A GoFundMe campaign to help pay for funeral arrangements has been launched by a friend of the family.

COMMENTS (1)

Anonymous69
Who?

222

#DanielAddamsRIP

Wow, holy shit, terrible news.
#DanielAddamsRIP

I'm gutted. #DanielAddamsRIP

How is this real? #DanielAddamsRIP

He was so young. Oh my god.
#DanielAddamsRIP

Fiendish Books is one of the best indie presses
out there releasing top-quality shit. This is a
major loss for the horror community.
#DanielAddamsRIP

WTF?! #DanielAddamsRIP

Does anybody know what this means for all of
the authors contracted with Fiendish?
#DanielAddamsRIP

Is Fiendish going to close down now? Is there
anybody else even on staff? #DanielAddamsRIP

Does anybody know what happened to Daniel
Addams? Did he kill himself or what? I'm not
trying to be insensitive I'm just curious.
#DanielAddamsRIP

MAX BOOTH III

Soooo for everybody wondering why my bank account is suddenly in the negative, it might be because I just flew to San Antonio, paid for a hotel, then had to immediately fly back home after the convention was canceled ON THE MORNING OF. Still no idea if vendors are getting refunded. This fucking sucks.
#DanielAddamsRIP

Who the fuck is Daniel Addams
#DanielAddamsRIP

Yeah I was another vendor for the Fiendish Book Festival. I understand they just experienced a tragedy but a lot of us spent a shit ton of money to attend this thing and it's kinda unprofessional for nobody to respond to our inquiries. #DanielAddamsRIP

YOUNG TEEN VIRGIN SPLIT OPEN BY BIG BLACK COCK—CLICK TO SEE WHOLE VIDEO
#DanielAddamsRIP

Can someone actually tell me WHY the festival was canceled? Like I get that one of the people involved died and that's really sad but he wasn't the only one involved?? Why couldn't they have still let us set up and sell books? Seems a little strange imho and I don't understand the mindset here.
#DanielAddamsRIP

We here at Fracas Books are deeply saddened to hear about the passing of Daniel Addams. Sabrina had him on her podcast a few years back and she's always said it was one of her favorite episodes. The two of them really

bonded during that recording.
#DanielAddamsRIP

Does anybody know if orders on the Fiendish webstore are still active?? I bought a couple books from them last night and nobody's emailed me a shipping notification yet. Concerning . . . #DanielAddamsRIP

MILKY WHITE LACTATING TITS 24/7 LINK IN BIO #DanielAddamsRIP

For those asking—no, I have no idea what this means for THE CLUMSY MAN. Even before Daniel passed, I was sending Fiendish emails every day trying to get an update. They've been ghosting me for weeks. I don't imagine I will get an answer anytime soon. If anybody knows a good lawyer, LMK, thanks. #DanielAddamsRIP

I'm pretty sure it was a Fiendish publication that first got me interested in reading indie horror. I'll forever be thankful for what Daniel Addams provided all of us. #DanielAddamsRIP

Because many of you have been asking me, yes, there will be a portion of this week's show paying tribute to my good friend Daniel Addams. If you don't want to miss it, make sure you subscribe to the Rick Jenkins Horror Experience on iTunes and Spotify. #DanielAddamsRIP #RickJenkins #TheGuardiansofHorrorPodcast

Fiendish Books encouraged satanic practices in the "literature" they published and their imminent closure is the best we can hope for at this point. #DanielAddamsRIP

I'll always be proud to have considered myself a Fiend. My heart goes out to Eileen in this time. Please donate to the gofundme if you have the cash to spare. #DanielAddamsRIP

Hearing troubling rumors about how Daniel may have passed. Please reach out to your friends and tell them what they mean to you. #DanielAddamsRIP

Daniel Addams is a notorious huckster. This is not the first time he's faked an illness to scam people out of money. Anybody who thinks he's actually dead is a fucking idiot. Don't believe the lies. #DanielAddamsRIP

So is this going to impact the upcoming Fiendish Tales submission call? Because I've been working on a story for it and now I don't know if I should even bother. #DanielAddamsRIP

Just now hearing the news. Absolutely devastating. I'll write up more thoughts on Patreon (see link in bio). #DanielAddamsRIP

Truly telling how many of you are able to share a fundraising link for some c!s white man in publishing meanwhile there is a genocide going on and children are dying and none of you privileged fucks are lifting a goddamn finger to help - YOU ARE ALL COMPLICIT #DanielAddamsRIP

I BELIEVE IN MISTER BONES

Sooo was i the only one at the festival bar the night of Daniel's death? Like . . . y'all heard the way his wife was talking about him right?? Why is nobody talking about this???? #DanielAddamsRIP

Some of you guys are being fucking rude as hell. A person DIED. Why don't you give the rest of Fiendish some time to actually grieve in peace? #DanielAddamsRIP

Oh wow more publisher drama??? Must be a day that ends in Y #DanielAddamsRIP

This is exactly why I advocate self-publishing over working with small presses. They're all run by one-to-two people out of their kitchen. There's no backup plans in place. None of these authors know wtf is happening with their books. Fiendish needs to do the right thing, and soon. #DanielAddamsRIP

Will always remember meeting Daniel at a convention in Austin sometime before COVID. He told me he'd read and enjoyed my novel GARGOYLE ALLIANCE. I've decided to make it 99cents on Amazon for the rest of the week in his honor. Let's get this trending!!! #DanielAddamsRIP #KindleDeals #IndieHorror

Y'all are in for a rude awakening once more info finally drops on D*niels Add*ms from F*endish. Let's just say there's a reason he decided to end his life NOW. There's some shit about to drop that's gonna make you wanna puke. #DanielAddamsRIP #WhisperNetwork

MAX BOOTH III

I literally started my own press because of Fiendish Books. He was such an inspiration. I don't know how to process this. Fuck, man. I can't believe this is real. #DanielAddamsRIP

PUSSY IN BIO #DanielAddamsRIP

The following is a transcript from episode #299 of *The Guardians of Horror Podcast*...

RICK JENKINS: Hello and welcome to *The Guardians of Horror Podcast*. I am your host, Rick Jenkins, author of such renown works as *Sky Monsters, Ocean Monsters,* and *Ground Monsters*, among many, many other books that have been considered for award nomination. I would love to name them all right now, but honestly it would take up too much podcast time. You can look up the rest of my bibliography on the Rick Jenkins Wikipedia page, which I did not write. I am joined—as always—by my loyal cohost, Patrick O'Brien.

PATRICK O'BRIEN: It's a pleasure to—

RJ: There is a lot of stuff to cover for this week's show. Especially since next week is our very anticipated episode #300. Everywhere I go, listeners are telling me how much

they're looking forward to that one.
What will we do? They all want to
know. Well, we're keeping that under
wraps for now—aren't we, Patrick?

POB: I was actually going to sug—

RJ: But for today's show, here is what
you can expect to hear. We have
obtained exclusive information about
the next big MCU reveal, which I found
on Reddit. We will get into that, one-
hundred percent. I'll be discussing
the origin story of one of my most
acclaimed novelettes. We'll review the
latest episode we watched on our
current *Walking Dead* rewatch. But
first...I'm afraid we must begin with
some truly unfortunate news—which I
wouldn't say we're breaking here,
exactly, but we're certainly the first
news-trusted audio program to cover
it, for anyone keeping track at home.

POB: Yeah, Rick, you are absolutely—

RJ: For those who haven't already
heard the news, it appears that Daniel
Addams, co-founder and editor-in-chief
of Fiendish Books, passed away last
weekend. This happened on the night
before the Fiendish Book Festival
Daniel was organizing in San Antonio,
for which I was the front-running
guest of honor. I don't know if a lot
of people know this, but I was
actually one of the last people to see

him alive. He insisted on picking me up from the airport personally. That's the kind of fan he was of my work. Maybe one of my biggest fans. A case could certainly be made. That's all I'm saying.

POB: I never personally—

RJ: Now, I won't violate the privacy of what Daniel and I spoke about during that car ride, but I will say he was very grateful I could find the time to fly out for his festival. We had a lot of fun things planned for that weekend, which unfortunately never happened. He passed away the night before the fest was meant to begin. The rest of Fiendish had no choice but to cancel the event. At this time, it's unclear if they plan to reschedule the festival, or refund vendors and badge holders, or what. There's also a lot of rumors concerning the cause of death, which I've heard, but nothing official has been announced yet so it would be unprofessional for this podcast to seriously entertain any of them.

POB: I think that's probably—

RJ: I will say, however, that while Daniel did seem genuinely moved to finally meet one of his heroes—me—I would be lying if I didn't detect a certain sadness in his eyes. This was a man of sorrow. I won't sit here and speculate the cause, but I will say this, folks...I will say this: if you're someone who's out there right now feeling similar, if it feels impossible to move on, to wake up in the morning and put a smile on your faceplease, there's no need to suffer in silence. There are people out there who can help you. Take BetterHelp, for instance. BetterHelp is here for people just like you—just like Daniel Addams. I mean it, folks. Therapy isn't just for rich, successful people like myself. It's for the everyday man. It's for all of us. BetterHelp could be the very thing you've been looking for, the service you've been praying to come save the day. It's convenient, accessible, affordable, and entirely online. Fill out a brief survey and get matched with a therapist in no time. Visit BetterHelp dot com slash HORROR today to get ten percent off your first month. That's BETTER H-E-L-P dot com slash H-O-R-R-O-R...

ACT TWO
"HOLD MY BONES"

I believe in Mister Bones, and by the end of this book so will you.

EILEEN RECOGNIZED THE opening sentence. Daniel had certainly repeated it enough during the final weeks of his life. As she went through the book on her phone, other lines struck her as familiar. Things he'd said to her who knows how many times, all the while she was only half-paying attention, never truly as invested in any of this as he was—until it was too late. Until there was no saving him.

She read most of the manuscript while vaping in her car, parked alongside a neglected child's soccer field that never seemed to see much activity outside of stray dogs relieving themselves over gopher holes. There was a Walmart down the street that she relied on for food and restroom breaks. Sometimes she just walked aimlessly through the aisles attempting to pass the time. A person could only sit in their car so long before their spine started protesting. Getting anything accomplished in their—*her*—apartment felt unobtainable. Lately she only returned to bathe, sleep, or charge electronic devices.

Every time Eileen walked in through the front door, she saw the same thing waiting for her in the kitchen: Daniel, at the table, desperately cutting away at his own flesh.

MAX BOOTH III

She'd already contacted her landlord about exiting their lease early, but he was being a dick about the whole thing, so for now it looked like she was stuck there. She didn't have the money to fight it. Xiomara had launched a crowdfunding campaign for her to help with funeral costs, but there wasn't much leftover now that he was officially buried. A month or two of rent and that was probably being generous. Cremation would've been cheaper and far more logical, and Eileen regretted being too clouded by grief to have made the more sensible decision when it was time to do so. As if she wasn't still clouded by grief. As if this cloud even had an end to it. No, this was the type of storm that stretched on and on. A forever storm.

There was no running from weather like this.

Eileen twisted the cap off of the two-liter of Coke Zero stashed in her car and poured the last of it into her thermos of melting ice. What space remained in the thermos was then filled with several splashes of Jack Daniel's. The name of the whiskey was not lost on her. She pressed the lid of the thermos back on and shook the container in a circular motion before enjoying a long, content sip through the metal straw poking out of the top.

She took a break from reading the *Mister Bones* book and attempted to sneak a peek at the hundreds of notifications begging for attention on her overheated phone. Dozens of missed calls and texts—a few from family members, but mostly from Xiomara. She didn't want to speak to any of them right now. She didn't have anything to say to anybody. What *was* there to say? None of them were going to make her feel any better. There were no magical words that'd fix everything. Daniel was *dead*. Like, *no-longer-alive* dead. *Buried-in-the-ground* dead. He was fucking *gone*. There was no more *him*.

The calls and texts alone were enough to overwhelm, but when she glanced at the amount of unread emails and direct messages awaiting her, she forgot how to breathe. Everybody wanted a moment of her time. Many of them simply offering their condolences, and letting her know if there's anything they can do for her—*anything at all*—don't hesitate to let them know. As if there was anything they could realistically do. As if they didn't already know that. Empty gestures to make themselves feel better. She wondered what any of them would say if she responded with something like, *Actually, I need you to go clean out my apartment*, or, *How about paying back all of the book festival vendors for me?*

Because her inbox wasn't *just* full of condolences. The Fiendish Book Festival vendors were getting antsy. They wanted refunds on the table spots they'd reserved. Some of them were also demanding reimbursement for their plane tickets. A few badge holders had sent similar emails. Members of the Fiendish Discord assumed refunds were incoming for everybody who had spent money to attend the festival. Eileen didn't know how to break the news that there would be no refunds. Not for anybody. Eileen was broke, which meant the company was broke. There wasn't even a company anymore, as far as she was concerned. Fiendish had died with Daniel. She had zero interest in continuing it by herself—continuing it *without him.*

Could any of these people sue her? Probably so, she imagined. They'd taken everybody's money, spent it on book festival preparation—among other things—and then didn't make good on their end of the bargain. There was no festival. Eileen never officially canceled it. She didn't send out any updates the morning after finding Daniel. She didn't let anybody know anything. She called 9-1-1 and then, once the paramedics confirmed he'd ceased breathing, she had stopped functioning. Didn't reach out to anybody. People blew up her phone but she ignored them all. Sometime Sunday afternoon, Xiomara finally showed up to the apartment. They'd noticed everybody's concern online regarding Eileen's silence. First they tried to call, and when that didn't work they came knocking on the front door. Knocking didn't bring her to the door, so they let themself in. Eileen hadn't bothered locking it after the paramedics wheeled Daniel's corpse out of her life. They found her in bed, staring up at the wind chimes, feeling shattered, obliterated.

She'd read some of the shit people were posting online. How could she not? Even the assholes who weren't blaming her for Daniel's suicide were still, in some way, implying she was somewhat responsible. All the dumb things she'd drunkenly let slip at the bar. Those hadn't been strangers eavesdropping on her self-imposed therapy session. The building had been packed with writers and readers and publishers who had traveled all the way to San Antonio specifically to attend the festival. They all knew about Fiendish. They were aware of Eileen and Daniel. Some could've been described as industry acquaintances, but plenty of them she would have also considered friends. People they'd socialized with at previous conventions. People they'd joked with on Facebook for a decade-plus. These were the same people who overheard Eileen at the bar. The same ones who were now posting their half-remembered transcripts all over the internet, now that news of Daniel's unexpected death had been announced.

The cause of death had not been revealed anywhere—not in the *Alamo City Weekly*, and certainly not by Eileen—and yet the general consensus online had already settled on suicide. Which made the known timeline as follows: Eileen gets wasted at a bar while talking shit about Daniel, then later that night Daniel kills himself. The natural conclusion being that Daniel's actions were a direct consequence of Eileen's words. It wasn't true, of course. He'd started cutting himself before she ever made it home. He was already practically dead by the time she walked through the front door. The only way he would've known about Eileen's behavior at the bar was if someone had contacted him while it was occurring. She supposed that was possible. Most of these people were more Daniel's friends than hers. But still. He wouldn't have done what

I BELIEVE IN MISTER BONES

he'd done because Eileen had gotten a little too drunk and run her mouth off. It didn't make any sense.

She didn't even personally believe what had happened should be considered a suicide, despite what the police had concluded after taking a five-minute look around the apartment. Something drove Daniel to opening his own flesh, and it hadn't been depression. Delusion, maybe, although labeling it as such felt like betrayal. Daniel's intentions with the box cutter had not been to die. She had to believe that was true. Otherwise, she would be left with no choice but to join him.

Instead, he'd been *searching* for something—for evidence that he'd really been cursed, that his bones had been replaced by . . . some kind of boogeyman. He never wanted to die. He'd wanted to live. And unraveling his own flesh had been his way of doing so. He needed to see inside his arm. He needed to prove the bone was fake.

It was a terrible idea, and if Eileen hadn't abandoned him to go get drunk she would've been around to stop him. She would have told him to be patient, that they had an appointment the following week with a legitimate doctor, that they'd conduct every test conceivable to give him peace of mind. She would have assured him he was going to be okay. All he had to do was hold off until after the festival. Once the weekend was behind them, she would've been able to dedicate more time and energy into helping him. She would have done whatever he wanted her to do. As soon as the festival was over, she would've fixed him. It was a promise she'd made to herself over and over in the weeks leading up to the event, whenever Daniel displayed signs of being more unwell than usual. They had made too many commitments, sunk in too much money to do a half-assed job with this festival. They had to see it through.

It wasn't like she hadn't tried to get him help before then. They'd seen the pro bono doctor. He'd made his suggestions, and they were following them. They'd even purchased one of their terrible fruit pies. She made the appointment at his actual office with X-rays and all types of other machinery that would undoubtedly drive them into irreversible debt. It wasn't her fault nobody could see him until the latter half of March. None of this shit was her fault. She'd done what she could do, and what had Daniel done?

He'd killed himself, anyway.

He couldn't wait. He couldn't hold on.

That couldn't be on her. It couldn't be.

Then why did it feel like she was responsible for everything that had happened?

Why was she so convinced that Daniel was dead because of her and only her?

How had everything gotten so fucked?

And why did it feel like she'd just started her period?

There were probably tampons back at the apartment. The box was easy to picture—waiting under the sink for the next time its services were needed. She could have returned home and fetched them. If Walmart had been closed, she would've been left with no other choice. Fortunately, they were still open. She remembered, back before the pandemic, how it used to be twenty-four-seven. Nowadays, most places tended to close by ten. It was maddening, especially for nocturnal freaks like Eileen and Daniel. Well, nocturnal freaks like Eileen, at least. Daniel was no longer part of the equation, despite how frequently her brain kept lapsing on this fact. She imagined it would never quite readjust.

Why would she *want* it to?

Why would she want *any* of this?

The Walmart wasn't packed, but it wasn't empty, either. If they were open for business then there would be people there shopping. She popped in at all hours of the day to use the bathroom. It was never desolate. Even after hours, the parking lot saw plenty of activity. Unhoused people living in their cars. Stoned teenagers doing donuts while blasting unlistenable garbage. Unsubtle drug dealers brandishing their products. This place was never dead. It was an organism in constant flourish.

First stop: the bathroom. No way in hell was she about to waddle around this store in her current condition. She'd end up leaving a crime-scene trail behind her.

The entrance on the merchandise side of the building was locked. Something employees did after eight for whatever reason. Some kind of shoplifting prevention, if she had to guess. Of course this was also the side where the bathrooms could be found. She entered through the grocery entrance and carefully made her way across the front of the store, toward her destination.

At the water fountain between the men and women's bathrooms, a guy in a black hoodie straightened up and wiped his mouth dry. He must've been no older than twenty. There was something about the way he stared at her as she approached the area. She just knew he was going to say something, that he was going to try engaging with her. *Not right now*, she thought, *not ever*. She contorted her face in an attempt to look extra bitchy. It didn't work.

"Excuse me, ma'am," he said, holding out his hand to stop her, "could I trouble you for a moment of—"

"No," she said, maneuvering around him and slipping into the restroom. There was a brief, paranoid moment when she feared he might follow her inside. All he ended up doing was muttering something about her being a cunt and then thankfully fucked off to go bother somebody else. There wasn't even time to breathe a sigh of relief. Especially once she discovered the tampon dispenser was busted. Someone else had already come along and emptied it of its goods. Whatever. She could still make do. At least she was in a bathroom, and the bathroom was mercifully replenished with an abundance of paper towels. She wet a handful under the sink, then grabbed another wad of dry ones before seeking refuge in the ADA-accessible stall. The extra leg room would be more than necessary for the cleanup job she was about to take on.

Once she was finished and had temporarily plugged herself with enough toilet paper to replace the Hoover Dam, she stepped out and washed her hands. Splashed some water on her face to jolt her back to reality. Studied her reflection in the mirror and wondered if a ghost was staring back at her. *Is this me?* she wondered. *Is this really me?*

She took her time building up the courage to exit the bathroom. For one thing, it didn't matter how hard she scrubbed her pants, there was still visible spotting. But more importantly, she was afraid the hoodie guy might've returned to the water fountain. She imagined him standing out there, pretending to hydrate, just waiting on her to reemerge from her hideout. Whatever he was so eager to discuss with her, she wasn't interested in finding out. There was nothing she wanted to say or hear from anybody. Silence was what she needed. Silence . . . and tampons. Possibly some chocolate, too.

A display at the front of the store was decked out for Easter. The holiday was either coming up soon or had recently passed. Who could say? Eileen had stopped processing time the way normal people did. She wasn't even totally positive if it was March or April at this point. In her mind, there was *Before Daniel Died* time and *After Daniel Died* time. Anything falling on A.D.D. time was perceived through the blurry lens of a nightmare. Impossible to comprehend.

Either way, a bunny made out of chocolate and peanut butter sounded goddamn incredible. She added two of them to her hand basket. The urge to rip one of the boxes open right then and chomp off a bunny head was strong. Decapitation via teeth. The only appropriate method of consuming bestialized foods. She wasn't a religious woman by any stretch, but these peanut butter bunnies made Eileen almost relieved Christianity had been invented.

I BELIEVE IN MISTER BONES

The clothing area wasn't far from the seasonal section. She found a pack of cheap underwear and some sweatpants hanging from the discount rack, then beelined toward the feminine hygiene aisle, which she noted was parallel with the dog food. *Coincidence?* she wondered, and fantasized how she might sound if she were to bring it up to any of the apathetic clerks stumbling around the store counting down the clock. Would they call her crazy? Would they kick her out? Ban her from the premises, perhaps? Some of the employees here had surely come to recognize her. She showed up far too often solely to take advantage of their toilets not to have fallen on *someone's* radar. Was she breaking some rule here? Violating a loitering policy they could nail her on? She doubted any of them cared. She wasn't disturbing them. And sometimes she *was* a paying customer. Like tonight.

Tampons and pads acquired, Eileen turned to exit the aisle and found herself face-to-face with the hoodie guy from the water fountain. The one who she was seventy-five-percent sure had called her a cunt. Ninety-nine-percent sure. Ninety-nine-point-nine.

Standing in a wide enough stance to block her path. There was no dodging him without making physical contact—which he was fully aware of, judging from the smug smirk spreading across his highly-punchable face.

"Ma'am, I was hoping to—"

"Please move," she said, hating herself for choosing politeness in this moment. This man was invading her space. He was confronting her when she'd already made her feelings about confrontation plenty clear.

He opened his mouth to say something else, so she spun around with the intention of leaving from the opposite end of the aisle. Except, her path was blocked *that* way, too. Another guy of a similar age, also in a hoodie. This one held up a cell phone with both hands. Deep in focus. The camera lens was pointed directly at her. There was zero doubt in her mind that she was being recorded.

"What's going on here?" she asked, question directed at either of them.

The guy behind the camera didn't say a word. He wasn't meant to be acknowledged, she concluded. Whatever this was about, it concerned the other guy—the one who'd first noticed her back at the water fountain. So she focused on him and repeated her question.

"Yes, ma'am," he said, still grinning, "as I was trying to tell you earlier, my name is Marshall and my TikTok has over one hundred thousand followers. I was hoping to interview you real quick for my channel. If so, I can compensate you with the crypto equivalent of fifty US dollars. I assume you're already familiar with the blockchain."

It took her a moment to process what she'd just been told. She was aware that they were filming her *now,* regardless of her consent. "Um, get out of my way, please," she said, and gritted her teeth—again with the word *please!*—before brushing past him, using her hand basket as a barrier between their bodies.

She could hear them following, pleading for her to *wait up* and reassuring her it would only take *just a moment.* Something clicked in Eileen's head. The one guy—the way he'd smiled. His face was familiar, recognizable. She couldn't place him until he mentioned TikTok, but of course she'd seen his videos before. She didn't have a personal account or the app even downloaded on her phone, but a lot of his videos were cross-posted over to Facebook, and people lost their shit over them—especially members of the community group, since the guy was local to San Antonio. She and Daniel had often ridiculed this idiot whenever the algorithm decided to punish either of them by cramming his face in their newsfeeds. These types of streamers who confronted people in public were toxic scum. They were all the evidence she needed that society had rotted. An inbred offspring of reality television stretched to its most grotesque.

I BELIEVE IN MISTER BONES

Still—she never thought in a million years one of these fuckers would approach *her*. And tonight, of all nights, while mourning her dead husband and shopping for tampons—it felt almost comical, like this was all some cosmic prank.

Instead of the checkout lines near the front, Eileen found herself fleeing through the lawn equipment and gardening section just beyond the pet food. There was no destination in mind. She just wanted to escape the two guys following her with cameras. The thought of screaming *rape!* briefly crossed her mind, but the amount of different attention that might bring upon her sounded almost as grueling. She'd rather take her chances shaking them off by herself.

She turned into a new aisle a little too frantically. One foot tripped over the other and she went tumbling forward. She would have collapsed on her ass if not for a display of tubular crystals dangling within reach. It wasn't until they all started clanging against each other and conjuring a discordant orgy of whines that it dawned on her what, exactly, the display was selling.

Wind chimes.

Eileen backed away, unable to take her eyes off them as they did their horrible little dance. *Of all the aisles*, she thought, *of all the fucking aisles . . .*

The two guys were standing on either side of her now. They picked up on her sudden discombobulation and were eager to take advantage of it.

"Excuse me, ma'am," the guy said, the one from all the other videos she'd seen, "I just wanted to ask you a couple questions." Approaching her like they hadn't just spoken. Making it look like this was a natural meeting in the fucking wind chimes section of all places. "If you had to pick between the Holocaust and the slavery of African Americans, which one would you keep and which one would you erase from history?"

He waited a couple seconds for her to respond. She did

not. She didn't even look at him. All she focused on was the display in front of them. They were still clanging together and she was concerned they'd never calm again.

"Okay, next question," the guy said, and cleared his throat. "Which would you prefer? Universal free health care for all American citizens, or women's equal rights?"

He giggled a little as he asked this second question. The sound was enough to snap her out of the wind chimes' trance. "Wh-what?" she said.

He repeated it.

"I'm—I'm not doing this," she said. "I don't want to be interviewed."

She tried to walk around him, but he held up his hands to block her path. "But ma'am, what about your basket?" He gestured to her basket, which was spilled all over the floor. She had no memory of dropping it. "You're not going to just leave all of this stuff, right? What about the poor, underpaid employees who'll have to pick it up and figure out where everything goes?"

"Oh, shit," she whispered, and bent to retrieve the items.

As she was on the floor, the guy stood over her and continued his interrogation. "Oh, my," he said, a perverted kind of humor on the tip of his tongue, "this sure is an interesting assortment of goods you've decided to purchase at this time of night."

Before standing back up, Eileen took a moment to close her eyes and grit her teeth. A calming exercise that failed instantly. She stood and attempted to walk away. Predictably, the TikTok guy had no plans of letting her get away so easily.

"One last question, since I know it's your *special* time of the month, and I would hate to get you too hysterical," he said, still smirking. "If you had to break either both of your arms or both of your legs, which would you pick, and why? Bonus question, would you be willing to flash your boobs for my followers? We'll obviously censor the nipples."

I BELIEVE IN MISTER BONES

A mask of heat slipped over her face. "What the fuck did you just say to me?"

It was his turn to take a step back now. She matched it with a step forward. His smug grin disappeared. "Hey, I was joking. You don't have to show us anything you don't wanna."

"What do *you* know about breaking bones?" she asked, practically shouting at this point and not giving a single shit. Spit sprayed from her mouth and she hoped some of it splattered directly into the slimeball's eyes. "What do *any* of you mother*fuckers* know about breaking bones?" The question not just directed to the host and the cameraman, but also to all the voyeuristic creeps viewing the meltdown from home. Were these streams recorded *live*? Or were they uploaded at a future date? She didn't know how any of this stuff worked. Daniel always took care of the social media promo for Fiendish. She didn't want anything to do with it.

"Ma'am," the host said, "I think maybe you need to—"

"Have any of you *cock*suckers ever broken a bone in your whole miserable existences?" she screamed. "*Huh*?" When neither of them responded, she swung the hand basket at the host's head. The poor, stupid boy was too naive to believe she would ever try to hit him. The basket smashed into his unguarded face and he dropped like a sack of potatoes.

Behind her, the cameraman cried, "Hey, you can't do that! We're minors!"

She spun around and, in one smooth motion, collided the basket against the side of the cameraman's skull. He didn't go down as easily as his knucklehead partner. Two additional strikes from the basket were required. The phone flew out of his hands. The sound of its screen shattering against the floor was the best thing she'd heard all week, competing only with the sound of the two TikTok guys groaning at her feet.

"You don't know shit about breaking bones," she told

them, and spat on each of their bodies. "You don't know shit about anything. You're just pathetic. Both of you."

She stepped over the host's body and exited the aisle. Directly ahead of her was another display that caught her attention. Not wind chimes this time, though.

Shovels.

THE CEMETERY WAS easier to infiltrate than anticipated.

Eileen expected tall fencing sporting pointy ends wrapped with barbed wire. Ferocious guard dogs and blood-thirsty gunmen on patrol. Anything, really, to discourage the public from trespassing after hours. Even a sign with a vaguely menacing threat would've been better than nothing at all. The first—and, until tonight, *only*—occasion she'd stepped foot onto the property had been during the day, to witness a pair of hired gravediggers lower Daniel's casket into the earth. She'd understandably been a little too distracted to take note of the site's security precautions.

Would other widows have returned sooner? Lay some flowers down on the grave, maybe? Kneel in the grass and whisper a little prayer? No, not a prayer. Neither of them had ever been the praying type. Kind words, then. A sentence or two about how much she missed him. Like it would have done any good. She'd be better off alone at the apartment, talking to the wind chimes. At least those would respond with a little touch. Any further conversations she might engage in with Daniel would be one-sided.

There *was* a gate at the front of the cemetery. Unsurprisingly locked and preventing Eileen from driving her car onto the land. She could've parked in an empty lot next to the gate, but feared drawing unwanted attention from someone driving past. There was a hardware store up the road that had closed hours ago. Even better, its small parking lot was located on the backside of the building, disguised from curious eyes. She collected her bag of Walmart purchases, the shovel, and the bottle of Jack Daniel's before locking up the car. She hung the bag under the spade and leaned the shovel against her shoulder, cartoon-hobo-style. It was only a five-minute walk back to the cemetery.

It turned out the gate was designed solely to block vehicles. Pedestrians—anybody on foot, really—could easily slip through the wide gaps on either side of the structure. Was this a flaw in the architecture? Or was trespassing not a major concern here? Either way, she was grateful. Although she'd only been here once, it didn't take too long to locate Daniel's grave. Light from the moon and her cell phone guided the way. The mound still appeared fresh. It hadn't smoothly readjusted back into a flat piece of unassuming land yet. Anybody strolling past the spot could take one glance at it and understand someone had recently been buried here.

When the workers had dug up the hole originally, they had used heavy machinery with steel claws specifically built to scoop up large mouthfuls of dirt. Eileen wouldn't have access to anything that convenient. If push came to shove, she was sure she could figure out how to operate it, but the noise would be too loud at this time of night. Someone would hear. There would be an investigation before she'd finished what she'd come here intent on doing.

There was no point in wasting any time. She knew this wasn't going to be a quick and easy job. If she was lucky, she'd be finished and out of here by sunrise. Who knew what time people started clocking in at cemeteries. Hell, she still wasn't sure if the property was empty *now*. Why wouldn't this place have a guard stationed somewhere? She just had to hope that they were as bad at their job as most people.

I BELIEVE IN MISTER BONES

The first shovel strike was painless, as were the second and third plunges into the earth. But on that fourth go-around? The enormity of this project fully hit her. This was going to fucking suck.

She took a swig of whiskey and got back to work.

Her phone died about an hour into the dig. Eileen's own fault for insisting on keeping the flashlight tool enabled. It didn't matter. The moon was full tonight, just as eager to discover the truth as Eileen.

Several feet later, her body collapsed into the hole, defeated. How much time had passed was impossible to tell. Hours. It had to've been. Her lower back was howling. Her hands were on fire. Bleeding from her fingers, her palms. Bleeding between her legs. Bleeding everywhere. What the fuck had she been *thinking* coming out here like this? She spent the majority of her days and nights formatting books. Her body was not prepared for this level of exertion. She was more liable to die out here than reach any kind of satisfying conclusion. She'd been so goddamn stupid to believe otherwise.

Slowly, Eileen climbed out of the hole and sat on the edge. Her legs dangled in the air, feet just missing where she'd paused digging. She wiped her bleeding hands against her pants and tried not to worry about what kind of bacteria might be entering any open wounds. There had been a whole shelf of gardening gloves next to the shovel display. Why hadn't she grabbed a pair?

Nothing had been thought out. Everything that'd unfolded tonight had been fueled by desperation and spontaneity. Otherwise, she would have stopped and considered the logistics of what she planned on doing. Instead, she was doing the considering *now*, when it was far too late to give up and go home. She'd already committed. She had *bled*. She had opened herself up. At this point there was less dirt in the grave than flung alongside it. Stopping was no longer an option. A break, on the other hand, was more than necessary—to catch her breath, to dry her hands, to calm her heartbeat. To devour half of a bunny made out of chocolate and peanut butter.

It was then, as her teeth chewed mushy sweets, that a new worry crept up. Something she would have considered earlier if she hadn't been in such a rush to take action. This hole was already deep enough that she couldn't step out—climbing was required. It would only get deeper. Any further progress and she wasn't so sure she'd be able to pull herself back up to the surface. These things were six-feet deep, right? Wasn't that the one universal fact everybody knew about graves? There had been an HBO show named after it, for crying out loud. Well, Eileen sure as hell wasn't six-feet tall. Not even close. What would she do then? She'd be trapped. Stuck until someone noticed her in the morning. Was grave desecration a felony? What if the suspect failed in her quest to reach the casket? Realistically, she hadn't desecrated much more than dirt. Practically nothing, in the grand scheme of things.

She took a hit from her vape and contemplated the predicament. Things would've been a whole lot easier if she drove around with ropes in her trunk. Shit, imagine how pretty she'd be sitting right now if she'd thought to bring a ladder along. No, all she had in her trunk tonight was a lousy dolly. The same one Daniel and her had utilized countless times to set up at vendor events. A tool they hadn't realized was necessary until after tabling at the first-ever Alamo City Comic Con, and found themselves forced to carry numerous boxes through hordes of zombie cosplayers. In the moment, it'd felt like one of the most frustrating and stressful experiences of their careers. Neither of them went to sleep that night in a pleasant mood. But after enough time had passed, the memory of the incident was romanticized through anecdotal retellings. It had only strengthened their bond, mythologized their relationship. If they could survive the San Antonio Zombie Walk, then goddammit they could survive anything.

I BELIEVE IN MISTER BONES

Or so they thought, anyway.

Maybe the dolly wasn't completely useless. A half-assed idea formed. She imagined propping the dolly at an angle inside the hole, the bottom nose plate digging into the dirt while the handle leaned against the interior wall, so the whole thing was at a slight angle—but sturdy enough not to tip over on either side. Then she could just climb up it. Use the dolly as a mini ladder of sorts. It could work. It would *have to*. Plus, if she somehow succeeded in removing Daniel's body from the grave entirely, she could use the dolly to wheel him out of here—although she wasn't very optimistic about her own strength there.

She walked back to her car and collected it from her trunk. Then she turned the key in the ignition just enough to wake up the battery and display the time on the dashboard. Nearly three in the morning. What time had she gotten here? Hard to keep track of stuff like that. She'd come over straight from Walmart, right? The store closed at ten, and she remembered thinking how close she was cutting it when she first entered the bathroom—which meant she would've arrived at the graveyard sometime shortly afterward. Had she really been here almost five hours already? Jesus Christ, she needed to speed shit up.

Eileen wheeled the dolly back to the cemetery, glancing over her shoulder every couple seconds, flooded with paranoia that someone was going to catch her in the act. Every step forward blossomed a new ache within her body. She had no idea how she was going to continue digging. It would have been easier—and preferable—to simply crawl into what she'd already unearthed, and wait for someone to fill it back up with her still inside. The idea could stay in her back pocket for now. A last-resort kind of plan. Until then, she got back in the hole and resumed work with the shovel.

Wrapping her hands around the shovel had become significantly more painful since before this last interlude. Each additional shovel strike felt like someone hammering a nail into a mini-Eileen voodoo doll. It had to be done. She had to finish what she'd come here to do. Way too much progress had been made to give up now. That's what she kept telling herself, anyway. It seemed to work. She kept going at it. Even when her hands started bleeding again. Eventually she started sobbing, but that didn't stop her, either. She sobbed and shoveled. Snot and tears streamed down her face. She didn't bother wiping any of it away. Let it drip, far as she cared. It could all join the blood leaving her body elsewhere. Let it become part of tonight's ritual.

With her phone dead, she had no idea how much time had passed since retrieving the dolly from her trunk. Another couple hours, it felt like. The night sky looked exactly the same. Had the moon shifted? If so, she couldn't remember where it'd previously been positioned. The whiskey was gone. So were her peanut butter bunnies. She didn't feel drunk or high or anything beyond exhausted. All of the liquor and weed had sweated out of her system. She smelled so fucking rancid. How much deeper would she need to dig? How much deeper *could* she dig? There was nothing here. Witnessing the workers lower the casket into this grave had been nothing more than a false memory. Nobody had ever buried Daniel. Then where was his body? Where was his *corpse*? It was being hidden from her. Locked away in some secret storage facility by the government. What didn't they want her to discover? What were they terrified of becoming public?

The shovel hit something hard. A *thud* reverberated up the handle. Scared her so bad that she screamed. A scream on top of the sobbing. She hadn't stopped since she started. Something had broken in her, had come unraveled. There was no fixing it. She struck the shovel down again. Another *thud*.

"Oh, fuck," she cried out, collapsing to her knees inside the hole. The moment the shovel had made impact with the smooth, hard surface hidden in the dirt, Eileen became convinced that she'd just touched concrete. She

I BELIEVE IN MISTER BONES

remembered reading once how modern burials sometimes poured a cement vault around the caskets to prevent them from shifting in the earth. She *had* thought about this possibility earlier, when she first started digging, but after racking her memory she couldn't remember any such process occurring during Daniel's funeral. Wouldn't she have noticed? Wouldn't she have *known*?

Now, after hitting *something* with her shovel, she was sure she'd misremembered. They *had* poured in the cement. Of course they had. Daniel's casket was protected by a concrete vault, and Eileen had just wasted all night breaking her body for the unobtainable.

Story of my fucking life, she thought, then swept a handful of dirt out of the way to reveal the brown tarnish of a casket.

The sobbing ceased.

Oh.

Eileen stood back up and retrieved the shovel. A few minutes later, she'd finished clearing the remaining dirt covering the wooden surface. *Holy shit, holy shit.* A new gust of energy and refreshed determination possessed her. She tried to open the casket, but it wouldn't budge. At first, she blamed herself for standing on the lid. How the hell was she supposed to open this thing without also being on top of it? But after closer inspection, she concluded the lid was sealed shut. Glue, possibly, or a locking mechanism hidden in the darkness of the earth. She wasn't going to pull it open regardless of her position. It wasn't like she could remove the whole casket from the hole, either. Not without any equipment. This box was staying right where it was.

Grave-robbing was a logistical goddamn nightmare. How the fuck did people do this kind of thing? Did nobody break into graves anymore? A crime of the past, now extinct thanks to modern burial renovations?

No, there had to be a way. There fucking *had* to.

She scooped up the shovel and raised it high above her

head, sucked in a deep breath and then drove the tool down as hard as she could. Ignoring the pain in her hands. Ignoring everything.

The tip of the spade cracked the wood.

Yes, yes, yes.

She repeated the action, over and over, until thoroughly obliterating the lid of the casket. At least the top half of it. There was no reason to break open the whole lid, right? Shit, come to think about it, there had really been no reason to dig up the entire length of the grave. She could have saved so much time by unearthing only a portion of the length while maintaining the same depth, then broken through part of the coffin and pulled the corpse out through the hole. She could have been done *hours* ago.

Whatever. It didn't matter. Too late to dwell over hypotheticals. The job was done. The grave was dug and the casket was penetrated.

And inside the casket, there he was.

Daniel.

Still in his funeral suit, despite the fact that he'd *loathed* wearing suits. If Eileen had been a good partner, she would have let them bury him in his I CAME ON EILEEN shirt. One last good laugh.

His eyes were shut. For some reason she'd been expecting them to be wide open, staring up at her. Be grateful for small things, she supposed.

The smell hit her hard. She tried not to react too strongly, out of respect. Seeing him like this, she expected to start sobbing all over again, but there were no more tears left in her. She was done crying. The corpse beneath her was not her husband. This was just a body. A husk of decaying flesh.

Eileen fantasized, briefly, about somehow lifting the corpse from the busted-open casket and carrying him out of the grave. Forget the fact that she was utterly exhausted and on the verge of passing out. Disregard the condition of her

I BELIEVE IN MISTER BONES

bleeding, defeated hands. If none of that had been a factor, she still wouldn't have been able to accomplish this objective—not in a million years. For one thing, there was a considerable weight difference between the two of them. Had that changed much in death? She supposed it was possible. But there was still the getting-him-out-of-the-grave aspect that she considered near-impossible. She was already worried about getting *herself* out of the grave. Add a whole other person? A *dead* person? It wasn't going to happen.

But that was okay. She hadn't come here to steal his whole body.

Only a piece of it.

Gripping the shovel once more, she lined the tip of the spade against the corpse's left elbow.

The arm separated easily enough. Only a dozen or so strikes of the shovel. She reached into the casket and pulled the severed appendage out. It was still wrapped in the sleeve of his funeral suit. She tossed it out of the grave, followed by the shovel. Took one last look at his face. Waited for his eyes to suddenly pop open. For his mouth to unhinge into a nightmarish screech. Nothing happened. He was still dead.

She thought about saying something. Final words or whatever. If this were a movie, she would've had some emotional, unprepared speech bursting out of her right now. But this wasn't a movie and she didn't have anything to say. Even if she *could* think of something worthwhile, there was nobody else here to hear her. Daniel's listening days were long gone.

The dolly was already in the grave. Fortunately, she hadn't been stupid enough to leave it up in the grass. She tilted it to the side, so the top of the handle leaned against the dirt wall of the grave, and the nose plate sort of dug in between the corpse and the interior side of the casket. It wasn't as sturdy as she imagined it being, but the plan still worked. She boosted herself up and rolled out of the grave, gasping for air like a newborn emerging from the womb.

I BELIEVE IN MISTER BONES

It would've been so easy to fall asleep right there. She nearly did, too. A nice, cool breeze caressed her filthy face as she lay in the grass. The only thing that stopped her from giving in and closing her eyes was the knowledge that when she opened them again, there would undoubtedly be several cops hovering over her. It was already bad enough that she had no intention of filling the grave back up. She had reached her physical limit hours ago. The hole would have to remain unearthed. Someone would notice the scene, the missing arm, everything. Probably first thing in the morning. There would be an investigation. Would they suspect Eileen? Maybe, maybe not. Why would the wife want to do something as insane as desecrate her husband's grave? What possible reason would she have to steal his left arm? They'd probably chalk the whole thing up to drunk teenagers or aspiring satanists. A new stupid TikTok challenge, perhaps. Unless the cemetery had a security camera somewhere. Then she would be fucked.

Assuming there wasn't a camera, Eileen would make sure to collect anything incriminating before leaving. The bag from Walmart. The shovel. The dolly. The empty whiskey bottle. Anything else she might discover while cleaning up her mess.

But first—there was something else she had to do.

The whole reason she'd come here in the first place.

The arm.

She found it near the shovel, where she'd thrown both items. Removing the suit sleeve was easy, now that the arm was no longer attached to a body. The flesh was pale, and felt slimy. But she wasn't here to study what his skin felt like. She was more interested in what was hidden *beneath* the skin.

She approached Daniel's gravestone. The engraved text was simple and to the point. His name, his birthday, and his death day. No *Loving Husband* or anything like that. She couldn't remember anybody asking her what she wanted on the stone. She wouldn't have known how to answer if someone had, anyway. It was better this way. It's what he would have wanted. Or maybe he would have preferred cremation. She didn't know. They'd never talked about it before. They *should* have, but they hadn't. So oh well. This was what he got. He'd just have to live with it. Or not.

She held the arm from either end, then centered it over the top of Daniel's gravestone.

Hesitated a moment, knowing that there was no reversing what she was about to do. Once this was done, there would be no more ambiguity to hide behind. Either Daniel had been insane, or everything he feared had been true. There was only one way to find out.

So fuck it.

Eileen smashed the arm down.

SUNLIGHT **BROKE THROUGH** the night sky sometime while driving across town. The clock on Eileen's car radio claimed it was just past six in the morning. She'd been digging up Daniel's grave for nearly eight hours. That was a full shift at most jobs. No wonder she ached all over. No fucking shit everything hurt. She was filthy and damp and bleeding and her skull wouldn't stop screaming but goddammit she'd done what she'd set out to do. If only that meant things were over.

She devoured three breakfast tacos and a large ice water in the parking lot of a shitty fast food Tex-Mex restaurant. Anything would have tasted divine to someone in her condition. She tried not to curse herself too much for neglecting to bring water with her last night. How she hadn't passed out from dehydration was beyond her knowledge. She should have never been able to walk back out of that cemetery. Her body should've shut down hours ago. Somehow she had fought through total system failure. But now . . . now it was catching up to her. Consciousness would not last much longer.

Xiomara lived on the west side of San Antonio. She had only been to their house a handful of times, back when the two of them were still teenagers. Xiomara had moved out when they were in their early twenties, only to return in the wake of divorce. Both of their parents had passed away, leaving behind only Xiomara's abuela. She and Xiomara lived together now. A nurse visited once a month to check on things but otherwise she remained in Xiomara's care. The house was small, but unique. Not the way most new houses looked nowadays. Its exterior had a faded purple coating that Eileen had always loved. Nothing modern was allowed to be painted purple, it seemed. Everything was boring, bland.

Eileen parked in front of the house along the curb. The sun was already cooking her through the windshield. It would only get hotter. She sat behind the wheel for a few minutes longer with the AC blasting her face. Debated leaning her head back against the car rest and closing her eyes until Xiomara noticed her and woke her up. It was still too early for most people to be awake. Especially someone like Xiomara, who treasured sleeping in at all costs. The Ghouls & Boils shop didn't open until the afternoon—assuming this was a day it wasn't closed. Eileen couldn't remember the schedule. Maybe she'd never taken the time to learn in the first place. It didn't matter. Xiomara's car was in the driveway. Clearly they were home.

She got out of her SUV and walked across the front lawn. Daniel's detached arm hung from her grasp, swinging against the side of her thigh as she approached the front door. It did not worry Eileen that someone might spot her out in the open carrying a severed appendage. Nobody would believe it was real.

And they wouldn't be wrong, would they?

It *wasn't* real.

The way Xiomara gasped at her when they opened the front door told her everything she needed to know about how insane she looked.

"E*ileen*? What the hell happened to you? I've been trying to call you. Is that an *arm*?" They were dressed only in a black tank top and underwear, and had a look in their eyes like they'd just been sound asleep only a handful of moments ago. That look, naturally, had since been mutated to better fit someone staring at a severed arm.

Eileen's legs felt like rubber. The bottoms of her feet burned as if her shoes were constructed of hot coals. A small knife was being twisted in her lower spine, over and over. Every part of her wailed for relief. "Can I . . . can I come in? Please?"

Felt weirdly like a vampire asking a question like that. Unable to enter until invited. Desperate to find shelter before the newly-arrived sun finished cooking her flesh. But that wasn't everything, was it? She was a changed woman. She had seen things most people are lucky to never see. She possessed a deeper knowledge of the universe.

Xiomara stepped aside and allowed her to enter. What else were they going to say? *Actually, friend I haven't been able to get a hold of for over a week who just showed up on my porch at six-thirty in the morning covered in dirt and blood and holding somebody's arm, I have plans today—can you come back another time?* Of course they were going to let her inside.

The house was lit only by the television radiating across the living room. Seated in front of the set, watching a Spanish-dubbed episode of *The Simpsons*, was Xiomara's abuela. A faded, withered afghan draped over her lap as she glanced up at their new guest from her rocking chair. She smiled a toothless smile and said, "Hello, dear."

"Hi," Eileen said, weakly. Her lips had cracked and it was painful to open her mouth. Not that it mattered. The old woman's gaze had already returned to her cartoons.

"Come on, follow me," Xiomara said, and led her into the kitchen. They flipped on the light and gestured for her to sit down at the table. Eileen didn't need to be told twice. As she slowly bent her sore legs and lowered herself into the seat, Xiomara filled a glass with tap water and brought it over to her. "You, uh, want some coffee?"

She nodded as she gulped down the water. "Yes, please."

Xiomara eyed the arm still dangling from Eileen's hand. Its fingers scraped against the floor. "I think I'll brew a full pot."

Nobody said anything further until the coffee had finished and Xiomara had poured each of them a mug. They sat across from her at the table and waited for Eileen to say something. Like Eileen knew what the fuck to say. She could barely *think* right now, much less articulate.

"Sooo," Xiomara said, tapping their fingers against the coffee mug, "are you going to tell me what the hell's going on, or do we need to play some kind of questions-and-answers game?"

"He was right," Eileen said, on the verge of nodding off. She sipped her coffee with the hand not holding her husband's arm. It was hot enough to burn her tongue. She took a deeper drink. The pain jolted her awake. "Xio . . . he was *right*."

"Okay," Xiomara said, slowly. "I'm going to need you to elaborate a bit. *Who* was right about *what*?"

"Daniel."

They gulped and set down their coffee mug. "What was he right about?"

Eileen tossed the severed arm on the table between them.

The two of them stared at it for a moment, nobody saying anything, until recognition dawned over Xiomara.

"Eileen . . . who . . . uh, is that . . . like, a *real* arm? Who—it's not *his*, right? Don't tell me it's . . . "

"You know whose arm it is."

Their eyes widened and they shielded their hand against their mouth. "How the fuck did you even—what did you—how—?" They paused and reexamined the physical state of Eileen, then let out another gasp. They jumped up from their seat and took a step back, running their hands over their shaved scalp in a frenzy. "Eileen? What the fuck? Did you *dig him up*? Like, did you fucking dig up his goddamn grave? *Eileen*?"

She nodded.

I BELIEVE IN MISTER BONES

The answer shocked them so much that they had to lean against the kitchen counter to support their weight. "How the *fuck* did you do that?" they shouted, then glanced in the direction of the living room, concerned, and lowered their voice to an outraged whisper. "*Why* the fuck did you do that? Holy shit, Eileen. *Holy shit.*"

"I wanted to see," Eileen replied. "I *had* to see."

"You wanted to see *what*?"

She set down her coffee and picked up the arm. Without any hesitation this time, she bent the limb upward, until the decaying fingers made contact with the point of severance at the elbow. The shape formed a ghoulish oval. The bone did not crack. It barely struggled against her strength. It was more like manipulating a birthday party balloon.

"I don't understand," Xiomara said, and Eileen didn't believe them. They understood perfectly. But she explained it, anyway.

"It's not real," she said. "It's fake." And then, because she felt like it was worth repeating—now, and forever: "*Daniel was right.*"

There were plenty of knives in the kitchen. The problem was picking one sharp enough that Xiomara would be okay with immediately discarding it to the trash. "Because," they reminded Eileen, "there is not a goddamn chance in hell I will be reusing it in the future." They settled on an old steak knife with a blade stained from some ancient food that never fully scrubbed clean. It was good enough to do what needed to be done.

Xiomara held the arm firm against the kitchen table while Eileen cut into the rotting flesh. Before proceeding, Xiomara had insisted on putting down a towel between the arm and wooden surface. They'd still have to eat on this thing, after all.

MAX BOOTH III

The knife cut through the skin like it was nothing. Butter wasn't an appropriate comparison. Solidified pudding, maybe. Daniel had already splayed open a starting point at the wrist for them, where he'd been sawing before succumbing to blood loss. Within five minutes, Eileen had removed the bone from its putrefied casing. What she pulled out resembled the standard type of arm on any given skeleton prop. The bones were white—whiter than she imagined. Like they were painted that way. A hand, connected to the radius and ulna, which were connected to the elbow section—the humerus? Whatever the hell it was called. The terminology was inconsequential. This wasn't a *science* issue. The freaky shit they were dealing with here belonged to the strange and fantastical.

"What are you girls doing?"

Xiomara's abuela stood in the kitchen archway, neck craned to peek at the table. They had not done a very good job of hiding their project from view of anyone who might've entered the room.

"Um," Eileen said.

Xiomara sighed and tossed the shedded skin in a nearby trash can. "Abi, go back to the living room. We're busy with something."

"But I need my juice."

"I'll bring you your juice. Go on."

She shook her head and started waving her finger at Xiomara. "You don't pour it like how I like it."

"What does that even mean? How many ways are there to pour juice?"

The old woman glanced at Eileen and gave her a look like, *Do you see what I have to deal with?* If she noticed the skeletal arm in Eileen's hands, she wasn't letting on.

Xiomara let out another dramatic sigh and stomped over to the sink to wash their hands, then brought down a clean glass from the cupboard and removed a carton of diet cranberry juice from the refrigerator.

I BELIEVE IN MISTER BONES

Their abuela stepped forward. "You better just let me do it."

"I *got it*—all right?" Xiomara made a big show of slowly twisting off the cap and pouring the juice to the halfway point of the glass, then handed it to her. "Go ahead. Taste it and tell me if I did it wrong."

She stared at the glass for a long moment, as if afraid to consume it, then raised it to her lips and sipped.

"Well?"

The old woman frowned. "It's not how I would have done it."

Xiomara exhaled a deep, calming breath. "Abi, you gotta get out of here. Okay? I love you, but you gotta scram."

She held up the juice. "What should I do with this?"

"You should take it with you and drink it when you're thirsty again."

"I don't think I'm going to want . . . *this*."

"Abi. Please."

She looked back to Eileen and gestured at the glass. "Are you thirsty, dear?"

"*Abi!*"

"Okay, okay!" she exclaimed, and whispered, "Don't have a cow, man," before hobbling out of the kitchen to the living room, reluctantly carrying the juice with her.

Xiomara apologized for the interruption and sat back down at the table. Their irritation faded as they were reminded of the reason for Eileen's visit.

Eileen, who had already returned her attention to the arm. Released from their fleshy prison, the arm bones bent with less resistance now. The bones were soft, and cool to the touch. "What does this feel like to you?" she asked, sliding the arm across the table to Xiomara.

They pressed their fingers against the limb from all angles. Soft at first, and then harder. "It's like . . . clay?" they said, uncertain. "Like the shit teachers would let you play with during art class. You know, like . . . fuckin' *plasticine*?"

"Yeah, that's what I was thinking, too."

Xiomara brought it up to their nose and sniffed, then jerked away, grimacing. "Smells fucking awful."

"Well, it *did* just come out of a decaying corpse."

"Do you think his whole skeleton is like this?"

Exactly the question Eileen had been mulling over. "Yeah," she said, and believed it. "I think by the end there, this stuff had overtaken him."

"How was he able to even stand, or walk around, or . . . ?" Xiomara drooped their head and fell silent, then whispered, "Or . . . you know, do *anything*?"

"I don't know how it works," Eileen said, omitting, *And I don't think we ever will*.

"What I don't get is, like, wasn't his body *looked at* by anyone? You know, like, *after* he died? Wasn't there an autopsy or whatever?"

Eileen shrugged. "I don't think they do autopsies on suicide victims."

"But *still* . . . wouldn't *someone* have noticed? How did he just get *buried* like this without anybody saying anything?"

"Maybe nobody cared enough to pay attention," Eileen said, "and he just . . . slipped through the cracks."

Xiomara fooled around with the bones some more. Bending them and experimenting with what shapes they could be manipulated into. It did not take long for Xiomara to morph Daniel's severed arm into an erect penis with two massive testicles.

"You mind if I keep this?" Xiomara asked, holding up the pseudo-cock.

"I . . . think I need to shower," she said.

"You wanna take this with you?"

"Uh, I think I'm okay."

"Suit yourself," they said, and resumed fine-tuning the sculpture.

I BELIEVE IN MISTER BONES

The water was scalding as it slapped against her flesh. Eileen's body was a chaotic road map of open cuts. Most of them she had no idea how they'd even spawned. The mysterious consequences of excavating your husband's grave and removing one of his arms, she supposed. She could've tweaked the temperature and made the water a little cooler, but what would've been the point in that? The pain was good. The pain was necessary. It was a reminder of what she'd done, what she'd accomplished.

Accomplished?

What exactly had she accomplished here? She dug a big hole and discovered something Daniel had been trying to tell her for over a month. If she'd stopped and actually *listened* to what he had to say instead of disregarding his concerns as mental illness or something else only a doctor could treat, then maybe they could have figured out a real solution before it was too late. Maybe they could have beat this thing.

No, this pain wasn't a reward. It was a punishment. A reminder of what could've been avoided—if only she hadn't behaved like the spouse in practically every fucking horror movie that's ever been shot. Daniel hadn't needed a Scully. He'd needed a Mulder. And she had let him down. He was so determined to prove to her that this shit was real, that his bones had been swapped out by some goddamn boogeyman, he'd literally killed himself trying to find evidence.

Well, now she had that evidence, but what was she supposed to do with it now? Daniel was gone. There was no bringing him back. No erasing what had already been done. Taking it the police wouldn't solve anything other than incriminating herself for corpse desecration. It probably didn't matter that the corpse had once been her husband. 'Til death do us part, and all that. So then what was she supposed to do with the arm? What was she supposed to do with the *knowledge*?

This Mister Bones fucker . . . this *boogeyman* . . . he'd infiltrated their lives and stolen Daniel from her. He'd destroyed not one life but two. All for what? Fresh bones? Did he *eat* them? What was he *doing* with these bones that he so desperately craved? The novella hadn't gone into specifics there. The narrative's lore reveled in its ambiguity. Goddamn she yearned for the opportunity to be in the same room as the scumbag who'd slipped the manuscript into their inbox. She'd already abandoned the idea that this whole thing had been a submission for them to consider for publication. The fact that they were publishers was irrelevant, she suspected. There were no *business* aspirations involved here. It was why the sender had chosen a moniker as ridiculous as August Skeef and hadn't bothered responding to any of Daniel's messages. The intention had not been to strike up a partnership. This was not a two-sided operation. The book wasn't a submission.

It was a curse.

And Daniel hadn't been the first one affected by it. She thought about the guy who had video-called him. The one who'd ripped his own jawbone off. Eileen hadn't believed that had happened, either. A trick video, she'd suggested. Some kind of AI voodoo. That's what she told him. Refused to believe otherwise. The alternative was too horrifying to accept. But she accepted it now. She accepted it all. Including the other stories documented in the *Mister Bones* book. The ones that spanned over a century of violence.

She wished she could confront the little freak herself. Mister Bones. The boogeyman. This Babadook, Freddy Krueger wannabe bitch. Drag him out of whatever hiding nest he'd set up shop in and make him answer for all the horrors he'd put the two of them through. Not just them but everybody else, too. All of his victims. Was there a way to kill him? Nothing in the book presented any information regarding weaknesses or viable killing methods. Intentional, she knew. The narrator wanted to sell Mister Bones as this unstoppable nightmare. But that was bullshit. Nothing was unstoppable. *Everything* could be killed. There wasn't a thing in this world, or any other, that lasted forever.

If Daniel hadn't been this creature's first victim, then it was safe to presume he wouldn't be his last, either. There would be others. The curse would continue spreading. It might take some time, but there would be another bone broken under the extremely specific circumstances required to summon Mister Bones, and the cycle would begin all over again until the poor son of a bitch unlucky enough to have done the summoning had lost every bone in their body.

Unless Eileen ended it, once and for all.

But how the hell was she supposed to do that?

It wasn't like she could infiltrate Marrowland and kill him on his home turf.

She didn't even know how to find this fucker.

Well, that wasn't true, was it? If she knew *anything* about Mister Bones, it was how to find him. Or, more accurately, how to make him find *her*.

She didn't think about it. Didn't consider the pros or cons. Her brain was empty. Wiped clean. What she did next was fueled purely by her heart.

It took a total of three kicks to the bathroom faucet before she could no longer move her big toe. By then, Xiomara had rushed in to investigate the commotion. Evidently she'd been screaming. She hadn't noticed.

"What *happened*?" Xiomara shouted, turning off the shower and helping Eileen sit in the tub. Their eyes were wide with panic—with fear. "What's *wrong*?"

"My toe," Eileen cried out, pointing down at her foot. It was bent at a nauseating angle, and already becoming discolored. "Is it broken?"

They followed her gaze to the toe, and gasped. "Jesus Christ, Eileen, what the fuck did you do?"

What needs to be done, she might've replied, if she'd been coherent enough to form a full sentence. Instead, she continued crying, and didn't stop—not fully—until an hour later, once the sleeping pills Xiomara gave her post-shower finally kicked in, and she passed out in Xiomara's bed.

It was nighttime when she regained consciousness. The windows were black, like they'd been painted that way. No longer at Xiomara's house but back at her own apartment. The wind chimes were gone. Had Xiomara come in and removed them all for her? She couldn't remember, but she was grateful for their absence, all the same. She wasn't sure how she would've reacted if the first thing she saw upon opening her eyes had been wind chimes. The ceiling was also painted black, she realized. As were the walls. Had they always been this way? It was difficult to recall. Everything seemed perfectly normal yet subtly disquieting. She was naked. Had she gone to bed without any clothes on? It didn't seem likely. She hated sleeping in the nude. But why? There had to've been a reason. But what was it? What was the reason? *Rise and shine*, spoke a voice from across the apartment. Daniel's voice. Only, no, he wasn't across the apartment. He stood in front of their bed. He was wearing a suit. It was *filthy*. What little of his skin was exposed looked so, so pale. His eyes were concealed by the shadows but she could still feel him watching her. *Rise and shine,* he said again. Now he was bending forward and rubbing her legs. Her calves. Her ankles. Her feet. She stretched her limbs for him, wanting him to touch her all over, hopeful that he would lean a little bit farther and plunge his face between her thighs, maybe crawl all the way inside her and wear her skin as a coat. He stood back up. Now he was nude, too—except, no, wait, that wasn't exactly right, was it? He *hadn't* removed the suit. It was still on him—partially. The rest had . . . what? Melted off. Liquified. But not just the suit. His *flesh*. Daniel's flesh had turned to goo. It was dripping off his skeleton, revealing overly-white bones beneath. He had never looked sexier. She desperately needed to fuck him. He had her left foot in his skeletal hand. Rubbing the arch softly as he guided it toward his face. He was standing tall and she was still on her back. Her leg was extended straight up for him. Exposed. Vulnerable. Feverish. His eyes were no longer hidden. She could see everything now. Daniel's eyeballs were murky, like they'd been spiked with cataracts. Half of his face had slipped off his skull. But he still had lips. He still had a tongue. And he put all of this to good use by slipping her big toe into his mouth. He started sucking and licking and slurping and kissing and nibbling and she moaned and begged for him to never stop and she could feel the bone in her toe suctioning out from her skin, detaching from the rest of her own skeleton and becoming part of *his* skeleton, and the ensuing orgasm was so strong that the bed itself was vibrating, the whole goddamn apartment was shaking. A warm wetness gushed out from between her legs with the intensity of a firehose. More than warm. *Hot*. It burned coming out of her but it wasn't painful. Oh god no it wasn't painful at all. She thought maybe she was pissing, but the liquid was . . . red. It was *blood*. Her blood. Erupting out of her. Spraying against Daniel as he feasted on her toe, ravenous. Soaking into him and lubricating his glistening skeleton. Turning the white a beautiful, erotic red. And all she wanted, all she truly needed, was for Daniel to never—

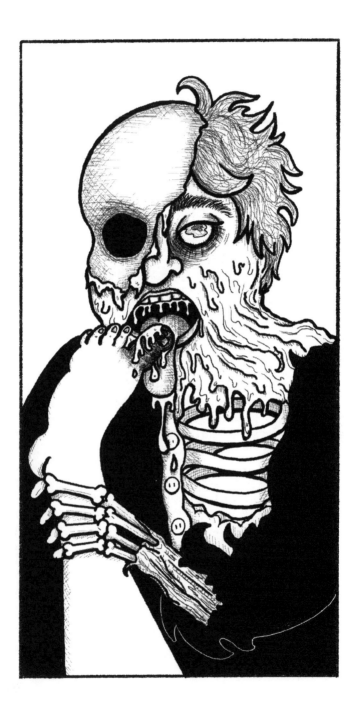

BACK AT XIOMARA'S HOUSE. Eileen had never left, after all. When would she have? *Why* would she have? She was never returning to that apartment again. To hell with the lease. She didn't care anymore. That place was just as cursed as Daniel's bones.

She pulled the blanket off and glanced down at her foot. It looked *fucked*.

But it also felt weird. Not in the way she expected.

None of it hurt—not anymore.

The pain had been replaced with a curious numbness. Like the front half of her foot had fallen asleep. The whole thing *tingled*.

All very similar to how Daniel had described various parts of his body leading up to his death.

She realized she was naked and barely remembered falling asleep. Xiomara had helped her out of the tub and given her a towel to wrap herself with, then some medication to wash down with a fresh glass of water. What happened after that? Xiomara had told her to use their bedroom, to lay down and try to rest, and they'd talk more when she woke up. She remembered she couldn't stop crying. The pain in her toe had been agony. Getting dressed never crossed her mind. She must've collapsed in bed and curled up under the covers and sobbed until the pills kicked in. It made sense. The only logic for why she would have gone to sleep without putting on any clothes. Sleeping in the nude usually gave her bad dreams. She didn't know why. Something with being vulnerable, she supposed.

Bad dreams.

It was already fading, whatever she'd dreamed. The details were fuzzy. She remembered Daniel being in it, though. Something with his flesh. His skeleton. She'd woken up horny. What the fuck?

The Walmart bag was on the dresser across the bed. Xiomara must've brought it in for her. Now Eileen regretted not adding more clothes to her purchase. At least she had the sweatpants and underwear—and, most importantly, tampons and pads. She turned back to the bed and cautiously lifted the sheets. *Fuck.* Xiomara was going to be pissed. Whatever. Nothing that couldn't be resolved with some cold water and hydrogen peroxide.

Putting any weight on her left foot felt strange—*risky,* even. Like she was daring her ankle to give out with every step. Made her paranoid. How much control did she really have of her own limbs? Who—or *what*—was really in charge here?

So far, the numbness hadn't spread beyond her foot. Not that the rest of her body wasn't suffering from an entirely different form of torture. Everything ached. Her spine was screaming. An impossible knot twisted in her stomach. Flames sizzled her calves and arms. She thought the pain wouldn't have gotten any worse than it'd been last night while doing the actual digging. Somehow, sleep had only intensified everything. She needed . . . she didn't know what she needed. There wasn't a medication invented that could fix what she was experiencing. She was just going to have to deal with it. Let the pain serve as a reminder of what she was doing, and why.

She searched through Xiomara's closet for a shirt that might fit. The two of them had never exactly worn the same size—even before Xio's top surgery. Now? Not a chance any of this shit was going to work. Except for maybe . . . there, almost hidden away in the closet, an oversized black jersey.

I BELIEVE IN MISTER BONES

The white head of a bull blowing steam out of its nostrils was stitched across the chest. Unmistakable as the logo for the San Antonio Rampage, even for someone like Eileen who'd never watched a second of hockey in her life—professional, or otherwise. It would fit. That was all that mattered. She collected it from the hanger, tossed it in the bag with her pants and underwear, then wrapped the bath towel around her waist before tiptoeing into the bathroom across the hall. There was no point in dressing until she'd had a chance to clean up some of the horror movie between her thighs.

Afterward, she found Xiomara on the couch in the living room. They had a laptop out on a TV tray, scrolling down some dimly-lit webpage. Their abuela was still watching Spanish-dubbed episodes of *The Simpsons*. A digital clock beneath the television set claimed it was a quarter 'til six. Nearly the whole day had been slept through.

Nobody noticed her standing there, so she cleared her throat and said, "Hey."

Xiomara's abuela nodded at her, smiling a big, toothless smile, before returning her attention to *The Simpsons*. She had a full glass of diet cranberry juice on the table next to her rocking chair. Eileen wondered which one of them had poured it this time.

"That's my jersey," Xiomara said, staring up at her from the couch like someone might behold a roadside oddity.

"It was all I could find that fits."

"Just be careful with it, okay? Don't go, uh, necromancing in it or anything. It's an antique."

"An antique?" She sat on the couch next to them, wondering where she'd set her phone. The battery had died back at the cemetery. She hadn't *left it* there, had she?

"Yeah, dude. The Rampage aren't even a team anymore."

"What are you talking about? What happened?"

"I don't know. They got sold or something. Las Vegas, I think? Renamed and everything."

"Who would want to play ice hockey in Nevada?"

Xiomara laughed. "Who would want to play ice hockey in Texas?"

They made a fair point.

"Hey," Eileen said, "have you seen my phone?"

Xiomara reached over the armrest of the couch and unplugged it from some out-of-sight charger and handed it to her. "Thought you'd want it juiced up."

"Thanks," she said, taking one look at the number of unread messages flashing at her and clicking the power back off.

"I should probably confess something," Xiomara said, nervous sounding. Purposely avoiding eye contact.

"Confess what?"

"When you were sleeping, I got on your phone and went through your email."

Eileen twisted reflexively in her seat. "Um, why would you do that?"

"Don't worry. I didn't read anything private. At least, I tried not to."

"Xio, what were you—"

"I used it to forward myself the book."

"*What* book?"

"You know. The book."

"*Mister*—"

"Yeah."

"But why would you—"

"That's why I've been trying to get a hold of you."

"To read it?"

They hesitated, choosing their words carefully. "Well, to compare."

"To compare *what*?" Eileen resisted the urge to reach forward and strangle the information out of them.

"To, um, well . . . to compare the other version I found online."

I BELIEVE IN MISTER BONES

"*What* other version?"

They licked their lips and finally made eye contact with her. "The first draft."

"The *what*?"

From across the living room, their abuela turned around and shushed them, then passive-aggressively raised the television volume.

"Maybe we oughta take this to the kitchen," Xiomara suggested.

"Where's the arm?"

The kitchen table was suspiciously absent of her dead husband's fake arm.

"I couldn't keep looking at it," Xiomara said, preparing a fresh pot of coffee. They lightly kicked the cabinet door beneath their sink. "It's under there, stashed in a trash bag."

They'd set their laptop on the table when the two of them first entered the room. Eileen was seated next to it and kept trying to steal glimpses of the screen.

"Don't, uh, look at that yet," Xiomara said, somehow spotting her with their back turned. "We gotta talk about a few things first—before I show you anything."

"Talk about what?" Eileen asked. "Xio, what the fuck is going on?"

They sat at the table across from her. For a moment, the only sound in the kitchen came from the coffee pot percolating. Then they asked her how her toe was.

"It hurts," Eileen said. "How do you think it is?"

"Does it, though?"

"Does it what?"

"Does it really hurt?"

Eileen's turn, now, to take her time responding. "Not like earlier." She cleared her throat, focusing on the sensations emitting from her foot. "It doesn't hurt at all, actually."

"It's numb, though—right? Like it's fallen asleep. Maybe your whole foot?"

"Most of the foot. Not the whole thing."

"And why did you do it?"

"Why did I do what?"

"Was breaking your toe not on purpose?"

"Xio, you said you found another—"

"*Eileen*," they said, stern, "please answer the question."

"You know why I broke it."

"Punishment or revenge?"

"What the hell does *that* mean?" Eileen said, feigning confusion.

"Are you trying to summon Mister Bones so he'll kill you—or so you can kill him?"

The question sounded so goddamn ridiculous coming out of their mouth. She felt even sillier answering it sincerely: "I *am* going to kill him."

"Do you know how? Like, what's your plan?"

"I don't—no, *enough*," Eileen said. "Tell me what's going on. You're freaking me out, Xio."

Xiomara nodded, like *fair enough*, and got back up to fix them each a cup of coffee. With their back turned on her again, they said, "Well, like I said. I've been trying to contact you. I've called, I've banged on your door—"

"I haven't been home."

"Well, yeah, I gathered that."

"I've been sleeping in my car."

"Oh?"

"In a field."

Xiomara paused and glanced over their shoulder, brow cocked. "Well, you do you, babe." They brought the mugs over to the table and sat across from her. "So, while you've been doing . . . uh, all of that, I've been going a bit crazy online."

"Crazy how?"

"Like, Bernstein-and-Woodward crazy. I could not be deeper in the rabbit hole right now."

I BELIEVE IN MISTER BONES

Eileen bit her tongue, then sipped the coffee Xiomara had fixed her. Anything to stop herself from screaming, *JUST FUCKING TELL ME ALREADY*.

"Especially now that I've gotten a chance to read the book y'all received, so thanks for that," Xiomara continued. "Plus, obviously, after seeing . . . uh, that." Their eyes flicked to the sink cupboard for a second. "Um, thanks for that, too, I guess."

"What did you find out?" Eileen asked. "Daniel did the same thing. He searched and searched online. He never found anything besides that guy on Twitter, and he didn't find him. *He* found Daniel." On top of that, Eileen silently added, she had been doing the same thing on her phone while hiding at the field in her car. There was nothing of any use online. Nothing that was going to help them.

Xiomara nodded, like they expected Eileen to say that. "Right, totally. It was the same with me, for the longest time. Lots of red herrings. Things that referenced the name Mister Bones but didn't have anything to do with *our* Mister Bones."

Eileen didn't care for the way they'd used *our* in that last sentence. As if Xiomara and Eileen somehow shared ownership rights over the miserable fuck who had killed her husband.

"For example," Xiomara said, "I'm sure you guys also found that Mr. Bones' Wild Ride thing."

"It was some kind of meme, right?"

They cringed at the response. "Kind of, I guess? It was a ride some 4chan dipshit had customized in a game called *RollerCoaster Tycoon*. The whole shtick was, like, anybody who boarded the coaster was on it for a really long time, or something? Or maybe it never ended. Someone wrote a creepypasta about it afterward and it became this whole thing. Anyway, not related to our Mister Bones."

"Daniel and I already figured that."

"There's also some Star Wars android with the same name."

"And a comic book villain, right?" Eileen said, remembering all the research she'd done in her car, high and drunk off her ass.

"Mmm-hmm. DC, I think? I saw a picture of him. Motherfucker isn't even a skeleton."

"Yeah, we found all of this. None of it led anywhere."

"Frustrating, right?" Xiomara said. "Like, how the fuck can there just be *nothing*? Shit, I nearly gave up, too. Until, that is, I checked the *ACW*." Meaning the *Alamo City Weekly*. "Did you ever take a look at the article they posted about you guys?"

"The obituary?" She wasn't sure if that could be considered an obituary. More of a death notice, than anything. If there was a difference. She didn't know. "They asked me for a quote, but I didn't know what to say. I still don't."

But Xiomara was shaking their head. "No, not that. I mean the interview they did with y'all to promote the festival."

"Oh." It had gone live a few days before everything happened. In truth, she'd forgotten it existed. "What about it?"

"Well, at the end of the interview, Daniel gave a shoutout to . . . you know, the *Mister Bones* book, and asked for people to contact him if they knew anything about the author."

"Oh, my god," Eileen said. "I forgot he did that. Wait, nobody's contacted us, though. I've been checking all of the emails." Which was only sort of true. Most of the time, she didn't make it past scrolling through the unread subject lines before getting overwhelmed and closing the app.

"You know how everybody always says not to read the comments?" Xiomara said, giddy with excitement. "It turns out, at least under these extremely specific circumstances, reading the comments was a very good thing."

They clicked one of the numerous tabs opened on their

I BELIEVE IN MISTER BONES

laptop and pushed it across the table for Eileen to get a better look.

"Inaugural Fiendish Book Festival brings horror authors to San Antonio this weekend" the headline read.

There was only one comment, from a now-deleted user. Miraculously, the content of the comment itself had remained unmoderated:

wtf i havent thought about bones since the fugue steaks days?? lmaooo

"Is this supposed to mean something to me?" Eileen asked, reading the comment over and over and failing to decipher anything recognizable.

"Nah, it looked like gibberish to me, too," Xiomara said. "But there was something about that phrase—'fugue steaks'—that kept gnawing away at me."

"I assume they meant fugue *states*, right? It's a typo, isn't it?"

"I mean, that's what *I* assumed, yeah. But still. It *is* a pretty funny typo, don't you think? I couldn't get it out of my head. Kept saying it out loud at random times throughout the day. Fugue steaks. *Fugue. Steaks.* How great of a name would that be for, like, a weirdo meat company? You just *know* they'd be based somewhere in Austin, right?" They laughed, then got serious again when Eileen didn't join in. "Anyway, I did some digging around for *fugue steaks*. Obviously at first Google tried giving me the *did you mean 'fugue states'?* runaround. Then I filtered out the autocorrection filter, and started seeing something interesting."

"Something interesting for . . . fugue steaks?" Eileen said, feeling like they'd accidentally fallen off track somewhere. What did any of this have to do with Daniel, or Mister Bones?

"I started coming across these *references* to fugue

steaks on different sites. Usually on forums, sometimes old blog posts. Nothing that ever really explained what they *meant*. Just offhand comments. Except, sometimes, the phrase was used almost like . . . nostalgically? For example: I found this writer's old video game blog, and one of the comments on an article he wrote about *Resident Evil* said something like, 'I've been following your shit since fugue steaks, keep up the great work.' Which is still . . . weird, right? Like what does that mean? What the fuck is fugue steaks?"

"I assume, since we're having this conversation, you figured it out."

Xiomara lit up like a Christmas tree. "You're goddamn right I figured it out."

"Well? What did you do?" Eileen instinctively glanced toward the sink cupboard, then back at them. "What does it mean?"

"Well, what I did was the simplest, no-brainer shit imaginable."

"Which was?"

"I typed in fugue steaks dot com into my web browser."

"What came up?" Eileen asked. Her friend's excitement was contagious. Her legs were bouncing, jittery. Casting tingling jolts of numbness up her foot.

"Nothing came up," Xiomara admitted, but continued grinning like they had another trick up their sleeve. "Nothing came up, *unnntiiiilll* I tried entering the same URL into the Wayback Machine."

"The *what*?"

"The, uh, Wayback Machine?"

"I don't know what that means."

Xiomara threw up their hands, feigning outrage. "Eileen, come on, dude. We're the same age!"

"Okay, and?" Eileen shrugged, already annoyed by this digression. "Do you know how to eliminate widows and orphans on a novel in QuarkXpress? I know my shit and you know yours, so just tell me what it means."

I BELIEVE IN MISTER BONES

"QuarkXpress? What fucking year do you think it is right now?" They dropped their jaw in horror, choking back laughter. "Wait, how to do *what* to widows and orphans?"

"It's a formatting thing, it's not important," Eileen said, joining in on the restrained laughter and hating herself for finding humor in a life post-Daniel. "The Wayback Machine?"

"Oh, yeah." They recomposed themself and drank some coffee. "It's part of the Internet Archive, and it's like . . . a time machine, I guess? In the dorkiest way possible, really. Not, like, a *real* time machine or anything. It just preserves copies of web pages that no longer exist. So, for instance . . . if there *used* to be a website called Fugue Steaks, and then the owner removed all of its content and shut it down, or maybe stopped paying their hosting bills and it expired into the ether, theoretically one should still be able to access certain remnants of this site via the Wayback Machine."

"Theoretically?"

"Okay, that's exactly what I did, and what do you know? The shit worked."

They clicked another tab on the laptop, revealing a shoddily-designed website with half of its images replaced with gray squares.

FUGUE STEAKS! the top banner proclaimed, followed by a subtitle: *YOU'LL FORGET YOU EVER VISITED US.*

To the far right of the banner was a logo drawn with MS paint of a mortified cow in the process of fading from existence.

The rest of the homepage consisted of a grid. On the left, sprawling down, was a row of category links like Deep Thoughts, Aimless Rambling, News, Movies & TV, Music, Books & Comics, Gamers Corner, etc. To the right of these links were other rows tallying how many topics and posts could be found in each category. The farthest row on the right listed the latest post someone had made in the category, along with a date and time.

"What the fuck is this?" Eileen said, even if she already knew. It was just the only question she could coherently form in her brain at the time.

"It's a message board, dude," Xiomara said. "Surely you remember those, at least."

"Yes, but—"

"—But what does it have to do with our situation?"

Exactly the question she wanted to ask. She nodded and waited for further context.

"You need to read something," Xiomara said. "I could try to explain it, but I think it's better if I just show you."

"Read *what*? Show me *what*?"

"There's a thread on these forums—from, like, a decade ago. Shit, older than that. Just . . . would you read it? I'll get you some more coffee. I know I sure as fuck need some more." Xiomara clicked another tab they had open, taking the screen to the first page of a thread titled **The Not-Philip Experiment**. They reached down to retrieve Eileen's empty coffee mug, then paused, scrunching up their face like something had just scratched the inside of their skull. "Oh, wait, shit. Forgot to mention something. You know that name? The one listed on the email y'all received with the book?"

"August Skeef?"

"Yup, that's the one."

"What about it?"

"It's, uh, it's an anagram."

"For *what*?"

Xiomara sighed, like they already knew what they were about to say sounded dumb as hell. "Uh . . . for 'fugue steaks.'"

"Excuse me?" She had heard what they said, but she was also sure she *hadn't* heard, either.

"Yeah, and, uh . . . from what I could gather, *all* of the forum members have usernames that also work as anagrams."

I BELIEVE IN MISTER BONES

"For 'fugue steaks?'"

"Yup."

"But . . . but why?"

Xiomara shrugged. "Because people on the internet are fucking weird, dude."

FUGUE STEAKS
|—{} AIMLESS RAMBLING
| |—{} THE NOT-PHILIP EXPERIMENT

Pages: [1] 2 3 . . . 39

Author	Topic: The Not-Philip Experiment
	(Read 3,760 times)

Faustus Geek
Administrator
Karma: 279
* Offline

The Not-Philip Experiment

<< on: September 16, 2011, 08:51 AM >>

Alright you foog faggots it's been entirely too dead lately so let's liven shit up. Take a break from jerking your dicks and molesting your dogs and put your goddamn heads in the game. I wanna try something.

A couple weeks back Skue posted in Books about some science bullshit she'd just finished reading and I keep thinking about it. Here's what she said, in case any of you cocksmokers missed it:

> **Quote from: SkueGustFae**
> *Any of you guys ever hear about the Philip experiment?? I got this book at a yard sale the other day called CONJURING UP PHILIP: AN ADVENTURE IN PSYCHOKINESIS &*

I BELIEVE IN MISTER BONES

I've been flipping through it here & there & let me tell you it is a fucking trip!! It's a nonfiction thing about these scientists in Toronto back in the 70s who try to . . . . . . make up a ghost?? Like out of thin air!! It's this whole official study & everything. They all get together & the plan is to make up this fictional spirit & then see if they can communicate with him & eventually materialize him into the real world. What they wanna answer is whether or not all physical manifestations actually come from the spirits of the deceased or maybe humans can project some kind of weird energy on physical objects or whatever &......just like the title of the book!!!......CONJURE UP a ghost. They come up with like background autobiographical details & how the ghost died when he was a person (SUICIDE!!) & everything. They name him Philip & do all of these tests like seances & stuff with chairs & recording devices & whatever. There's a few scenes where they're like "OH SHIT IS THAT PHILIP??" because the table they're all sitting at moves or makes a noise but in the end it was kinda disappointing?? I mean don't get me wrong they did produce SOME cool stuff. Like they would ask questions & the table would make a banging noise to answer, one bang for yes & two for no. But that was kind of it I guess? It wasn't much better than some lousy ouija board. Like they didn't actually "conjure" him up or anything like that. I wanted this ghost to come out & lay on a thorough spook!! I hate an anticlimactic

MAX BOOTH III

> ending, I tell you what!! (Hank Hill,
> anybody??) Anyway it just got me
> thinking about how cool it COULD have
> been. Maybe nonfiction isn't my thing I
> don't know guys!! I know one thing for
> sure & that's foogs could have done a
> way better job with something like this.
> At the very least it wouldn't have been
> so dang boring!!

So, I looked this shit up and turns out
it's real. The experiment was carried
out by a group called the Toronto
Society for Psychical Research. Sorry
to have doubted you Skue but
sometimes you say crazy shit on
here. Anybody can go search for "the
Philip experiment 1970 Toronto" right
now and find the same thing. Also
just watch this video SpiritSeekers
uploaded last year:
https://www.youtube.com/watch?v=X
2IGPT2J1cc

I would love to try something similar
here. Skue made an excellent point.
We COULD do a way better job than
these faggoty nerds. Plus I'm so
fucking bored. There isn't shit to do
over here. It's fucking Friday and I
have nothing at all lined up this
weekend. So we're going to do this.

I don't want to do a ghost though.
Ghosts are fucking gay. Let's conjure
up something way cooler than a
ghost. Some kind of monster or
something.

I BELIEVE IN MISTER BONES

And we aren't fucking naming him "Philip" either. That's the gayest name I ever heard in my life.

What do you sons of bitches think?

---

august skeef
Beef Enthusiast
Karma: 53
* Offline

Re: The Not-Philip Experiment
<< on: September 16, 2011, 08:59 AM >>

Ummm yesss this sounds like it could be a lot of fun. Good idea, Geek (and uhh also Skue?).

FETUS KEG USA
Sex Wizard
Karma: 358
* Offline

Re: The Not-Philip Experiment
<< on: September 16, 2011, 09:05 AM >>

AGREED

GHOSTS LOVE SUCKING COCK

SkueGustFae
Meathead
Karma: -45
* Offline

Re: The Not-Philip Experiment
<< on: September 16, 2011, 09:44 AM >>

Oh how cool!! Yes Geek I'm so happy you want to do this!! But how would we......you know, DO this?? In the book everybody got together in the same room & like.....fed off each other's energies & stuff?? How do we recreate that HERE??

MAX BOOTH III

ass_guku_feet

Meathead
Karma: 11
* Offline

Re: The Not-Philip Experiment
<< on: September 16, 2011, 09:48 AM >>

> **Quote from: FETUS KEG USA**
> *GHOSTS LOVE SUCKING COCK*

Do ghosts spit or swallow?

FETUS KEG USA

Sex Wizard
Karma: 358
* Offline

Re: The Not-Philip Experiment
<< on: September 16, 2011, 09:53 AM >>

THEY SWALLOW BUT THE CUM
IMMEDIATELY SLIPS OUT OF THEIR
JUICY GELATINOUS ASSHOLES LIKE
SLIMER FROM GHOSTBUSTERS

I KNOW THIS BECAUSE I AM A GHOST

Faustus Geek

Administrator
Karma: 279
* Offline

Re: The Not-Philip Experiment
<< on: September 16, 2011, 10:02 AM >>

> **Quote from: SkueGustFae:**
> *But how would we......you know, DO this??*

Obviously we'll need to make some
tweaks given our circumstances. But
also consider the fact that these
Canadian fags didn't exactly succeed.
There was no "mission
accomplished" for them. Their goal
was to conjure a physical
manifestation of a spirit of their own
design. At best their

I BELIEVE IN MISTER BONES

subconsciousness tricked them into believing something besides their own knees were tapping the underside of a table. That's it.

Another thing they did was waste a lot of fucking time. The first entire year of their experiment consisted of them all getting together and just...talking about Philip. Having conversations about the imaginary backstory they provided for him. Then, seriously, a year later they decided that was retarded and it was time to do some real science shit like seances. We're not going to waste a year like them. In fact, we're not even going to come up with a backstory for this monster. Backstories make monsters boring as fuck. We want this bitch to be scary.

But first we do need to decide what KIND of monster this is going to be. The way I see it, there are a plethora of classics we can pick and choose from, then try to make our own. You got your vampires, zombies, werewolves, swamp creatures, mummies, eldritch beings, or maybe something more slasher-centric like Michael Myers or Jason Voorhees. No ghosts, though. And, I'll say this too before anyone suggests it—no gay-ass leprechauns.

I'm open to ideas from everybody. I think for this to work it needs to be a group project. Not just one person coming up with all the ideas. We all need to feel involved.

feagues_tusk
Meathead
Karma: -8
* Offline

The Not-Philip Experiment
<< on: September 16, 2011, 10:21 AM >>

Surprised you preemptively banned leprechauns for being too gay but nothing about vampires being too sparkly. Is it possible Geek is becoming a weak admin, my fellow foogs? Has he just accidentally outed himself as a TWILIGHT lover? Is mutiny necessary at this stage, or shall we wait for more damnable evidence to build up?

Faustus Geek
Administrator
Karma: 279
* Offline

The Not-Philip Experiment
<< on: September 16, 2011, 10:56 AM >>

feagues_tusk has been banned for also being too gay

---

fake tug uses 6969
Beef Enthusiast
Karma: 125
* Offline

The Not-Philip Experiment
<< on: September 16, 2011, 1:22 PM >>

It would be cool to make a monster that hasn't already been done to death. I'm sick of zombies and vampires. There's nothing that exciting about werewolves, too. They're predictable. What about something that doesn't already have a pre-established lore?

I BELIEVE IN MISTER BONES

FETUS KEG USA
Sex Wizard
Karma: 358
* Offline

Re: The Not-Philip Experiment
<< on: September 16, 2011, 01:46 PM >>

> **Quote from: fake tug uses 6969**
> *What about something that doesn't already have a pre-established lore?*

WELL THAT FORFEITS YOUR MOTHER FROM CONSIDERATION

---

keefasGUUTS
Meathead
Karma: 14
* Offline

Re: The Not-Philip Experiment
<< on: September 16, 2011, 03:37 PM >>

IDK if we're going to be able to just come up with a brand-new original monster. If it was so easy wouldn't we have more than the same old shit we always see by now?

U Tu Seek Fags?
Sex Wizard
Karma: 198
* Offline

Re: The Not-Philip Experiment
<< on: September 16, 2011, 06:53 PM >>

The key is to take an older monster and put a new spin on it. Like what if we DID choose a vampire...but this time the vampire is a black man??? And what if he goes to Brooklyn, New York???

---

keefasGUUTS
Meathead
Karma: 14
* Offline

Re: The Not-Philip Experiment
<< on: September 16, 2011, 07:05 PM >>

Are you sure that's not the Eddie
Murphy movie VAMPIRE IN
BROOKLYN?

U Tu Seek Fags?
Sex Wizard
Karma: 198
* Offline

Re: The Not-Philip Experiment
<< on: September 16, 2011, 07:52 PM >>

Not even remotely the same thing.

---

feat. Kegusus
Meathead
Karma: 19
* Offline

Re: The Not-Philip Experiment
<< on: September 17, 2011, 05:59 AM >>

what about a skeleton

---

keefasGUUTS
Meathead
Karma: 14
* Offline

Re: The Not-Philip Experiment
<< on: September 17, 2011, 08:07 AM >>

What ABOUT a skeleton??

I BELIEVE IN MISTER BONES

feat. Kegusus
Meathead
Karma: 19
* Offline

Re: The Not-Philip Experiment
<< on: September 17, 2011, 09:37 AM >>

I don't know. I've just always thought there's not enough spooky skeletons in horror. Seems weird there's not, like, an iconic one that comes to mind. Can anybody think of a famous one?

FETUS KEG USA
Sex Wizard
Karma: 358
* Offline

Re: The Not-Philip Experiment
<< on: September 17, 2011, 02:44 PM >>

WHAT IF THE SKELETON HAD A HUGE "BONER"

Faustus Geek
Administrator
Karma: 279
* Offline

The Not-Philip Experiment
<< on: September 17, 2011, 03:11 PM >>

Skeleton could be cool maybe. What would be so scary about him?

FETUS KEG USA
Sex Wizard
Karma: 358
* Offline

Re: The Not-Philip Experiment
<< on: September 17, 2011, 03:14 PM >>

THE SIZE OF HIS DONG

Faustus Geek
Administrator
Karma: 279
* Offline

The Not-Philip Experiment
<< on: September 17, 2011, 03:19 PM >>

If it's at all possible for you, Fetus Keg, I'd like to take this a little more seriously.

FETUS KEG USA
Sex Wizard
Karma: 358
* Offline

Re: The Not-Philip Experiment
<< on: September 17, 2011, 03:22 PM >>

OKAY THEN WHAT IF HE STEALS YOUR BONES WHEN YOU'RE SLEEPING

Faustus Geek
Administrator
Karma: 279
* Offline

The Not-Philip Experiment
<< on: September 17, 2011, 03:26 PM >>

Holy shit.

SkueGustFae
Meathead
Karma: -45
* Offline

Re: The Not-Philip Experiment
<< on: September 17, 2011, 04:44 PM >>

That is genuinely unsettling?? Oh my god haha

I BELIEVE IN MISTER BONES

FETUS KEG USA
Sex Wizard
Karma: 358
* Offline

Re: The Not-Philip Experiment
<< on: September 17, 2011, 04:50 PM >>

AND HE HAS A HUGE HARD-ON
WHILE HE'S DOING IT

---

august skeef
Beef Enthusiast
Karma: 53
* Offline

Re: The Not-Philip Experiment
<< on: September 18, 2011, 12:43 PM >>

No joke...I've always sorta fantasized
about not having any bones...for my
body to just melt into a puddle of
goop...is that normal...?

U Tu Seek Fags?
Sex Wizard
Karma: 198
* Offline

Re: The Not-Philip Experiment
<< on: September 18, 2011, 02:13 PM >>

how the fuck would a monster steal
your bones when you're asleep
though? wouldn't you wake up?
wouldn't you be like "HEY CUT IT
OUT!!!"?

---

feat. Kegusus
Meathead
Karma: 19
* Offline

Re: The Not-Philip Experiment
<< on: September 18, 2011, 04:01 PM >>

Maybe he's also an expert surgeon.
His weapon could be a scalpel. And
he's always going around cutting
people open and removing their
bones then sewing them back up
before they're awake.

MAX BOOTH III

The Not-Philip Experiment
<< on: September 18, 2011, 04:21 PM >>

I think this needs to be something we could all realistically believe, and a skeleton performing surgery sounds way too fucking retarded for my tastes, sorry. It needs to be simpler. Simple and weird is scary. Stressing out about the logistics of something is only going to make this dude lame as fuck.

Re: The Not-Philip Experiment
<< on: September 18, 2011, 05:03 PM >>

EXPLANATIONS ARE FOR PUSSIES

LET MYSTERIES BE MYSTERIES

I BELIEVE IN MISTER BONES

FUGUE STEAKS
|—{} AIMLESS RAMBLING
| |—{} THE NOT-PHILIP EXPERIMENT

Pages: 1 . . . 8 [9] 10 . . . 39

Author	Topic: The Not-Philip Experiment
	(Read 3,760 times)

fake tug uses 6969
Beef Enthusiast
Karma: 125
* Offline

The Not-Philip Experiment
<< on: September 23, 2011, 06:47 PM >>

> **Quote from: august skeef**
> *It feels like something is missing.*

That's because there IS something missing. You guys aren't thinking about this shit from a grander scope. Every monster has a weakness. A way to defeat it. So far, we just have this evil skeleton that haunts your dreams stealing your bones until you die and that's it. All good horror stories still have some taste of hope...even if its only purpose is to be crushed at the end. So where's the hope in this story, or whatever the hell this is meant to be? What choices do people have to survive?

---

august skeef
Beef Enthusiast
Karma: 53
* Offline

Re: The Not-Philip Experiment
<< on: September 23, 2011, 07:25 PM >>

Is there something that's known for killing bones?

MAX BOOTH III

feat. Kegusus
Meathead
Karma: 19
* Offline

Re: The Not-Philip Experiment
<< on: September 23, 2011, 08:33 PM >>

Makes sense to me that if it's a ritual (bone breaking while concentrating on his existence) that summons him after you, then it should be another ritual that reverses it, or something.

---

august skeef
Beef Enthusiast
Karma: 53
* Offline

Re: The Not-Philip Experiment
<< on: September 23, 2011, 09:09 PM >>

What do you mean by "reverses it"? Like the victim starts stealing bones from the skeleton? (BTW we really do need a name for this fucking thing at some point)

---

keefasGUUTS
Meathead
Karma: 14
* Offline

Re: The Not-Philip Experiment
<< on: September 24, 2011, 01:37 AM >>

I know you guys are sick of hearing about vampires but my brother and I were watching that Gary Oldman Dracula movie the other day, and I was losing my shit once I realized Tom Waits plays Renfield, the weirdo who eats bugs and worships Dracula and basically acts as his servant. What if USER is right and there is another ritual, and what reverses here is the motivations of the skeleton. Instead of coming after you

I BELIEVE IN MISTER BONES

he's now worshipping you. He does whatever you want. If you want someone dead then he'll kill them for you. Really anything you might desire. He'll even jerk you off, is what I'm trying to say here.

---

fake tug uses 6969
Beef Enthusiast
Karma: 125
* Offline

The Not-Philip Experiment
<< on: September 24, 2011, 08:59 AM >>

What kind of ritual would that even be? What would be the opposite of breaking a bone?

---

feat. Kegusus
Meathead
Karma: 19
* Offline

Re: The Not-Philip Experiment
<< on: September 24, 2011, 09:06 AM >>

Uhhhh healing a bone?

---

fake tug uses 6969
Beef Enthusiast
Karma: 125
* Offline

The Not-Philip Experiment
<< on: September 24, 2011, 09:11 AM >>

Well how the fuck would you do that, dumbass

---

feat. Kegusus
Meathead
Karma: 19
* Offline

Re: The Not-Philip Experiment
<< on: September 24, 2011, 09:23 AM >>

With......uh, lots of rest and relaxation. A sling or cast might also be necessary.

---

fake tug uses 6969
Beef Enthusiast
Karma: 125
* Offline

The Not-Philip Experiment
<< on: September 24, 2011, 09:28 AM >>

Boring.

SkueGustFae
Meathead
Karma: -45
* Offline

Re: The Not-Philip Experiment
<< on: September 24, 2011, 02:55 PM >>

You know, last weekend I went to the flea market. I'm here in Pennsylvania where everybody is real big on hunting, so it's natural to see lots of that kind of shit for sale at these events. Camo & gun cases & whatever else, including lots & lots of animal skulls. But not just skulls. These rednecks do all types of crazy shit with bones. The one thing that impressed me the most, though, probably because I've never seen one before in my life, was this one lady who had WIND CHIMES made out of bone for sale. They sounded

I BELIEVE IN MISTER BONES

GREAT. I would have bought one if they weren't so expensive...

Any of you guys ever see a bone chime before? Are those common or no? Because the more I think about it as I type this, the more I think how cool it might be to incorporate one of these somehow. Like what if instead of animal bones the chime was made out of real human bones. You could summon the skeleton by clacking it all together.

SHIT come to think about it...it IS kind of like the opposite of breaking a bone? One ritual involves the DESTRUCTION of something...& this one could be the CREATION of something (music).

Did I just solve this thing or what??

U Tu Seek Fags?
Sex Wizard
Karma: 198
* Offline

Re: The Not-Philip Experiment
<< on: September 24, 2011, 04:13 PM >>

I don't know wind chimes are kinda gay

MAX BOOTH III

FETUS KEG USA
Sex Wizard
Karma: 358
* Offline

Re: The Not-Philip Experiment
<< on: September 24, 2011, 04:17 PM >>

WIND CHIMES ARE THE GATEWAY TO THE SOUL

AND ALSO MY ASSHOLE

---

keefasGUUTS
Meathead
Karma: 14
* Offline

Re: The Not-Philip Experiment
<< on: September 24, 2011, 04:33 PM >>

I think that means Fetus is voting "yes" for the wind chimes idea.

---

august skeef
Beef Enthusiast
Karma: 53
* Offline

Re: The Not-Philip Experiment
<< on: September 25, 2011, 10:49 AM >>

It can't be as simple as just ringing wind chimes though. There needs to be something more to it.

---

keefasGUUTS
Meathead
Karma: 14
* Offline

Re: The Not-Philip Experiment
<< on: September 25, 2011, 11:43 AM >>

What about an incantation? All good rituals have an incantation.

I BELIEVE IN MISTER BONES

U Tu Seek Fags?
Sex Wizard
Karma: 198
* Offline

Re: The Not-Philip Experiment
<< on: September 25, 2011, 12:11 PM >>

What the fuck does that mean

---

fake tug uses 6969
Beef Enthusiast
Karma: 125
* Offline

The Not-Philip Experiment
<< on: September 25, 2011, 12:26 PM >>

Magic words, dipshit

U Tu Seek Fags?
Sex Wizard
Karma: 198
* Offline

Re: The Not-Philip Experiment
<< on: September 25, 2011, 12:30 PM >>

Like abracadabra? Red rover, red rover, send Mr. Bones on over (let's just call this guy Mr. Bones who cares)

FETUS KEG USA
Sex Wizard
Karma: 358
* Offline

Re: The Not-Philip Experiment
<< on: September 25, 2011, 02:03 PM >>

KLAATU BARADA NIKTO

SkueGustFae
Meathead
Karma: -45
* Offline

Re: The Not-Philip Experiment
<< on: September 25, 2011, 02:14 PM >>

Like from Army of Darkness?? Haha

---

fake tug uses 6969
Beef Enthusiast
Karma: 125
* Offli...

The Not-Philip Experiment
<< on: September 25, 2011, 02:45 PM >>

Ummm if you think that shit is just from AoD then you need to turn in your foogs credentials and get off this message board...

SkueGustFae
Meathead
Karma: -45
* Offline

Re: The Not-Philip Experiment
<< on: September 25, 2011, 02:53 PM >>

It's literally the only place I've ever heard it before??

---

keefasGUUTS
Meathead
Karma: 14
* Offline

Re: The Not-Philip Experiment
<< on: September 25, 2011, 04:13 PM >>

I'm pretty sure it originated in THE DAY THE EARTH STOOD STILL but it's been in a bunch of other shit too

---

I BELIEVE IN MISTER BONES

Faustus Geek
Administrator
Karma: 279
* Offline

The Not-Philip Experiment
<< on: September 26, 2011, 02:55 AM >>

I doubt we'll come up with anything better. It's a neat homage. Let's use it.

---

fake tug uses 6969
Beef Enthusiast
Karma: 125
* Offline

The Not-Philip Experiment
<< on: September 26, 2011, 12:50 PM >>

So, just to clarify, this secondary ritual—which summons the skeleton and forces him to become your servant—involves ringing a wind chime made entirely out of human bone, and then chanting KLAATU BARADA NIKTO?

U Tu Seek Fags?
Sex Wizard
Karma: 198
* Offline

Re: The Not-Philip Experiment
<< on: September 26, 2011, 12:53 PM >>

Sure why the fuck not

---

august skeef
Beef Enthusiast
Karma: 53
* Offline

Re: The Not-Philip Experiment
<< on: September 26, 2011, 03:19 PM >>

Is nobody else curious how anyone is going to realistically gather human bones for this?

U Tu Seek Fags?
Sex Wizard
Karma: 198
* Offline

Re: The Not-Philip Experiment
<< on: September 26, 2011, 03:23 PM >>

Is that really our problem? And besides, if the ritual was easy where would the fun be in that? Let's make them really work for it.

SkueGustFae
Meathead
Karma: -45
* Offline

Re: The Not-Philip Experiment
<< on: September 26, 2011, 09:00 PM >>

Wait do we actually think people are going to take any of this crazy shit serious enough to try it??

U Tu Seek Fags?
Sex Wizard
Karma: 198
* Offline

Re: The Not-Philip Experiment
<< on: September 26, 2011, 11:43 PM >>

Ideally, yes.

I BELIEVE IN MISTER BONES

FUGUE STEAKS
|—{} AIMLESS RAMBLING
| |—{} THE NOT-PHILIP EXPERIMENT

Pages: <u>1</u> . . . <u>12</u> [13] <u>14</u> . . . <u>39</u>

Author	Topic: The Not-Philip Experiment
	(Read 3,760 times)

fake tug uses 6969
Beef Enthusiast
Karma: 125
* Offli

The Not-Philip Experiment
<< on: October 01, 2011, 08:43 PM >>

I can't believe the best fucking name any of us can come up with is Mister Bones.

---

august skeef
Beef Enthusiast
Karma: 53
* Offline

Re: The Not-Philip Experiment
<< on: October 01, 2011, 09:09 PM >>

I personally love it. It's child-like...almost innocent, but at the same time it has this creepy mystery to it. You almost don't want to take it seriously but at the same time...you wanna keep your guard up, just in case...

Faustus Geek
Administrator
Karma: 279
* Offline

The Not-Philip Experiment
<< on: October 01, 2011, 09:31 PM >>

We're past that. I'm sick of wasting time debating the name. We'll be here forever trying to come up with the perfect choice that doesn't exist. There's nothing particularly scary about the name Michael Myers either.

311

MAX BOOTH III

That shit is just some dude's name. It's what he DOES that makes him scary—and, as consequence, his name.

And we already know what Mister Bones does...but what we need now are some actual stories. Anecdotes. I want you guys to start coming up with short-ish snippets detailing how people have been haunted and killed over the years. Don't be restricted by time or location. If he's entering dreams from "Marrowland," then I don't see why he can't be summoned by anybody anywhere.

Please try to exercise proper spelling and grammar. Follow the guidelines we've already brainstormed earlier in the thread. Also stay grounded in some sense of realism. We want these things to be somewhat believable, right?

I will be following along and compiling everybody's entries into a separate document. Depending on quality, I'll also edit them. Feel free to post multiple ones. Just don't get butthurt if I don't include yours for some reason.

I've already written one as an example, before any of you schlong-lovers start whining about not knowing what to do. You'll see the style and mood I'm trying to achieve here. Something along the lines of that old kids show, ARE YOU AFRAID

I BELIEVE IN MISTER BONES

OF THE DARK? You sons of bitches remember the Midnight Society? If not, do yourself a favor and look that shit up. It's great.

Anyway here's what I have. I call this one STEPHEN, FROM BALTIMORE...

FUGUE STEAKS
|—{} AIMLESS RAMBLING
| |—{} THE NOT-PHILIP EXPERIMENT

Pages: 1 . . . 25 [26] 27 . . . 39

Author	Topic: The Not-Philip Experiment
	(Read 3,760 times)

SkueGustFae
Meathead
Karma: -45
* Offline

?

Re: The Not-Philip Experiment
<< on: October 08, 2011, 12:44 PM >>

Just finished going through the document Geek shared & my only question is what's with the redacted wind chime chapter?? I thought that was a pretty good idea...

U Tu Seek Fags?
Sex Wizard
Karma: 198
* Offline

?

Re: The Not-Philip Experiment
<< on: October 08, 2011, 02:03 PM >>

He already explained it here:

> **Quote from: Faustus Geek**
> *Before anybody asks, I decided not to use the wind chime shit after all. In the end it just felt too convenient. Too*

distracting from the whole point of what we're trying to do here. I don't think it's relevant enough. But I did leave a section for it in case I change my mind later. Plus, to be honest, I sort of like how it currently looks now, like some forbidden secret's been censored from the reader. It's exactly the kind of detail that will burrow into someone's brain and make them obsess over our little skeleton creation.

SkueGustFae
Meathead
Karma: -45
* Offline

Re: The Not-Philip Experiment
<< on: October 08, 2011, 02:14 PM >>

Oh...

FETUS KEG USA
Sex Wizard
Karma: 358
* Offline

Re: The Not-Philip Experiment
<< on: October 08, 2011, 02:33 PM >>

ALSO MAKING A MISTAKE BY NOT EMPHASIZING THE SIZE OF HIS MASSIVE, MASSIVE DONG BUT THAT'S JUST MY OPINION

I BELIEVE IN MISTER BONES

Pages: <u>1</u> . . . <u>37</u> [38] <u>39</u>

<u>Faustus Geek</u>
Administrator
Karma: 279
* Offline

The Not-Philip Experiment
<< on: October 29, 2011, 11:50 PM >>

PLEASE READ THIS
Okay, foogs, shit is about to go down
real fucking soon, so I thought I
would quickly remind everybody of
what they need to be doing, and
when.

As previously discussed, if we're
going to do better than the Toronto
retards did with Philip the gay ghost,
we need to severely step up our
game. Which means doing a ritual of
our own. A shared experience done
by all of us at exactly the same time.

A little over 24 hours from now, on
Halloween MORNING. I'm sick of
debating what day to do it on. The
night of Halloween makes no sense
because by then the witching hour
won't occur until well past midnight.
Doing it on the morning of Halloween
still falls on actual Halloween, so
that's what we're doing.

Monday, October 31—3:00 A.M.
EASTERN STANDARD TIME.

MAX BOOTH III

If you're in a different time zone, make sure you do the homework and figure out the time difference on your end. Don't fuck this up because you don't understand math.

For this to work, we all need to do it at the EXACT SAME TIME.

As far as what bone you decide to break, I think that's your choice. The specific bone doesn't matter as much as the act itself. As long as you intentionally snap a bone in your body at the right time, you should be good.

And, of course, please clear your mind beforehand and leave room only for Mister Bones. Do not think about anything else. Visualize him and lock that image in. Throw away the fucking key. Do not take your eyes off of what truly matters here. Reread the document we created over and over leading up to the time. Lose yourself in the lore.

And then break that fucking bone.

Personally, I'm going with my pinky. But you guys do whatever you want. I recommend something that isn't going to be a pain in the ass in your day-to-day lives, though.

Will this actually work? I have no idea. But I feel like it's worth a shot. We've come up with something special here. I want to see it through.

I BELIEVE IN MISTER BONES

Worst-case scenario is we all break a
bone together and look like
dumbasses. It's not like we're fucking
killing ourselves or anything.

But best-case scenario?

We conjure up a motherfucking
monster.

EILEEN READ THE full thread without making a sound. A valid argument could've been made over whether or not she'd blinked until reaching the end of the discussion. She *thought* Xiomara had been seated beside her the whole time, re-reading over her shoulder, but truthfully anything beyond the scope of the laptop screen had ceased to exist for however long it took Eileen to make it through everything.

Afterward, she leaned back in the chair and slumped her shoulders. Her vision softened into a welcomed blurriness. She wished she could claim that none of this made any sense, that it was all some prank, maybe something Xiomara themself had photoshopped. It all felt so goddamn silly that she didn't *want* it to be the truth. She didn't want *any* of the dumb shit she'd just read to be linked to Daniel's death. He deserved better than that. *Everybody* deserved better than that.

"Well?" Xiomara said. "What do you think?"

Eileen had no choice but to laugh. The question was too ridiculous to take seriously. What did she *think*? What the fuck *could* she think?

"I *think*," Eileen said, "that we need something stronger than coffee."

"I have some Malibu," Xiomara said, then got quiet, concerned, "but . . . "

"But what?"

I BELIEVE IN MISTER BONES

"It's, uh, under the sink."

Like Eileen cared about coming in contact with the arm. After all, who had been the one to dig it out of the ground? Who had dismembered it with a shovel and brought it over here in the first place? An arm didn't scare her. Not even an arm planted by a conjured-up boogeyman. She got up and dug through the cabinet until finding the bottle of coconut rum. Behind her, Xiomara fetched them each a glass.

"Do you want a mixer?"

Eileen scoffed at them. "Not for *Malibu*."

They shrugged. "Some people use mixers for Malibu."

"Yeah—weaklings."

"When was the last time you ate something?"

"I don't know," she said, but that wasn't true. She remembered exactly when, and what. Last night, while excavating her husband, she'd devoured two peanut butter bunnies. Her hands had been covered in dirt and blood and chocolate and it had all tasted so goddamn good. But wait. No. That wasn't true, was it? She'd had those breakfast tacos afterward, before coming here. She'd almost forgotten. Her brain was at capacity. Memories were struggling to compete with each other. "Why?"

"Because, if we're about to get drunk, we should probably have something in our stomach. Plus, shit, I know you gotta be hungry. You've been here since like six in the morning and you haven't had a single thing to eat."

Truthfully her stomach *did* feel hollow. Gnawing. "Okay, yeah, good idea."

Xiomara preheated the oven and, once it'd clicked on, took out a foil-wrapped pan of leftover enchiladas from the fridge. As it baked, they each helped themselves to a half glass of rum. Neither of them had brought up the Fugue Steaks message boards yet. Eileen was still letting it all simmer, trying to process exactly what she'd read. At least that's what she told herself. The shit wasn't rocket science. There were things she didn't understand, of course.

Obviously she had questions. Lots of them. She didn't expect Xiomara to have the answers—unless they somehow knew more than what they'd already shown her tonight.

She took a long drink from her rum, then paused and examined the glass.

"What's wrong?" Xiomara asked, grimacing from the post-swallow of their own liquor.

"Are you sure this isn't water?" she asked.

"What?" Xiomara started giggling. "Are you already drunk somehow?"

She shook her head. "This stuff smells like . . . nothing? And it's tasteless, too. I think something's wrong with it." Then it clicked, and she shifted her tingling foot beneath the table in a useless attempt to wake it back up. "Wait. Never mind."

Xiomara stared across the table at her like someone might with a loved one dying from cancer. "The same thing happened to Daniel, too, right?"

"Yeah," she said, no defense mechanism in place to fight off the overwhelming feeling of failure falling over her like a blanket. "There was a point where I thought maybe he had COVID, because of that. He wasn't coughing or showing a temp or anything but, like, losing your sense of smell? Not being able to taste anything? Classic COVID symptoms, right? I remember suggesting it to him and he gave me this look, like, *Why can't you just believe me?* He didn't bring it up again. I pretended like he regained his senses and he pretended like I thought he wasn't losing his mind. Anyway." She took another sip of the bland rum. "Joke's on me, I guess. Now I'm the one going crazy."

"You know, they talked about that in the forum," Xiomara said. "Someone came up with that idea. That you'd lose those senses. You, Daniel, and anybody else who summons him."

"I saw."

"They came up with everything."

"I know," she said, clenching her jaw. Pissed off but

unsure at who, or what. At the Canadian paranormal researchers for first inspiring the idea? At the message board "foogs" who came up with this game, and made it a reality? At Mister Bones, for being birthed into this stupid, fucked-up world by strangers on the internet and forced to obey a bizarre occult ritual every time some idiot breaks their bones while thinking about him? Or maybe at Daniel, who fell for what was essentially an email scam and pushed everything aside—the company, their marriage—attempting to publish something that was never a submission in the first place? Pissed at all of them, including—most importantly—herself. For not matching Daniel's curiosity at the beginning of his investigation. For not taking his concerns seriously in the days following his wrist fracture, and the weeks leading up to his death. For letting stupid work shit get in the way of what really mattered. For sinking all of her time and energy and money into a community that never really gave a shit about her. For everything.

The oven started beeping. Xiomara pulled out the enchiladas and set the pan down atop the stove, then turned back to Eileen. "You know, one thing I can't get over? How long ago this all happened. Two-thousand-eleven? That's, like, a fucking *eternity* in internet time. How did so many years pass without anybody ever posting about it elsewhere? How did it manage to stay isolated to that one forum thread, but *also* involve members emailing the book out to random people like that, for years and years? I mean, for fuck's sake, they're still doing it, right? The one y'all got is all the proof you need. Why is nobody else *talking* about this shit? Why does it all feel so weird and lonely?"

Eileen shrugged. It didn't feel that mystifying to her. Not after spending the time sitting here at the kitchen table collecting her thoughts. Plus, despite its lack of flavor, she suspected the coconut rum was starting to finally kick in. Words were spilling out of her in a smooth, uninterrupted flow that only a healthy buzz could inspire. "I don't know. I guess if you think of it as spam—which is what it is, right?—how many people actually open those types of emails? Most of them get deleted unread. A lot of the time, they get filtered and never seen at all. And for the very, very small percentage of people who ever even open them? How many of *those* people are reading an entire novella's worth of text? And, of those who *do* read it all, how many of them are going to do anything more besides laugh and delete it, or maybe forward it to a friend to do the same? How many of them are going to actually take it seriously? How many of them are going to believe it's real? And then—how many of *those* people are going to end up breaking a bone while *actively thinking about the book*? The odds are so astronomically small, and yet . . . "

Xiomara nodded, knowing where Eileen was going with this. "And yet, it happened to Daniel."

Eileen closed her eyes, fighting back a fresh wave of tears. "It happened to Daniel."

"And now you, too," Xiomara reminded her, setting two plates down on the table, and told her they'd be right back before taking a third plate into the living room for their abuela.

Left alone in the kitchen, Eileen stabbed her fork into the enchiladas and took a big bite, unfazed by the steam drifting out of the food. A little hot, but beyond that she didn't taste anything. She helped herself to another forkful. Same result.

When Xiomara returned, they asked Eileen how it was.

"Same as the rum."

"Shit, babe," they said, taking a bite from their own plate. "You're really missing out. This shit is delicious."

"Oh, gee, thanks," Eileen said, smiling despite how she felt.

"I wonder if that stuff will come back to you, once we stop . . . um, whatever you wanna call it. The curse?"

Eileen paused mid-bite. "And how do you think we're going to do that?"

I BELIEVE IN MISTER BONES

"What? Stop it?" Xiomara cocked their head, like they were being pranked. "You read the same thing I did, right? About the wind chime?"

She nodded and swallowed. "The one made of real bones."

"Don't you think that might be, like . . . you know, *the key* to fixing all this shit?"

"It wasn't in the book, though," Eileen said. She'd already thought about this. "The whole chapter was marked as redacted."

"I realize that," Xiomara said, pausing to chew, "but what if it's still part of the lore, anyway? It wasn't like anybody else had flat-out rejected the idea when it was first suggested—like the ten-foot dick, for instance. Everybody was all in on the wind chime chapter until the admin decided to omit it at the last minute. I mean, shit, Eileen, like you just said—there's even still a placeholder for it in the book y'all received. It still has to be relevant somehow, right?"

"What did it say again?" Already Eileen was having trouble focusing. The exhaustion from last night's physical activities had not faded. Her next sleep could not come soon enough. "Something about being able to control him, right?"

"Not only that, but it's how we get him to come out of hiding." They snapped their fingers, powered by a refreshed jolt of excitement. "It's how we do the thing those Toronto ghost people failed to do with Philip whatshisface. We conjure a physical manifestation. No more hiding in your dreams. We get him out in the open. We get him *here*, and then, uh . . . "

"And then what?"

Xiomara deflated back in their seat. "I don't know. I guess we fucking kill him or something."

Eileen ran her hand through her hair, still half-convinced this was all some nutty nightmare she couldn't wake up from. "And how do we do *that*?"

"I guess we could just beat the shit out of him? Like, won't he just be a skeleton? Get some hammers or whatever and clobber the son of a bitch until he falls apart. And then, I don't know, burn the remains? Cremation-style."

"Hammers?" Eileen started cracking up. "This thing *steals bones*. Do you really think we're going to defeat him with hammers?"

"Dude, have you ever gotten hit with a hammer?"

"No, I can't say that I have."

"Well, trust me, it sucks." They raised their index finger to cut her off from replying. "*Or,* consider that we might not even *have* to kill him."

"What do you mean?"

"I *mean* . . . you read the forum posts. The whole point of the ritual is to gain control of the fucking guy, right? To make him your little Renfield. Oh no, now you have a free skeleton butler. What a travesty."

"I don't want a free skeleton butler," Eileen said. "Especially a skeleton butler who *killed my husband*."

"I don't think we can really blame him for that, can we? Knowing what we know now. It's not his fault some internet freaks designed him to be a monster."

"Maybe you're right, but I'm not about to start feeling *sorry* for him, either."

"Holy shit. Wait."

"Wh-what?" She was almost afraid to find out.

"This whole time, I've been thinking how this all feels like a knockoff *Elm Street*."

"Okay . . ."

"But it's not."

"What is it then?"

Xiomara grinned. "It's a knockoff *Frankenstein*." They paused, grin intact, letting the silence between them do the talking. Like they'd dropped a massive bombshell and were proud of it.

Until Eileen said, "Wait, how?"

I BELIEVE IN MISTER BONES

"How *what*?"

"How is this like *Frankenstein*? The doctor didn't create him with the intention of making him a monster. It was the townspeople who mistook him for one."

Xiomara's face contorted into a frown, and they rubbed their temple. "I guess it's been a minute since I've watched it . . . *wait*, why does that fucking creep create him in the first place, then?"

Eileen shrugged, struggling to remember. "I guess just to see if he could?" What the hell were they talking about right now? "Besides, even if we wanted to try this . . . unless you have a collection of real human bones somewhere, I don't know what we're going to do. I'm sorry, but I've already dug up one grave this week. I don't think I have the stamina for a second."

They looked at her like she was a lunatic. "Who said anything about grave digging?"

"Well how else are we—"

"Babe," Xiomara said, "if you don't think I can get us some human bones *tonight*, then I don't even know how we're still friends."

"But . . . how? What—what are you going to do?" Eileen asked, not quite sure she actually wanted the question answered.

"Why don't you just refill our Malibu, and let me worry about the rest?" they said, reawakening their laptop from hibernation. Within seconds, they were fully focused on whatever they were machine-gun firing against the keyboard.

Eileen got up and cleared both of their plates, then rinsed them off and stuck the dishes in the sink. The bottle of rum was still on the counter. She poured their glasses to the brim. What was the point in exercising conservatism at this point? Xiomara was in the process of trying to track down *human remains* so they could perform an occult ritual to summon an imaginary boogeyman. Tonight, getting drunk would be a necessity.

Ten minutes later, Xiomara leaned back from the laptop and cracked their knuckles. "Okay," they said.

"Okay what?" Eileen asked, holding the rum up to her lips.

"Okay, someone's bringing over a skeleton in two hours."

"*What*? Like a *human* skeleton?"

"Well, I sure as hell hope so," they said. "I would hate to report them for false advertising."

"What the fuck are you *talking* about? How? *Who*?"

But all Xiomara did was smile. "Don't ever underestimate the weirdos on Facebook Marketplace.

THE DOORBELL RANG two hours later on the dot.

Eileen and Xiomara crept up to the front door together. The idea being that the type of person selling skeletons on social media would be less likely to murder someone if they were in a pack of two. From everything either of them had ever read, serial killers typically turned chicken when outnumbered.

Xiomara's abuela was still wide awake, curled up in the rocking chair watching *The Simpsons*. She was visibly annoyed by the doorbell noise, and making a big show of raising the volume with the remote held high over her high.

"Sorry, Abi," Xiomara said, "I know it's late."

"Doesn't she ever go to bed?" Eileen asked.

Xiomara turned toward her with a flat expression. "I've known this woman my entire life. Not once—not even for a *second*—have I ever seen her sleeping. Nobody has."

To confirm, Eileen glanced back at the old woman, who was now making eye contact with her. She winked, smirked, then redirected her attention to the television set. Eileen mouthed *what the fuck?* and decided to forget about it for now. She could wait to investigate this new mystery until after they'd killed Mister Bones.

Xiomara opened the door, revealing a bald man with a goatee standing out on their porch. It was late by then. Eileen wasn't sure the exact time. Close to ten, maybe. The man wore baggy blue jeans and a dark green polo shirt. He held a duffel bag at his side. Easy guess as to what was inside it. A name tag attached to his breast read "JOE."

"Any of y'all order a goddamn human skeleton, or what?" he asked, chuckling.

"Jesus Christ," Xiomara said, glancing outside to ascertain whether anybody was within earshot. "Why don't you come in before you get a SWAT team knocking down my door?"

Joe chuckled again in a way that made Eileen want to punch him. "Shit, you ain't gotta tell me twice."

On the way to the kitchen, he paused in the living room to inspect the television. "Ah shit, I love this show." He watched for a moment, then squinted. "What the fuck, are they speaking Spanish?" He glanced around at anybody who would listen to him. "How the hell did they do that? Is this a bootleg or something?"

Xiomara's abuela maxed out the volume and crossed her arms, fuming at all of these unwanted guests interrupting her cartoon time.

In the kitchen, Joe nodded at the bottle of Malibu on the counter. "Shhiiieeet, are we about to have ourselves a party?"

"Do you have the skeleton?" Xiomara asked.

He nodded, enthusiastically. "Y'all wanna see it?"

"Well, that's why you're over here, isn't it?"

Giddy, the man placed the duffle bag on top of the kitchen table and unzipped it.

Eileen stood across the kitchen, spine leaning against the sink. It was becoming increasingly more difficult to balance on her left foot. She craned her neck, trying to get a good look inside the bag. There were certainly bones of some sort in there.

Xiomara walked right up to it and reached in, then brought out a stray bone to examine it closely. Looked like a femur to Eileen. "I thought they'd all be connected, or something," Xiomara said.

I BELIEVE IN MISTER BONES

"I'm sure they could all be reconnected if you had a strong enough glue," Joe said, standing next to them and grinning at the bag of bones. "Ain't no problem at all that glue can't fix." He glanced back at Eileen, making sure she was part of the conversation. "Or duct tape, for that matter."

"I guess so," Eileen said, not wanting to debate the man selling a duffle bag skeleton.

"Where did you get this thing?" Xiomara asked, holding up a second bone and squinting at it with one eye shut.

The man let out a full-on belly laugh. "Hey, shit, how do I know you two ain't the law?"

Eileen opened the cupboard at her feet and pulled out Daniel's severed arm, then waved it at him. It was still sculpted into the shape of a penis, which she'd forgotten about until removing it. "Do we look like cops to you?"

The man named Joe turned his hands into rock n' roll devil horns and raised them as a salute. "Fuckin' far out."

Meanwhile, Xiomara was giving her a look like *are you out of your goddamn mind?* Which shouldn't have been a question at that point. Of *course* she was.

Eileen returned the dick-arm to the cupboard and kicked the door shut. It had served its purpose for now. "So why don't you answer their question then?"

"Huh?" Joe said, devil horns slowly dropping.

"Where did you get the skeleton, Joe?"

The man gasped. "Holy shit, y'all know my name?"

"It's on your shirt, man," Xiomara said, sighing. "Plus, we talked on Facebook . . . "

Joe inspected his chest and defensively covered the name tag with his hand. "Oh, right," he said, blushing. "I sell phones for a living, by the way, in case anyone here might be in the market . . . "

Neither Eileen nor Xiomara responded.

Joe cleared his throat, nervous, and said, "Y'all ever heard of Dylan Polk High School? Over on Armadillo Drive?"

Eileen and Xiomara glanced at each other like *what the hell?*

"Uh, yeah," Xiomara said. "That's where Eileen and I graduated."

"No shit?" Joe grinned. "Me too." Then he cocked his head at Eileen. "Shit, I actually recognize you? What year were y'all?"

Reluctantly, Eileen answered, and a weird, flabbergasted gasp escaped him. "Well holy shit, folks, I think we all went to high school together. Y'all don't recognize me?" He tapped his bald head and said, "Imagine hair down to my shoulder?" He ran both fingers over his lips, to his ears. "Plus a chopstache? Y'all remember Lemmy?" When nobody responded, he said, "Motörhead?"

"Shit," Xiomara said, "I *do* remember you."

He didn't strike a chord with Eileen, but that didn't mean much. She'd mostly kept to herself in high school. Xiomara had been her closest friend in those years. There were a few other girls she'd hang out with occasionally, converse with during lunch, but for the most part she kept her face stuffed in a book. Stephen King, Anne Rice, and V. C. Andrews—the holy trinity. There were at least a hundred guys with the exact hairstyle Joe described. He could have easily been one of them. It wasn't like any of them had ever spoken to her. Not that she would have wanted them to, anyway.

Regardless, Eileen nodded and said, "Oh, yeah, that's right." Then, because she was paranoid nobody believed her, she added, "How have you been?"

Without realizing it, she'd refilled her glass of rum and was already taking a desperate drink.

"Oh, you know," Joe said, "like I was telling y'all earlier, I sell phones now. Y'all got T-Mobile? I'm with T-Mobile. Decent pay. Good benefits. I can hook you ladies up, if y'all are ever in the market. Hey, you still write?" The question was directed to Eileen.

She tried to drown herself in the rum before responding. Jesus Christ, how did he know about that? "No, not really," she said. "Um, what about you?"

I BELIEVE IN MISTER BONES

He nodded, excited. "Oh, here and there. Maybe not as much as I used to. I remember, back in English, you was always filling up them notebooks? I always wondered what you were writing about."

The truth wasn't very exciting, and something she hadn't thought about in years. Short stories about being a depressed girl in Texas. Suicidal ideation poetry. Failed openings of novels that subconsciously plagiarized whatever book she might've been reading at the time. She'd given up writing long ago. Too many rejections. Too many people telling her she wasn't good enough. She wasn't cut out for it, no matter how good she felt when doing it. Being on the other side of the business—the publisher—that was different. Easier, in a way. She still got a chance to be involved in the industry without all the crushed-hope heartache that came with submitting her own work.

"She actually runs a publishing company now," Xiomara said, and if Eileen had been closer to them she would have elbowed them in the ribs. Why would they go and bring *that* up?

"Oh, no shit?" Joe said.

"I used to," Eileen said. "I don't think I'm going to continue it." Was that the first time she'd admitted this out loud? It felt oddly satisfying. Like a heavy weight lifting from her chest.

"Well that's a damn shame," Joe said. "You know—"

"Why are we talking about any of this?" Eileen asked, finishing her latest helping of rum. "Why did you bring up *high school* of all things? What does this have to do with anything?"

"Oh, yeah, right," Joe said, scratching his head nervously. "I was asking if y'all knew about Dylan Polk 'cause that's where I got, uh, *that* from." He nodded to the duffle bag of bones.

"From the high school?" Xiomara said, and stepped away from the bag, as if it might be contaminated with all of the bad memories they associated with the place.

"Yeah, well," Joe said, "as y'all might or might not be

aware, it closed down a few years back. Ran out of money or something. I don't know the specifics. But it was abandoned. A lot of shit was left behind. Doors and windows boarded up and everything. NO TRESPASSING signs posted everywhere. Real official and shit."

"What did you do," Xiomara said, "break in and steal the skeleton from the science lab or something?"

"Um." He scratched his chin, puzzled. "Yeah, actually, that's exactly what I did. How the heck did you know that?"

Xiomara shrugged. "Pretty easy guess? Where else was this story going? Plus," they pointed to the duffle bag, "there's a femur in there with a tag attached to it that says PROPERTY OF DYLAN POLK HIGH SCHOOL SCIENCE LAB."

"Ah, shit. Sorry, I meant to take that off." Then, perhaps agitated that he was deprived the chance to tell the story on his own terms, changed the subject to payment. "Anyway, y'all got the cash or what?"

"Two-fifty, right?" Xiomara asked, reaching into their pocket for the money. Before he showed up, they had already separated the bills from their wallet. Figured if this guy was coming here to rob them, it'd be better not to let him see where they kept the rest of their money. Eileen had promised to pay them back as soon as she could, and Xiomara had waved a dismissive hand at her and said, *Nah, I'm gonna keep this thing after we're done with it, anyway. It'll be a cool decoration for my store.*

"That'll do it," Joe said. He looked over at Eileen and explained, "My original asking price was three hundred, but seeing how close y'all were, I figured a discount was in order. Saves me the hassle of tryin' to figure out how to mail human remains."

"Okay," Eileen said.

"I also offered to throw in a free cow esophagus, but I guess y'all don't got any use for one of those."

"You steal one of those from a school, too?" Xiomara asked, handing him the money.

He unfolded the bills and slowly counted them. Two

hundreds and a fifty. Theoretically, it shouldn't have taken him more than a second to confirm it was the correct amount owed. *Theoretically.*

"No, no," he said, "I got this one customer. I always give him a good deal on the latest phones. He hooks me up with organs." He paused and looked up from the cash. "Not human organs. Cows, deer. Normal organs."

"What do you do with them?" Eileen asked, unable to help herself.

He chuckled. "What do I do with them? Honey, I eat 'em." He patted the open duffle bag. "Speaking of, what are y'all planning on doing with the skelly?"

"I don't think that's any of your business, actually," Xiomara said.

"Oh?" He looked around the kitchen, face frozen in a goofy smile. "Wait a second, y'all ain't planning to do any freaky intercourse shit with this thing, are you? A little lesbian skeleton ménage a trois, perchance? Because if so, I'd be willing to waive my entire fee if I could watch. I don't need to touch or anything. My eyes are good enough. I've always fantasized about something like this, tell you the truth."

"You've always fantasized about lesbians having a threesome with a skeleton?" Xiomara said, more intrigued than disgusted.

All traces of humor faded from his expression as he said, "Yes."

"Hmm." Xiomara walked over to Eileen and held her hand. "What do you say? Wanna fuck this bag of bones with me?"

Behind them, Joe made a noise like he'd just ejaculated in his pants.

"Um, I think I'm going to have to pass," Eileen said, uncertain if Xiomara was joking or not.

"Sorry, Joe," Xiomara said. "Maybe another time."

"Goddammit," he said, looking like he was about to cry, "I *knew* this was too good to be true."

XIOMARA TOOK THE lead when it came to constructing the wind chime. They'd always been crafty and skilled with tools, even back in high school, opting for wood shop over home ec. Eileen wasn't useless about this stuff, either. She'd taken wood shop *with* Xiomara, hadn't she? Maybe she hadn't been as naturally observant, but it wasn't like she'd *failed*. In fact, when it came to her relationship with Daniel, she was always the one who fixed stuff around the apartment and put together furniture.

Xiomara designated the top of the skull as the base for the wind chime. Typically, they told her, you'd use a flat chunk of wood or titanium for the base, something sturdy enough to support the weight of the tubes and also flat enough to balance without being a pain in the ass about the whole thing. *But*, the way Xiomara figured it, the less artificial substance that went into the design the better their chances of this insane ritual actually working. It was bad enough that they'd have to use string for it. If only the skeleton still had its hair. Now *that* would have some proper voodoo.

"Actually," Xiomara said, thinking it over some more, "what about *your* hair?"

Eileen nearly dropped her umpteenth glass of rum. "What *about* my hair?"

"Instead of string, we should use strands of your hair,"

they said, then tapped their own scalp. "I would do it, but uhhh, I'm fresh out. But also, you're the one summoning him, anyway. It makes sense, right?"

"Sure, I don't give a shit," Eileen said. She wasn't precious about hair. She wasn't precious about anything anymore. She'd already broken a toe on purpose. What were a few strands of hair? She'd tear out her own tongue, if Xiomara suggested it might help. She'd rip off her whole fucking jaw.

As they drilled into the bones, Eileen scavenged for a pair of scissors from the bathroom and cut off a couple locks. She avoided her reflection in the mirror. No interest at all in seeing what she looked like tonight. Her imagination had already speculated its own idea, and she was too terrified to find out if it was accurate. She *did* use the opportunity to pee, however. All that rum and somehow her bladder hadn't broken until now. A mini miracle, if she really thought about it. She inspected her tampon afterward, decided to go ahead and change it out. It'd already absorbed its fair share, and then some. Plus, who knew when she would have another chance to slip away to the bathroom after this. Better to go into this ritual fresh and rejuvenated. Before leaving, she splashed some water in her face, but kept her eyes shut until stepping out of the room.

Xiomara had finished drilling holes in the bones. They took the locks of hair from Eileen and threaded them through the openings. Single strands wouldn't have supported the weight without snapping, so they banded together multiple locks to create something firm enough to hold the bones in the air. The process seemed so smooth and flawless, she wouldn't have been surprised to discover this wasn't the first wind chime of bones they'd ever made.

After the task was complete, Xiomara held up the wind chime by its upside-down skull base and said, "Ta-da."

"Holy shit. It looks great."

They performed a small bow and said, "Thank you,

thank you, thank you," before setting the object on the table next to its unused companions. The wind chime itself had only required a couple leg and arm bones. Four, in total—five, including the skull. The rest of the skeleton remained in the duffle bag it'd arrived in.

It was late. Nearing midnight. Xiomara suggested maybe they hit the brakes for the night before starting the ritual in earnest. Do it first thing in the morning, after breakfast. Eileen shook her head. She was wide awake. Electrified with the excitement of how close they were to accomplishing something monumental.

"Maybe you're not tired because you slept all day," Xiomara pointed out.

"And maybe I don't want to go to sleep because I know what's waiting for me in my dreams," Eileen countered.

"Frederick Krueger?" Xiomara said, starting to laugh and then abruptly stopping. They sunk their jaw to their chest, deep in thought about something.

"What's wrong?"

They shook their head, sniffling back snot and aspiring tears. "Nothing. Let's just kill this fucking thing already."

The ritual would happen outside, it was decided. Well, really, *Xiomara* decided. Eileen didn't have a preference either way—just as long as it happened.

As long as it worked.

Neither of them realistically had any idea what the consequences of the ritual would be. The Fugue Steaks message board had left the details vague enough to allow room for multiple interpretations. The exact size of Mister Bones was also unpredictable—assuming a physical manifestation did, indeed, summon from Marrowland. Xiomara didn't need some supernatural skeleton fuckhead making a mess of their house or upsetting their abuela during cartoon time. It made more sense to do it in the back yard where there was plenty of space for a creature of any size to materialize. And, although there weren't any perimeter fences out here, neither of them was too concerned about nosey neighbors. The back of the house faced the woods, and the people who lived on either side of Xiomara were geriatrics who rarely left their beds. Friends and family members never seemed to visit. For all Xiomara knew, both of her neighbors had died ages ago. The surrounding houses could all be inhabited by severely-decomposed corpses.

"Besides," Xiomara said, "even if someone *did* see us and call the cops, what law would we be breaking, exactly? Spooky magical skeletons don't have rights. This is *my* property. If anything, we'd be standing our ground."

It made sense to Eileen. It also sounded batshit crazy.

Which was the norm these days, of course.

They'd long departed the land of safe and cozy.

Xiomara hung the bone chime under the awning that expanded over a square of concrete at the back door. The night felt bizarrely windless. Still. Silent. The woods ahead of them were calm, as if waiting for something. Were trees patient? They must've been. Look at how long it took them to grow.

Despite the backyard security light being enabled, it was still remarkably dark.

"Are you sure you don't wanna wait until we can actually see shit?" Xiomara asked.

"It'll be fine," Eileen said, forcing herself to sound confident. It had to be tonight. It had to be *now*. Going to sleep again was not an option. She wasn't going to lose any more bones. She wasn't going to offer up another piece of her body. The momentum was too strong to pause. They had the bones. They had the wind chime. Moving forward was the only option. If they put it off until tomorrow, what would be stopping them from putting it off another day, and then another? It would only get easier and easier. Until Eileen's skeleton was a match for the one buried in Daniel's grave. She shook her head. Not a chance. That wasn't going to happen to her. "We're doing this," she said. "We're fucking doing this."

She gripped the shovel she'd bought from Walmart. The wooden handle reignited the wounds poorly healing on her fingers and palms. It was hard to believe that twenty-four hours ago she was using this same tool to dig up her husband's grave. Hard to believe but not impossible. The pain pulsating through her exhausted body was plenty enough evidence. That had really happened, and so would this.

Next to her, Xiomara wielded their own weapons: two hammers, one in either hand.

The plan was stupid, but simple. Summon Mister Bones into the corporeal world and then see if Eileen could control him. If not, then they'd bludgeon him with hammers and a shovel until he was nothing more than a pile of bones that they could set on fire. If *that* didn't work, then they'd run like hell and hope someone else knew how to stop the thing. This was Texas, after all. Monster or not, Mister Bones would not make it too far before some gun-toting patriot tried to blow him the hell up.

"Okay," Eileen said, "are you ready to do this?"

"I mean, no?" Xiomara said. "Are you?"

She shook her head. "Where do you think he's going to come from?"

They shrugged. "I guess I assumed the woods." The two of them took a moment to study the outline of the trees. "It'd be the most cinematic entrance, at least."

"Yeah, feels right to me."

"Man, it's going to suck if we just, like, get killed immediately," Xiomara said. "I don't have anybody else lined up to open the shop tomorrow."

"Nobody's getting killed."

"Besides the skeleton?"

"Well, yeah," Eileen said. "Obviously besides the skeleton."

I BELIEVE IN MISTER BONES

"Okay. *Okay.*" Xiomara clapped their hammers together, pumping themself up. "Okay, fine, fuck. Let's do this."

Eileen rested the shovel against her leg, the spade balanced on the concrete patch beneath their feet. "So I just shake the bones and say the words, right?"

"While thinking about him."

The reminder seemed comical to Eileen, who couldn't have removed the mystical creature from her mind if someone was paying her.

"You remember the words, right?" Xiomara asked. "You're not going to cough your way through them, or anything?"

"My name is not Ash Williams," Eileen said. "I remember the words."

She wondered what Daniel would think if he saw her now. If he would have been relieved to witness her finally taking this stuff seriously, or depressed to learn the consequences of ever retrieving the *DO YOU BELIEVE IN MISTER BONES?* email from his trash folder. Not that any of this could have been predicted. Sometimes life was fucking crazy, and all you could really do was hold on until you couldn't anymore. And then what? You let go. You let inertia guide you to wherever you were meant to fall.

Well, she wasn't ready to let go. Soon she would, but not yet. Not while she still had some fight left in her. Most of her skeleton remained. She was still *her*. But not for much longer, if she didn't put an end to this bullshit. If she didn't *do something*.

Eileen reached up and shook the wind chime, thinking *Mister Bones, Mister Bones, come on out wherever the fuck you are*. Thinking, *Mister Bones, Mister Bones, let's see your stupid fucking face*. Thinking, *Mister Bones, Mister Bones, you belong to me now*. The bones rattled together, creating a hollow melody. It was soothing, weirdly enough. Calming. It gave Eileen the confidence needed to recite the magic words chosen by a bunch of anonymous nerds on the internet:

MAX BOOTH III

"*Klaatu . . . barada . . . nikto.*"

The bone chime went still.

Other than a Spanish-dubbed episode of *The Simpsons* playing from inside the house, the night was silent.

Eileen and Xiomara stood at the edge of the concrete wielding their weapons. Bodies tense. Minds focused. Waiting.

Nothing was happening.

"How long do you think it'll take?" Eileen asked, already wincing at the pain in her hands from gripping the shovel.

Beside her, Xiomara shrugged. "I don't know. The message board didn't specify." They lowered their hammers. "I guess I thought it would be sorta instantaneous."

"Me too."

"Unless it didn't work."

"I said the words correctly, didn't I?"

"I mean, I think so?" They scratched the back of their neck with one of the hammer claws. "It sounded right to me, at least. You *were* thinking about him? Like, picturing him in your head as you did everything?"

Eileen relaxed her blistering grasp on the shovel. "Yes, I was *thinking* about him." She nodded at the wind chime. "Are *you* sure you made that correctly?"

"It's a wind chime, Eileen, not rocket science." With one of the hammers, they tapped the bones and caused them to rattle together again. "Sounds like a wind chime to me." The two of them listened to the bones for a moment, then Xiomara said, "Shit, maybe we got ripped off."

"Ripped off how?"

"I don't know how to tell whether or not human bones are authentic—do you?"

"You think that guy sold us something fraudulent?" Eileen said. Weirdly, the possibility had never crossed her mind until now.

"I don't know. *Maybe?* What do you think?"

I BELIEVE IN MISTER BONES

"Should we try it again?"

"What—the ritual?" Xiomara sounded horrified at the prospect.

"What do we have to lose?"

They started laughing to hide their fear. "What if it's like when you take an edible and don't feel anything, so you take another one, and an hour later suddenly you're melting on the ceiling?"

"What the fuck are you talking about?"

"What if by doing the ritual twice you summon *two* of these fuckers, or something?" Xiomara raised both hammers, for emphasis. One, two.

"You think there's more than one?" Eileen re-tightened her grip around the shovel, as if two evil skeletons were about to leap out of the darkness and attack.

"I don't know *what* I think, babe. I'm just . . . you know, speculating. Anything could be possible, you know?"

"Maybe you're right," she said. "Not much time has passed. Maybe it'll still happen."

"Should we just . . . uh, stand out here like this until it does?" They nodded to the back door. "Or do you want to go back inside?"

"I guess I haven't really—"

"*Shh*," Xiomara shushed, finger to their lips, eyes wide.

Eileen, suddenly scared out of her mind, mouthed the word *What?*

"Do you hear that?" Xiomara whispered, leaning close to Eileen's ear.

She tried to focus, but still couldn't pick up on anything. "Hear what?"

They shook their head, slowly, waiting for it to register with Eileen. "Nothing," they whispered. "I don't hear anything." Then, in case she wasn't getting it, they added, "What happened to *The Simpsons*?"

Eileen hadn't noticed until that moment, but Xiomara was right. The television noises from inside the house had quieted. Now the night truly was devoid of sound.

"Maybe she shut it off?" Eileen said. "Or paused it to use the bathroom?"

"You don't understand," Xiomara said, arms trembling, "that TV? It never shuts down. It's *always* on. One time I tried to turn it off and she *burned my hand with a cigarette.* Do you understand?"

"Well," Eileen said, not quite sure what they were implying here, "let's go check on her then."

She took the lead now. Xiomara followed closely behind, breathing down her neck. Eileen readjusted the shovel in her grip, despite how silly it made her feel here in the house. What was she going to do with it? Bludgeon a little old woman to death because she stopped watching cartoons?

The television was still on. Its volume, however, had either been drastically lowered or muted altogether. On the carpet, between the rocking chair and the TV, Eileen spotted the remote. Perhaps it'd fallen, she thought, and the MUTE button had accidentally pressed in upon impact. Next to the remote was an empty glass. The carpet surrounding either object was stained dark. Something had spilled. Something like diet cranberry juice.

The television's glow was just bright enough to illuminate Xiomara's abuela in her chair, rocking in a rapid, spasmodic tempo. Her afghan had fallen off her waist and was now piled up at her feet.

"Ab-Abi?" Xiomara said, voice cracking, and pushed past Eileen to check on the woman. They dropped both of their hammers to the floor as they neared her, then flinched back and gasped. "*Abi?* What's wrong? *Abi?* Estás usted bien? Estás herido?"

Eileen limped farther into the living room, fighting the numbness overwhelming her left foot, refusing to let go of the shovel. Something bad was about to happen. Something bad *already* was happening. She just hadn't caught up to speed yet.

The old woman's hands clenched either armrest of the rocking chair. Her spine was straightened back, flat against

I BELIEVE IN MISTER BONES

the wooden structure, face tilted toward the ceiling. Eyes wide, mouth unhinged in a dry croak. Her body wasn't just rocking—it was *vibrating*.

"Xio, what's wrong with her?" Eileen asked. Part of her hoped this was a regular occurrence, that their abuela just needed a pill or an injection of something. That this was normal, and not at all related to what the two of them had just been fooling around with in the back yard.

"I don't know," Xiomara cried, shouting things in Spanish at the woman and not receiving any answers. They held her head against the rocking chair backing to prevent a concussion. Unrestrained, her skull would've bounced harder and harder against the wood until something cracked—either in the chair, or herself.

Eileen's feet remained planted on the carpet. She couldn't move. Couldn't do anything but watch the scene unfold, helpless and terrified. *Is this our fault?* she kept thinking. *Did we do this?*

Something in the old woman's face changed. The skin grew taut, like it was being pulled against her skull. The dry croak evolved into a moist scream. Like she was drowning, choking.

"Abi? Jesus Christ, Abi, what the fuck?"

It wasn't just her face growing tighter. Her arms and hands, too. Gone were the wrinkles and loose flaps of flesh. Eileen imagined the skin beneath her clothes was doing much of the same. But *why?* What would tighten the flesh like that?

Her body—the old woman's body, it was getting bigger. She was *growing*.

Growing from within.

But *what* was growing?

What was inside her besides . . .

Besides a skeleton?

—fuck fuck fuck—

Eileen opened her mouth to warn Xiomara of what was about to happen, but it was too late.

A split in the old woman's face emerged in the middle of her forehead, then expanded vertically in either direction, through her hairline, through her nose, her mouth, her chin, her throat . . .

Xiomara screamed and stepped away, as helpless as Eileen.

There was no preventing this.

Whatever this was.

It was happening.

Her face, now divided into two wet chunks of rolled-back flesh, continued shrinking as it birthed a skull entirely too large to have ever belonged to an elderly grandmother. The eye sockets were wide, hollow, black. The mouth had teeth, unlike Xiomara's abuela. Teeth that were sharpened—and eager to be used. This wasn't the woman. This was something else.

Mister Bones.

He was hatching out of the woman's body.

Bursting from her flesh like it was nothing more than a barrier—no, a *portal.*

A portal leading from Marrowland to Eileen's world.

Because she had beckoned him.

She had summoned him.

—not like this not like this not like this—

The rest of the old woman's skin sloughed aside as a creature comprised only of bones finished emerging from her shriveling carcass.

He had finally arrived.

"Holy fucking shit, holy fucking shit, holy fucking shit." Xiomara repeated the words like they were a chant. Eileen couldn't have said it better herself. *Holy fucking shit* summarized the situation perfectly.

Mister Bones—the abnormal skeleton who had just hatched from the old woman's body—scrambled off the rocking chair and landed on the carpet, in the same spot as the fallen remote and spilled juice. Behind him, the television's volume abruptly returned, erupting the living

room with Homer Simpson shouting something in Spanish. The noise seemed to spook him. He *flinched*.

Eileen expected the creature to make a noise. A growl, or something threatening. Something *monstrous*. But did he have any lungs? Did he have *any* organs? The skeleton did not growl. He didn't scream. He didn't say anything at all. The only noise originating from his proximity came from his many knotted bones rubbing and clacking together as he fled from the obliterated corpse of Xiomara's abuela. His exact size was too impossible to determine in the darkly-lit living room, especially since he moved in a standing frog pose, legs bent out, hips stretched down. Necessary, Eileen realized, to prevent his skull from crashing through the ceiling. What the fuck had they just unleashed?

"Get him!" Xiomara shouted, and she stared at them like they were crazy. *Get him?* Did they not see this thing? There was no *getting him*.

The skeleton scurried past, knocking over random furniture in his tornado of chaos. Did he even *notice* Eileen and Xiomara standing there, dumbstruck? He moved like a wild animal trapped in a house. A creature conditioned to the wilderness suddenly contained. What were they supposed to do? Leave all the doors and windows open and hope he escaped without causing too much damage?

The thing had just *burst* through Xiomara's abuela. The ceiling and walls were now painted with her innards. The television's glow had turned red from gore dripping down the screen. Mister Bones was a danger. An uncontrollable killing machine. A monster. Maybe the people on that message board hadn't given him a choice when creating him, but that didn't mean much *now* with him in Xiomara's house, wrecking everything and everyone within reach.

Eileen cracked her knuckles against the shovel handle. Beside her, Xiomara retrieved the hammers from the carpet. The two of them glanced at each other, but didn't

I BELIEVE IN MISTER BONES

say anything. The fear in their eyes spoke plenty. It asked, *What the hell have we done?* It asked, *Are we actually about to do this?* It asked, *Are we really this stupid?*

Eileen and Xiomara followed the sound of destruction into the kitchen. Mister Bones had knocked everything down from the counters. Dishes and appliances were scattered across the floor. What was he searching for? A way out, of course. An exit. Back to Marrowland? Eileen wondered if he'd ever been summoned like this before. Was tonight his first time visiting their world as a physical being? Had he ever ventured beyond the unassuming dreamscapes of his victims? She imagined it must've been terrifying. Once again, she was reminded of a rabid animal.

She'd read *Cujo* the week it was published. There was only one thing a person could do with an animal that'd gone crazy.

"Hey you fucking piece of shit!" Xiomara shouted from across the kitchen.

Mister Bones turned around in a quick *snapping* motion, moving almost like a spooked crab while remaining in his standing frog pose. Back pressed against the counter, his impossibly-long arms stretched around either side of the kitchen. *Where were his hands?* Despite the emptiness of his eye sockets, he still managed to look surprised to find them here—to learn he wasn't alone.

Sections of his skeleton were still wearing bits and pieces of Xiomara's abuela.

Then, finally, a *growl*.

But not from Mister Bones.

From Xiomara.

Both hammers raised, they charged forward and started swinging wildly. Eileen didn't leave her hanging. She followed, bringing the shovel back like a baseball bat, ignoring the pain burning into her hands as she swung at his head. The back of the spade connected square against his skull and he flew back against the counter.

His mouth snapped like a hostile dog, barely missing her arm. *Don't fuck with me*, the gesture said. *You don't know what I'm capable of doing.*

She swung again, this time at his teeth, and knocked his entire jawbone to the floor.

Meanwhile, Xiomara had already demolished half of his midsection with the hammers.

If he was fighting back, she couldn't tell, and she certainly didn't want to give him the time to regroup and defend himself. They had surprised him. The opportunity wouldn't present itself twice.

Another strike of the shovel took the rest of his skull clean off. It hit a cabinet behind him and bounced to the other side of the room.

The kitchen flooded with the adrenalized screams of Xiamara and Eileen as they took turns bludgeoning the skeleton with their weapons of choice. Neither of them stopped until there was nothing left to hit, until every bone in his macabre anatomy had disconnected and scattered on the floor with the rest of the junk he'd knocked down. Until the two of them were standing there, out of breath, surrounded by a pile of inanimate bones.

Until it was over, finally fucking over.

UTTERLY EXHAUSTED, the two of them dropped their skeleton-slaying tools and collapsed in the detritus of their carnage, holding each other and sobbing, leaning against the cabinet storing Daniel's severed dick-arm.

"Is it *done*?" Eileen asked, snotting into Xiomara's shoulder. "Did we do it?"

"I think so," they said, face pressed against Eileen's own shoulder. "Shit, I think so. Shit. Holy fuck. I think so."

Neither of them would open their eyes and witness the destruction they'd caused. It was all too much to bear, to process, to accept. Embracing each other was all they could do. The only cathartic release available outside of further beating the shit out of the skeleton's lifeless bones.

The longer they held each other and kept their eyes shut, the longer they could prevent the reality of what awaited them not just in this kitchen but, more importantly, back in the living room. *The Simpsons* could be heard from where they sat. The television's volume had kicked back on after Mister Bones stepped on the remote. Nobody had bothered shutting it off again. It was better with it turned up like this. Made it easier to pretend Xiomara's abuela was still in there, in one piece, breathing normally for a woman her age and sipping diet cranberry juice from a perfectly-poured glass.

"*Eileen*?" Xiomara's voice sounded sticky and raw. The

tears and snot kept coming. Eileen could feel them soaking against her shirt. She knew she was doing the same to Xiomara's bare shoulder. "*Eileen*, I gotta tell you something."

"It's okay," Eileen whispered, "it's over, we did it."

"Something happened . . . "

"It's over."

"Eileen, I fucked up . . . "

Eileen tried to push away from them and get a better look at their face, but Xiomara tightened their hold around her arms, keeping their bodies smushed together.

"Eileen," they said again, throat clogged with mucus, "I fucked up, I fucked up so bad . . . "

"What do you mean? What are you—"

"I was there, that night. Eileen, I was there."

"What night?"

"The night. You know. The night. The fucking night. When Daniel . . . I was there."

Eileen returned the intensity of their hug. "I know, Xio. Remember, you told me? You brought him my car keys."

"No, you don't understand. Something *happened*. Eileen . . . something happened . . . "

Her arms loosened from Xiomara, and this time they didn't try to stop her as she pushed away. "What are you talking about?"

Xiomara wiped snot from their face and told Eileen everything they'd been keeping a secret since the night of Daniel's death. Everything that had been slowly killing them, poisoning their guts and boiling their blood.

They told her how they'd given Daniel the car keys and ate dinner with him and how they'd informed him of all the terrible, ugly things Eileen had been saying about him at the bar.

How they hadn't left the apartment right away, but stayed with him. How they'd offered to help package the swag bags, and how that'd immediately evolved into something else—a massage, their hands upon him, then his hands upon them.

I BELIEVE IN MISTER BONES

How they'd ended up in the bed Daniel and Eileen shared.

How they'd undressed each other.

And what happened afterward.

Including what Daniel tried to do to them, when they were finished.

How he'd tried to break their finger, to pass the curse onward.

How it hadn't worked, how his grip hadn't been secure, how they'd managed to wiggle free.

How they'd pepper sprayed him and ran out of the apartment, afraid he was going to give chase, convinced that their life was in danger.

No way of knowing that it wasn't *their* life coming to an end that night.

No way of knowing what Daniel would do to himself shortly later.

How *could* they have known? How could *anyone* have known?

Eileen listened to Xiomara talk, feeling a space between them grow wider the longer words continued spilling out of their mouth. What was she supposed to say to this? How was she meant to react? It didn't make any fucking sense—and yet, at the same time, everything suddenly clicked into place.

Daniel's death really had been a suicide.

It had nothing to do with the fraudulent bones corrupting his skeleton.

This was about *Eileen*.

She'd abandoned him to get drunk and shit-talk his entire existence—and Xiomara, the fucking snitch, the little rat, had come right on over to tell him all about it. To tell him every stupid thing she'd said about him.

And how had he responded?

In the most boring, predictable way possible.

He'd cheated on her and then killed himself.

Too spineless to confront her about it with words.

Instead, he'd opened himself up. He'd dug the box cutter in nice and deep. Something he'd been wanting to do, anyway, she imagined, and now Xiomara had finally given him an excuse. They'd provided him a way out.

"Would you please say something?" Xiomara sobbed. "Please, Eileen, *say something.*"

"What do you want me to say?" Eileen asked, voice soft, emotionless. She had stopped crying halfway through their confession. Now she didn't know what to do.

The two of them were still seated on the floor, but now a decent gap of space separated their bodies.

Xiomara shrugged, wiping their face on the inside of their tank top. "I don't know."

"Yeah, I don't know, either."

"What are you thinking?"

"You don't want to know what I'm thinking."

Upon hearing that, they buried their face in their hands and resumed sobbing and apologizing.

Eileen didn't feel any sympathy for them. If anything, this sloppy display of emotions only made them appear more pathetic. They weren't the one who should be crying right now. They weren't the one who had been betrayed by their best fucking friend. Eileen should've been the one flipping out right now. She should've been crying and breaking shit and throwing a tantrum, but she wasn't. She was too *tired.* There was no more energy left in her to be loudly devastated. So instead, she just sat on the floor and watched Xiomara do the heavy work for her, and all she could think was, *Goddammit, why did you have to go and tell me this?*

What should've been a moment of triumph now felt short-lived, aborted, flushed down the toilet.

If Xiomara had still wanted to maintain any semblance of a friendship between the two of them, they would have kept this a secret. They would have let the burden eat them from the inside rather than unload it all on her mere moments after slaughtering a spooky skeleton together.

I BELIEVE IN MISTER BONES

The way Eileen figured it, by spilling their guts out like this, they'd effectively killed not just Daniel but also their relationship with Eileen. After tonight, the two of them were finished. How could she ever interact with them again without thinking about Xiomara and Daniel fucking each other? Not just that, but everything else. Making Daniel think Eileen no longer loved him. *Pepper spraying* him. Running away from him like he was some kind of freak. Would he have taken the box cutter to his wrist if Xiomara had never shown up that evening? It seemed extremely unlikely. Goddammit. God*dammit*. They sure as hell weren't kidding when they'd said they had fucked up.

Something in the kitchen moved in her peripherals. Eileen presumed it was Xiomara finally standing up and leaving her alone to process the news, but when she lifted her head Xiomara hadn't shifted from their position at all. Their face remained hidden behind their hands. The crying had quieted, but not died. Their nose was putting in extra effort controlling the levels of snot leaking between their fingers. A good friend might've offered them a box of tissues. Too bad Eileen wasn't feeling the "good friend" vibes at that moment.

Something was still moving, though.

Behind Xiomara.

The bones.

They were *moving*.

From all over the kitchen, they were sliding toward the same spot behind Xiomara, who remained oblivious.

Toward the base of the skeleton. Like it was a magnet recalling its minions.

He was rebuilding himself.

Xiomara was too focused on feeling sorry to notice what was happening behind them. It wasn't like this was a *quiet* process, either. Bones banging against bones, slapping trash on the floor, bumping into the cabinets. All Eileen could do was remain seated and witness the scene unfold, equal parts horrified and fascinated as the skeleton reanimated.

And then, there he was, once again.

Mister Bones.

His arms weren't as elongated now. Maybe they could expand and contract when desired. Either way, both hands were visible. *How many fingers did he have?* More than five, certainly. Beyond that, she couldn't tell. They were thin, and long, contorting over each other.

Hovering over Xiomara.

"Oh my god," Eileen managed to whisper, only succeeding in prompting Xiomara to look up at her.

"*What*?" they said, moments before the skeleton reached down and dug his sharpened nails into their face and pulled the skin clean off their skull in one quick, powerful motion.

Xiomara slumped aside, sans a face, blood gushing to the floor.

Then, with the intensity and meticulousness of an ant colony consuming dropped food crumbs, Mister Bones shredded Xiomara's clothes off and proceeded to rip open their skin, starting from the top of their back down to their ass. There was no hesitation as he reached inside their body and pulled out their spine, and then the rest of Xiomara's skeleton. Everything collected from her annihilated flesh was piled behind him, as if he was guarding the bones from anyone trying to take them back.

Eileen didn't get up. She didn't try to run away. Escape never crossed her mind. *She* had summoned him. *She* had made this happen. Fleeing the scene would be meaningless.

There was nowhere for her to go, anyway.

Let him take her next. Fuck it.

She didn't need a body anymore. She didn't need her bones. She didn't need a goddamn fucking thing.

She was *done*.

Nearly fifty years on this planet and not a thing to show for it, not a single reason to continue breathing other than being scared of the alternative.

I BELIEVE IN MISTER BONES

Well, she wasn't scared anymore.

This life was nothing but one bullshit thing after another.

So, once more, with feeling . . .

Fuck it.

She closed her eyes and leaned her head back against the kitchen cabinet—the same one, she realized, that currently housed Daniel's arm. It made her feel connected to him, in a weird way, despite the bones being counterfeit. Like he was still with her. And if that wasn't the perfect moment to get ravaged by a reanimated skeleton, she didn't know what was.

When an uncomfortable stretch of time passed without feeling anything, or *hearing* anything beyond *The Simpsons* playing in the living room, she opened her eyes again and found Mister Bones in front of her. He was crouched in the standing frog pose again, spine too complex to straighten in a house of this size. He'd been *watching her*. Waiting for her to wake up.

"Well?" she said. "Why don't you just get it over with already?"

The skeleton did not react.

"What's your problem? What do you *want*?"

She climbed to her feet, careful to avoid eye contact with Xiomara's deboned corpse. When she stepped to the other side of the kitchen, Mister Bones's head turned with her. Still watching her. Waiting for something. She weirdly did not feel threatened by him. If he was going to kill her, dismember her, rip her to pieces, why hadn't he already followed through with it? That's not what he wanted. Then what *did* he want?

Earlier this morning, he'd been after her bones. The numbness in her left foot was a constant reminder of that. But the situation had changed, right? She'd summoned him again—this time, through the proper channels. She had summoned him on *her* terms. The bone chime had been triggered, the incantation recited. It was supposed to be different now. He wasn't supposed to be after her. He was supposed to *serve her*.

But if that were really true, then why had he killed Xiomara and their abuela?

Why had he slaughtered everybody in this house except for Eileen?

"Well, what's the plan now?" Eileen asked.

Predictably, the skeleton had no response.

Too exhausted to stand, she picked up one of the fallen kitchen chairs and sat down at the table. Patted around her pocket for her vape pen and could have cried when she felt it not only safe and sound, but also charged. She took a couple hits, eyes glued on Mister Bones as he crab-walked through the trash and gore toward where she sat. Why did his mannerisms remind her of a dog, following her around like this? He wasn't a dog. He was a distorted skeleton so large he couldn't even fit in the house. He was an evil, fucked-up monster responsible for the deaths of at least three people, if not more.

She blew a cloud of weed vapor in his face. It disappeared in his perpetually-unhinged mouth and dark, hollow eye socks. She imagined the skeleton getting high and starting to behave like someone out of an '80's stoner comedy. Saying shit like, "Radical, dude!" and inhaling spray cheese. All types of wacky shenanigans. If it affected him at all, he was good at hiding it. The skeleton stood perfectly motionless. Sorta reminded her of the King's guards. Those dorks with the goofy hats everybody was always trying to make laugh. Could Mister Bones laugh? What type of sense of humor did he have?

She remembered the dream she'd had earlier that morning—skeleton-Daniel sucking on her big toe—and thought she had a pretty good idea of what kinda sick shit this creature found funny.

Her left foot tingled against the floor as she sat at the table. How many bones had he replaced the last time she slept? And what would happen next time she closed her

I BELIEVE IN MISTER BONES

eyes? Now that he was summoned from Marrowland and supposedly her servant, would the bone stealing cease? Would her dreams be safe again?

"Are you done fucking with me?" she asked him. "Are you done taking what's mine?"

No response.

But it did get her thinking—where *had* her foot bones gone? If he'd replaced them with the same clay-like substance as Daniel's skeleton, then where did the *legitimate* bones go? Same question for Daniel's bones. Where *were* they? What was he *doing* with all of these things? Eating them? She didn't think so. Wouldn't she have witnessed him munching on Xiomara's insides? Instead, all he'd done was set them aside, saving them for something. But *what*? The message board had never addressed these questions. Either the idea never occurred to anybody there, or it was considered "spookier" to leave such details ambiguous.

After seeing him up close, she had her own theory brewing.

This creature's anatomy didn't align with the skeleton of any other species on Earth. That was because he *wasn't* of this planet, or even this world. He was the figment of an internet collective's imagination. Created out of nothing. A true mythological invention hailing from an equally mythological world. *Marrowland.* That wasn't *real.* The message board had made it up, just as they'd made Mister Bones up. His structure did not make any logistical sense. The length *and* volume of bones consisting of his skeleton seemed to readjust and improvise every time he shifted position. Even the way he moved around felt inherently anachronistic. He was not a carefully thought-out entity and *because* of this negligence he'd ended up becoming far scarier than any of his creators could have anticipated, but perhaps not in the way they might've intended.

What Eileen couldn't stop thinking about was *how* he'd materialized. Where had all of these bones forming his bizarre skeleton *come from*? She suspected the answer was simple. He was constructed of the bones of his victims. The people he'd violated throughout the years, sabotaging their dreams from the safe confines of Marrowland, somehow managing to literally remove sections of their bodies without ever actually stepping foot in the same realm. Some heinous variation of astral dreaming. Astral *haunting*, she thought. Collecting more bones than anyone or anything would ever need, crafting his very own physical vehicle to possess should the moment ever come that someone insane enough would ring a bone chime and chant the incantation.

Meaning the skeleton watching her hit the weed pen right now had been manufactured with the bones of several dozen—if not *hundred*—dead people.

Including her husband.

Assuming she wasn't off base here, then the bones that had once resided within Daniel were now assembled somewhere in the creature currently smeared with Xiomara's guts.

In a weird, deranged, absolutely fucked-up way, Daniel was a part of Mister Bones now—just as Mister Bones was now part of Daniel. The two were linked together, forever. If she chose to think about it a certain way, then Daniel wasn't completely dead, was he? Not while this magical skeleton was here, at least, bones still connected to each other. Because if Mister Bones remained alive, then—to some extent—so would Daniel.

Right?

She took another hit of the vape, uncertain of which possibility she wanted to convince herself was the truth. Thinking about *any* of this right now felt sick and morbid. Seated in the same room as her dead friend. Her friend who was now dead because of Mister Bones. She'd never told him to kill them. She'd never asked for this. So why the *fuck*—

Except . . . how true was that, really?

I BELIEVE IN MISTER BONES

As Xiomara confessed to everything that had happened, as they'd sobbed and snotted all over the place, hadn't Eileen fantasized about reaching over and strangling them?

Hadn't an intoxicating rage clenched her nerves, pleading for a release outlet?

Wasn't it then possible that Mister Bones had absorbed this vicious energy from her, someone he was now undeniably connected to thanks to the bone chime ritual?

That he'd interpreted these feelings of betrayal as a command to end their life?

An intuition between summoner and servant.

But if that was the case, that didn't explain what had happened to Xiomara's abuela. She'd never thought a negative thing about her before. There was no beef between them. As far as she knew, the old woman had never slept with Daniel. Then *why*? She remembered thinking how it'd looked like the creature had been hatching out of her. Like she was an egg in the midst of cracking. Maybe if Eileen spent more time brainstorming, she could come up with some theory about Mister Bones requiring an unassuming, weakened body to transport from one world to the other. Someone who wouldn't be able to fight back. How it would be ridiculous to assume he'd materialize out of thin air. Where else could a skeleton come from *besides* a body, right?

But the truth was, Eileen had no fucking idea why he'd come out of her like that.

The truth was, she didn't care so much about the old woman.

Not in that moment, not while seated at the kitchen table, studying the creature's skeletal structure.

Right then, only one thing was on her mind.

One thing she wanted to know.

"Daniel?" she said, voice cracking. "Daniel, is that you?"

She held out her hand, waiting for something to happen, nervous that something actually would.

Too afraid to watch, she closed her eyes once again, seeking the comfort of self-imposed darkness.

Never in a million years did she seriously expect the skeleton to grab her hand.

Which was why, when he did exactly that, she let out a little scream.

FROM THE WAY the gas station clerk was staring
at Eileen as she stumbled through the automatic
doors, she imagined his hand was already hovering
under the little red emergency button behind the counter.
The one he was trained to press when someone barged in
wielding a shotgun and demanding the contents of the cash
register. She didn't know if the gas station actually had a
button like that. They always did in movies, though, and
when had movies ever lied?

One glimpse of the overhead security mirror was
enough to make Eileen recoil at her own appearance. The
gas station clerk's restraint was impressive. There wasn't
a laundromat on earth that'd be able to clean Xiomara's
vintage hockey jersey after this. She looked like a goddamn
zombie fresh from the grave. Which only reminded her of
the San Antonio Zombie Walk incident from their early
days as publishers. Instincts brought her hand to her
pocket, intending on pulling out her cell phone and texting
Daniel about it. He would have gotten a kick out of the
observation. Except she couldn't text him—not now, not
ever again. Actually, patting around her pants, she realized
she couldn't text *anybody* right now. Her phone was back
at Xiomara's house.

Who the fuck would she have texted, anyway?

Whatever. It didn't matter. At least she'd remembered
her debit card.

MAX BOOTH III

Hopefully there was enough of a balance to purchase the two items she'd come here to collect:

A bottle of lighter fluid, and a box of matches.

The skeleton was where she'd left him. Thinking of him as "Mister Bones" felt weird and silly. Mister Bones was someone from a book. The thing waiting for her in the woods was more than that. He was palpable. He was *real*. It was better for her sanity to refer to him as just "the skeleton." Less cartoonish feeling. Less like a joke.

Together, they'd departed Xiomara's house and entered the woods from the back yard. It was only then that she'd seen how large the skeleton really was, no longer burdened by spatial limitations. Stretching her neck up to behold his full size reignited an ache in her shoulders she'd temporarily forgotten existed. The two of them walking side-by-side like that reminded her of *The Iron Giant*, a movie she hadn't thought about since watching it at the drive-in during the summer of 1999. If she remembered right, it had played alongside that godawful *Inspector Gadget* movie with the guy from *Ferris Bueller's Day Off*. She'd gone there alone, intrigued by the advertisements for *The Iron Giant*, and found herself crying behind the wheel of her shitty hand-me-down Ford Pinto while little kids ran around the exterior speakers playing freeze tag and throwing popcorn at each other. She wondered if Daniel had ever seen it. If so, she wondered if he'd also cried at the end like she had cried. She hoped so. She really did. There were few things in this life more emotionally satisfying than crying during a good movie.

There was a clearing in the woods not too far from Xiomara's house. Eileen remembered it from her teenage years. The two of them would come out here and smoke pot and talk about dumb shit that didn't matter then and certainly didn't matter now. Eileen led the skeleton to this

I BELIEVE IN MISTER BONES

clearing, then told him to wait. To *stay*. She promised she'd be back, and she'd kept that promise. He was still exactly where she'd instructed him to be standing. Spine straightened out to rival the length of some of the trees out here. What would somebody think if they caught them? What *was* there to think besides *wow, that sure is a big fucking skeleton?*

She considered holding his hand again, but feared she'd never do what needed to be done if they shared one more single ounce of intimacy. It would be better just to get it over with before she chickened out. Before she was stuck taking care of her own personal Iron Giant.

"I'm sorry," Eileen whispered, avoiding eye contact with the skeleton as she sprayed the lighter fluid across his bones, getting as much of it on him as possible. She made sure to soak in a decent puddle of the stuff in the dirt at his feet. "This is the way it has to be," she told him. "I hope you can understand that. I hope that you know this is what has to happen."

The skeleton stared down at her without reacting.

Waiting for her to do it.

Just as eager for this to be finished as she was.

Okay, then.

She lit a match and tossed it between his feet.

But of course that didn't work.

If Eileen had been thinking coherently, she would have anticipated her plan's failure. Logic, unfortunately, had gone on vacation for the time being.

There was a reason funeral homes invested in crematoriums. Reducing bones to ash was no easy task. Just as books required a certain temperature before catching fire and burning, so did humans. Only humans were much tougher than paper. Between 1400- and 1800-degrees Fahrenheit was what it took to cremate a person,

I BELIEVE IN MISTER BONES

she would learn later, once curiosity annoyed her enough to search for the answer online. Nowhere near the temperature she could achieve out in the woods with a bottle of lighter fluid and a couple matches. Of course this thing wasn't exactly a *person*, but the internet didn't have a solid answer for an appropriate burning temperature when it came to mythological creatures.

The point was—it didn't work.

The skeleton remained alit for a few strong minutes. Just long enough to convince Eileen that the situation was almost resolved.

If the flames were painful, he did not express any discomfort. He didn't express anything at all.

Slowly the fire faded. The bones appeared unharmed, aside from being searingly hot to lay hands upon. Once it became clear that the plan was a bust, Eileen lost her shit. Blame sleep deprivation. Blame hunger. Blame her period. Blame grief. Blame whatever. But she freaked out. Fell to her knees. Started punching the dirt and screaming. Full-on temper tantrum at its finest.

"You *have* to die! Don't you understand? This can't continue. *None of this can continue,*" she told the skeleton. "Please die. *Please . . .* you *have to die.* You *have to . . .* "

And, to her immense relief, the skeleton seemed to be listening.

Not only that, but he seemed to *understand.*

One by one, pieces of him started dropping to the ground.

Disconnecting.

Separating.

Crumbling.

Until he was nothing but a pile of bones in front of Eileen.

Eileen, who understand perfectly what the skeleton had just done for her.

Eileen, who now found herself faced with a choice to make.

Leave the bones here in these woods, or take them back to her apartment?

The rest of the lighter fluid was donated to Xiomara's house. Eileen didn't know if burning it down was the right decision, but when she thought about leaving the corpses in their current condition she felt sick to her stomach. Someone would eventually stumble upon the grisly scene and be forever traumatized. Going the pyromaniac route felt more responsible. If the arson led back to Eileen, then she'd face the consequences. What was she going to do, go on the lam? Flee to Mexico? No. She wasn't going anywhere but back home, to the apartment that she had been trying her best to avoid since discovering Daniel with the box cutter. There was no more hiding from it. There was no more running. She was too fucking tired.

That night, Eileen passed out the moment her head hit the pillow.

It was a deep, dreamless sleep.

When she woke up, her left foot was still numb.

But that was it. Just her foot. The sensation hadn't spread.

The curse had become stagnant.

Isolated.

It took some doing, and a lot of how-to videos on YouTube, but eventually all of the wind chimes in the apartment were switched out with new ones. Ones she had crafted herself. The skeleton had provided her with plenty of supplies. She figured why not? Almost like the antithesis of the curse, when she thought about it. Replacing artificial material with real bones. Sometimes, when the weather was nice enough outside, she opened the windows and let the chimes sing to her. If she closed her eyes tight enough, she swore she could hear Daniel's voice.

The *Mister Bones* book needed some revisions before it could be published. A proper ending was required. Some kind of closure, even if it wasn't what readers were hoping to find. And, since she had no way of contacting the Fugue Steaks message board users, Eileen was left with little choice but to assign herself the task of writing it.

The title of the chapter was easy enough: *Daniel, from San Antonio*.

Recalling everything that had happened, and writing the details down in a way that felt both entertaining *and* authentic would be challenging, but not impossible. Eileen could do this. If *anybody* could do this . . .

The hardest parts to write were the parts that weren't true.

Like the very end, when it was revealed Daniel had conquered Mister Bones once and for all.

That Daniel had survived long enough to write this very book in the reader's hands.

That he'd ensured no one else would ever fall victim to this curse again.

That it was over, that everything was going to be okay now.

Because the more people who read it, and believed that was the true ending, then maybe—just maybe—it would no longer be a lie. Maybe it really would be over.

Yeah, it took her a long time to write that part.

But she did it.

She finished it.

And then she formatted it.

MAX BOOTH III

There was no more money in the account to hire a cover artist, so she made one herself. Nothing fancy. All she did was take one of the bone chimes out where there was good lighting and snap a couple photos, then chose the least shitty option. *Voilà.*

The title was already decided, and the credited byline felt like a no-brainer. Anybody who had a problem with it could go to hell for all she cared. They'd had plenty of time to reach out.

I BELIEVE IN MISTER BONES the top of the front cover read.

And, below it:

A NOVELLA BY DANIEL & EILEEN ADDAMS.

He had started it, and she had finished it.

One last collaboration together.

This would be the final publication ever released by Fiendish Books, a small press that everybody would forget existed within one year of officially shutting down, outside of the occasional, "Hey, remember those guys?" muttered by drunk introverted writers at horror conventions.

And, as time progressed, more and more the answer would be, "Never heard of them."

But that was okay, Eileen thought.

It was how these things usually ended, anyway.

ABOUT THE AUTHOR

Max Booth III is the publisher of Ghoulish Books, a small press and bookstore that they co-run with their wife, Lori. They also organize and host the Ghoulish Book Festival every year in downtown San Antonio, TX.

It is at this point in the bio that the author feels it is necessary to once again remind the reader that the novel they just read was fictional and any real-life resemblances within the text are purely coincidental.

Seriously. Let's not get weird about this.

Learn more about Max at FuckMaxBooth.com.
Learn more about Ghoulish Books at GHOULISH.RIP

Printed in Great Britain
by Amazon